'What changed
for one not satis

'The party hasn't started

His voice took on a persuasive tone that brushed over her skin like velvet. He seemed to draw something from her that she'd never known she had. Was she out of her depth with this one?

'Do you think I'm going to abandon my hostess responsibilities for a frolic across the sheets with you?'

He raised a dark brow. 'Are you?'

The scary thing was she had a feeling that was exactly what was going to happen.

He closed the door, muting the sound of the party below.

She clutched the edge of the dressing table on either side of her hips. If she touched him she might not be responsible for her actions, and with him she very much needed to be responsible.

His head dipped...his mouth hovered. 'I'll admit to a little curiosity of my own,' he murmured, and touched his lips to hers.

Dear Reader

Brie's story hadn't fully formed in my mind when I began writing my last book, MISTLETOE NOT REQUIRED, where Brie makes her first appearance. Brie supported her friend Olivia when she had to make some heart-wrenching decisions. Likewise, Olivia was there for Brie as Brie struggled to improve her relationship with her long-lost brother, Jett.

Because that's what friends are for.

From the start, Olivia's party-loving friend was demanding to be noticed—so much so that I had to promise her a book of her own, and here it is.

Digging into Brie's past to find out why she's such an attention-seeker was the fun part—giving her a worthy opponent even more so.

Leo Hamilton is a short-term, casual kind of guy when it comes to women and relationships. His brutal past and consequent responsibilities have made him a bit of a control freak, and this aspect of his personality immediately clashes with Brie's sassy independence.

He's also a man of integrity—as Brie is about to find out for herself...

Anne

THE PARTY DARE

BY
ANNE OLIVER

Published in Great Britain 2014
by Mills & Boon, an imprint of Harlequin (UK) Limited,
Eton House, 18-24 Paradise Road, Richmond, Surrey, TW9 1SR

© 2014 Anne Oliver

ISBN: 978-0-263-25023-7

Printed and bound in Spain
by Blackprint CPI, Barcelona

Anne Oliver lives in Adelaide, South Australia, and with its perfect location and relaxed lifestyle why would she want to leave?

In another life Anne was an early childhood teacher, but not long after she began writing paranormal and time travel adventures as a weekend escape she knew it was more than a hobby. Eventually preferring the fun of writing contemporary romance, she dreamed of swapping yard duties for the life of a published author.

It happened in December 2005, when she was accepted by Mills & Boon® for their Modern Heat™ series. The dream continued when her first two published novels won the Romance Writers of Australia's Romantic Book of the Year in 2007 and 2008. She considers herself very lucky to have been a finalist for the same award in 2012 and 2013.

Other interests include animal welfare and conservation, quilting, astronomy, all things Scottish, and eating anything she doesn't have to cook.

Visit Anne at her website: www.anne-oliver.com

Other Modern Tempted™ titles by Anne Oliver:

MISTLETOE NOT REQUIRED

DEDICATION

To make a friend you first have to be one.

With thanks to my critique partners:
Kathy, Linda, Lynn and Suzie.

Thanks also to my editor, Meg Lewis,
who read the story and asked the right questions.

CHAPTER ONE

'I SHOULD FOREWARN you the purchaser intends to reno-vate. Big time.'

'Renovate? *Big* time?' Breanna Black blinked at her soon-to-be departing next-door neighbour, Carol. 'Do you know what that involves, exactly?'

'I overheard elevator and wall demolition to make way for indoor pool mentioned. Amongst other things.'

The words were still echoing in Brie's head at Carol and George's farewell dinner more than twenty-four hours later. She shook her head as she rinsed her hands in Car-ol's upstairs bathroom. The Reece-Bartons had sold their beautiful mansion, East Wind, to a moron. East Wind was a mirror image of Brie's West Wind next door, built by brothers in the late nineteenth century. Obviously Leo Hamilton—her new *clueless* neighbour—didn't appreci-ate historical structures or their significance. She swiped up the hand towel, rubbing away at the excess energy she didn't know what to do with. *An indoor pool?* For heaven's sake. If he wanted—

'Apologies for the interruption, George.' An unfamil-iar voice drifted up the stairs. 'I didn't realise you had company.'

Deep and rich and silky, the timbre seemed to harmo-nise with the foyer's warm wood-panelled walls where she imagined the recent arrival standing. Pushing the bathroom door wider, she cocked an ear in the direction of the stairwell and listened.

The actual words were muffled by the flautist's rendition of "Greensleeves" and the disorder of mingled conversations from the twenty or so guests, but it was the tone that hooked her attention. Would he look as scrumptious as he sounded? she wondered. A shiver of lust shimmied down her spine. Would he sound the same in bed?

Then George and his visitor moved from the foyer, their voices merging with those at the dinner party.

Wow. Brie straightened away from the wall she'd been leaning against and moved to the mirror. She hoped he'd stay for a drink at least so she could get a gander at him but she took her time repairing her make-up, determined not to give in to temptation and rush downstairs merely to satisfy her curiosity. Whoever he was.

Finally, she slid her lip-gloss into her purse and exited the bathroom. He was probably married with six kids. Except he didn't sound married. 'And what exactly does *married* sound like?' she scoffed out loud. He had to be short, then—being six foot tall herself had its disadvantages. Except she couldn't imagine anyone with a voice like that being anything but...

Perfect.

He appeared on the top stair as if she'd conjured him up, and her normally forthright and confident 'Hi' turned into a breathless schoolgirl sound of awe and appreciation.

He gave a brief half-nod. Said, 'Evening,' in that sexy as sin voice. One hand on the newel post, he stepped onto the upstairs landing. Thirtyish. Tall. Taller than her. Close-cropped dark hair, steel-grey eyes. Whipcord lean and tanned—her idea of a perfect man in one succinct package from his clean-shaven jaw to his crisp white business shirt and twilight-blue tie to his perfectly pressed charcoal trousers...with security pass clipped to his belt.

Leo Hamilton.

She almost groaned aloud. Perfect to look at but sadly that was where it ended.

Her smile remained frozen in half bloom on her lips. She refused to be seduced by his better than gorgeous looks. Beauty was only skin deep after all. Wasn't it great timing that she'd just fixed her lip-gloss? She frowned at the ridiculous thought that popped up from nowhere. *No.* It wasn't great at all.

What she really wanted to do was tell him exactly where to stick his renovation ideas. But she straightened slowly, drew in air tinged with the faint scent of skin-warmed cotton and reminded herself there was nothing to be gained by rudeness. *Pull yourself together, Brie. Smile. Forget those pesky little renovations he's planning and try the neighbourly, welcoming approach.*

To start with at least.

'Mr Hamilton. I couldn't help but notice your name.' *Oh...* Wrong place to look. She gave a little shrug—*wrong place to wear it*—and dragged her eyes from his crotch and up to meet his grey impenetrable ones. 'I'm Breanna Black.' She stepped forward, stuck out her hand. 'Your next-door neighbour.'

He nodded, all unsmiling and enigmatic. 'Breanna.' He took so long to extend his own, Brie wondered for a moment if he intended responding at all.

When he did, at last, take her hand in a decisive grip, she didn't reciprocate like some weak-willed female meeting her teenage idol but with the same strength and intensity as he. He looked startled. His eyes widened and his jaw tightened and she got an impression of hard, wide, slightly roughened palm before he released her. Or had she pulled free first?

Whatever, that first contact was as brief as it was disconcerting so she followed up quickly with, 'Call me Brie.

I've heard you're moving here from Melbourne?' *And a few other not so good things besides.*

'It's more of an investment, but yes. You heard correctly.' The way he said that last, almost accusatory, made it sound as if she were the town busybody when *he* was the ignoramus with no appreciation for history or architecture. And okay, she was interested only because he was going to be living next door—*and renovating*—which might affect the property value of her own home.

'Bad week at the office?' she murmured. 'Thank God it's Friday?' When he simply stared at her and made no attempt to reply, Brie continued, 'Carol told me. That you're from the mainland.' She defended what she considered her reasonable query, even if he did not. 'She and George are more friends than neighbours. So, you've big plans for this place?' The words shot out before she could stop them. 'An indoor pool, I hear?'

'Do you believe everything you hear?'

His cool stare matched his barely veiled criticism then he glanced down the stairwell, giving her time to check out his profile. The neat shape of his ear, the pinprick of evening stubble along the sharp jawline. Her trained therapist's eye couldn't help but notice his suntanned skin would benefit from one of her men's all-fruit facials, and her mouth tingled at the errant thought of licking it off— *Stop.*

She pressed her lips together. Unlike the Reece-Bartons, this man was *not* her friend. In any way. If she could just convince her woman's body of that fact. 'Not at all, but I believe Carol. Are you aware that this home is a signific—?'

'Chris, up here.' He raised a hand to some unseen body below, effectively cutting Brie off.

The lifelong sense of powerlessness she'd always felt at being repeatedly ignored bristled along her spine. *'Excuse me?'*

His focus turned sharply and wholly back to Brie. She wasn't being ignored now and the words she'd been about to say melted off her tongue. They stood almost eye to eye. Mouth to mouth. Breast to chest. Her nipples tightened. So did her belly. Somehow he made her feel dainty and petite, an achievement no man had ever accomplished. His gaze seemed to check her out from the roots of her hair to her low-heeled boots and every place between.

'My architect,' he said, finally.

Architect. Chris. Right. Now she had his attention back, she struggled to regather the thread of their conversation. 'What does he think of your plans?'

But she was suddenly speaking to empty space because, without a second glance, he was headed back the way he'd come, his masculine scent drifting on the air behind him.

Rude. Inexcusably, unjustifiably rude. Brie saw a blonde clutching a tablet device to her ample bosom, which was plumped over an inappropriately low neckline. She watched the woman move to meet him at the foot of the stairs. His architect. Female. Of course. He actually smiled at the woman and Brie fought a stab of pique. He wasn't ignoring *Chris.*

She watched them compare notes, converse a moment, then George appeared and both men walked towards the front door while Chris and her tablet headed towards the kitchen. The guys shook hands but just when Brie thought he'd forgotten she'd ever existed, Leo Hamilton turned his head and that enigmatic silver gaze found her, skimming her entire body again.

Her skin prickled, as if he'd given her an all-over body scrub with one of her salon's best exfoliating mitts. She shivered and resisted the urge to soothe her arms.

A corner of his mouth lifted. A smile? Or a smirk... As if he knew the effect he'd had on her. She narrowed her eyes. Damn. She was a confident woman when it came to any man, hunky or otherwise, so why this particular man wielded that power she had no idea—he was irritating and arrogant and dismissive. And a bunch of other things she refused to waste her time thinking about.

If he began to raise his hand in some sort of belated farewell, she didn't see it. Eyes averted and head high, she started downstairs. She heard the front door close and aimed a smile George's way. 'I hope I didn't scare him off.'

'I'd venture your new neighbour's not a man who scares easily,' he said, returning her smile. 'He had a plane to catch.' George fell into step beside her as they headed back to the dinner table. 'You'll have plenty of time to get acquainted,' he said with the devil in his voice.

A half-laugh caught in her overheated throat and she had to clear it. 'He's not my type.'

'No?'

'*No.*' Granted, conservative senior citizen George probably thought every man was her type since he'd probably never seen her turn into her driveway with the same guy twice.

But he'd be wrong. She enjoyed men but she was discerning in her choice of partners. The arrogant guy next door with the mellow bedroom voice? No way.

She shook off the double distraction of Leo Hamilton and her bedroom in the same image. Apart from finding out what his intentions were for East Wind—which she could do by talking with his architect if necessary—she couldn't wait to ignore him the next time she saw him.

Leo leaned back against the prestige cab's headrest as they headed for the airport. What the hell had happened back there? His whole body was still vibrating, as if he'd been blasted sideways by a sonic boom.

The after-effects of the shockwave that was Breanna Black.

His libido had jolted awake and demanded breakfast, an occurrence so unexpected and so irrational given his usual taste in women that he'd left Chris with the calculations he'd intended checking through alongside her.

He barely noticed Hobart's lights winking as he crossed the Tasman Bridge. A neighbour who could light his fire with just a look was a complication he didn't need. Perhaps he could oversee what needed to be done via email? He dismissed that idea with an impatient snap of fingers against his thigh—this project was as personal as it was important.

Whereas *she* wasn't important. In any way. He refused to alter his plans on a woman's account. Particularly one he'd just met.

And now he was going to be at the airport half an hour earlier than planned where he'd no doubt spend that time digging her out from beneath his skin.

He didn't have time for the attraction. The distraction. Or whatever the hell Breanna Black was.

Still, if he had to choose one word to describe her it would be stunning. Not in the usual way one called a woman stunning but in a stun-gun kind of way—and he was still feeling the burn.

She was all about impact rather than beauty. There was nothing subtle about her. Her cheekbones were too wide and too sharp for her face. Then there was the eye-popping lime tasselled top that stretched taut over firm, round and very generous breasts. Her mouth…ripe and red and damned if he hadn't wanted to move in and—

He closed his eyes but the woman's image blistered the back of his eyelids. Her hair a shiny river of blackberry silk flowing over her shoulders. Midnight eyes flashing with an inner fire, which made him wonder if that apparent passion for knowing other people's business extended to her bedroom.

Leo pinched the bridge of his nose to alleviate the tension building between his brows. He wasn't being entirely fair. Breanna had introduced herself at least, whereas he'd not exactly been Mr Congeniality.

Nice work, Hamilton. Way to antagonise the new neighbour. His sister needed an ally in this new community—another woman she could rely on when he wasn't around—not an adversary.

So he wouldn't be telling Sunny about bumping into Ms Black yet, he decided. If he happened to see Breanna next weekend—and he didn't intend going out of his way to do so, but if he did—he'd make more of an effort. For Sunny's sake.

Two hours later the Melbourne night wrapped its chill around his bones as he jogged up the shallow stone stairs of home. The evocative strains of violin drifted from within. Sunny was weaving her magic and he listened with brotherly pride. Little wonder she'd been accepted into Hope Strings, which performed as part of Tasmania's prestigious Philharmonic Orchestra, and at the ripe old age of twenty-four.

Rose and amber light spilled through the front door's stained glass, and as he pushed it open the delicious aroma of Mrs Jackson's slow-cooked bouillabaisse filled the air. His highly valued daytime housekeeper, and worth every cent he paid her.

He shrugged out of his coat and paused, a feeling of warmth seeping through him. Unlike his childhood, these days coming home gave him a comforting sense of peace and achievement.

But circumstances were about to change yet again. With Sunny's exciting new career taking off, despite her physical challenges, his little sister had demanded her independence. In no time at all, she'd be in her own home, in a new state. Alone. She'd point-blank refused his offer to employ a live-in housekeeper but had agreed to a cleaner on the condition she paid the woman's wages herself.

He zoned out and let the violin's sweet melancholy wash over him. *Enjoy the moment while you can.*

The house fire had robbed Sunny of the use of her now withered right leg and deformed foot, but had that slowed her down? Not on your life. If anything it had made her stronger, more determined.

She'd have that autonomy with his blessing—and some conditions. He'd arranged to install a personal emergency alarm system and insisted she wear a distress pendant at all times while in the house. And—*yes, Ms Black*—he had indeed checked out the feasibility of a pool.

Tasmania's climate didn't favour an outdoor construction, so he'd been considering alternatives. Sunny loved swimming; she found the weightlessness liberating. But not when she was alone. Which was why, in the end, he'd decided against the pool. It wasn't in keeping with the home and he didn't trust her to stay away from a pool when he wasn't there.

His freelance environmental management consultancy business took him to Tasmania on a regular basis and he anticipated dropping by her place at every opportunity. He also intended purchasing a suitable apartment nearby for himself. She could yell *control freak* and *uncompromising jerk* as often and loudly as she liked—he was immune as far as her insults were concerned, and was more than comfortable with any label she threw at him so long as she was safe.

'Why are you standing there all by yourself and looking like the world's about to end?'

'Hey, Suns.' He realised he'd been lost in thought awhile. 'I was listening to you play and thinking how quiet it's going to be here.'

'Doesn't say much for my skills then; I stopped five minutes ago.' She was leaning on her elbow crutch in a slant of light studying him with a half-smile on her lips, blonde hair curling in wisps around her face.

He nodded, coming out of what felt like a daze. 'I'll want a CD of your music.' He was going to miss her. Sunny by name, Sunny by nature.

'Already working on it.' She cocked her head. 'Problem with the new house?'

Why did her question immediately conjure a certain dark-haired dynamo rather than his latest property acquisition? 'A few surprises, that's all.'

That famous Sunny mood dimmed. 'So there *is* a problem.'

'Nothing I can't handle.' He walked to her, clasped her shoulders with both hands and smiled his reassurance. 'I'm ravenous. Did you wait for me?'

'Of course I did.'

He squeezed her shoulders and released her, and she accompanied him down the passage, her crutch tapping lightly on the tiles. They both preferred the cosiness of the little kitchen alcove over the formal dining room. Because he knew she wanted him to, Leo sat down and let her ladle the fish stew into two bowls without assistance.

She'd raided his wine stash. He poured two glasses of pinot noir from the bottle she'd set on the lace-cloth-covered table. 'Celebrating again?'

'Can't seem to stop,' she said with a laugh. The table was arranged flush against the bench to accommodate Sunny's disability and she carried the bowls to the table one at a time. When she was seated, she raised her glass. 'To the next adventure.'

Crystal chimed against crystal. 'Wherever it is you'll find it, Suns.'

'I was thinking more along the lines of *your* next adventure.' Her blue-eyed matchmaking gaze winked back at him.

He leaned back and studied his glass. 'We seem to be talking at cross purposes again.'

'What happened with that pretty little brunette you sent fifty red roses to then escorted to the theatre last month? Aisha, wasn't it?'

Ah, Aisha. Perfectly lovely, perfectly amenable. Or so he'd thought until she'd expected him to pay the cancellation fees for the overseas honeymoon she'd booked in anticipation of his marriage proposal.

Sunny and his love interests were very separate aspects of his life, except that she'd caught him ordering the roses. 'You know me.' He broke open his bread roll. 'Short-term casual all the way.'

'You're right, I *do* know you. And it's just sad.' She pointed an accusatory finger at him then shrugged and sighed rather dramatically. 'Okay, so you're looking for ways to make your next million.'

'Accumulating wealth.' He drank deeply then tilted his glass towards her. 'I thrive on the challenge.'

She grinned, picked up her spoon. 'I love a challenge too. Swimming in the Australia Day Big Swim on Sydney Harbour, for instance.'

Leo set his glass down and blinked at her while she tucked into her meal. 'Are you serious?'

'I've put my name on the list for swimmers with disabilities,' she said around a mouthful of fish. 'January's nine months away. Plenty of time for you to agree to be my swim buddy.'

'We'll need to have that conversation at some point,' he growled and got stuck into his own meal. But of course he'd agree—what was more, she knew it.

She tolerated her scars and deformity without a whisper of complaint or self-pity. Her wish to live independently was her choice, not his.

'I'll be fine,' she said, reading his mind.

'Mum would've been proud of you.'

'She'd have been proud of *us*.' Spoon halfway to her mouth, Sunny eyeballed him. 'I know what you're thinking. Don't.'

Sunny's pain was physical and would last a lifetime. Leo's anguish was deep and every bit as enduring. Guilt. Regret. His memories of the night twelve years ago when their lives had changed forever was as stark and real and terrifying as if it had happened yesterday.

He'd saved his sister but had been too late to pull their bruised and battered mother from their burning home. If his father hadn't goaded him into swinging that punch earlier in the evening, maybe the monster wouldn't have come back later and torched the place. The only justice was that he'd also died in the blaze.

'I wish she could have been here to see me perform in Sydney,' Sunny was saying. 'She'd always wanted to attend a concert at the Opera House.'

'*I'll* be there,' he said, pushing the past away and raising his glass to her.

'I'm counting on it. It's my last gig with the gang before I join Hope Strings. Three weeks, don't forget.'

'I won't,' he promised.

How could he forget? He only had to oversee the renovations, secure his own rental accommodation in Hobart and check out the environmental practices of a new client on the east coast of Tasmania in addition to his existing workload.

And to top it off there was the nosy neighbour with the attitude.

He tossed back the last drop of wine and set his glass

on the table with a decisive *plunk*. He absolutely, positively, without a doubt, didn't have time for a distraction like Breanna Black.

CHAPTER TWO

ONE WEEK LATER on Saturday afternoon, with Eve's Naturally closed for the rest of weekend, Brie made her way to East Wind's back door trailing her small plant trolley. She and Carol had exchanged keys years ago for those times when either of them were away. Before she handed her key to the agent Monday morning, she'd made arrangements to reclaim several dozen potted herbs and flowers she'd given Carol over the years. She'd intended collecting them during the week but had been working insane hours and they'd slipped her mind.

Taking a last look down the driveway to make sure Mr Hamilton of the husky voice hadn't decided to turn up in the last two minutes, she deactivated the alarm and let herself in. Not that she expected him—apparently he wasn't able to collect the keys until Tuesday. Carol hadn't elaborated and Brie was thrilled with herself for not asking for more details.

The glass-walled atrium formed a semicircular structure at the back of the home; soothing and familiar scents greeted her as she crossed its old brick floor. The sun's warmth on nutrient-rich, damp soil. Basil. Oregano, mint and lemongrass. 'Hello, my little treasures.' She trailed her fingers over a variegated thyme. 'I've come to take you home.'

Positioning the trolley near the workbench, she collected

the smaller pots, and to keep the more delicate plants going until she had time to deal with them tomorrow, she filled a spray bottle and began misting them.

She caressed the thick leaves of a large aloe vera in an elegant waist-high blue pot. 'You're going to be a challenge to lift, aren't you, my pretty? Maybe I should ask our friendly as a frozen fish neighbour for help.'

Huffing out a breath, she plugged her ear buds into the smartphone in the hip pocket of her jeans, switched on her favourite playlist. 'He'd have to acknowledge I'm alive first.' In time with her music, she shot off three hard squirts at a struggling coriander. 'And I sure as heck am not going to be first to acknowledge *him*.'

He'd barely given her the time of day. As if she'd been invisible.

Story of her life.

Well, not quite. She knew she stood out in a crowd *now*, thanks to her late growth spurt at the age of fifteen. She'd had years to practise how to garner attention—and she'd learned well. Even if it hadn't always been attention garnered for the right reasons and had landed her in trouble more often than she cared to remember. Her rebellious years.

These days she didn't have to work hard for that attention. Except from people like Leo Hamilton. And why did that irk her?

'I'm very much alive, Mr Big, Bad and Built,' she told an overgrown cactus with delusions of its own importance. 'And I'm going to make it my business to show you I *do* exist.'

Aiming her bottle at it, she squeezed the trigger. Hard. Seemed she wasn't done with rebellion yet.

Arms crossed beside a potted kumquat tree, Leo leaned a shoulder against the door jamb and watched with some amusement while his new neighbour drowned the arid-loving cactus and his reputation as a usually well-mannered guy. With those bits of plastic in her ears, he wondered if she even knew she was voicing her opinions aloud. Yeah— she existed all too clearly and, despite his best efforts to the contrary, his body responded, the tension tightening with every squeeze of her slender fingers on that trigger bottle.

He wasn't hiding but he was counting on her not seeing him just yet—he hadn't witnessed anything as fascinating as Breanna Black making herself at home in *his* atrium since his pubescent self had ogled the naked female form for the first time.

He'd wandered around the back of the house with some landscaping ideas on paper to find the door open. He was ticked off that she still had the key George had mentioned and, worse, she was still using it. Obviously she had the security code as well. He intended familiarising her with the concept of privacy…soon. Right now he couldn't take his eyes off her. She had the sexiest backside, especially when she wiggled it as she was doing now in time to music only she could hear.

Her top was a yellow-raincoat yellow, and, from what he could see in profile as she moved, cling wrapped to those abundant breasts. The short hem flared over black leggings that clung to long, long legs. She looked like the sunflower she was standing next to.

She continued squirting, flicked her long black plait back over her shoulder. His fingers itched to free it from the confines of its elastic band, to watch it shimmer the way it had that moment at the top of the stairs last week, to feel its silky texture against his palms. To bring it to his nose and inhale. Slowly. Deeply.

Pull yourself together.

She was a neighbour, and, right now, a damn nuisance. He'd worked past midnight every evening this week so he could be in Hobart over the weekend to check out some nearby short-term accommodation for himself while the electrician ripped out the guts of this place and installed new wiring throughout. The plumbers were going to be here, and the kitchen renovation crew.

He did not want this woman in his space. Nor did he need her sensual perfume wafting his way and clogging up his sinuses with scents better appreciated in the bedroom.

She plunked the sunflower on the trolley, gave it a drenching. 'He'd better not be planning any external changes that will affect the value of *my* home. An elevator, for crying out loud? And if he even thinks about getting rid of that foyer chandelier...' Her rant trailed off— presumably she was contemplating what she'd do to him in the event.

Wearing skin-tight leather and brandishing a whip.

The image of the two of them engaged in bodily combat flashed before him. The slippery slide of that black leather against his flesh. His teeth finding the vulnerable place under her chin while she screamed in pleasure. He clenched his jaw—he could literally feel his blood pressure spike.

He'd heard enough. He wanted her out of here, now. Before he said, or did, something detrimental to his state of solitary well-being.

Uncrossing his arms, he pushed off the door frame.

'Now why would I want to do that?'

The low murmur near her ear at the same instant someone removed her ear buds had Brie practically leaping out of her skin. 'What the...?' Fists raised, she spun around. *'You.'* Her fists uncurled and she lowered her arms to the workbench. 'You startled me.'

She was still startled, but in an electrifying, breath-stealing way, and her strength seemed to drain out of her under the force of his steely eyed gaze.

He wore casual today—faded denim and a matching soft-looking jumper, and he smelled of warm wool and that indefinable masculine scent she recognised from the last time she'd seen him.

'Then again, if I did want to do that...' He didn't appear concerned that he'd scared ten years off her life and looked her up and down in a manner that wiped whatever she had been talking about from her mind.

'Do...*what*? And...and what are you *doing* here?'

'Shouldn't I be asking you that question?' His voice was all reason and calm. Not to mention husky and low and seductive.

'I thought George told you about the key,' she went on, since she did owe him an explanation. 'And the plants.' She began picking up pots at random, setting them on the trolley. 'I apologise, I meant to get around to it during the week but I was busy.'

One dark brow rose, his expression clear. *Doing what?*

'You're not the only one who works, Mr Hamilton.'

He slouched casually against the workbench. 'You can rest easy—I have no intention of removing the chandelier. The elevator's not happening and there'll be no exterior changes—I love the house's old-world charm and I appreciate that the two buildings share a history, which I believe should be retained. Apart from some electrical and plumbing work, I'm doing some kitchen renovations, which involve shifting a wall about fifty centimetres, but they won't compromise the integrity of the place. You okay with that?'

She breathed a sigh of relief and slapped a hand to her chest. 'Thank goodness. I've been thinking about you—about *it*—about your *renovations* all week.' *Busted.* 'And I've been thinking other stuff out loud too, haven't I?'

No reply as his gaze stroked over her again.

Her blood rushed through her body and heat bloomed beneath her skin. 'I'll, um, get out of your way.' She tossed the rest of the pots onto the trolley willy-nilly. When had she ever been so scatter-brained talking to a man?

'You wanted me to give you a hand with this one, right?' He indicated the aloe vera.

He gave no outward hint that he'd heard her 'friendly as a frozen fish neighbour' comment, but she knew he had, and cringed inwardly. 'That'd be great,' she muttered. 'Thanks.'

'Reckon you'll need to keep it steady,' he said, lifting it on board the trolley as if it weighed no more than an empty bucket. Which drew her attention to the movement of the muscles beneath his jumper. The way they stretched the wool tight across his chest and bunched beneath the sleeves.

He glanced her way. 'Your back yard, I presume?'

She shifted her focus to his eyes. *Only* his eyes. 'No need for you to bother. I can manage, thank you.'

'Wouldn't want that pot to shatter.'

Wouldn't want her self-control to shatter either. She wanted to be away from him asap. Away from his warm man smell that made her want to burrow against his chest and breathe deep. She didn't *want* to like her new neighbour but her body had a mind of its own.

Best to let him play Mr Macho then and get it over with. Get *him* over with and she could go back to whatever she'd been doing before. If she could just remember. 'Okay. Thanks.'

They proceeded outside with rattling pots and trailing greenery as he manoeuvred the trolley towards the driveway.

Probably not wise to tell him she'd entered his property this way but, 'There's a gap between our fences.' Brie lifted a chin in the general direction, holding the pot steady with both hands. 'Carol and I used it to save time. I was going to close it after I got the plants,' she told him.

When he said nothing, she continued, 'We looked out for each other. As neighbours should. Don't you agree?'

'I'd say it depends on the neighbour.' They reached the gap and he stopped to inspect it. 'I'll organise a tradesman.'

'Fine. Thanks.' He seemed so keen to take charge, she'd let him. *This* time.

'Which reminds me.' He held out his hand, palm up. 'You have my key.'

Brie glimpsed scarring on the inside of his forearm as she retrieved the key from inside an empty ceramic pot and dropped it in his palm. 'Thanks, it'll save me a trip to the agent.' Flipping her hand, she grinned at him. 'And while you're at it, you might want to change the security code.'

'Yes. I will.'

Then he smiled back. Kind of. As if he hadn't meant to and it was a surprise to him too, generous lips quirking at the corners. She glimpsed a twinkle of humour in his eyes.

Her stomach fizzed, her limbs went soft and her fingers tightened on the rim of the pot as her inner flirt demanded she come out and play. *No*, Brie told her.

He looked away, resumed pushing the trolley again. 'So, Ms Black. Breanna—'

'Brie.'

'Brie. How do you earn a living?'

'I'm a beauty therapist. You?'

'Environmental management consulting.'

Her brows lifted. 'And what does an environmental management consultant do, exactly?'

'I freelance to businesses who want advice on their environmental practices.'

'You must charge a fortune for your services.' She gestured towards her garden shed as they crossed the square of lawn bordered by recycled pink bricks. 'You might as well know I'm a tell-it-as-it-is kind of girl—I know how much you paid for the place.'

He cleared his throat. 'My clients seek me out, not the other way around.'

'Really? With those interpersonal skills I witnessed last week?'

'I was in a hurry.'

'Because of me?'

He made a strangled sound, cleared his throat again. 'No excuses. I apologise.'

Hmm, uncomfortable. How charmingly appealing. She loved having that effect on a man. Her resolve to keep her distance was weakening by the second. 'Accepted. You had a plane to catch, right?'

'Correct.'

'And a date waiting?'

'Not precisely. Are you always this…?' He seemed to struggle for the word.

'Straightforward?' Not the word he'd have used, she'd wager, and his 'not precisely' answer clarified nothing. 'Pretty much. You mentioned this was an investment, so will you be here often?'

They stopped at the shed and unloaded the pots.

'I'll be stopping by to check on the progress. And I've just taken on some new clients in Tasmania so I'll be on the island most of the time. Where do you want the aloe vera?'

'Inside the conservatory. Thanks.'

She watched him push the trolley to the rear of the house, then, once inside, she helped him unload the pot where she wanted it. 'Would you like something to drink? I have a chilled fruit tisane in the fridge.'

He regarded her blankly. 'Thanks, but no thanks.'

'Sure? It's a very refreshing beverage.'

'I'm a coffee man, myself. And I'm due to check out

some rental accommodation in the Arcade Apartments.'
He checked his watch, displaying a thick wrist dusted with
dark hair. 'Twenty minutes ago.' Grimacing, he yanked out
his phone, sent a voice message apologising and advising
he'd make a time later this afternoon.

Millionaire's accommodation, the Arcade. 'Where are
you staying at the moment?'

'A bed and breakfast two minutes away.'

She nodded. 'That'll be Hannah's Hideaway. How much
are you paying for an apartment at the Arcade?'

'More than it's worth.' He spoke briskly, pocketed his
phone with a similar movement. 'Proximity's important.'

Brie, always on the lookout for extra funds for Pink
Snowflake, came up with an instant light-bulb idea. 'How
long are you looking at?'

'Few weeks.' A tiny frown dug between his brows.
'Why?'

'What would you say to living right next door?'

'I'm not interested in a room.' Penetrating eyes considered hers and he took his time answering. 'If that's what
you're offering.'

'I'm not offering you a room.' She matched his gaze.
'My brother, Jett, and my best friend, Olivia, are on their
honeymoon and I'm house-sitting their new health retreat
from next week for a couple of months or thereabouts. It's
totally flexible. So, you could stay here, have the entire
place to yourself and the rent money could go to the Pink
Snowflake Foundation instead of the Arcade owner's over-
inflated bank account.' She grinned at her own ingenuity.
'It's win-win.'

'Hmm.' He squatted in front of the blue pot, tested its
stability on the uneven green tiles recycled from the sixties and laid with her own fair hands. 'What's the Pink
Snowflake Foundation?'

'Jett and Olivia are opening a luxury holistic retreat

for cancer patients to recuperate after their treatment and Pink Snowflake is Olivia's project of love that made the whole thing possible. It's ahead of schedule but the happy couple are overseas. They asked me if I'd like to spend a few nights a week there. Soak in the spa, enjoy the pool and solarium. Use the gym. Explore their private cellar. Naturally I couldn't refuse.'

'Naturally.' The tone was dry. Rising, he hooked his thumbs in his jeans pockets and looked about. 'You own this place? You live here alone?'

She nodded. 'I inherited it when my parents died and, yes, I live alone.'

'So I'd have the entire place to myself? No unexpected interruptions. Until the job's done?'

'All yours. Although I may need to come by and collect the odd outfit or whatever. But you'd have all the keys and I'd ring first. I wouldn't just drop in.' *Unless you invited me.*

As if he'd heard her private thought, his eyes dropped to her mouth. He looked away fast, checked his watch again and she pounced before he could refuse. 'When would you want it by?'

His eyes flicked back to hers. This time they held. 'Next weekend.'

Was it her imagination or was there something in the way he said that? A glint rapidly masked behind that quicksilver gaze?

'Sold,' she told him before she could think of all the reasons why inviting a man she knew nothing about—except that he turned her on—into her private sanctuary might be a bad idea. 'The Pink Snowflake Foundation thanks you.'

'Okay, we'll give it a try,' he said finally. 'I'm all for a good cause.' He pulled out his mobile, cancelled his appointment with the Arcade rep.

'"We" as in you and a partner?' Brie spoke more sharply than she meant to.

'"We" as in you and me.' The way he linked them together in that low, husky voice while he held her gaze prisoner made her pulse race with excitement. 'I want to see it,' he said, sliding his mobile back into his pocket. 'If it's not an inconvenience.'

'Not at all.' She gestured him towards the far side of the conservatory while she got herself under control. 'Family area's through here. Layout's the same as yours,' she said, whisking a basket of washing off the sofa as she passed. 'Have a seat and I'll get you a drink. I have fourteen kinds of tea, hot or cold— Oops, you're a coffee m—'

'Thanks, but there's no need,' she heard him say. 'I'm meeting my architect in ten.'

The busy blonde with the over-exposed boobs. 'Chris.' She raised a brow. 'Thought you weren't planning any major changes?'

'Just that kitchen wall I told you a…bout…' Leo's voice trailed off as he took in the visuals. He'd walked into chaos.

What appeared to be an entire wardrobe of party dresses was strewn across an armchair. As he entered the kitchen, a variety of foodstuffs covered every available surface but he had no idea what she intended cooking. He gave a mental shudder, comparing it with his own ordered world, from his computer files to his DVD collection to the way he arranged his ties.

Had she thought this idea through? He doubted it. By all appearances, it seemed she was one of those impulsive people who never stood still, gravitating from one interest to the next as the whim took her.

'Excuse the mess. I've been experimenting with some nature-based facial masks and steams.'

Which explained the bowl of pink mash that smelled like strawberries and peppermint. But not the fifty or so plastic beer and wine glasses stacked alongside a large box of Moroccan lanterns. 'I'll come back later,' he told her. When he'd reconsidered.

'Hey, if you're in a hurry now, why don't you come by this evening? I'm having a party—ten o'clock on—you could check out the place then.'

Fine for some. He had a Saturday night date with his laptop. To ease the pain, he was planning to help the evening along with a nice Tasmanian Cabernet Shiraz. He intended stopping at the trendy upmarket bottle shop he'd seen nearby. But that wasn't the only reason. An evening with Breanna Black in party mode was a bad idea. 'No can do. I've got work to finish.'

'Don't we all? But on a Saturday night?' She clucked her tongue. 'That's just sad.'

'Some might say so.' But he was proud of his consultancy business. His alone. He'd built it from the ground up, with nothing but determination and hard work and it was the first and only part of his life he'd ever had absolute control over. It was worth a few sacrifices.

'I'll leave you my contact number.' He placed his business card next to a row of a dozen or so unusual teapots on a distressed wood sideboard then turned to her. 'If you'll tell me your details, I'll come by tomorrow. I'm presuming afternoon'll be best?'

She smiled. A naughty smile that seemed to make him an accomplice in whatever racy plans she had for the evening, and almost had him wishing he'd accepted her invitation, bad idea or not.

Temptation beckoned with the luscious curve of those full lips. 'Give me your phone.'

Holding out her hand, she stepped close. Too close, and into his personal space. Feminine scent enveloped him; the tips of her extended fingers brushed his jumper.

He stepped back. She wasn't getting her hands near

his contacts list—or anywhere else for that matter. His groin tightened at the erotic thought. 'Just tell me, I'll remember.' He had an exceptional memory for numbers and facts—except right now he was having trouble remembering his own name.

She rattled off a series of numbers as he walked to the door.

'We'll work out the details tomorrow,' he muttered.

He didn't stop till he reached the new SUV he'd picked up only hours ago. Sliding onto the caramel-soft seat, he tipped his head back and closed his eyes, lust and frustration building a fire below his belt.

Hadn't he stayed away from her? Minded his own business?

Had it made a scrap of difference?

The woman wasn't merely a nuisance, she should come with a warning label. *Approach at your own peril.*

So much for working without being disturbed. Brie didn't have to be physically present to mess with his head.

Tonight was going to be a long, uncomfortable night.

CHAPTER THREE

Brie, an experienced hostess, was running late for her own party. Her plant rescue expedition had taken longer than she'd anticipated. The reason for that was an enormously sexy man and he was still centre stage in her thoughts. And didn't she love the fact that here was a man who more than matched her height? She set out nibbles, arranged tea-lights and lanterns for lighting later while she thought about her impulsive offer to rent her home to him.

She doubted he'd expect the use of the entire house but it was going to be a race against time to have the place tidy and the stuff she wanted to take to the retreat packed by next weekend. On top of that, the thought of Leo Hamilton sleeping in her bed, on her sheets, sent a shiver through her, along with the question: did he sleep naked? There was no alternative. It was the only room with a bed long enough and wide enough to accommodate a man his size.

Two hours before her guests were due to arrive, she drove to the liquor shop. She'd paid for her order, the cartons already stacked in her car with a friendly staff member's assistance, when she remembered she'd intended to buy a bottle of sparkly to enjoy after work in the retreat's spa later in the week.

And there he was, the most recent object of her private fantasies perusing the classiest labels in the red wine section. Labels so out of her price range, she could only imagine the smooth, rich flavour. No doubt the two of them had vastly different tastes. And not only in wine.

Come on, Brie, when has that stopped you?

It might be fun at that.

She picked up the nearest bottle of sparkling white while she watched him from the corner of her eye. She'd glimpsed a sense of humour this afternoon. Even traded flirty looks with him. Whether he acknowledged it or not, Brie knew when a guy was interested.

She also knew that the moment the renovations were done, he'd leave the property in his agent's hands and move on to his next million-dollar investment. He was that kind of guy. She smiled to herself. And *that* made him the perfect kind of guy—perfectly constructed, perfectly casual, perfectly short-term.

When Brie set her sights on a man, he didn't stand a chance. But their fun times never lasted long—these days she made sure of it. Since Elliot, her motto was *no heart, no hurt.* Worked for her every time.

Heat stroked Leo's left cheek like a glove and the hairs on the back of his neck seemed to move antenna-like in the same direction.

He knew why before he looked up.

He'd seen Breanna and her puppy-dog assistant stacking up her car with booze and thought she'd left. But no, she was walking towards him, holding a bottle of bubbly and wielding her flirtatious smile like a challenge. His fingers tightened on his two-hundred-dollar bottle of Barossa shiraz cabernet and, with a vague nod towards her, he moved to the refrigerator section.

Like an inevitability, she kept coming. He selected a black olive pâté and his favourite cheese—a Tasmanian Brie—before he realised the irony of his choice.

Too late to swap for a Camembert. Was this some kind of cosmic conspiracy?

She'd loosened her hair and it slid over her shoulders, straight and thick and glorious. She stopped in front of him, noted his product choices and wielded that smile some more. 'Party for one?'

'Might as well get some enjoyment out of the evening while I work.'

She flicked her hair back in an artful, well-practised feminine move. 'Why do tonight what you can put off till tomorrow? I have some crackers at home that would go nicely with that Brie.' Her eyes seemed to say *the type of cracker that goes off with a bang.*

'I'm sure you do. *Brie.*' He refused to be seduced by her smoky-voiced invitation with its barely subtle innuendo. To prove it, he maintained his nonchalant gaze towards her as he drew out his wallet. He was all in favour of seduction, but he wanted to be the one doing the seducing. Wherever and whenever *he* was good and ready. He ignored the fire in his chinos insisting that time was fast approaching. 'I'll see you tomorrow afternoon. As arranged.'

'Fine,' she said, not looking away. 'However you want to play.'

Hard and fast. The unspoken words singed the air between them.

He waited for Breanna to break the searing eye contact first. The tension stretched out for several long seconds. Only when she finally glanced at her watch then delved into her bag for her purse did he turn towards the cash register at the end of the aisle.

'Afraid you might enjoy yourself, Mr Hamilton?' she teased behind him. 'Or is it me you're afraid of.' It wasn't a question.

He turned, caught her teasing, tossed it back. 'Not at all. Parties aren't my scene. Too many people.' He intentionally lowered his tone. 'But a party for two…' He watched the teasing light in her eyes flare to frank awareness and a distinct attraction before she looked away. Score two to him.

I'm as eager to find out as you are, baby doll. But he had no intention of acting on it. Yet. *He'd* decide the if and when and it wouldn't be tonight. Still, he couldn't help grinning as he walked to the counter and set his platinum card down.

She followed, stood a good arm's distance along the counter from him, considering the bottle in her hands. 'I think I'm going to need two or more of these,' she murmured to herself.

'Best to be prepared, I say.'

That startled a laugh out of her. 'You're not what I expected, Mr Hamilton.'

'Should I interpret that as a good thing?'

'I'll let you know. Later.' She dared him with a hot glint in her midnight eyes, a quick curve of those glossy lips.

Which had him wondering how those eyes would look dazed with passion, how her lips would feel pressed against his own. How they'd feel against other body parts…

He gritted his teeth as his body responded to that tempting glimpse of paradise. He refused to be dictated to by his hormones. Or Ms Black. Swinging away, he raised his bottle in farewell as he moved to the door. 'Enjoy your party.'

Yanking open his car door, he shook his head. Unbelievable. He was walking away from an opportunity to share the evening with a hot woman who obviously wanted the same thing he did.

He slid inside, sat a moment, staring through the windscreen. His next-door neighbour. Correction: *Sunny's* neighbour. She and his sister looked about the same age, had the same feisty personalities—they'd probably get on well, even long-term.

Whereas he and Breanna? It would be hot and temporary, like that firecracker she'd made him think of. A whizz-bang, short-term fling.

But unlike the easy-going, casual women he hooked up with, this one would clash plenty with him. Give him a whole lot of drama he didn't need.

He'd endured more than his share of emotional trauma. As a kid hearing his mother's broken pleas when her violent husband exercised his conjugal rights and slapped her around while doing it, her sobs in the dark after he'd gone.

For more than half his lifetime he'd been powerless to change the situation. And every time his young self had tried, his mother had copped the beatings and the bruises.

Then there was the fire. Sunny's arduous recovery and rehab. The relentless questions that nagged at him: what could he have done differently? What *should* he have done to change the outcome?

His breath fogged up the windscreen and he swiped a hand over the glass, switched on the ignition. High drama? Not him. No way. He'd planned his evening—a meal in one of the city's upmarket restaurants overlooking Sullivans Cove, a few hours of work in the cosy sitting room accompanied by his favourite shiraz. Nothing and, more specifically, *no one* was going to interfere with those plans.

At ten-thirty, Leo powered off his laptop and stretched cramped muscles. The decision to postpone opening his wine had given him a clear head to work. His latest client was a new six-star eco lodge on Tasmania's east coast with the beguiling name of Heaven. He'd finished reading their initial commentary and had noted his suggested changes and added his in-depth report an hour earlier than he'd anticipated.

It left him at a loose end for the rest of the evening.

Was that why he'd subconsciously postponed opening the bottle in the first place? Frowning, he dismissed it.

He never felt the need to self-analyse. Until tonight. Until Breanna had burst into his life.

Her name alone brought her to sparkling life behind his eyes in a thousand different images, like seeing her through a kaleidoscope. Each one bright and sassy and unique.

Unsettling.

He paced to the window, stared past the rain pattering lightly on the night-darkened glass, in the direction of their homes, a two-minute drive away. He'd seen a substantial amount of liquor ferried to her car this afternoon. Was that a regular thing? He drummed his fingers on the pane. She was obviously a girl who enjoyed fun times. Were her parties noisy and boozy and out of control?

Tonight was an ideal opportunity to check things out and ensure his latest and most important acquisition was in Sunny's best interests. It wasn't as if he hadn't been invited, he reminded himself, and, picking up his bottle, he grabbed his car's remote.

The unmistakable sounds of revelry greeted his ears when Leo strode up Breanna's rain-slicked path with his bottle of wine a short time later. Bass thumped. Loud, but not loud enough to intrude on her neighbours' peace. It scored Breanna a conditional nod of approval, even if her taste in music did nothing for him.

It appeared to be an open-door policy so he let himself in, crossed the foyer lit by a chandelier that matched his own. As he stepped into the formal lounge room, the atmosphere, overly warm with too many bodies packed into one place, enveloped him. Glow from the Moroccan lanterns splashed the shadowy room with splotches of orange and watermelon pink.

He waited for his eyes to adjust, expecting to see Breanna standing tall amongst the crowd wearing some eye-popping creation. Guests were gyrating in time to the pounding beat, others were loading plates at the spicy-smelling buffet in the corner.

But he didn't see Breanna. He exhaled on an impatient breath. Where was she?

An attractive redhead in a slinky purple number found her way through the dancers and bobbed up in front of him. 'Hi.'

Her smile was friendly interest. He was surprised to find it did nothing for him. 'Hi there,' he said, only half listening while he continued to search out the only reason he was here.

'I'm Samantha. We haven't met, have we?'

'No, we haven't. I'm Leo.' He nodded towards the empty wine glass she was caressing. 'Where can I get a couple of those?'

'Drinks? I'd love—'

'Glasses.' He held up his bottle. 'You don't know where Breanna is, do you?'

'She's not far—I saw her a few moments ago talking with Bronwyn.' Her smile evaporated and she waved towards the kitchen. 'Glasses are that way.'

'Thanks.'

On the lookout for the hostess, he made his way through the crowd, grabbing two clean long-stemmed wine glasses from the kitchen. The room looked marginally tidier than it had this afternoon. He spied a gaggle of girls in the family area where clothes had been scattered earlier, but saw neither Breanna nor her clothes. He checked the atrium where guests talked over booze and chips. The downstairs loo.

With the rest of the rooms in darkness, their doors shut, he presumed they were off-limits. Which left the next floor.

Familiar with the layout of his own place, he walked straight towards the master bedroom. He knew Breanna must be there since it was the only room with a light on.

The sensual fragrance he'd come to associate with her—the one he'd taken to calling midnight temptation—drifted in the air. Anticipation swarmed through him and his pulse quickened.

He could hear movement and tapped on the semi-open door. 'Breanna.' When there was no reply, only a fast rustling sound, he tapped again. He was impatient to see her now he was here. 'Breanna. Are you decent in there?' In that instant it occurred to him that she might not be alone. Something hooked in his gut. Was that what he'd heard—two desperate would-be lovers trying to cover up fast? The thought of some other man touching her the way he'd been thinking of touching her shocked him into movement and he walked in without further preamble.

Leo was here? Brie scrambled up, tugged the hem of her new vermilion dress down, her heart jack-hammering. She swiped at a lock of hair that had fallen over her brow. He was the *last* person she wanted to catch her on her hands and knees searching under the bed for a DVD she'd borrowed from Bron and forgotten about.

She'd almost composed herself in front of the mirror when he entered *without* waiting for her invitation. Still, she could hardly hurl accusations—the door was open and he *had* asked permission. She'd just chosen not to answer until she was ready.

She still wasn't ready and her heart was still thumping but she dragged her eyes to his reflection and locked gazes with him in the mirror while her fingers fumbled with the dress's neckline. She could almost see the heat haze shimmering on the glass. Still watching his reflection, she saw him set his mega-expensive bottle of wine and two glasses on her bedside table.

He wore black casual and oh…my. She didn't know what possessed her but to demonstrate just how cool and

unruffled she was, not, she whirled around, sashayed over
to him and planted a firm kiss on his mouth. Then she
whirled back to the mirror.

Her lips were on fire. Her whole body was burning. She
felt like a teenage rookie and glanced at him from beneath
her lashes. *Think cool, think cool.*

He hadn't moved. He shook his head. 'What was that?'

She shrugged, the laugh catching in her throat. 'A
whim. I was curious.'

Now she was even more curious. What would a full-on
sensual assault be like? Trying for casual, she picked up
her brush, ran it through her hair. Her arm felt strangely
weak, as if she were coming down with a fever. 'What
changed your mind?'

'I finished sooner than I expected.'

'Ah.' She nodded wisely. 'Party for one not satisfying, huh?'

'The party hasn't started yet.' His voice took on a persuasive tone that brushed over her skin like velvet. 'Nice.'

He meant her slinky dress—at least she thought he
did—except his gaze seemed to skim only the bare thighs
its short hem didn't cover, sending goosebumps over her
flesh.

'Nice of you to notice.'

Setting her brush down, she turned from his reflection
to look at the real man. And reminded herself to breathe.
He seemed to draw something from her that she'd never
known she had. Was she out of her depth with this one?
'Do you think I'm going to abandon my hostess responsibilities for a frolic across the sheets with you?'

He raised a dark brow. 'Are you?'

The scary thing was she had a feeling that was exactly
what was going to happen. She loved playing the catch-
me-if-you-can game almost as much as reaching the winning post but this time she seemed to be tied to the starting

gate. 'You've got a high opinion of yourself, haven't you?' She wasn't going to make it easy for him.

He nodded. 'I'm comfortable with who I am. How about you?'

'At the moment I'm feeling pretty relaxed.' Not exactly answering his question. She smiled to hide the fact she was strung out like wet washing in the wind.

He closed the door, muting the sound of the party below. Taking his time, he peeled the foil off the top of the bottle, unscrewed the cap and splashed some wine into the bottom of the glasses. 'Do you like a good shiraz?'

'I do. I should—'

'This one's my favourite. I didn't expect to find it here.'

'Me either,' she murmured. She could delay her hostess duties a moment. Or possibly the rest of her life.

She leaned her backside against her dressing table for support as he stopped in front of her, both glasses in one large hand. The other he wrapped around the back of her neck, holding her skull in such a way so she was looking right at him. Up close his eyes were pewter flecked with cobalt. He smelled of fresh rain on cotton, shampoo and soap. She clutched the edge of the dressing table on either side of her hips. If she touched him, she might not be responsible for her actions, and, with him, she very much needed to be responsible.

His head dipped, his mouth hovered. 'I'll admit to a little curiosity of my own,' he murmured and touched his lips to hers.

Firm and warm. They moved gently; testing, teasing, tasting. Taking his time, showing her how devastating one long, drawn-out kiss could be. How a woman could be seduced into forgetting her own identity. Her fingers tightened on the wood behind her. She could feel his body heat radiating between them and her fingers itched to explore but still she didn't touch him.

She'd never been one for slow. This leisurely pace was new. Mesmerising. As her body melted against his her blood grew sluggish and flowed like clotted cream through her veins.

Even the sound of the rain on her window faded and all she was aware of were his fingers massaging the back of her scalp, his lips on hers, and the rich, dark promise of more. She yearned. When he raised his head, she bit back a sigh.

He lifted his hand from the back of her skull to trace a path just once down the side of her face, fingertips leaving a trail of tingling nerve endings. 'Breanna.' He slid his thumb over her bottom lip then took a step back.

He looked bemused, she thought. The way she felt right now. 'That was…that's a lot of curiosity.'

He reached out, flicked a strand of hair behind her ear. 'Unlike your "whim", I enjoy taking my time.'

'I noticed,' she said, feeling as if she were floating a few centimetres off the floor. She struggled to rein in her far-flung thoughts and ground herself. 'There are at least fifty people downstairs who'll be wondering where I am.'

'They seem a pretty self-sufficient lot. Try this.' He handed her a glass.

She took it with nerveless fingers and sipped, letting the rich mellowness caress the inside of her mouth. 'Mmm.'

He drank too. 'I doubt they'll notice you're missing for a little while.'

She sipped again. 'Someone could turn up here at any moment.' Bron, for instance.

'Does that bother you?'

'No.' It should, it really should but right now she couldn't bring herself to care. 'You're bad.'

He grinned, as if seducing women at their own parties was a regular pastime, and raised his glass. 'Your opinion?'

'Of the wine? Or the kiss?'

He watched her over the rim. 'We both know we enjoyed the kiss.'

He had that right and the knowledge shimmered through her. 'The wine's beautiful—smooth and rich.' *Like you.* Worth every cent he'd paid? Probably not. Still, she wasn't complaining and sipped some more.

But she'd not eaten since lunch and the wine's potency on an empty stomach spread through her limbs like an approaching anaesthetic. Her senses were filled with him, her mind reeling and already cloudy. Intoxication was a definite possibility and one she couldn't afford.

She set her glass on the dressing table. 'I'll just slip downstairs to check everything's okay and get us a dip and some of those crackers I promised you.'

Leo watched her slick a new layer of gloss over those luscious-tasting lips. He couldn't wait to muss her up some more. He wanted to see the real Brie first thing in the morning with no make-up and satisfied with a long, slow night of sex.

As if reading his thoughts, she grinned at him in the mirror. 'I'll be right back.'

As she crossed the plush sage carpet his eyes followed the sway of orange silk-clad hips and he imagined how those barely covered, shapely long legs would feel entwined with his.

Man, oh, man, he needed to sit down. He sank into a cream wicker rocking chair in the corner to wait for his body's response to partially subside—as if that were remotely possible. Not with Brie's midnight temptation fragrance permeating every corner of the room. The tantalising taste of her lips on his own. The girl knew how to kiss and no doubt a good deal more.

Taking a long, slow swallow of his drink, he focused on

the way it slid warm and satisfying down his throat rather than the *un*satisfying ache in his groin.

For his next distraction, he turned his attention to her bedroom. He'd expected something bold and out there like the woman herself but her room was feminine and whimsically romantic—if you ignored the shamble of clothes, paperbacks and boxes scattered every which way. Deep green walls showcased John Waterhouse prints—The Lady of Shalott, Narcissus and The Awakening of Adonis.

On the queen-size bed lay a heap of flamboyant outfits that looked as if they'd been tried on then hastily discarded. Beneath, he glimpsed a rose-coloured floral quilt. He stared in growing consternation. Was this the room she expected him to sleep in while he stayed here? This bed? Surely she had other rooms and other beds?

He ran a perplexed hand over his hair. He hadn't come here tonight with the intention of starting something with Breanna—his temporary landlady and Sunny's future friend.

His observations so far confirmed she was nothing like the type of women he enjoyed—soft, cuddly, *organised* women willing and happy to let him take control. Women who were aroused by dominant men.

So why the blazes would he want to start *anything* with Breanna Black?

He already had.

And why not? With a body like hers? Pushing up, he paced to the door, craned his neck to see if she was on her way. He couldn't wait to get her naked and beneath him and find out what really turned her on. Then set about driving her slowly mad with wanting it. Taking her to the brink of ecstasy with his hands and mouth, watching her eyes plead and burn with passion as he dragged her over the edge at last screaming his name—

Clenching his jaw, he checked the time. Where the hell

was she? She'd all but dared him to come to this bash and he'd played right into her hands. With Breanna he couldn't seem to think rationally. He was *still* playing into her hands, waiting in her room like an obsessed fool until she condescended to return. He shook his head to clear it.

She might have others fooled into playing her games, but not Leo Hamilton.

It took a tall tumbler of iced water under bright kitchen lights to clear Brie's cotton-wool head and remember that she had a duty to all her guests, not just the man waiting for her in her bedroom who did crazy things to her internal organs and just wanted sex.

'Hey, party babe.' Samantha popped her head around the door. 'A guy was looking for you.' She gave the thumbs up as she crossed the room. 'Did I forget to mention he was pretty damn cute?'

Cute? 'He found me. Thanks. Would you take this to the table, please?' Brie slid a plate of crackers with smoked salmon pâté and dill out of the fridge. 'I'll be right back.'

'Take your time,' Sam told her, reaching for the platter with a conspiratorial twinkle.

'I'll be right back,' Brie repeated firmly. There was a party happening. *Her* party. *Her* friends. Her priority.

'Brie?'

She was halfway down the hall to invite the *cute* Mr Hamilton downstairs to join the fun when the distressed voice had her turning back. Megan swayed in front of her, brow creased, lips white.

Brie gripped her friend's arms. 'What's wrong, honey?'

'I'm fighting a vicious migraine and the migraine's winning. I've been looking for you.'

'Oh, Megs, I'm so sorry.' Guilt crawled through her as she propelled Megan to an unoccupied room off the hall, pushed her gently onto the nearest armchair. Leaving the light off, she squatted down in front of her. 'I'd invite you to sleep it off here, except the noise…'

Megan closed her eyes. 'Thanks but I need to go home before I throw up. Can you find Denis?'

'Sure.'

It took a few minutes to locate Megan's boyfriend having a smoke on the front veranda and a few more to help Megan to the car and see them off safely.

She was at the bottom of the stairs when Leo appeared at the top with that stern and uncompromising expression she'd seen him wearing last week. 'Hey, there. I—'

'We can make arrangements tomorrow,' he said as he descended. 'To work out the rental agreement.'

Had he added that last bit in case she thought he was referring to something more explicitly sexual when it clearly wasn't? Prepared to cut him some slack because she'd left him alone for longer than she'd meant to, she smiled, tried again. 'I'm sor—'

'Not too early, right?' he added, his eyes cool, shuttered. 'So you can party into the wee hours. Enjoy yourself.'

He hadn't given her a chance to explain. Hadn't bothered to hear her reasons, and he was leaving. Just like that. She clenched her fists against her sides. Let him think what he would—after a childhood of being a social outcast, she was done letting other people's assumptions and prejudices hurt her. 'Is this a bad habit of yours?'

'Is what?'

'Forget it, it's a waste of time.' She was doubly angry he could affect her to such an extent. *Why him?* she wanted to scream. When he reached the bottom of the stairs, she stepped in front of him and poked his chest with a finger. 'You know something? I *will* enjoy myself. They don't call me Party Babe Brie for nothing.'

Twisting away, she marched across the foyer, glared at him as she slipped off her shoes beneath the graceful arch leading to the entertainment area. She ran her hands down the sides of her dress in a deliberately provocative manner that had the cool in his eyes turning molten, the cobalt flecks darkening. So satisfying to watch that handsome jaw clench, as if he hated himself for responding.

She grinned. His fingers flexed at his sides. *Ooh, yeah, baby. Gotcha.* Still watching him, she picked up her strappy stilettos, spun them above her head. 'Hey, everyone, time to get this party swinging.'

CHAPTER FOUR

AT FIVE A.M. Sunday, with the last guest gone, Brie dragged her dance-weary feet upstairs to bed. A couple of hours' sleep… She blinked at Bron's DVD forgotten on the dressing table next to the half-empty bottle of shiraz. Leo Hamilton's fault.

She crossed to her en-suite bathroom and grimaced at what she saw in the mirror. Her make-up had worn off, leaving her skin pale and revealing darker than usual smudges beneath her eyes. 'One too many drinks, Party Babe Brie,' she told her reflection.

Her nightly cleansing ritual completed, she applied her own pre-mixed moisturiser then climbed into bed. She stared at the ceiling, wide awake, body still buzzing despite the fatigue. Her mind refused to shut down. Leo was no different from any other male in that he liked to look at the female form. Boys had started looking at her when she'd rivalled them in height during her fifteenth year and grown a pretty decent pair of boobs.

Which had hurt at the time because, in their twisted little adolescent minds, boys automatically thought she slept around. An easy lay, she'd heard Billy Swanson snigger before she'd decked him with her backpack. She still hated that men could enjoy a fling and were considered playboys or studs whereas women who enjoyed the same were gossiped about in less than flattering terms, but nowadays she didn't let it get to her.

And nowadays mature men saw her as more than boobs and legs—mostly. And if they didn't…did it matter? It wasn't as if it was long term. And she enjoyed being in the company of a nice-looking man. She enjoyed being swept off her feet and wined and dined and danced. Most of all she enjoyed how they made her feel at the end of the night.

She knew without any doubt at all that Leo could make her feel *really, really* good. But unlike other men she'd enjoyed spending time with, even hours after he'd gone, Leo's potent energy lingered in her room and she dragged the covers up over her face as if to shield herself against its force and gritted her teeth.

Men. They filled a basic human need but, like parties and new experiences, they were to be enjoyed and appreciated before moving on to the next. She was careful to choose a partner on the same wavelength and with the same expectations and moral code as herself. Cheating was out. She never lied because she knew bitterly how it felt to be lied to. She expected—no, she *demanded*—honesty in return.

Unstructured, temporary relationships were her thing. Since Elliot. Eight years ago she'd been so dazzled by the rich young executive she'd seen nothing but the stars he hung in the sky exclusively for her pleasure. When he'd started sending floral apologies for missed dates, she'd made exceptions for him, and excuses. Until the stars had faded and she'd seen him clearly for the lying, cheating rat he was.

Leo's sudden arrival in her room had both surprised and excited her, transporting her to another place with his unexpected but fun spontaneity and slow-burning kiss.

Until it had ended in disaster less than fifteen minutes later. How did he get away with his appalling lack of so-

cial skills? Yeah, looks and sex appeal—they worked every
time. No, not every time and not with her. He had some
major grovelling to do before she'd let him anywhere near
her person again.

But she smiled into the darkness remembering his reaction on the stairs. Pure molten lust and powerless to act
on it. Because, in that situation, *Brie* had held the power.
For her, that power had been the only thing that had saved
the moment. She fell asleep at last with the smile still on
her lips.

While her raspberry mint tea steeped, Brie plodded outside
with a carton of cans and bottles destined for recycling.
She winced at the glare—nine a.m. on a Sunday morning
was unspeakably early to be up after an all-nighter. But
preferable to being assaulted with dreams of a man she
didn't want to think about and whether he tasted as good
in the morning as he had last night.

She emptied her recycling into the bin with a loud
clanking of glass and metal.

'Good morning.'

The familiar voice resonated crisply in the chilly air.
She swivelled to see the man himself watching her from
the gap in the fence a few metres away. How dared he look
so refreshed? So together? So attractive? Unlike the way
she knew she looked without a scrap of make-up and less
than three hours' sleep. 'We aren't meeting until this afternoon,' she said, turning her back to him. She gathered
bottles from a patio table, tossed them in the bin.

'I was outside and heard you busy there. We could meet
this morning if you prefer to get it out of the way.'

To avoid looking at him she wiped the table top with a
rag and wished he'd go away so he wouldn't see her. 'This
morning doesn't suit.'

He paused, obviously unused to people not falling in

with his plans. 'Okay. I've drawn up a schedule. Shouldn't take long. We can grab a coffee in town somewhere and work it out. Say one o'clock? I'm on the three-fifteen flight out.'

She rose, not avoiding his gaze now but looking him straight in those silvery eyes. 'I don't drink coffee. Work it out?' She said each word as if she were talking to a dim-witted child—which wasn't much of a stretch, considering last night's behaviour. 'Work what out, exactly?'

Genuine surprise crossed his expression. 'The details of the agreement you persuaded me was a win-win for both of us. Or have you forgotten already?'

'Ah. *That* agreement.' Temper seethed hot through her veins but she kept her cool. 'I thought you might be going to work on your apology for walking out last night without waiting for me to tell you that I was detained by a guest who'd been taken ill.' Brie waited a beat for that piece of information to sink in. 'This might be hard for a guy like you to comprehend but she took priority over anything you and I might have had going.'

At least he had enough smarts to look uncomfortable. 'Why didn't you say so last night?'

Incredible. 'You're making it *my* fault?'

He frowned. 'It's not about who's right or—'

She slammed the lid of the bin shut. 'Of course it's not.' A man like Leo was never wrong. 'Did you give me a chance to speak last night?'

A muscle popped in his jaw. 'Is she all right?'

'A migraine—she gets them sometimes. She'll be okay.'

'When you didn't come back I assumed—'

'Never assume, Leo.'

'Th— What's burning?' His voice sharpened, nostrils flaring, his head whipped towards her house. He didn't wait for a reply, pushing through the gap in the fence and hurtling towards the atrium.

In that instant Brie smelled it too and remembered. *'Omigod.'* She heard Leo's footsteps pounding behind her as she sprinted up the path and into the kitchen.

They arrived in the doorway together. On the stovetop flames licked the inside of her frying pan and acrid smoke billowed towards the ceiling. She froze for an instant, the terrifying crackling sound filling her ears as she tried to remember how to put out a grease fire.

In that same instant Leo's heart stopped and his mind spun back twelve years. Only for an instant but he saw it all, every last detail while he switched off the gas, grabbed Breanna's tea towels and shoved them under the tap. *Dragging Sunny from their burning home, the fallen beam trapping her leg as his mother screamed for help from inside the inferno. Impossibly far away.*

He relived it in horrifying and vivid Technicolor as he wrung the cloths out then laid them carefully over the pan. *Hands restraining him as he tried to go back inside for Mum, her screams lost in the commotion of falling debris and the wail of sirens.*

More smoke issued forth as the damp cloths snuffed the flames. The instinctive scream rising up his throat almost overwhelmed him, then he looked at Breanna, staring wide-eyed with shock at the blackened stove top. His first reaction—was this his fault for distracting her away from the kitchen? No. She'd broken a cardinal rule by turning on a frying pan and walking away. 'Are you okay?' he asked her.

'I will be. In a moment. Thank you.'

His nerves shattered, Leo scanned the ceiling, fear of what might have happened masked by anger. 'Where the *hell* is your smoke detector and why the *hell* wasn't it working?'

'There isn't one.'

'No smoke alarm.' He pressed his stinging eyes with the heels of his hands and ordered himself to simmer down. The muscles in his legs vibrated; his anger teetered on a dangerous edge. 'You're telling me there are no smoke alarms in this house?'

'Afraid not. I've been meaning to get around to it but—'

'You've been meaning to get around to it.' He lifted his gaze to hers, unable to believe what he was hearing. 'I don't suppose there's a fire extinguisher either?' When she shook her head he threw up his hands in frustration and shouted, 'So, what, you don't value your own life? Can't be bothered to keep yourself safe?'

'It's okay, the fire's out,' she said, waving an almost casual hand. 'You're overreacting to this whole thing. Of course I—'

'You have no *freaking* idea, do you? Not a bloody clue. Have you *seen* what burns can do to the human body?'

'N—'

'Obviously not.' Two strides, he gripped her upper arms. 'Woman, I could shake the living daylights out of you.'

She nodded like a puppet on a string. 'Okay, point taken. Can you let me go?'

What in hell was he doing? He released her so fast she almost stumbled back.

Blinking rapidly, she nodded again, glanced towards his scarred arm. 'I'm sorry. I've…you've…'

'No.' He stepped back. He loathed the fact that Breanna had witnessed his runaway outburst, and worse, that she'd been physically subjected to it. Emotional displays indicated a lack of control and, to his mind, constituted a weakness.

Leo Hamilton did *not* do emotion. He did *not* lose control. Forcing his gaze back to hers, he blew out a slow breath to steady himself. 'You sure you're okay?'

'I'm okay.'

Did he detect a bit of a wobble in her voice? For her own safety, he hoped so. 'Look, if I—'

'I got the message—smoke alarms are on top of my list.'

He wondered just how sincere that intention was. Easy to forget now that the emergency was over. Easy to forget if you'd never had a personal tragedy with fire. 'A change of plans.' He pulled out his phone, scrolled to her name. 'Tell me your email address and I'll send you the schedule I've drawn up. Let me know if there are any points you want to clarify. If not I'll see you next Saturday.'

She recited her address then added, 'No going out for coffee, then?'

Biting back a four-letter word, he shook his head. 'You don't drink coffee. Remember?' He slid his phone back into his pocket.

'You know what I mean. And I'm flexible—I can make an exception. For you.'

'Some other time.' He was still dealing with the stresses of the past few moments and the haunting memories they conjured up—he didn't want to deal with their attraction and Breanna's disturbing lack of concern at the same time.

A few seconds longer and it could have gone the other way. Chills chased down his spine and he knew he couldn't simply let it go. He strode to the door, let himself out, relieved she didn't try to follow.

Brie's legs shook so badly she slumped onto the nearest stool and closed her eyes. Her thoughts were on spin cycle and a swarm of bees buzzed in her ears. Now that Leo had gone she gave in to the shock of nearly setting her house on fire. Even worse; he'd seen it all—and saved the day.

Reaching for her teapot, she poured a mug with trembling fingers, barely managing to bring it to her mouth without sloshing it over the rim.

She'd like to think she'd have reacted with Leo's speed

and clarity. His scarred forearm—he'd had personal experience. Which was none of her business unless he chose to share it. Which he hadn't.

Forty-five minutes later she was scrubbing her grungy stove, still counting herself lucky, when she heard footsteps on the path. She heard a knock as Leo called her name and the sound of the screen door opening and closing.

He appeared in the doorway as she wiped her hands on a clean tea towel. She noticed how his frame seemed to block out most of the light and her heart pitter-pattered faster for the second time in an hour and for an entirely different reason. 'Did you forget something?'

'No. You did.'

Then she saw he carried a fire blanket still in its pack and an extinguisher under one arm.

'Is that to put out the sparks?' She knew it was a delayed shock reaction but she had the crazily inappropriate desire to laugh. 'You're hot, but not that h…' She trailed off beneath his steel gaze.

'Don't push me, Breanna. I'm not in the mood.'

She nodded, pressed her lips together briefly then said, 'Sorry. And thanks. Thanks heaps. I was trying to lighten the moment. Guess not, hey.'

Ignoring her response, he set his purchases on the table, scanned the kitchen walls. 'You got a couple of hooks? I can hang the blanket for you.'

'I can manage a couple of hooks. Really,' she said when he looked sceptical. 'I'll do it today, I promise. And thanks again, I mean it. How much do I owe you?'

'Don't worry about it.'

'But—'.

'Buy me a drink some time.'

She might have taken him up on it, but he was already walking to the door.

In ten seconds flat he was gone. Back to Melbourne.

She wasn't disappointed, she told herself, unpacking the blanket. All work and no play wasn't her type. Busy business-focused men weren't her type. They'd drive each other mad; she had no doubts about that at all.

Still… She hugged the blanket to her chest, remembering that kiss last night. Wouldn't it be fun discovering if she was right?

She should have found him those damn hooks.

On Wednesday evening Brie noticed a light on next door as she pulled up in her driveway around six-thirty. Apprehensive, she squinted through the night-darkened foliage for a better view. It was way past business hours and Leo was still in Melbourne. At least, she presumed he was, and she felt a surprised little flutter at the possibility that he'd come back earlier than expected.

She was about to check whether his car was under the car port when a guy in overalls ambled up her drive. He raised a hand. 'Ms Black? Mr Hamilton told me to come.' He dug in his overall pocket, pulled out a piece of paper. 'Name's Trent Middleton and I'm installing a smoke alarm for you this evening.'

Brie frowned at the work order. 'I didn't order a smoke alarm.'

'It's all paid for, just needs installation. Mr Hamilton told me to wait till you came home.'

Had she missed a text or something? 'My goodness, how long have you been waiting?' She could have been gone for hours. What if she'd gone out for drinks or a movie? Had Leo even considered that?

Trent shrugged. 'Since four. He paid me to wait.' He grinned. Obviously being paid to do nothing suited him well.

Brie could hardly send him away now. 'You'd better come in, then.'

She didn't like that Leo had taken it on himself to install an alarm. Nor did she want to be beholden to him for the cost. Breanna Black paid her own way, thanks very much.

Leo was one of those men who needed to have a handle on every situation and took it as a personal failure if he didn't.

She didn't want him having a say in her personal circumstances, or her life if it came to that. But she couldn't pretend she didn't feel a warm fuzzy that he was concerned enough to do this for her.

So later that night when she climbed into bed, she called his mobile.

'Good evening, Breanna,' he answered over the distant sound of a television. There was an unexpected hint of relaxed in his usually laconic tone. 'I was expecting your call.'

Hearing his dark velvet voice close to her ear sent a rush of heat through her body. She tried not to imagine him lying next to her and saying much more interesting things into her ear and said, 'So you know I'm a well-mannered person who always says thank you.'

'You're welcome.'

'You should also know I don't accept charity.'

'Wasn't charity, Breanna. A fire alarm's mandatory for residential rentals. As a property owner, you—'

'Enough said.' She waved a hand in empty space. 'I'll be reimbursing you for the cost if you'll send me the invoice. I'm making it clear right now, I pay my own way.'

There was a pause. 'So you'd be the type of woman who likes to lead on the dance floor.'

'For your info, when I'm on it, I *own* the dance floor,' she informed him. 'And you'd be the type of man who likes a woman to lie back in bed and let you do all the work.' She switched off her night light, stretched out on her crisp cotton sheets and indulged in the tempting image.

'We seem to have shifted from dance floor to bedroom in rapid succession,' he said, sounding amused. 'You want to test that theory of yours, Breanna?'

'I'm a direct kind of woman, so I might. But we were talking about fire alarms and the paying of them. Business is business and, as your landlady, I get to reimburse you.'

'We'll toss for it, then. Winner pays for the alarm. You call, I toss.'

'No deal.' She laughed. 'You think I'm that gullible?'

'I'll text you a photo of the result.'

'R-i-i-ght.'

'Okay. Something else.' The sound of the TV faded as if he was moving to another location. 'I'm home, are you?'

'Yes. What something else?'

For some reason she imagined him settled in a large wingback chair in front of a roaring fire with a brandy. Her pulse stepping up, her mind already a million miles ahead. She could do a lot with that big chair and brandy scenario…

'Three statements about yourself. One's a lie. I guess which one, then it's your turn.'

Could be interesting. 'Okay.'

'First to get three wrong…'

But Brie didn't hear the rest because her focus had shifted to the female voice that suddenly piped up in the background. She couldn't make out the words but it hardly mattered: He was chatting up one woman on the phone while entertaining another in his home. No wonder he'd moved to another room to talk. *Sucked in, Brie.*

She sat bolt upright. 'One, I'm twenty-six. Two, I've circumnavigated the earth in my bi-plane. Three, I'm not interested—and I'll give you a hint: *that's* not the lie.' She stabbed a finger in the air. 'I don't play those kinds of games.' Pressing the disconnect button, she glared at the dim light coming from the window, furious with him, furious with herself for being so easily manipulated. Again. Hadn't Elliot taught her anything?

She absolutely refused to admit to being disappointed. This thing with Leo was only a flirtation. And now it was over.

When the phone buzzed a moment later, with his name on the screen, she ignored it. The next time his name popped up she muted all calls, tossed the phone onto her bedside table with a clatter and rolled over. The way she always handled unwanted calls.

Nobody lied to Brie and got away with it. Not any more. She wished Leo Hamilton to the bottom of the Pacific Ocean.

CHAPTER FIVE

BRIE STILL WISHED Leo Hamilton to the bottom of the ocean the following morning. He wouldn't have still been on her contacts list but for the fact that he owned the house next door and she was darn well going to pay him for his darn fire alarm.

So she was beyond angry with herself when she answered her phone the following day during her lunch break without checking the screen and heard his voice in her ear.

'*Don't* cut me off.'

Her finger hovered over End Call. How creative a liar was he? 'You've got ten seconds.'

'I've figured out why you—'

'Five.'

'Sunny's my sister.'

'Your sister was with you last night?' Brie laughed. 'You think I'm that naïve?'

'No, but it's the truth—we share a house.'

'You share a house with your *sister*?' He'd mentioned a sister. She really wanted to believe that he was telling the truth. But... 'Why?' What was wrong with him that he'd share a house with his sister?

She thought she heard him hesitate, then he said, 'It's a big house. Our separate living areas are off-limits to the other unless invited and we meet on neutral grounds in the kitchen for meals.'

'You'd better not be lying.'

'Why would I lie to you?'

'Oh, I don't know, why would you?' *How about because you only have to smile or say one word and I want to believe everything you say?* Just as she had with Elliot. Maybe she had to start giving guys a chance. It was too depressing to believe they were all Elliots.

His rich low chuckle flowed around her like melted chocolate. 'I'm curious, Brie. Were you jealous?'

She rubbed a hand over the place where her heart had skipped a huge beat and coughed out a laugh. 'You called me Brie.'

'I guess I did.' He sounded surprised. 'So, were you?'

'Jealous? I wouldn't go that far.' *Moving right along.* 'I've read your email.' She picked up a sandwich triangle but didn't eat it. 'I looked over your schedule and everything seems to be in order.'

'Yes. You indicated as much in your emailed reply twenty-four hours ago. You don't remember?'

Oh. 'I only wondered if a busy man such as yourself would find time to check all his emails.'

'If I didn't, I wouldn't have a business, would I?'

'Right. Well.' She checked the time and composed herself. 'I run a business too. My next appointment's a chest and back wax then I have an aromatherapy treatment and two Brazilians and I haven't finished my lunch—'

'Chest and back wax,' he repeated, seemingly stuck on that next appointment.

'Yep.' She bit into her sandwich, spoke around it. 'Huge, hairy, masculine—you get the picture.'

There was a choking sound followed by, 'I'll let you get on with it, then.'

He disconnected and Brie grinned, popped the rest of her sandwich in her mouth and went to check the temperature of her wax.

* * *

On Saturday afternoon Leo strolled around the corner and into West Wind's back yard and did a double take. Breanna's face was caked with a layer of dark mud, her hair swathed in a magenta terry-towel turban while she massaged some product into her toes, the nails of which were an electric blue. She wore maroon leggings under a loose green shirt.

He'd known it was a useless exercise over the rock beat hammering away inside her house, but he'd rung the front door bell anyway then sent her a text. She'd answered neither, so he'd made his way around the back to the atrium.

Leo preferred to think she'd simply lost track of the hour but it seemed more probable she'd forgotten he was coming today. The more he looked, the more likely it seemed she'd forgotten he was coming at all. She was wearing those ear buds again—in addition to her sound system—and there was no sign of any packing or urgency to do so. As he drew closer he saw that the wrought-iron table was covered in little make-up pots and bowls along with a tall jug full of cubes of watermelon and lemon slices and a bowl of chocolate mousse.

Just another casual Saturday afternoon prepping for the next social event on her calendar? *Party babe Brie,* she'd informed him last weekend, sassy-mouthed as Scarlett O'Hara on steroids. And tonight was Saturday night, after all.

Leo didn't know what irritated him more: the fact that he'd been looking forward to this afternoon more than she obviously had or that she'd not even bothered to organise this arrangement that she'd suggested in the first place.

When he stopped in front of her, she glanced up, screamed and yanked out her ear buds at the same time. Her horror-stricken expression made him grin. 'If it isn't the party princess.'

'Party princess?' Covering her lower face with her hands, she glared up at him with those gorgeous black-as-midnight eyes and spoke through her fingers. 'Why do you have a problem with that? I have a social life even if you don't and you weren't due till *tomorrow*. Why do you have to keep sneaking around and startling me?'

'I tried the doorbell, and sent you a text. Our agreement was Saturday; you *did* read the schedule—didn't you? And I distinctly recall mentioning Saturday the last time I saw you. In your kitchen. Remember? Pan on fire, no smoke alarm? That day.'

Oh peachy. Just peachy. Brie wanted to go some place dark and hide for the next twenty years. 'You said a lot that morning but I don't remember you saying Saturday,' she said from behind her hands while she rose, stepped into her shoes.

'It's on the schedule,' he informed her, obviously enjoying her discomfort. He had a twinkle in his eye as he spoke. At least she *thought* he did—she wasn't looking too closely.

He waved an all-encompassing hand. 'And I seriously doubt you'd have been ready by tomorrow in any case, judging by this confusion.'

She'd been testing her products before using them on her clients, and of all the days to get carried away, when a silver-eyed hunk in tight black jeans, snowy open-necked shirt and tan jacket came to tell her she'd misread his precious schedule.

'Probably not,' she admitted, struggling to keep it together. 'I've been busy and a bit distracted this week.'

He gave an almost imperceptible nod, which had her wondering if he'd been distracted too, and for the same reason, then he grinned again and said, 'By the way, mud's a good look for you.'

'Is that supposed to be a compliment?' she snapped. Embarrassment prickled and she was sure a rash was breaking out all over her neck. Snatching up a damp cloth, she swirled it in her bowl of cool water, turned her back on him while she cleaned off the mess in front of her little mirror on the table. 'It's not mud. It's my chocolate and avocado mask.'

With her face cleansed of its rich goo, her skin naked and baby-soft, she turned back—reluctantly—to find he'd closed the distance between them. She leaned back, held up her palms. 'Too close. I'm not wear—'

'You're stunning without make-up.'

'I wasn't angling for a compliment.'

'It's not a compliment, it's a fact.'

The wonder of his gruff words filled her with light; she felt the glow to the soles of her feet. 'I'm no make-up model but thank you anyway.'

But he was still seeing her at a disadvantage. To get even, she dipped a finger in the chocolate concoction. 'How would you look with a moustache?' She smeared it slowly just above his upper lip. 'Made from all natural products. Cocoa powder, avocado, coconut milk and oil.

'More?' she asked, when he didn't move, just watched her as if he were made of stone. Leo Hamilton was no Sensitive New Age Guy. 'Relax,' she soothed. 'Ever been out with a beauty therapist?' She smeared another dollop on his chin, rubbing in a gentle circular motion, enjoying the feel of masculine stubble beneath her fingertips.

'No.'

She smiled at his mouth. 'You have the most irresistible cupid's bow I've ever seen on a man.'

She reached out a finger but he grasped her hand and held it away. 'I've been fantasising about kissing you again all week.'

Their eyes clashed, silver on black. 'I know,' she murmured.

Her pulse leapt as he slid his lips over hers. Once. Twice. Brushing back and forth in that unhurried way he had that she was fast learning to savour and appreciate.

Only their lips touched. His were rich and firm and promised pleasures yet to be explored and enjoyed. Pure pleasure. Physical enjoyment, nothing more, she told herself.

But it felt like a lot more and her body shivered though the afternoon sun shone warm on her skin. The fragrance of his freshly soaped skin mingled with the surrounding scents of basil and thyme and lemon verbena.

Then he nibbled on her lower lip with his teeth, so lightly she wanted to cry with the bewildering gentleness. She tipped her head back, arched her neck, silently pleading for more, but Leo wouldn't be drawn. Not yet.

'*How* do you know?' he muttered against her mouth.

'I just know.' She also knew men like Leo—powerful men supremely confident in their sexual magnetism and charm—wouldn't be entirely reassured by that cryptic wise-woman answer.

She tilted her head so that she could see his fine masculine features properly. 'I've been fantasising about you too.'

'I know.' His mouth twitched with humour.

She reached out to touch the full bottom lip. 'Why wouldn't I? I'm a healthy single woman and you're a single, attractive man. Right?'

He dipped a finger in her bowl of chocolate, dabbed a smudge on her chin, then licked it off with one unhurried swipe of his tongue.

Her eyes drifted to half-mast as her body ached in an unfamiliar way. He was good. Slow was good, slow was—

'You could use some sweetener.'

Her eyes snapped open and she snorted at his grimace of distaste. 'It's not meant to be body paint.'

His eyes sharpened, the glint of a sword in sunlight, tempting her with its promise of silvery delight.

'But it could be,' she suggested, silkily. 'Some other time.'

'When?'

She smiled her best seductive woman's smile at the sexual need in his voice and ran a finger from his Adam's apple to the bottom stud on his expensive leather jacket, lingering tantalisingly above the growing bulge in his jeans. 'I'll let you know.'

But before she could step away, he dragged her against him with both hands, the promise in those sharp eyes morphing to impatience. His own reactive emotion obviously annoyed him. 'I don't respond well to being manipulated, Breanna.'

Biting back a grin, she blinked up at him. 'Is that what you think I'm doing?'

His hands shifted from her arms to her spine to her bottom, where he crushed her against his body. 'You know exactly what you're doing.'

The hot, rigid length of him pressed against her and she let him know with a tiny subtle shift of her hips just how much she was enjoying it. 'I'm not manipulating you.' Smiling, she met his eyes and her hands hovered at the waistband of his jeans. 'Yet.'

His nostrils flared, his jaw tightened, those eyes smouldering silver with honest-to-goodness lust. Warning her not to start something she didn't intend to finish.

'When I do,' she continued confidently, 'you'll know about i—'

His mouth swooped on hers, snatching the rest of her words. Dominating, demanding, determined. She felt that tight leash of his slip a notch, as, with ruthless insistence, his tongue forced her lips apart and dived inside to duel with hers.

Heat sizzled along her lips, her veins, while images whirled through her mind. The two of them right there on the uneven bricks finishing this.

And even though she felt the urgency humming through him, through them both, even though he didn't relinquish his tight grip on her bottom, he gentled his kiss, settled in. And, oh…the sweet, seductive flavour of him. His need hot, matching her own.

Leo was having a hard time staying upright as soft feminine hands tugged at the hem of his shirt and slipped beneath. His stomach muscles contracted violently. He hadn't intended to kiss her; he'd wanted to teach her a lesson in… he couldn't remember what…and now—hell—he was in all kinds of bother.

Somehow, he pried his lips from hers long enough to drag in air and relinquish his hold on her jersey-covered butt. She gazed up at him, cheeks flushed with desire, mouth damp and wide and wicked. He swore silently and hoped she hadn't noticed his restraint was ready to snap.

Her fingernails scraped over his nipples, sending darts of lust twanging through his body. His breath hissed out and he shuddered, capturing and restraining her hands.

Brie thanked her stars he'd had the willpower she seemed to be lacking. It made it marginally easier to pull her hands out of his grip and step back and…*breathe, Brie.*

How could she have got so carried away? It was just a kiss. *Just a kiss.* And she had a zillion things to do. On the top of her list was organising West Wind for her new tenant. 'No body painting today.' Forcing casualness into her voice, she inhaled a long breath while she waited for her pulse to slow. 'Or tonight. I have a previous engagement.'

The frank transparency of lust faded from his eyes as he stuffed the front of his shirt back into his waistband. He glanced at her make-up stash on the table. 'A previous engagement?'

She glared at him, annoyed at the ridiculous question she saw in his gaze. Annoyed that he obviously assumed tonight's engagement was a party. She could clarify, but *why should she when he was ready to assume the worst*?

'I would *not* have kissed you if I was dating another man tonight, let's get that clear.' She should *not* have to explain herself. Not to him, not to anyone. She turned away and began stacking her pots back into plastic containers, glad she had something to do. More than annoyance, his doubts and assumptions tore at a vulnerable place inside her. The place Elliot had helped sculpt, the place she'd taught herself not to acknowledge.

The place she reminded herself now that did not exist.

'That didn't come out the way it was meant to.'

'Is that an apology?' She waved a hand in his general direction as she packed then thought better of it. 'Forget I said that and we'll call it even.'

A few heavy seconds passed, then he asked, 'Are we good?'

'We're good.' Picking up her box, she headed for the back door, leaving him to follow. At the door she turned to him. 'Really. We're good.' She smiled, impatient to demonstrate he couldn't get to her emotionally but not quite able to meet those eyes. 'I apologise that the house is still a mess. I'll get right on it.'

'I can see if there's a room available in town for this evening.'

'*No.*' Plonking her box on the kitchen table, she heaved an inward sigh at the mess in front of her. 'You *will* have a place to sleep here tonight.' Somewhere.

'In that case, I've got a few errands in the city. I'll need a key if you're going out before I get back.'

'The spare's on the hook next to your fire blanket if you want to take it now.' She gestured to it while she cleared the table and loaded the dishwasher.

The moment he left, she slammed the dishwasher shut, grabbed water and detergent and set to work with a scrubbing brush.

Annoyance turned to severe aggravation, made worse by his lingering scent in her nostrils, which in turn lent her speed and energy as she moved like a dervish through the kitchen chores. He assumed too much and too frequently and so far his assumptions had been unreasonable and way off the mark. Her house party and sick guest confrontation for starters. She also had a gut feeling he'd turned up at her party last Saturday in the first instance because he'd *assumed* they were boozy affairs and wanted to check. Yep, that would fit his personality profile.

She loved to party and she loved to flirt and did so regularly and often. But when friends or others, even people she didn't know, needed her help or support, as with Megan and her migraine, there was never any question— they were her priority.

Hands fisted on hips, she scanned her kitchen, rarely tidy, now sparkling like new beneath the down-lights. Ready for Mr Hamilton to use—if he ever cooked. He probably had a personal chef-cum-housekeeper.

They had this extraordinary attraction thing going on but, away from the fantasy world they seemed to be playing in, who was Leo Hamilton? She did know he was quick to criticise. Ready to assume the bad. She dusted off her hands. So for tonight, let him assume.

Staying out of Breanna's way was the wisest course so Leo didn't return until seven o'clock. In case she hadn't had time to eat, he'd bought her a pizza when he'd bought his own.

He needn't have bothered because she was long gone. He found a note addressed to him on the kitchen table.

Leo, I've made up a bed in the bedroom at the far end of the passage. Apologies, the bed's a bit small but it's only for tonight. B
PS Don't wait up xx

Kisses from the girl who'd put him in the bedroom furthest from hers?

He wanted more than paper kisses. A lot more. He'd never met a woman who intrigued him so. Then again, he'd never met a woman quite like Breanna. No, that wasn't entirely true. He'd met those confident, liberated women, but had avoided getting tangled up with any of them. After the sex went stale, what did they have in common? They were too independent, too confrontational.

Too much trouble all round.

So why was he walking through her house, having struck a deal with her, and checking out the rooms they'd agreed he could use—including her bedroom with the only bed big enough to accommodate his height?

En route he saw a couple of suitcases and cardboard boxes stashed by the front door ready for her to take with her to her brother's retreat tomorrow. Great, he told himself. Out of his way. Out of temptation's way.

Every one of those pre-agreed-on rooms was tidy, with the exception of her bedroom, which was still in the throes of a battle not yet won. Because he didn't think he could sleep comfortably beneath rose florals and flounces, he'd purchased a Lincoln green quilt cover and plump feather pillow for his stay. But for tonight they'd be sleeping under the same roof, a few short steps apart.

Five hours later, he was stretched out on the sofa in the living room and asking himself why he was still awake and wondering what time party princesses came home. Or if they came home…

Breanna had been adamant she was going solo this evening, insulted that he'd suggested otherwise, but what if she'd met someone tonight? The thought bothered him more than it should. And *that* bothered him. Because what self-respecting man would choose to hook up with a woman as temperamental and stubbornly independent as Breanna Black?

He heard her car pull up and realised his appearance downstairs would suggest he'd been doing what she'd told him not to do: waiting up for her. He remained where he was because he didn't respond to demands; furthermore, to retreat now would only make him appear guilty of same.

His first glimpse of her in a sexy black dress had him wanting to sit up straighter and take notice. Of every dip and every curve, the long, lean, toned muscles in her legs and arms as she tossed a long-haired black and maroon jacket onto the sofa.

'You're still up.' Her bag followed the jacket down.

He shifted his inspection to her face and noticed dark smudges beneath her eyes. Socialising too hard and too often could do that. His cynicism or personal experience? 'I'm never in bed till one.' Unless…

'So you weren't waiting up for me.'

'No.'

'That's a relief, 'cos I'm stuffed.' Crossing the room, she collapsed onto the armchair opposite him and yawned. 'So, do you go to bed late by choice, or do you work late hours?'

'Both.'

'When I get the chance, I like to curl up at seven and sleep for twelve hours.' She kicked off her black patent stilettos, closed her eyes and murmured, 'Unfortunately, the opportunity doesn't occur very often.'

It was her choice to party, but she looked somehow vulnerable with her black lashes resting on paler than usual cheeks. He'd bet she didn't make a habit of allowing that aspect to reveal itself. He almost felt sorry for her and volunteered, 'I could have picked you up,' before he could censor himself.

'Whatever for?' Her eyes snapped open. 'Let's be clear here. I enjoy spending time in a man's company. I enjoy it a lot and I enjoy it often. How I choose to spend that time depends on the man, the timing.' She flipped a hand. 'Even the weather. Point being, I like men but I don't need one to look after me.'

Fascinating. Leo hadn't noticed until this moment how irritation caused the outer corner of her left eye to twitch and how both eyes glinted with tiny speckles of gold in the Tiffany lamp light on the table beside her. How the more fiery she became, the fuller, and more tempting, her bottom lip appeared to be.

'You conduct your sexual activities according to the weather?'

'Whatever.' Her eyes slid closed once more and Leo could almost see the feistiness drain away. 'I need to sleep,' she murmured.

That much was obvious. 'Do I offer to sweep you into my arms and upstairs?'

'Not necessary. Nor do I need tucking in—in case you were wondering.' She rallied enough to lever herself off the chair, grab her bag and stumble her way barefoot to the foyer. 'Breakfast's on you,' she said, over her shoulder. 'Night.'

'Goodnight.'

He heard her door close and imagined her falling face down on her bed, maybe slipping off her dress first...

Like unwelcome guests, those provocative images refused to leave. Lust licked through him, hot and restless and unassuaged. So he strolled to her bookcase to check out her taste in reading material. Flicked through a couple of classics, a biography of Amelia Earhart. He discovered an entire shelf of first editions in pristine condition behind glass and was settling down with Stephen King's *Carrie* when he heard a jingle coming from inside Breanna's jacket.

He considered answering it but what would be the point? When the second call came two minutes later, he was curious enough to take her phone from the inside pocket and check caller ID. Sam. No surname, no photo. No telling if Sam was male or female. And none of his business.

On the third call, because there was a possibility of some kind of emergency, he answered. 'Breanna Black's phone. Leo Hamilton speaking.'

'Oh.' The female voice sounded flustered, as if she might be catching Breanna at a sensitive or inopportune moment. 'Is Brie...is Brie there? Are you...?'

'Her new tenant,' he clarified before the woman could jump to the wrong conclusion. 'Did she mention renting her house out for a short while?'

'She did. You're the guy from the party last weekend, right?'

'Yeah. And you're...?' He tried to recall meeting a woman called Sam.

'You were looking for a couple of glasses?'

'Ah, *Samantha*.' The redhead. 'Brie's gone to bed. She left her phone downstairs. Can I help?'

'You certainly can. If Brie hasn't mentioned her purse is missing then she hasn't noticed yet but she dropped it on the footpath outside her salon tonight. We share the same professional rooms—I'm a remedial massage therapist and we had a session here this evening. Can you tell her I've put it in our safe? That way she can come by and collect it when she wakes up.'

Breanna hadn't mentioned her salon this afternoon. Her face had been covered in goo while she massaged her feet with some sweet-smelling concoction—her focus on partying and looking good while she did so. 'I'll let her know.' He was about to disconnect but Sam got in first.

'Great, thanks. Hopefully she'll get a decent sleep. On top of cleaning up the house for you, she's worked her butt off this past week.' Sam sounded as if she considered it entirely his fault that Breanna had left the place in a mess until the last possible moment.

'If I don't see her, I'll leave her a note.' He sat down then stretched out on the sofa, letting his fingers run through the strands of Breanna's long-haired jacket. 'So, she was working tonight?'

'Yes. She looked done in when she got here but she refused to postpone because she didn't want to let them down.'

Leo frowned. Hadn't she been going to a party? Glamming up for an evening on the town?

Not according to Sam.

Yet she hadn't challenged his party princess gibe. Further, she'd accepted full responsibility for her lack of organisation and the whole forgotten schedule business without saying a *damn thing* in her defence. What had happened to the straight-talking Breanna? And who were the mysterious *them* she hadn't wanted to let down? 'You said a session. What do you mean by that?'

'Brie's been working with cancer survivors on a monthly basis,' Sam explained. 'Demonstrating how to care for their skin after chemo and radiation and using her home-made natural products, which she experiments with in her spare time. And that's on top of salon hours, which includes taking on extra patients who can't afford to pay.' Sam ended her glowing testament with, 'She's one of a kind.'

In other words, *Brie's more than you think*. 'Thanks for letting me know,' he said. 'I'll make sure she hears she's appreciated.'

He disconnected, his legs hanging over one end of the sofa while he caressed Breanna's jacket some more. He'd have been none the wiser if Sam hadn't filled him in. There was much more to Breanna than he'd first thought. And he meant what he'd said—he intended letting her know.

CHAPTER SIX

LEO SET UP Breanna's dining room as his temporary office. He'd been up since the crack of dawn, due in part to the cramped bed he'd been assigned but mostly because he had a business commitment this evening and he wanted to ensure everything was organised before taking Breanna out to breakfast and seeing what other activities she'd planned for today.

She might spend the early part of the afternoon with him before he left for his three-hour drive to Heaven. He was due to dine with the owners and developers of the east coast's luxury eco-lodge this evening.

He wanted to make up for yesterday's badly timed visit. He wanted to know why a straight-talking woman like Breanna hadn't set him straight about her evening's plans. Most of all, he wanted a little more up close and personal time with her.

Earlier, he'd brought in a load of groceries and made room for them in a kitchen cupboard. He'd made himself space on a refrigerator shelf until Breanna took what she wanted when she left. He didn't need much; he rarely cooked. He'd left his new pillow and quilt on the tiny half-bed he'd slept in last night before taking a brisk walk in the early morning chill followed by an almost as chilly shower.

Over a quick breakfast of instant coffee he found hiding at the back of the cupboard and thick, buttered toast,

he logged on to the internet and did some banking trans-
actions. He went over his report for this evening, made
a couple of last-minute changes. By the time he phoned
Sunny she was having brunch with friends in one of Melbourne's trendy arcades and shopping was on her afternoon
agenda. Seemed nothing slowed his sister down.

He made a couple more calls, then surfed the net for
relevant articles on current environmental trends while he
waited for Breanna to wake.

At ten-fifteen, he was onto his second coffee when he
heard movement upstairs, then the splash of Breanna's
shower. His skin started to itch. He rubbed at the back
of his neck and stared at his laptop's screen. He tried to
concentrate on the words but the cascading sound from
above made him think of shower sex. Of sweet-smelling
soap and slippery rose-petal skin. Of how long it had been
since he'd indulged in that particular activity.

Which had him wondering: when had he stopped thinking of Breanna as Sunny's neighbourly support person and
started thinking of her as his next lover? The thought unsettled Leo as much now as it had that first time he'd laid
eyes on her and he itched in a way he'd never itched before.

He itched some more when Breanna appeared beneath
the dining-room arch smelling fresh and looking fabulous
in indigo-blue jeans and a tight navy sweater that showcased her assets to full advantage. She wore her jeans
tucked into caramel-coloured calf-length boots and her
hair swung free about her face. Stunning.

She saw him watching—ogling—and smiled. 'Good
morning.'

It was a good morning now. She was like the sun rising
on a beautiful day. 'Morning.' He cleared a sudden husk
from his throat and asked, 'How did you sleep?'

She shook out an orange scarf covered in little black

owls. 'Very well. I suppose the same can't be said for you? I'm sorry about the bed.'

'You could have offered to share yours.'

Her grin was quick and lively. 'Is breakfast still on?'

'You bet.'

'Great, I'm starved.' She wound the scarf around her neck, slung her bag on her shoulder. 'Shall we go? Or are you busy?' She tagged the last on as an afterthought.

For her, this morning, he was prepared to drop everything and go just to be with her. 'I'm free until later this afternoon.'

'In that case I've changed my mind about breakfast. There's a new wine and cheese place in Richmond having an open day today on their lawns. The weather's going to be fine, it's only a half-hour's drive and I've been dying to try it.'

She switched from one idea to the next so fast she made his head spin. He was learning she only had one speed: fast forward. 'Wine on an empty stomach?'

'Today's my first day off in two weeks. I've got twenty-one hours left before I have to go back to work and I don't want to waste it.'

'It's a date, then.'

'Nuh-uh. Not a date.' She shook her head but her eyes danced. 'Sunday sessions don't count as dates, especially in the morning.'

'Okay, it's a non-date.'

He watched her cross the room to fetch last night's jacket, which was still on the sofa, then she caught sight of her phone on the coffee table and frowned. Looked straight at him with accusing eyes.

'Samantha rang last night,' he informed her.

'You answered my phone?'

'When it rang three times in succession, I figured it might be important. I was right. You dropped your purse outside your salon. Sam said to let you know she put it in the safe.'

'Really? Jeez….' Her expression turned appreciative. 'Thanks. I hadn't even noticed…what is wrong with me lately?' Her shoulders lifted and she rolled her eyes at the ceiling.

'Coffee—or whatever it is you drink—before we go? You look like you need it. I'll make it—I was going to make another coffee for myself anyway.'

'Okay. Thanks. Green tea. Red tin with yellow cows, on the shelf above the kettle.'

Brie followed him into the kitchen, sat down and took in the view as he reached for the tin. She was going to have to keep her hands from straying to that soft mohair jumper he was wearing that matched his eyes perfectly. And those sexy-as-sin jeans.

'Do you cook?'

'Not if I can help it.' He set a steaming cup in front of her then set the sugar and the carton of milk on the table between them. Finally, with his own mug, he slid into the chair opposite.

'Join the club—I'm no cook either.' She laughed. 'We'd be no good as housemates.'

He poured in milk then cradled his mug between his hands. Steely eyes studied her. 'Why didn't you tell me about last night?'

So Sam had blabbed. Brie wondered how much. She raised the tea to her lips, took a long, slow sip—soothing and fragrant—and said, 'What about last night?'

'Sam told me, so don't pretend you don't know what I'm talking about.'

'I know exactly what you're talking about.' She smiled at him over the rim of her mug, knowing he'd expected a different answer. 'As for why I didn't tell you, I'll let you figure it out for yourself, Leo.'

Jaw rigid, he stared at her for a long minute, his eyes turning a darker shade of grey. He gulped down the rest of his drink, set his mug down with a clunk of china on wood and leaned back in his chair.

He really didn't get it, she decided, and drained the last of her tea. It wouldn't occur to him that Leo Hamilton, obvious chick magnet, might draw a wrong conclusion when it came to women. And she wasn't going to enlighten him. She pushed up from the table and rinsed her mug, set it on the drainer. 'Okay, while you're thinking about it, let's make a start before it rains.'

'Didn't you say the weather's going to be fine today?'

'It's four seasons in one day here—you'll be used to that, coming from Melbourne.' She shrugged into her jacket. 'I have to pick up my purse before we head out of town. Are you driving or will I?'

'Is that a serious question?'

'Why wouldn't it be?' She searched her pockets for gloves, stuffed them in her bag. 'It makes sense; I'm local and—'

'It's not a problem,' he interrupted, swiping up his leather jacket and producing a set of keys from the pocket. 'I might not be local but I do know my way around Tasmania's main roads. We'll take your luggage as well, get it out of the way.'

'We'll do that later,' she said, refusing to let him have it all his way. 'We don't have time now. Brunch beckons.'

Fortunately he didn't argue or it might have got nasty. She climbed into his car and they drove the five minutes to Eve's Naturally. Even in his spacious vehicle it felt too close, too intimate. Breathing in his scent. Aware of his long tanned fingers on the steering wheel. The way her body seemed to lean towards his a little too much whenever they took a left turn. And even when they didn't.

'I only meant we need more time at the retreat because I want to show you what the Pink Snowflake's been able to achieve.'

'No worries, so long as we're there before three.' He negotiated around a bus. 'I have a dinner meeting at six this evening but it's a three hour drive if I stick to the speed limit.'

'Which you will, of course.'

'Of course.'

'So you'll be staying there overnight, then?'

'Yes.'

'And this client needs your environmental management consulting expertise?' She checked out his strong, masculine jaw in profile. 'Did I get it right?'

'Yes and yes.'

'So where are you going that takes three hours?'

'Heaven.'

She laughed. But she didn't laugh so much as sigh at the way he glanced at her after he said it. As if… 'Say a prayer for me when you get there.'

She watched his lips curve but he kept his eyes on the road as he asked, 'Have you ever been?'

'To heaven? Yeah, I've been. But you're talking about the resort. Not at those unaffordable prices.' She indicated Eve's Naturally amongst a row of spacious offices on the left. 'You can stop here. I'll be two secs.'

Then they were on their way out of suburbia, headed towards the historic town of Richmond with its charming little cottages and her favourite old-fashioned English sweet shop.

Brie kept up a running commentary, pointing out local places of interest, telling him what she knew about the Blue

Bandicoot winery they were going to be visiting, which they would reach before the town of Richmond itself.

Leo checked his speed as Breanna chatted on about the passing scenery and the area's history. Her tour-guide conversation kept his mind from straying to impure thoughts about how they might turn off onto one of the narrow side roads, pull over, recline the seats and engage in creative and mutually satisfying sex.

The more he tried to concentrate on her words, the more vivid and creative his imagination grew and the stronger the ache in his groin became. His gaze slid sideways. She was looking out of the side window, giving him a view of her neck, pale and creamy and exposed as she talked. He forced his eyes straight ahead and tried to concentrate on the road.

'Am I boring you?' The sharp tone of her voice a moment later pierced his lusty thoughts.

'What? No. Of course not. I've driven on this road before but I can say, in all honesty, it's never been such an interesting journey.'

She snorted. 'You don't say.'

'I do say.'

'Nuh-uh.' He heard her shift sideways in her seat to look at him. 'What were you *really* thinking, Leo? While I was telling you about the history of the winery?'

'If I told you, we'd have to take a detour and stop for a bit and I don't have time today.'

The car filled with a wordless anticipation. 'Forget the wine and cheese,' she said slowly. 'Brunch is overrated.'

He ignored her sensual tone that slid through his lower belly like a hot knife. 'I've been up since six and I'm hungry. Enough of the tour-guide talk, tell me about you.'

'How about what I'd like to do to you right now?' She sucked in a breath between her teeth. 'Or what I'd like you to do to me?'

'We both know it's a bad idea to pursue that particular conversation while I'm driving. Something less...vivid.'

'Oka-ay. So when my father died six years ago, I discovered I have a half-brother. It took me three years to track Jett down in Paris, so I was technically an only child growing up. And now he's just married my best friend, so—'

'*You*, not your brother. Tell me about *you*.'

'I love vanilla ice cream drenched in hot chocolate sauce.'

'Do y—?'

'I love the contrasts of hot and cold on my nipples. And I especially love it when someone—'

'Stop. You're deliberately provoking me.' And he was responding exactly the way she wanted him to. *Not going to happen, Breanna.* He tightened his hands on the wheel.

'Provoking you? Mmm, I hope so,' she murmured, and he could almost feel the trail of her fingernail down his upper arm even though he knew her not-so-innocent hands lay innocently in her lap. 'You could pull over...and...'

'We could, but I'm hungry.' A tingling sensation akin to pins and needles danced down his left arm and into his fingers.

Heat, desire and an altogether different kind of hunger was building within the car like a tropical thunderstorm. He switched off the heater, flicked open the upper air vent and tugged at the neck of his jumper. He didn't find over-confident women a turn-on; why was his body responding so carnally to this one?

'According to the GPS, the turn-off to the winery's in one kilometre,' she said. From the corner of his eye he saw her stretch her arms over her head. 'Your last chance.'

'Or what?' Checking the rear-view mirror, he pulled to the side of the road, tyres skidding on the gravel as he brought the vehicle to a fast stop. He tossed his sunglasses on the dash, unclipped his seat belt and leaned over so that their faces were centimetres apart. He could still smell her shower scent, the subtle fragrance of her make-up. 'Are you saying there won't be another?'

She took off her sunglasses too, drew a circle on his thigh with a fingertip, looked at him from beneath sooty lashes. 'I'm not saying that at all. I meant last chance before lunch—or brunch. Whatever. So kiss me.' Her demand came out more like a needy plea.

Better, he thought, watching her pupils dilate, her glossy lips part slightly in expectation. 'You're not interested in exercising your feminist proclivities and kissing me first?'

She wiggled closer on her seat, fingers spreading warmth over his thigh, breasts tantalisingly close to his chest but not quite touching. *Tempt and tease.* 'I liked how you kissed me yesterday and I want you to kiss me again.'

His gaze dropped to her mouth, yesterday's spicy memory, today a sweet anticipation. 'Then we can go and eat?'

'If that's all you want from me.'

To his surprise, her direct gaze changed, became almost vulnerable. As if deep down she feared rejection and had made a lifetime of proving she didn't. 'Not even close,' he murmured, taking her face between his hands and laying his lips on hers.

But there was nothing hesitant about the way she kissed him back. Her kiss was as warm and full-flavoured as he remembered, her competent therapist's fingers firm as she slid them around his neck and into his hair.

He didn't know how long their lips remained locked together. Didn't much care. He was still determining how far to take this here on the side of a reasonably busy road when she made the decision for him, pulling away with a breathless, 'Whoa. We're forgetting we're in public here.' Her cheeks were flushed; her eyes still held that hint of lost kitten.

'I hadn't forgotten.' Surprised, he raised his brows. 'That bothers you?'

'No. Yes. We should get going.'

With a finger on her chin, he tilted her face to his before she could scrabble to put her sunglasses back on. Her tempt and tease routine was a façade. She was maintaining an emotional distance, if not a physical one. Which was more than fine with him. Still, he wondered what had spooked her. He shifted back behind the wheel, slid his own sunglasses back on. 'Let's go find something to eat.'

The wine estate was a celebration of colour, sound and flavours. Even though the vines had been pruned and tied in preparation for spring growth, the sky was blue, the last autumnal foliage still clung to deciduous trees, giving the atmosphere a glorious golden hue despite the chill in the air. A jazz band played in the barn area of the vineyard's historic stables, wine sparkled, the aroma of cheese mingled with fried onions from the nearby barbecue.

Despite the undercurrent of low-grade sparks that sizzled between them, Leo found Brie's wit and humour complemented his own as they worked their way through a variety of wines and cheeses and the inevitable sausage sizzle. True to typical Tasmanian tradition, the clouds eventually rolled in and the party turned soggy. They shared his umbrella on the way back to the car while she fed him pieces of quince-paste-lathered cracker.

As a responsible and sober driver, he drove them back, allowing plenty of time for Breanna to show him the McPherson retreat, named after a generous benefactor. But Breanna was dozing ten minutes after leaving the winery, catching up on her lack of sleep. He ought to be relieved, but, oddly, it was disappointment that dragged at him for the rain-soaked drive back to Hobart.

* * *

When Brie pried heavy eyes half open, she was looking at
the familiar high-walled gate of the retreat through Leo's
rain-washed windscreen. His voice was low, his warm
breath tickling her cheek. She couldn't make out what he
was saying but she wanted to slide back into sleep with
that sexy murmur against her ear.

'Wake up, baby doll.' Sharper this time.

She blinked at the ridiculously incongruous term as it
applied to her and snorted, 'That's a first.' She pushed up,
annoyed that she'd dozed off in front of Leo. More annoyed
that he'd woken her from such exciting dreams.

'Security code.' He sounded vaguely impatient, as if
he'd asked her a few times already.

She recited it to him, then forced some energy into her
voice and said, 'I need my stuff. And my car.'

'All taken care of.' The gates slid back and he drove
through. 'Your stuff's in the back but you won't be driving for a few hours yet after that alcohol. I'll drop you back
at your house on my way to the coast if you want to stay
there tonight and drive here tomorrow.'

He'd stopped and loaded her gear and she hadn't woken?
How was that possible? Maybe it had something to do with
how super-relaxed she was feeling with the wine's pleasant warmth still buzzing through her system. 'Thanks,
anyway, but I'll be staying here tonight. And thanks for
loading my stuff. I appreciate it. I'll catch a cab to work
tomorrow morning—I can pick the car up later.' She'd
been hanging out for her regular soak in the retreat's spa
all week and nothing was going to keep her from it.

She climbed out and the ground beneath her feet tilted
a bit. 'Come on in,' she said, digging out her keys.

She pushed open the front door, smiled and breathed
deep as the fresh smell of new work met her nostrils. 'I'll

be moving Eve's Naturally here as soon as Jett and Olivia return. I can't wait to be a part of Livvy's exciting vision.'

'You sound as if you're trying to sell it.'

'It sells itself. And even better, we're able to offer subsidised rates to disadvantaged clients, thanks to generous ongoing donations through Pink Snowflake—which your valuable and generous rent is going to.'

They spent a few minutes unloading her gear before she showed him around. She was so proud to be able to talk up and show off the professional services in addition to personal fitness coaches, the range of areas from solarium to meditation and yoga plus a fully staffed kitchen specialising in organic food. She pointed out the gorgeous bushland and river views visible from floor-to-ceiling windows.

'It's going to open for business as soon as the happy couple can drag themselves back from honeymoon-land,' she told him, switching on the heating and shrugging out of her jacket. 'It'll be a couple of months yet but we already have clients booked in.'

'I can believe it.' Leo wasn't easily excited about the projects he saw on a daily basis but this unique set-up was something else. The creative use of space. The sparkling fixtures, recessed lighting, marble and honeyed Tasmanian Oak. The relaxing use of muted colours: mulberry and charcoal, blue and cream. The way it harmonised with the surrounding environment.

And the foundation that had made it possible.

He held a growing respect for these guys who'd pulled it together. 'I'm impressed. And I don't say that often.'

'Of course you are, and I'm sure you don't, Mr Hamilton.' There was a smile in her voice as she tugged off her boots and nodded to another wing they'd not yet explored. 'Take off your shoes then come and see my favourite place to relax in.'

He did, and moments later he saw an indoor pool with a blue and grey and green vista stretching all the way to the coast. Today the view was misty and waterlogged with rain sluicing down the huge panes. 'I see why you love it.'

'We're not quite there yet,' she said with a glint in her eyes and moved towards an archway on the far side.

He followed her to a massive shiny white spa surrounded by marble and gold and enclosed in glass. The same panorama of flora and river spread out before them. Privacy with a view.

'But if you want a change in scenery…' Breanna pressed a remote.

Panels slid down on silent tracks, blocking all light and sound from the outside and leaving them bathed in a soft blush. Leo noted vaguely that the architect had designed a curvature in the panels, which prevented the light from the pool filtering into the spa's area. The rest of the world ceased to exist as the watery sound of a harp trickled like silver over imaginary moss. The stresses of the last few days slid away. Afternoon turned to hot summer night as the floor beneath his bare feet warmed and he drank in the sight of Brie surrounded by a pink aura.

Her close-fitting dark clothes showcased her long limbs and slender body, her rounded breasts and mysterious eyes. It was almost as if he were under a spell.

And he might have spoken to tell her how amazing she looked, how much he wanted her and damn the consequences, but to speak would somehow seem irreverent at that moment.

He heard the sound of bare feet on marble as she crossed the room and lit half a dozen fat candles. The scent of sandalwood soon drifted on the air and he breathed slow and deep. It was almost as if she was seducing him.

Except she'd done nothing overtly provocative, nothing to entice him to play her game. Whatever her game was.

Should have heeded that glint in her eyes earlier.

Shaking himself out of the fog that enshrouded him, he concentrated on opening and closing his fists. Taking short sharp breaths.

What time was it? He checked his watch, swore under his breath. With the weather the way it was, he'd take longer to get to the coast than he'd planned. 'I have to go.' He flicked an impatient hand at the walls. 'If you'd remove the privacy screens, please.'

'Are you sure I can't tempt you to stay a little longer?' But even as she spoke the panels slid away and the intimate mood vanished, replaced by the cool glare of a wet afternoon.

'It's a—'

'Three-hour drive,' she finished for him. 'I know.' They turned and retraced their steps to where they'd left their shoes.

He put his on then straightened to look at her. Barefoot, her hair tousled from her earlier car nap and the inclement weather. Again, as it had earlier, her expression tugged at something inside him but he dismissed it in the same heartbeat. 'Catch you later.'

'If you change your mind, or decide to come back early…' She stared up at him, eyes deep and dark and perceptive. 'You'll remember the code to get through the gate,' she said, reaching into her jeans pocket. 'And here's a keycard for the retreat. You might want to use it sometime.'

'I won't need it,' he told her, but found himself taking it anyway. It was warm from its proximity to her skin. An invitation he *would* resist.

'That's entirely up to you.' She walked to the door, opened it. A gust of wet wind blew in with a flurry of leaves. She shivered and folded her arms tight across her shoulders. 'Glad I'm going to be warm and cosy here.'

'I'm glad you are too,' he said. 'Have a pleasant evening.' And, turning before he could change his mind, he dashed through the downpour to his car.

There was no way he was going to be late for this meeting. No way in heaven.

CHAPTER SEVEN

WHO WAS BRIE? Leo pondered the riddle as he negotiated Hobart's Derwent Bridge in heavy rain. The playful tease or the little girl lost? The up-front woman who insisted on honesty or the compassionate campaigner he'd only glimpsed beneath that flirty exterior—a side he'd not known existed until his conversation with Sam.

Obviously she didn't do deep and meaningful relationships. And wasn't that what he wanted too? A hot and mutually satisfying no-nonsense fling with no drama when one or both of them called it quits and moved on?

Assuming he wanted a fling with a woman who liked to be in the driver's seat.

Thoughts of driving prompted him to check the time again. In this weather he was going to be later than planned. He'd call ahead when he was out of the suburbs and let them know the state of the roads and his ETA.

His thoughts turned relentlessly to Breanna again. *Did* he want a fling with a woman who called it as she saw it? A stunning and sexy woman who wasn't afraid to let him know what she wanted? He found her personality surprisingly stimulating and refreshingly different. He found their subtle power tussles a challenge.

Leo thrived on challenge.

She'd all but seduced him earlier; he still didn't know how she'd managed it without a touch, without one flirtatious word. Just that on-again off-again wicked glint in her eyes. So she wanted to play? He saw a U-turn opening in the road up ahead and flicked on his indicator.

Game on.

And he *would* win.

Brie was waiting for him on wide-cushioned matting at the edge of the spa when she saw his car pull up on the security monitor. Smiling, she rubbed her hands together in satisfaction—and spine-tingling expectation. She'd known he'd come back. She knew men. If there was a choice between a new lover and work they chose the sex every time. Leo Hamilton was no different.

So after he'd left this afternoon, she'd lowered the panels again. The light was a dim blush once more. She'd cranked up the temperature in the air and in the spa, changed the music to mellow blues and added a couple of essential oil burners to the candlelight for a soothing and relaxing atmosphere. She'd turned dismal day into sultry night.

A quick make-up repair then she'd changed into a long silk garment of midnight blue, leaving her feet bare. She'd wavered between sexy underwear or none at all, and had decided to initiate her new tangerine lace with black trim, which had cost her almost a week's takings. She hoped he appreciated it before she let him take it off her. Because it was all about the sex and what man didn't enjoy a little mystery to unwrap first?

And it was going to be good. Better than good. Because they understood each other from the start. He wasn't her type, she wasn't his but they had this *thing* going on. It would be casual, fun sex. Temporary. Something to enjoy and work out of their systems then move on. *No heart, no hurt.*

Suddenly there he was. Before she was quite ready for him. A darker silhouette against the dark panels. Only his eyes flashed in the wavering candlelight. Power emanated from that gaze. Strength. Control. Dominance.

And for the first time in her life with a new lover, she felt a flicker of nerves zip down her body.

Not fear. She knew on an instinctive level he'd never harm her. This was something deeper, something primal. Something that tore her open and left her defenceless. And a growing awareness that here was the potential for pain of a different kind. If she let there be..

'Come here, Breanna.' Calmly spoken, his demand bounced off the walls and vibrated through her body as he tossed his jacket down.

'It's more comfortable here,' she began. 'There's—'

'*Now,* Breanna.' All semblance of calm vanished, impatience rolled in like thunder to take its place. 'And bring that remote with you, wherever it is.'

She picked it up from the low table as she walked—in a deliberately relaxed fashion—towards him. *Relaxed?* Her insides were quivering, her knees liquefying.

His hand shot out, palm up. She met his gaze force for force as she handed him the remote. Up close he looked even more formidable. Almost the way he'd looked the first time she'd seen him. Her pulse hiked. 'If you want to change the music you pr—'

'I want to raise the panels.'

She blinked. 'Raise them?' Spoil the atmosphere she'd created with so much care and anticipation? But she knew by his demeanour not to argue. 'Green button, top left.'

The panels rose. The rain had eased and watery afternoon sunshine filtered in, highlighting the stark features of the man standing in front of her. Black pricks of stubble on his tight jaw, steely resolution in his eyes, those usually full lips compressed into a line.

Had she thought she'd influenced his decision to come back? She was no longer so sure. He didn't look like a man being coerced into doing something he didn't want to do as he tossed the remote onto the mat alongside his jacket. He looked like a man in control. What was worse, he was calling the shots—and Breanna was doing his bidding.

She found herself almost wilting under his scrutiny and drew herself up. 'I—'

'Don't. Don't say anything.'

For emphasis, or because he no doubt expected a fulsome retort from her, he reached out, pressed a thumb against her lips. He wrapped the other hand around her hair, twisted it around his wrist, forcing her to look up at him. 'We're going to do this my way.' He slid his thumb slowly along the seam of her lips. 'No messing about in dark corners.' He jutted his chin toward the windows where the light poured in then looked back into her eyes so there was no escaping that gaze. 'I want to see you well and properly while we do it.'

And she didn't say anything because, possibly for the first time in her life, she was speechless. Dumbstruck with a trembling and new kind of anticipation that swirled through her body. Gobsmacked because this wasn't happening how she'd planned. This was not how it was supposed to happen.

He gave her no time, laying a firm mouth on hers with ruthless and practised precision, sending tingles from her lips to the soles of her bare feet.

Her hands, which had hung useless at her sides for the past couple of moments, rose to his belt buckle only to be brushed aside by a strong hand. He lifted his lips barely enough to remind her, 'My way.'

'B—'

Okay. She closed her eyes and allowed herself to be swept away by pure sensation. Her breasts felt full, swollen, her nipples tight, and she wished he would just soothe the ache—anyhow he liked. She breathed in the scent of warm man and sandalwood. The slow seductive sound of blue moon jazz cruised on the air.

Crushing her mouth, he hauled her closer. *Finally.* All the way…pressed against him, from neck to knee and every place in between. His body was hot and hard, lean and fit. She moaned as his erection pushed against her belly, her hips instinctively arching to meet him.

Anticipation was pale comparison to the real deal and her body quivered, her heart catapulted against her ribs. She'd wanted more than a kiss with Leo, had imagined how it would feel but hadn't imagined it would ever be this intense. This raw, primitive need for him that transcended anything she'd ever felt before.

Releasing her, he drew back, watching her. He was breathing heavily, his eyes molten, his lips glistening from their assault on hers. 'I want you. In the daylight. No adornments, no frills. Just you.'

'Ever see me wearing a *frill*?' She had an insane desire to laugh but she couldn't seem to raise her voice above a murmur.

Humour glinted in his eyes. 'Good point.' His voice, however, was rough velvet and confident when he promised, 'I'm going to make you come.'

A glorious fist of desire slammed against her middle. *Thank the Lord.*

The backs of his fingers trailed shivers down her bare arm. 'I'm going to watch you while you do.'

Damp heat spurted low in her belly and she felt her tangerine lace panties grow damp. 'Yes.'

'As you already know, I'm a man who likes to take his time, so we could be here a while.'

No problem at all. But she felt obliged to remind him. 'Your dinner appointment?'

He walked to the non-alcoholic bar in the corner, picked up a stool. 'I've rescheduled.' Setting it in front of her, he sat down, hands on his thighs, fingers splayed, his gaze sending sparks all down her body. 'Wet road, poor visibility. It's a supper meeting now.'

'Ah...'

He'd rescheduled for her—for both of them—as she'd expected he would. But this man caressing her up and down with hot eyes and taking his time... She felt almost gauche and inexperienced, which was amazing and odd since she was always an eager and equal participant in her sexual encounters.

This was new. She licked her lips, tasted him. Couldn't stand the tension a second longer. 'So, are we going to get on with it?'

His eyes sparked with heat as he gestured with a jerk of his chin. 'Get rid of the dress.'

'You don't want to do it yourself?'

He shifted his position, spreading his thighs a little. 'I'd prefer to watch.'

Satisfied with that response, she smiled, untied the halter neck and let it shimmer down her body.

Fascination held Leo immobile as he watched the garment slide down, down, down. It caught for an instant on her breasts, then with a little wiggle it shimmied, light and shadow playing on its silky surface as it revealed the curve of her slender waist. A flat belly, then, to his surprise, a miniature strawberry stud twinkled at her navel. Something to talk about some other time.

Then those endlessly long legs he hadn't been able to stop fantasising about. Damn shame he wouldn't have time for the steamy spa she'd obviously planned for the two of them.

Like all women, he supposed she'd worn the sexy underwear for his pleasure. And he appreciated it. But it could only mean she'd thought about having sex with him. Not only thought about it—she'd anticipated it. Unless she always dressed prepared for a little seduction?

Either that or she'd *known* he'd come back… Something he hadn't known himself until a short time ago. And in that time, she'd showered and changed—he'd smelled fresh soap on her skin and a spritz of her midnight temptation perfume. And her choice of dress was chosen expressly for slipping off. The knowledge disturbed him more than he was comfortable with.

Who was playing who?

He twirled a finger in the air. 'Turn around.' He had the upper hand, at least for now.

Arms outstretched, she pirouetted while he admired firm, round buttocks. His palms tingled—tempting little handfuls he was itching to familiarise himself with some more. Her lingerie choice came a distant second to all that pretty skin. 'Nice colour,' he told her. 'Hot.'

'Like a sunrise,' she said with the confident smile that had no doubt seduced countless would-be lovers.

Seduced. 'Come here,' he demanded, absurdly annoyed with her self-assurance and his thoughts of her with other men. Annoyed, because jealous was not a word he associated with himself. Ever.

As she glided closer he wondered how long he could go without touching her.

He discovered the answer two quick heartbeats later when he slid his hands around her waist. He was right: her skin felt like warm silk and his fingers wandered up her ribcage, thumbs flicking over the underside of her breasts through her bra. Tight, wine-dark nipples pressed against the lace, temptingly erect, tantalisingly close. His erection throbbed in time with his pulse and he was glad he was sitting down. He breathed deep and slow and dug down deep for that last remnant of control.

Her hands rose to cover his. 'Let's—'

'Hands behind your neck. Clasped.'

She made a whimpering sound but did as instructed, which pushed her breasts closer, an irresistible provocation.

Pulling her to him, he closed his mouth around one nipple and sucked her through the lace, drawing the tight bullet into his mouth while he manipulated and drew out the other between thumb and forefinger.

And in those few stuttering heartbeats, nothing but naked skin would suffice. He leaned back to look at her, more than satisfied with the view. Desire and desperation in her eyes, cheeks flushed with arousal, lips parted. Hands still clasped behind her head.

Satisfied? Leo choked back a laugh. Hell, he wasn't nearly satisfied. His head spun with her scent, her taste and every part of his body screamed for more. For all.

Not yet.

He reached out to touch again and his infamous control slipped a notch. More. *To hell with it.* One swift tug and her panties were gone, rent in two and tossed over his shoulder. He glimpsed the shock in her eyes but he was already grasping that final flimsy barrier in his fist.

Brie gasped as the last of her clothing was shredded and flung who knew where. Not in fear, not in fury or indignation, but with rising excitement. His gaze swept over her naked body, raising goosebumps upon goosebumps. Dizzy with desire, she swayed towards him, quivering, shivering, craving more.

He slammed both thighs with his fists. 'Come here.'

Yes. She didn't need to be told twice. Brie watched his eyes turn smoky as she straddled him, opened her most intimate self to his smouldering silver gaze, her limp arms all but collapsing onto his shoulders.

His hard masculine hand moved down between them. Biting down on her lower lip, she arched upwards, the

ache, the tension in her lower belly almost unbearable. *Leo.*
'Touch me.' The words hissed out between clenched teeth.

He stroked her once, fingers gliding like silk over her
moist centre, their gazes fused as he watched her gasp
and shudder and moan at that first startling contact. Her
attention drifted to where his fingers stroked, slow and
steady, again and again. She could only whimper. The
man rendered her incapable of speech, incapable of co-
herent thought.

But she could feel that slow slide to paradise. Oh, *how*
she could feel. Sensation building on glorious sensation.
What Leo was doing to her went way beyond her wildest
experience—and she'd had her share of wild experiences—
yet paradoxically he was achieving it with his frustratingly
leisurely patience. Barely touching her—as soothing and
gentle as the misty rain on the other side of the windows.

She could smell the jasmine oil now, and magnificent
man and her own arousal, could hear the fast thud of her
heart, and, despite his keeping his movements slow, Leo's
quickened breathing. Then she heard him say, 'Look at
me.'

'I am,' she murmured, her gaze riveted by the impressive erection straining against his jeans. *Oh, my.* She
couldn't wait to wrap her hands around him but her own
needs took precedence when he pushed a finger inside. She
bit her lip and pleaded, 'Hurry, hurry, hurry.'

He did *not* oblige. 'No. Right now I want slow and wet
and slippery. And I want to watch your eyes when I take
you there so *look at me.*'

His words thrilled, excited, electrified. She lifted her
gaze. His brow was dotted with sweat, his grim-mouthed
expression telling her how much effort it was costing him
to hold onto that control he seemed determined to maintain.

Mindless passion, a sweet lingering endurance. They

watched each other as he took her higher, pressure building, slowly at first, then gaining momentum. Faster, faster
on her own runaway sky rocket.

He sent her soaring to heaven before she could scream
hallelujah.

It took a couple of stuttering heartbeats to reclaim some
shred of sanity, her arms trembling, hands clutching his
shoulders, his mohair jumper soft against her fingers.
'You...' she barely managed. 'Inside.'

She heard the rasp of his zip, the rustle of foil as he
protected them both and still his eyes didn't leave hers. It
was as if some force had brought them together and refused to let go.

He drove himself home in one fierce thrust, the force
expelling what little breath was left in her body. She raised
her hands to shoulder height, palms facing forward, and
exhilarated in the power she felt in the fingers that linked
with hers. Murmured his name as they rocked together
towards that final glorious peak.

She felt his release deep inside, her internal muscles
rippling around him in response as she climaxed a second time. On a shuddering groan, he threw back his head,
exposing the strong masculine curve of jaw and stubbled
chin.

Spent, she collapsed over him with a satisfied moan.
Finally, a man with the determined will to rival hers in
the bedroom—or wherever else they chose to do it. Until
Leo had come into her life, she'd not realised this sexual
power-play with a worthy opponent was what she'd missed
in a lover.

Not just sex, a tiny voice whispered. Something deeper.

Wasn't going to happen.

She caught sight of her ruined bra floating in the spa
and clutched at the distraction like a woman drowning.
'No appreciation for sexy underwear?' she murmured.

'Not so much as for what lies beneath it.'

His answer was just what she needed, keeping her in the now. Sexy and casual—what they both wanted. She'd have grinned but her face felt numb. 'That was my newest pièce de résistance.'

He pushed up, bringing her to her feet so suddenly she almost stumbled. 'I'll pay for the damages.'

'Hey, I wasn't complaining.'

'Nevertheless. Bathroom?' He was tucking himself away; his tone bordered on curt.

'Door on the left.' Brie pointed towards the far side of the pool. Was it her overactive hormones or was it the feeling that everything had just changed, making him seem remote and in a hurry to leave?

Her nakedness in contrast to his fully dressed state added to her intense feeling of vulnerability.

Of course he'd be in a hurry, she told herself, grabbing her dress and hauling it up her bare torso. He had a three-hour drive in slippery conditions. He'd be driving through dusk then full dark with heavy cloud and possible fog. The country roads would be horrendous if the rain started up again, as it threatened to.

He exited the bathroom looking casual and gorgeous and her heart did an unexpected somersault in her chest. She'd got what she'd wanted but she'd not factored in the serious cardio workout that had come with it.

She didn't need cardio; she got that at the gym. Especially not with him. He was short-term, like her. They both understood that. 'Are you sure it's wise to travel tonight?'

'You'd advise against it?'

'Yes. You could—'

'You think like a girl.' He swiped his jacket up off the mat.

'I *think* like someone who's concerned about you.'

He looked genuinely surprised, eyes widening as they

flicked to hers, fingers motionless for an instant on the soft leather. 'Don't be. I've been looking after myself since I was five years old.' His lips quirked as he shrugged it on. 'I've scored a suite in Heaven for tonight and I don't intend to waste it.'

Focused on his six-star accommodation. Not a word about whether the earth had moved for him. No suggestion of when, or even if, they might do it again. After such an orgasmic interlude, for her at least, he made Brie feel more than a little idiotic.

And she *was* an idiot to make such a big deal of it. 'Well, enjoy,' she said, making herself smile and be her usual laid-back self. 'I know I would.'

'Hey, you're in a good spot—what's not to enjoy here?'

'Absolutely. And I will.' She'd make sure she did.

'I'll contact you.'

Ha. Of course he would. She relaxed into her smile. 'I'll be here. Not that it matters where I am. The beauty of mobiles.'

'Yeah.' Quick flash of humour in his eyes. 'Because I need your banking details for the rental payments.'

Oh. 'Right. Fine.'

A small frown pinched his brow. 'Problem?'

'Not at all,' she said, tightly. Angry. And doubly angry that she felt the absolute need to lie but in this instance her damaged pride and her rare attack of vulnerability demanded it.

'Good, then.' He flipped a hand. 'Stay warm, I'll see myself out.' He turned, walked towards the main wing. 'Catch you later.'

Not if she could help it. But even as she muttered, 'Right,' she knew that wasn't true. Thin-lipped, she hugged her bare arms and watched him disappear, listened to his footsteps fade. 'Damn you, Leo Hamilton. You made me lie.'

It didn't matter, she reminded herself. *He* didn't matter.

It was just sex—spectacular, mind-blowing, earth-shattering sex. But that was all it was. *Had been,* she told herself, because there'd be no repeat performance.

Remember, Brie: No heart, no hurt.

CHAPTER EIGHT

LEO HAD MORE important things to think about. He repeated it over and over. More important things than the woman who'd stripped his mind clean of everything except having her again any which way he could. He crossed the Derwent Bridge for the second time in as many hours, relieved he had somewhere he needed to be and he needed to be there fast. Clients to impress, a reputation to uphold.

Business was his focus. His priority. His life. *Never forget it.*

His tyres sprayed water and brakes screeched as he hit them for a red light he'd not seen till the last second. Leo shook his head and glared at the wet road in front of him. *See what happens when you allow yourself to be side-tracked by a woman?*

No, sir. Not Leo Hamilton, happy-go-lucky bachelor. He had enough trouble handling his sister. Safest to keep relationships with the opposite sex simple, easy, uncomplicated.

Not so easy. Because he couldn't stop himself wondering what the woman he'd left behind less than thirty minutes ago was doing now. Indulging in a soak in her steamy spa or a vintage champagne from her brother's rare and expensive French collection? Given her mood when he'd departed, it was more likely champagne *in* that steamy spa.

She'd be hard at work, soaking her sulk away in a moun-

tain of froth, because every man knew when a woman said
'fine' in a tone that could slice through an iceberg at fifty
paces, she meant anything but.

Precisely the reason he liked his single, uncomplicated
life. Never get involved with a woman's sulks. He knew
Breanna had expected the afternoon to continue into the
evening. He'd been sorry to have to disappoint because
he'd have enjoyed the promised sex in the spa as well as
the next guy, but work took priority. There'd be other opportunities.

She'd not been able to get enough of him.

He smiled, remembering. But his smile faded. Was pleasure all it had been? Nowhere near an adequate description, but the alternative was too unsettling to contemplate.

She'd expected more from him. He'd been too afraid
of his own reaction to stay. And why would he stay? He
was late already.

Switching the radio station from jazz to pop, he shook
the edgy feeling away and tapped along with the beat,
overtaking a semi-trailer as he travelled through rolling
farmland beneath a bruised evening sky and rehearsed the
agenda for tonight's meeting aloud to keep his concentration focused where it should be.

But it wasn't long before his thoughts returned to Breanna and a pressing desire to hear her voice. 'Call Breanna
Black on her mobile number,' he told his smartphone. Then
changed his mind when he heard the ring tone. 'Cancel
that call.' Because what would he tell her? That the sex
had been incredible? That she was the most responsive
lover he'd ever had? She had a body that could keep a man
awake and tossing into the wee hours?

She'd be keeping him awake tonight.

And there it was again, plain as the purple clouds on the
horizon. *He'd* not been able to get enough of *her*.

He swore once—loudly—then, still muttering, shook

his head. She'd made it clear she couldn't wait and he'd
been so besotted with her uninhibited self-confidence, her
sheer abandonment when she'd come apart in his arms,
he'd not even considered his own reaction.

Or deliberately chosen not to.

He remembered that instant when he'd linked his fingers through hers as he pushed slowly inside her for the
first time. A fleeting notion that he'd been waiting his
whole life for that moment… He dragged a nervous hand
over his head. All just another facet of her mysterious
charm, he assured himself, but he had to work hard to
shove it to the back of his mind. Tonight he had a job to do.

The following morning, Leo breakfasted on juice, sweet-
corn fritters with smoked Tasmanian salmon and a giant
kick-start espresso coffee in Heavenly View, one of Heav-
en's three restaurants. The table overlooked the ocean
where the morning star hung like a jewel and a thin line
of approaching daylight spread along a pearl horizon.

Experiencing the newest six-star eco-lodge first-hand
had well and truly lived up to his expectations. The only
structure approved within thirty-five kilometres, it perched
on a hill forty metres above a pounding sea and pristine
white beaches. The team had done a great job blending
conservation and tourism while protecting the coastal wilderness. The building materials had been choppered in,
the sumptuous dining experience used fresh local produce exclusively.

He'd established new benchmarks for sustainable tourism including conversion of waste into clean irrigation
water and an extensive recycling programme. He'd also
kick-started the establishment of a fund supporting local
environmental projects, the final details of which he'd laid
out to the team last night.

This morning he was basking in the afterglow of success and a hefty five-figure deposit was due in his bank balance. Further, in appreciation of his work, he'd received a complimentary weekend break for two starting Friday evening with a seven-course gastronomic delight to be served in the most expensive suite the lodge had to offer.

He glanced at his phone, screen black against the snowy white tablecloth. His first thought on waking had been of Breanna and whether she'd slept as little as he. In the next moment, he'd wanted to share his good news and tell her his efforts over the past ten months had been rewarded and to ask if she was free this coming weekend.

Which was totally unexpected because he'd never felt the desire to share any aspect of his business or its success with any woman. Never mixed business with pleasure.

But the weekend of indulgence on offer was a different matter, he told himself as he flicked through the day's news on his tablet. It had to be this coming weekend because he'd arranged to be in Singapore on business for the next, and three weeks was ridiculously too far away. However, phoning a woman at six a.m. smacked of desperation. One thing Leo had never been was desperate.

A text, then, asking her if she was free, which she could read at her leisure. He shook his head. He'd call in and see her on his way home. She'd be at work…

He drummed his fingers on the tablecloth and glared at his phone again. What was happening to him? Until yesterday afternoon he'd considered himself a reasonably sophisticated guy when it came to women and the whole dating scene. Well, the jury was out on that one now.

Nor had he ever been gripped by indecision. *Just do it*. He reached for the phone at the same time it rang in his hand. Sunny's photo beamed back at him.

He beat back the tiny disappointment that it wasn't Breanna. And instantly castigated himself. 'Hey, Suns.' Hearing her voice raised a momentary concern. Sunny rarely rang him—it was always the other way round. 'Everything okay?'

'Everything's great. Only four days to go to the big Opera House gig. I'm super excited now.'

'I bet.' He relaxed as the tension eased with Sunny's bright enthusiasm. 'So what are you up to so early this morning?'

'Extra violin practice, but I should be asking you that question.'

He straightened in his dining chair as the tension crept back. 'What did I miss?'

'First up, you departed Melbourne a day earlier than you planned, with only a text to say you'd left. Then I don't hear from you for over forty-eight hours—you never let it go more than a day. What's going on?'

He picked up a butter knife, twirled it between his fingers and said, 'You expressed a need for space, said I was stifling you. "Control freak" has been tossed out there a few times, amongst other things.'

'Yeah, all well and good but since when have you listened to me, brother love? So who's the woman?'

'If you believe there's a woman involved, why are you checking up on me at the crack of dawn? It's still dark, for Pete's sake.'

'Shall I ring back later, then?' she asked, sweetly.

'No. I'm not with a woman. I'm in Heaven.'

'In heaven without a woman? That's not like you, Leo.'

'Sunny dearest.'

'Leo love. Who's the woman?' He opened his mouth but she spoke first. 'Never mind denying it. So—' her tone turned brisk '—how *is* Heaven?'

'Still looking pretty black from where I'm sitting.'

'Everything going okay over there?'

'Better than okay. I left home a day early because I needed to go over some minor adjustments in the kitchen with my architect and I had some details to finalise before the meeting here, which, by the way, was a major success.'

'Of course it was. Congratulations! Your architect's a woman, right?'

'And your point is?'

'Never mind. Have you met any of my neighbours yet?'

Breanna.

His body responded with all too easily remembered heat. Her face looking more stunned than stunning the last time he saw her. In a shimmery dress that was all but transparent from a certain angle; but of course she'd known that.

And the way she'd looked—the way he always left a woman—dishevelled and satisfied.

Except, this time… Something inside him twisted. He felt as if he'd left a tiny part of himself behind.

Since Sunny had specifically asked, there was no point putting it off; he felt obliged to fill her in. 'I've met West Wind's owner.' He cleared a husk from his throat. 'As it's turned out, I'll be staying there for a bit when I'm down in Hobart while she house-sits for her brother and his wife. So I'm right next door to our place. Convenient all round.'

'Yes. Very convenient.'

'She's absolutely not my kind of woman,' he stated. Too fast, too curtly.

'Did I ask?'

At the humour in her voice, he swore beneath his breath while leaping to his own defence. 'She's extroverted and argumentative.' *And sexy and honest and too intriguing for his own peace of mind.* 'The kind of woman who'd drive any sane man crazy. You two should get on well.'

'Really? Interesting. Are you a sane man, brother love?'

'You tell me,' he said, tapping the knife repeatedly on the tablecloth. He'd thought he was. Now he wasn't so sure. Brie had done that to him. They'd spent a handful of hours together over the past couple of weeks and Breanna had changed who he was in some way. She'd worked her unique and magic brand of seduction. How had he let that happen?

'You're so sane it's scary,' Sunny said. 'So, does *she* have a name?'

'Breanna Black. Beauty therapist with her own business. Eve's Naturally. Into natural stuff.' *Tisanes*—whatever the hell they were. Foody face masks. 'Talks to her plants.' His mind wandered back to that first weekend. 'They call her Party Babe Brie. Apparently. What does that tell you?'

'That she's fun?'

'Exactly my point,' he muttered. 'I don't have time to waste.' Not that he didn't enjoy fun—he did—but being with Breanna was like being on a wild ride at an amusement park and he'd never enjoyed that out-of-control, falling sensation at the top of a roller coaster...

'You've been avoiding her, then.'

'Yes. No. Not exactly. Listen, I have to get moving,' he told her, tossing down the knife and pushing back his chair, *needing* to end this conversation *now.* 'Some loose ends to tie up here before I leave.'

'Okay. Friday night, don't be late. I have too much to do to worry about reminding you.'

'In which case, I'll not intrude on your precious time for the rest of the week,' he said, making his way out of the restaurant.

She laughed. 'I'll be the girl in the sparkly black dress.'

'Ciao, for now.' He disconnected, almost walked into Heaven's senior accountant at the door. 'Gerald, good morning. I was hoping to see you before I leave,' he said, relieved to switch to business. 'I need another look at those figures.'

Because he was always straight with Sunny—except when it came to her sexy new neighbour—he made sure to find a few more of those loose ends before leaving Heaven.

They took longer than he'd anticipated and he made a couple of overseas calls to other clients so he had no time to phone that sexy neighbour until nine-thirty when he was halfway back to Hobart.

He called up her number, heard it ring, tapped his fingers impatiently. 'Come on, Breanna, pick up.'

'Hello. You've reached Breanna Black. I'm unable to take your call...' He let the sound of her low, sensual voice wash over him and tried to curb his impatience. He wanted to hear that voice up close and in person and moaning sexy things, not a detached greeting on some mechanical device. 'Please leave your name and a message and I'll return your call as soon as possible.'

'Leo speaking. Don't bother returning my call. I'll be at your salon in about ninety minutes.'

Brie took a mid-morning break in the lunch room she shared with Sam and Lynda, a physiotherapist. She wished she were fully booked and too busy for distractions today but her next client had cancelled. So she intended catching up on client info in preparation for the upcoming move to the retreat. She blew on her blackberry tea as she scrolled through her messages one-handed and saw she'd missed a call from the biggest distraction of all.

Her heart did a back-flip against her ribs, her palms instantly sweaty, and she almost dropped the phone. Her finger was poised to retrieve the voice message when she remembered. Leo—her new *tenant*—had said he'd contact her about banking details for the rent. As he'd all but bolted out of the door.

She plunked her mobile on the table, glared at it and took a sip of too-hot tea while she waited impatiently for her heart to settle down. She didn't want to hear his message. Why put herself through the humiliation and sheer awkwardness of hearing him ask about *banking details*?

She'd text him the information instead—now—so he wouldn't have to call back.

What was wrong with her that he'd obviously decided sex between them wasn't going to work? Yes, he'd been in a hurry for an appointment he'd postponed—for her. No. She crossed her arms, still glaring at the phone. For them. But mostly for himself.

After she'd tempted him to play her game, it was true. But his lack of response after their close encounter had left her feeling inadequate and dissatisfied. A word, a touch, a kiss… Anything to let her know he'd felt *something*.

She'd never had sex with a man who hadn't wanted more. And knowing that, she'd always held the power; she'd set the rules. Her rules. No-strings sex for as long as it worked for both of them and exclusivity while they were doing it.

Her rules didn't seem to work with Leo, who obviously set his own. She'd known that and had gone ahead and played anyway. With a man she realised now she didn't understand as well as she'd thought.

It was time to stop thinking, time to get moving. Brie drained her cup then rinsed it in the little sink. A quick draught alerted her to a presence behind her. Turning, she saw Leo just inside the room.

'The receptionist? Jodie?' He jerked a thumb over his shoulder. 'She said I could come on back.'

Brie just bet she did. It was a wonder she hadn't shown him the way personally.

'She offered to show me the way but I didn't want to waste time on polite conversation or wait while the both of you engage in useless office talk.'

'Okay.' She ripped off a piece of paper towel and wiped her mug with exaggerated care and was pleased to note the tightness in his jaw, the way he stood, fingers tense against his thighs. Fingers that had stroked her all the way to heaven mere hours before. 'What *do* you want to waste time on?'

'I wanted to see you alone. And I promise it won't be a waste of time.'

'No?'

'No.'

A tingle raced down her spine but, no matter how tempting his promise, she refused to play. Leo Hamilton needed to learn he couldn't treat women—her in particular—with such a cavalier attitude. 'So it's your lucky day,' she said with a smile, then tossed up her hands. 'Oops, too late. Break time's over.'

His lips compressed in obvious irritation. Without taking his eyes off her, he shut the door. 'Not yet. I juggled appointments to be here so—'

'Yeah, *so*? This is my place of work.'

'I know, I saw your office on the way through.' The way he spoke, she knew he wasn't impressed with the way she organised her desk—or not, as the case happened to be.

'*And* this room's a shared space,' she went on. 'I take my business reputation seriously and I have appointments too. You can't just—'

'Jodie told me your next client cancelled. You're free. So am I.'

'Am I supposed to be impressed that you've juggled your work to visit me here? Because it happens to suit you?'

'It doesn't suit, particularly, but I'm here anyway. To see you, as I've just explained.'

'Have you heard the saying, never mix business with pleasure?'

'Who said anything about business?' In two strides he was in front of her.

His fingers were firm and impatient on her shoulders

and excitement zipped down her spine, but she shrugged out of his grip. 'Who said anything about pleasure?'

'Breanna.' He spoke her name in a voice that was pure seduction with a glimmer of self-deprecating humour. 'You're annoyed with me.'

Yeah. Big time. 'How very perceptive of you.' To siphon her mad into positive energy she ripped off another square of paper towel, turned her back on him and began rubbing at tea stains on the sink.

'I had to leave, you knew that.'

'Yes.' She stopped, turned back and looked him straight in the eye. 'But it's the manner in which you left.' And the state he'd left her in.

He looked perplexed, brow furrowed. 'This is just sex with us, right? That's all you want? All either of us want,' he finished with a certain grim finality.

'Absolutely. Couldn't agree more.'

'So what's the problem?'

'A little post-coital conversation would have been…I think "polite" is the word I'm looking for. Maybe you're not familiar with the etiquette a woman expects after sex. Still, you could have stayed a few moments and proved me wrong.'

'Not when I have an important meeting I'm already running late for because I stayed longer than I should have with you. Longer than I meant to.'

'Okay.' Tossing the paper towel in the kitchen tidy, she swiped her tense fingers down the front of her navy skirt. 'So are you saying if you hadn't had that meeting scheduled, you'd have been happy to stick around? Be honest, please, because I got the distinct impression you couldn't wait to get out of there and I'd rather know now than be made a fool of.'

He nodded slowly, as if considering his words with care. 'I didn't sleep a wink in Heaven's softer-than-air bed last night; what do you think? And if you're under the impression I'd ever set out to deliberately make a fool of you, you couldn't be more wrong.'

He did appear a little worse for wear today, she noticed. Eyes bleary, lines etched deeper around his mouth. She sensed there was more he wasn't saying but she accepted his roundabout excuse for an apology for now, until she could get to the bottom of whatever it was that had disturbed him. Because he'd very neatly avoided her first question. 'I didn't sleep much either,' she confessed.

His smile was slow and shattering. 'I have something in mind I think you'll enjoy.'

To her shocked embarrassment she felt her cheeks *blooming* at his blatant promise of erotic delights. Like a teenager, for heaven's sakes. To hide it, she busied herself rinsing everyone else's coffee-stained mugs. 'I'm listening.'

'Is next weekend free for you?' he said close to her ear.

She pressed her lips together at the exciting sensation of her body vibrating in harmony with his voice. Struggled to answer with her usual flirty tone. 'It could be. If you make it worthwhile.'

'How about I take you to Heaven?'

A corner of her mouth lifted. 'You already have.'

'This'll be better. Sex *and* post-coital conversation with food and wine and stunning views. A weekend of heaven at Heaven. We can take our time returning after Sunday brunch. What do you say?'

Irresistible. How could she refuse? 'I say that sounds like a tempting offer, Mr Hamilton.'

'Make no mistake, Ms Black, it's a very tempting offer. Question is, are you going to take me up on it?'

'I reckon I might…'

'G—'

'Think about it,' she finished, with a smile on the inside.

Let him think about *that*. She stepped sideways to reach for the teapot but she found herself being spun around and pressed up against the kitchen bench by a hard, toned body.

Before she could utter another word, his lips crushed hers. His unique flavour was overlaid with impatience and desire, as if he couldn't get enough quickly enough and was damned annoyed about it.

To heck with fighting it, she decided, absorbing his hot, dark taste as his hands moved down her back, cupping her buttocks and dragging her closer to that hard ridge of masculine heat.

'What happened to slow?' she managed when he finally lifted his mouth to stare down at her.

'A change is good.'

Then somehow her skirt was ruched halfway up her thighs and her hands sliding like limp spaghetti over his shoulders. His hands were nowhere near as innocent, caressing her breasts outside her virginal white blouse, then rolling the hard nipples between his fingers as he tugged at an ear lobe with his teeth. 'Good?'

'Good.' Whimpering, she arched her back, rubbing her aching breasts against his palms, his rock-hard erection pressing against her belly. 'This is so *bad*…'

'Positively wicked.' His hands slid down her body, over her thighs, stroking her skin, then inching higher beneath the hem.

She smiled against his stubbled cheek. 'I like a bit of wicked.'

'I know.' He pulled away, staring at her with eyes that, for one fleeting instant, reminded her of a wolf with one foot caught in a trap. 'You're a fascinating enigma, Breanna Black.'

'And that bothers you.'

'I can handle it,' he muttered. 'And you.'

'I look forward to being handled,' she said. 'As long

as you're only referring to the bedroom. You're one very sexy man, Leo Hamilton, and, to my complete surprise, I find I like you. Shall we leave it at that?'

He fingered a strand of wayward hair at her temple that had escaped the clasp at the back of her head. 'I'll pick you up on Friday night. What time do you finish?'

'I'll be ready to leave by five. No, make it four-thirty. No sense waiting around—I'm an impatient woman.'

'So am I.' He slid a finger across her lips. 'Impatient, I mean.'

She sucked in a slow breath between her teeth. 'So, is this a dirty weekend or a romantic getaway?'

'What do you think?' He started to walk towards the door.

'I need to know what clothes to pack.'

He turned back. His gaze was molten silver, stroking over her. 'An overnight bag is all you'll need. And your contraceptive pill if you take it.'

Her pulse pounded, a carnival ride out of control. 'I do.'

'Glad to hear it.'

'Me too.' It was going to be okay. Just sex. Fun times. Temporary.

'I promise you a night you won't forget. Two, in fact.'

He grinned with wicked intent, which had her insides jumping erratically, and waved a hand towards her chest. 'But you might want to fix your blouse for now.'

Oh, cripes.

By the time she looked up again, he was gone.

CHAPTER NINE

LEO WAS FLAT out seeing clients in the north of the island state for the rest of the week. He had to adjust his schedule around losing Friday afternoon in order to drive back to Hobart then on to Heaven. There was no possibility of making up that time over the weekend because he intended spending every waking moment indulging in more fascinating pursuits.

Since he was working in a remote wilderness area west of Launceston, he had no mobile coverage from Wednesday morning onwards. Which was a good thing because it prevented him from picking up the phone late in the evening just to hear Brie's sensual bedroom voice and indulge in a little pillow talk to get him in the right mood for the weekend.

Not that he hadn't been in the right mood since he'd seen her on Monday morning at her office. He'd wanted her so badly his body ached. Still did. He'd not been able to focus properly on anything else since.

She was still a distraction he couldn't afford.

He reminded himself of that fact as he checked his phone messages at two p.m. on Friday. Moments ago he'd arrived back in Launceston and was taking a coffee break on the town's outskirts before driving on to Hobart.

Then he saw something that dashed his cheery anticipation into the ground. A check-in reminder for this af-

ternoon's four-thirty p.m. flight to Sydney. Sent yesterday
when he'd been out of range.

No freaking way.

His mood plummeted and he stared at the screen, disbelief tracking like tiny ice picks up his spine. *Not possible.*
Sunny's concert was *next* Friday. It had to be—he'd booked
the flight for the wrong week, that was all. But even as he
brought his calendar up on the screen he remembered that
next weekend he was due in Singapore.

He heard Sunny's voice echo in his ear from Monday
morning's conversation. *Don't be late.*

And there it was—the ugly truth. Stabbing him in the
eyes. Pounding away in his head. He was due in Sydney
this evening to watch his baby sister perform at the Opera
House. Sunny's dream gig—and now his waking nightmare.

He'd been so caught up with his own carnal needs and
wants, he'd forgotten the person who deserved his support
the most. Someone who deserved so much better than a
brother who forgot her important day.

He slapped cash on the table and dashed to his car.
Shoving it into gear, he all but fish-tailed out of the tiny
café's driveway and headed south to Hobart. The airport
was this side of town; he'd have to put his car in long-
term parking overnight. If he drove straight there instead
of going home to shower and change, he might just make
it before the final passenger call.

Wasn't it ironic? His flight was departing Hobart at the
same time he was due to pick up Breanna for their idyllic weekend away.

Brie squeezed her Friday afternoon clients in between the
morning ones, forfeiting her morning tea and lunch break
to do so.

She'd dashed out at three-thirty, and as she drove home

to change and get ready she hoped all the juggling was worth it.

It would be worth it.

As she hurried inside, she checked her mobile for the first time since midday and saw three missed calls from Leo, made every half-hour since two this afternoon. He'd not left a message so she had no idea what to make of them, but a bad feeling snaked through her gut. She was about to call him back when the phone rang. Leo's number.

'Hi.' Her voice sounded too breathless—she was aiming for casual. 'What's up?'

'Breanna.' She heard a pause, as if he wasn't sure how to say whatever it was. 'I apologise for the late notice but I can't make it this evening. I'm expected at an important function in Sydney and missing it is *not* an option.'

And here Brie was, thinking that their date was the most important event on his weekend's calendar. *Big mistake, Brie.* He didn't sound apologetic; he sounded terse, as if he couldn't wait to get off the phone. As if he made a habit of double booking and she rated a poor second after his work appointments. If indeed that was what it was… *Remember Elliot?* His appointments hadn't been work-related either.

Of course Brie wasn't an exception to a man like Leo. They weren't even in a proper relationship.

'It's only for tonight,' he went on when she didn't respond. 'I'll be back in Hobart tomorrow morning. It depends on flights, I need to change my booking. Thing is, my sis—'

'I was going to wash my hair anyway,' she cut in before she could hear his excuse. Her throat felt as if it was closing over—that old feeling she'd never wanted to suffer through again. 'No, I wasn't,' she said. 'I was going away with you, Leo Hamilton, because *you* invited *me*. But something better came up and you changed your mind.'

'I did *not* change my mind, Breanna. I messed up my diary and now they're calling my flight. Listen to me. My s—'

She disconnected, turned her phone off. For a moment she just stood and stared at the black screen as a chill wrapped around her. 'I don't want to hear your excuses,' she whispered through clenched teeth. 'I don't *want* to hurt the way Elliot made me hurt with his lies. The way my parents made me hurt with their secrets. And I know you could hurt me so much more than anyone else ever could.'

With the exception of her indulgent spa and champagne chill-out sessions, Brie didn't enjoy being on her own. If she had an evening free and found herself alone, she'd fill it: parties, work, colleagues, friends, distractions—it didn't matter.

That was the beauty of freedom. Freedom to choose what she did and who she did it with. Not being tied to a regular partner or schedule. Not having to be accountable to anyone but herself.

The only way to live. Right?

But tonight as darkness closed in, she couldn't focus on freedom or anything else. Leo had cancelled when she'd been looking forward to a weekend of fun and naughty surprises.

She needed something to take her mind off it.

Food, she decided, eyeing the fridge. The more calories and unhealthier, the better. She dug out two huge scoops of mango ripple ice cream, unwrapped the chocolate-coated almonds left over from last weekend's party and poked them in, then drizzled the lot with raspberry syrup.

She tucked in to the cold delight but Leo was still in her head. Something about the man tugged at her heart, and it terrified her. She wanted to believe he was a decent guy, an honest one. Like his concern for her safety when he'd had the fire alarm installed. For the umpteenth time tonight she wondered if she should have given him a chance to explain before he hopped on that plane to Sydney. To home.

Maybe the reason he lived with his sister was because she couldn't afford to live elsewhere, was jobless and had begged him to take her in? Brie never got involved in family issues with any guys she dated.

When the florist delivery service turned up on her security monitor with roses—four dozen yellow and a single black one with no card attached—her heart didn't stall or stop or turn cartwheels. It cramped. She redirected the driver to the local hospice. Grand gestures like that had always left her cold. It was too easy to order expensive flowers and forget the reason within moments. In her experience, flowers equalled a guilty conscience.

It was just the kind of thing her parents used to do. They'd toss a wad of cash at her and tell her to go spend it in the shopping mall, when all she wanted was for them to look her way. Nor had money bought friendships as a way out of her loneliness. She'd had to work hard for those.

Already overly full on ice cream, Brie poured herself a large glass of merlot. Setting it on the coffee table in front of the white leather lounge overlooking a forest of indoor plants, she put on a classical CD and found her knitting bag. She pulled out her home-spun alpaca yarn and in between mouthfuls of the ruby liquid she continued with what she called her stress scarf.

Leo's roses and the hospice threw up memories she'd never be able to forget. In his final hours at that hospice her father had revealed she had a half-brother.

The truth had changed her life. Clarified so much. Her whole life she'd been invisible to her parents and when her mother had been killed in a car accident nine years ago, Brie realised she'd never really known her.

Why couldn't they have just been honest?

All those missing years not knowing Jett hurt the most

of all. She knitted faster, needles clacking rhythmically like a train gathering speed.

Her parents' marriage had taught her what not to do so she'd made sure to end a relationship before she reached anything that might lead to deepening feelings. Until she'd met Elliot and made an exception—and what a disaster that had turned out to be. Which was why she'd be telling Leo it was over—because she was teetering on that dangerous edge again.

Falling for him wasn't an option. She loved her freedom, her lifestyle. She'd die of boredom if she was to commit herself to one man. Or so she told herself.

Totally out of sorts, she picked up her phone, tapped Samantha's number. When Sam answered, Brie didn't bother with preliminaries. 'What are you doing tonight?' then, 'Can I sleep over at your place? And you'll need to pick me up because I'm already over the limit.'

'You really care about this guy,' Sam said, over her margarita cocktail an hour later.

They'd found an out-of-the-way table in a chic bar with a view over Sullivans Cove—sheer luck for a normally busy ten o'clock on a Friday night.

'No. Yes. I don't want to. You know me—terminal party girl, no emotional entanglements. I'm not going to see him again.'

'Bit hard since you're his landlady and he's your next-door neighbour.'

'He's going to rent out his place when it's finished. All I'll see of him are his nice regular deposits into my bank account for the next few weeks or months, which will go to Pink Snowflake. So yay.'

Leaning on her elbows, Brie sucked a weak gin and tonic through her straw and stared at the waterfront and its light-rippling reflections. 'He cancelled our hot week-end—which I never asked for in the first place, by the way—for some unmissable function in Sydney.'

'Did he explain what it was?'

'I hung up on him before he could.'

'Brie. You have to stop doing that.'

'I can't deal with excuses and lies and rejection.'

'So you hung up and now you don't know if it was any of those or not.'

Brie slid a finger over the moisture on her glass. 'He's not into parties. See? He's just not my type.'

'Actually, I don't. He ticks all your boxes: looks, intelligence, charisma. So what if he doesn't like parties?'

'He prefers parties for two,' she murmured, then glanced sideways at Sam who was watching her with a smirk.

'There you are—he *is* your type.'

Brie looked back at the view. 'He sent roses.'

Sam slapped a hand on the table. 'The nerve of the man.'

'Flowers imply guilt.'

'Or an apology.'

'Or an easy out—call a florist, place an order and two minutes later the conscience is eased and the lucky recipient's forgotten.' Brie twisted in her chair to implore, 'Can we do lunch tomorrow? Just you and me. We can go to Salamanca first, I know you love the markets.'

'I've never seen you go to so much trouble *not* to see a guy who's obviously as interested in you as you are in him. And to be perfectly frank, I don't think you're being fair. At least give the guy a chance to explain.'

Brie shook her head. But Sam was right. Probably. 'I'm afraid of what I'll do if I do.'

Sam reached over and squeezed her hand. 'Okay. We'll do brunch and the markets, but the moment he contacts you and turns up—because you *will* tell him where we are, and he *will* turn up—you two are on your own.'

* * *

Sydney's fog was still hanging around but the curtain was beginning to lighten, the runway almost visible now. In the airport lounge, Leo shuffled his newspaper and checked the departure board. His flight was still delayed by at least an hour. He sent another text advising Breanna since her phone was still switched off. He was learning that it was Breanna's modus operandi. She was going to have to change because he didn't like it. Further, he wasn't going to put up with it.

She'd not given him a chance to explain and that was unacceptable. What the hell did she want from him? He'd had a floral arrangement delivered; he'd never known a woman who couldn't be persuaded with flowers. And very expensive they'd been too. But she'd remained stubbornly out of contact.

Breanna was untidy, confrontational and too out there for his taste. She was hard work. Why couldn't he forget her and move on since that was what she seemed to want? What made her so special that he couldn't wait to see her again? Or maybe that was what it was—those differences, those points of disagreement that challenged him.

And just to complicate things the other woman in his life was also intruding on his thoughts.

Before he'd left for the airport this morning, Leo had stopped by Darling Harbour at Sunny's invitation to have breakfast with her and the rest of Tasmania's Hope Strings ensemble who were also in Sydney to see last night's Opera House performance.

He'd been glad because he'd wanted an opportunity to meet the people his sister would be working with. Ensure she was accepted and happy. And from everything he'd observed, she looked radiant with a glow to her cheeks he'd never seen. She'd found her niche, so it was all good. Fantastic.

But he'd noticed one guy paying particular attention to her. Gregor Goldsworthy had spiked hair with a greenish hue about it, a piercing in his left eyebrow, a tattoo on the inside of his wrist—and who knew where else since the rest of his upper body was covered in some sort of long sheepskin coat that looked as if it had been resurrected from the sixties.

He was fine with that. Live and let live. The respected cello player obviously scrubbed up okay when a formal occasion demanded it. And Sunny was an attractive, outgoing and talented blonde; of course men were going to notice her.

But what Leo couldn't get past was the fact that Sunny had been paying this Gregor guy the same rapt attention. The knowledge stirred uncomfortably inside him like the curdled airport coffee he'd just disposed of.

Sunny hadn't mentioned Gregor—and why would she? She'd tell Leo to butt out of her private life. And he did. Mostly. Ditching his newspaper, he stalked to the windows where the sun was struggling through the rapidly dissipating fog. Ground crews were starting to move, the disembodied airport voice was announcing the first flights.

Time to go and have it out with Breanna.

Sam grabbed Brie's phone off the table where they were having brunch, checked it with a cluck of her tongue. 'You can only receive when it's switched *on*.'

'I've been checking,' Brie told her around a morsel of toast, since she was barely hungry. 'He texted his flight's due in at one-thirty. Fog delay. I switched it off so I don't have to talk to him.'

'Why'd you do that?' she asked, still playing with Brie's phone. She snapped a selfie of the two of them. 'You're the most confident woman I know when it comes to talking with men.'

'Not this time.'

She gulped her English breakfast tea. Why was it different with him? Brie had never felt so spun out after having one-off sex. Since those amazing moments with Leo she felt as if she'd been ripped open and all her insecurities laid bare. Had anything changed between them in the meantime? If so, how would she deal with it?

She didn't know yet because she hadn't let him explain.

Of course, if he had changed his mind she'd deal with it. If he'd lied and she found out, she'd tell him where to go. But deep down, whatever the reason, she'd die a little. A lot.

Because no matter how hard she tried to deny it, it *mattered* with him. Nerves were so bunched up in her throat that she could barely talk. 'I need some air,' she muttered. 'This place is stifling.'

'Let's stroll down to the markets,' Sam said, handing her back her phone. 'He'll ring when he arrives and you can tell him to meet us there. That way it won't look like you've been sitting around waiting for him to show up.'

'Which I haven't been.' Brie made a determined effort to improve her mood for Sam's sake. 'I'm just enjoying a lazy morning out with a girlfriend.'

The day was chilly and grey but Saturday's regular tree-lined Salamanca Market in Hobart was a sensory hive of activity. The aromas of pancakes and burgers filled the air. Umbrellas sheltering stalls displaying everything from carpets and cloth to bird feeders and lampshades set against the backdrop of historic Georgian warehouses.

When her phone jingled in her pocket just after two o'clock, Brie startled. She yanked it out, checked caller ID, and her pulse went into overdrive. 'Leo.'

'How do you like your crêpes?' His voice was caramel-smooth. 'Lemon and sugar or strawberry jam?'

She spun around, saw him at the food tent a few stalls

away. He had his back to her but he stood out; an unmiss-able head above the rest. To add to her agitation, her whole body readied itself at the sight, as if it were programmed to respond exclusively to him. 'How did you know I'd be here?' She looked at Sam as she spoke.

'Forgotten your text already?'

'Traitor,' she whispered to Sam and turned away to watch a busker playing French songs on his piano accordion.

'What was that?' Leo's voice.

'I was speaking to Samantha. *She* was the one who texted you. I'll have the jam, please. And stay where you are. I'll come to you.' She disconnected with a scowl. 'Bet all the women say that to him. As for *you,* my friend, I'll haul you over the coals later.' But she let Sam give her a quick hug before she made her way through the crowd.

She thought she was ready—calm and composed—when she tapped him on the shoulder and he turned around, his hands filled with crêpes, shiny dark hair riffling in the breeze.

And then she was leaning over to kiss his cheek, inhaling his warm scent before she could think about it.

Before she remembered yesterday.

'Hi.' She pulled back, stared into pewter eyes that reflected the sombre morning sky. 'I shouldn't have hung up on you last night.'

'I've noticed you do that a lot.'

She heard the disappointment in his tone. 'Yes. I know, and I'm sorry.'

'Is it a bad habit of yours or is it just me?'

'It's not you.' She clenched her hands, rubbed them together, not from cold but with nerves. 'Are you going to accept my apology or not?'

'I will. This time.'

His gaze grew so intense she had to force herself not to

flinch and look away. 'I know I didn't listen yesterday but I do want to know why you cancelled on me.'

His expression remained inscrutable, as if he was deciding whether to tell her or not. Finally he nodded. 'Okay.' He looked about them. 'Let's find somewhere quieter.'

'That way.' She gestured away from the crowds to the top of Salamanca Place where there were seats beneath a canopy of trees.

'I got the roses,' she said, to fill the silence between them as they walked. 'Pretty.'

'Glad you think so.'

'Expensive.'

'Not a worry.'

'What was the black one symbolic of?'

'Me? Your light to my shadow? Wh—'

'I sent them to a hospice.'

His steps slowed a little. 'You sent them to a hospice.'

'I know some of the patients there and know they'd appreciate them far more than me.'

'Okay. You don't like flowers—got it.' He didn't say more as he led her to a seat on a grassy spot beneath some trees, handed her the plate with the jam-laced crêpe, kept the lemon and sugar one for himself.

'I love flowers. Just not for apologies.' Her stomach was churning but she unpeeled the plastic wrap and picked off a corner of her pancake. 'So?' she prompted.

'As I tried to explain before you cut me off, I messed up my diary. Rather, I didn't add you to my diary because, frankly, I didn't need to. I couldn't think of anything—or any*one*—else. Which got me into all sorts of—'

'You promised me a night I wouldn't forget. You were right—I won't forget.'

'Breanna…'

She held up her hand, looked away to the sandstone buildings around Sullivans Cove so she wouldn't read what she might in his gaze. 'I've changed my mind. I don't want to know.' She didn't want to hear. Was too scared to hear. 'I'm sure you had a perfectly valid reason, but this thing between us, it's not going to work, best not to go any further.' She rewrapped her virtually untouched crêpe in plastic and struggled against nausea. And fear. Oh, God, the fear. 'I'm not going to Heaven with you, Leo.'

His sudden iron-like grip on her upper arm through her thick jacket had her jolting and swivelling her head his way. Her paper plate slipped off her lap and onto the grass.

'Listen to me, Breanna.' His eyes were stormy, his mouth a grim slash, the powerful image of this man on the edge of his steely control setting Brie's heart pounding with something between exhilaration and anger.

'Take your hand off me,' she warned through clenched teeth.

But instead of letting her go, his fingers tightened. 'Listen to me first. Weeks ago I made a commitment to watch my little sister perform at the Opera House. Can you put yourself in my place a moment and imagine how I felt when I realised I'd been so preoccupied, so infatuated, so obsessed with *you,* Breanna Black, that I'd forgotten I was supposed to turn up and show my support on one of the biggest nights of her life? Leo Hamilton, the only family Sunny has—the only family I have.'

Brie exhaled slowly, searching his eyes, falling into that confused gaze. Falling for him a little more with every passing second that he punished himself as he loosened his grip on her arm, then let her go altogether with a muttering of disgust obviously aimed at himself.

'You went to watch your sister. And you nearly forgot because you were thinking about me.' The wonder of it stole through her heart like gold. 'I should've let you explain.'

'Yes.'

'You didn't forget in the end and that's all that matters,' she said, watching the tension in his shoulders ease a little. 'You were there for her. What was Sunny doing at the Opera House?'

'She's a violinist.'

'Talented. You must be a proud brother.'

'Yes. And you hung up on me because…?'

'Because I didn't want to hear your lies. What I expected would be lies.'

'Your opinion of me is that low?' He shook his head.

'No. I…'

'You have trust issues. What did he do?'

She nodded, glad he'd guessed because it made it easier to tell him. 'A few years ago I was involved with a guy. Foolishly blinded by his dazzling attention. Until I learned that Elliot sent flowers whenever he cancelled his dates with me to fool around with other women.'

'Despite the popular rumour, not all men are bastards, Breanna.' He scowled, his expression dark. 'I'm sorry I brought back bad memories for you.'

'Don't be, it's not your fault. You didn't know. Bloody lies.'

'You mentioned once that you didn't know about your brother's existence until recently. What was that about?'

'My dad fathered Jett with another woman a few months after he married my mum. He confessed to me on his deathbed.'

'That's tough.'

'That's the poisonous nature of secrets and lies.'

He looked away towards the docks, then said, 'While we're sort of on the subject, I don't think I mentioned Sunny's going to be your new neighbour.'

'No, you sort of didn't. When did you plan on sort of telling me?'

'I'm telling you now. The house is for her—she has a new job with Hope Strings starting soon.'

'Sunny's with Hope Strings? That's great.' But living next door, not so much. Could be awkward. 'I look forward to meeting her.'

'I think you two will get along well. You're like her in some respects.' He turned, his gaze brightening as if he'd had a light-bulb moment. 'She's impulsive and loves spontaneity. Like you. Do you have a valid passport?'

Huh? 'Yes, why?'

'Ever been to Singapore?'

'No, but—'

'I'm there next weekend on business. Forget Heaven. Come with me to the Gardens by the Bay.'

CHAPTER TEN

'I CAN'T JUST fly off to Singapore with you.' But the very idea was already whisking her off on a magic carpet of thrilling anticipation. 'I have clients, appointments. People depending on me.'

'Business-class flight, Marina Bay Sands hotel,' he told her. As if that would make a difference.

She'd spent too much of her life struggling for acceptance and building a good professional reputation to risk it by abandoning her clients when they needed her, particularly those suffering through cancer treatments, just to run off with a man.

But not just any man. This was Leo Hamilton, and he was flying her overseas for the weekend, business class, and staying in that famous hotel she'd only ever dreamed about with its infinity pool fifty-seven storeys high and... and...

The very spontaneity of the idea appealed to her on so many levels.

A once-in-a-lifetime opportunity for the ultimate dirty weekend. Or maybe it was a romantic getaway this time. Brie's mind whirled; her heart did a little tap dance inside her chest. 'I...'

'If you can juggle a few appointments on Friday, we'll leave in the afternoon, and return early Monday morning. You'll be back at Eve's before morning tea break. Can that work? I—'

'Your proposal's accepted.'

Leo fought back a grin, relieved his powers of persuasion, at least, were still in good working order. 'That was quick.' And the best answer he'd heard all morning.

He gestured to a nearby bin and they headed towards it. He was still trying to figure out how he'd asked her to accompany him as they walked across the grass. He'd always kept his private and business lives separate.

What was it about Breanna that had him changing life-long habits? One look into her dark eyes and he knew. He couldn't wait to get her naked and he was prepared to do whatever it took to spend some quality uninterrupted time with her. Even if it meant taking her on a business trip. And if personal and business got a little tangled up, what the hell was wrong with that?

Things could end up getting a little knotted.

He refused to examine that thought further. He'd made his decision. Chucking their half-eaten pancakes in the bin, he rocked back on his heels, tossed the end of his scarf over his shoulder. 'Come home with me.'

'Home? As in West Wind?'

'Your place. My place. Who cares where?'

'Not West Wind. Because when it's over with us…' The air was calm but she tightened her arms around herself as if a cold gust had blown through her.

Yeah. He understood. And the knowledge, too, left him with a lead-ball sensation behind his breastbone, which was best dismissed. But he did know what they both wanted right now. And West Wind was never going to be an option for them. 'Where's the nearest hotel?'

'Hey.' Laughing, she tapped his chest. 'You *can* be spontaneous.' Grabbing his hand, she pulled him along. 'This way. And it happens to be a five star.'

'As long as it has a bed.'

'Who needs a bed?' She laughed again. He could get used to that sound.

The desk manager didn't bat an eyelid when they arrived at the lobby desk breathless and without luggage and requested a room. But Leo saw a glimmer in the man's eyes as he handed him their room key.

Leo wanted to tell the man he'd never done this in his life, that it wasn't what it looked like. That he wasn't spending a quick couple of hours heating up the sheets with some stranger he'd just met; that she wasn't a hooker. But Breanna was already dragging him towards the elevator bank.

The moment she pressed the button, the elevator doors opened and she grinned at Leo, anticipation sparkling in her eyes. No one else was waiting and they stepped in.

'Hang o—' The rest of his words were cut off when she yanked him close, pressed her mouth to his before the lift doors had finished closing.

She tasted of spicy heat and wild honey and he struggled to remain upright when she pushed up against him, knocking them both against the back wall.

He spread his feet for balance and placed his hands on her arms to steady them both. Which put him at a disadvantage when she reached down between them, found him rock hard and ready for action. 'Brie.' He swallowed as heat spurted into his lower belly. 'Slow down!'

It was no laughing matter but Breanna's eyes lit with humour as she cupped her hands around him. Moulded, stroked, squeezed. 'One speed, Leo, and it ain't slow.'

'But we're in a public lift.'

'You think like a girl,' she told him, an echo of his words not long ago. 'You're way too conservative, Mr Hamilton. Way too uptight and…'

She squeezed him again and smiled against his lips, sending more sparks shooting straight to his groin. Wondering vaguely if he might spontaneously combust, he tightened his fingers on her arms, hauled her closer, heard her muffled moan of approval as he devoured her mouth once more.

He couldn't recall whether either of them had pressed the button for their floor. He hoped one of them had because this could end badly for them. Then the lift dinged, the doors slid open and somehow they made it to their room without getting arrested.

She was stripping off her jacket as she made her way to the floor-to-ceiling windows overlooking the wharves where a pale sun cast a lemony square over the room's thick white carpet.

Tugging off her jumper, yanking off her boots and peeling her jeans down her long toned legs, the shining waterfall of black hair sliding over her shoulders. She stood in the patch of sunlight wearing only a playful smile and a strawberry charm that winked cheekily in her belly button while he pulled his jumper over his head, dropped it on the bed. She looked like some tall and gorgeous genie who'd won a temporary reprieve from her bottle home and wanted to make the most of her brief freedom.

Then she went very still, her smile gone. 'What *is* that?'

Leo was used to the reaction. Breanna hadn't seen it the last time they'd had sex because he'd not taken the time to undress. But he didn't see revulsion in her eyes, just concern as she studied the ugly scar that puckered the right side of his body from waist to hip to the front of his thigh.

'It's nothing.'

'It's *something*. What happened?'

He shrugged, not wanting to talk about it. 'We didn't come here to trade war stories.' Even now, his father was still trying to rule his life from the grave.

No frigging way. He was stronger now. In control of

his circumstances. Able to look out for Sunny the way she deserved to be.

'I can see why you freaked out about my dumb fire accident.'

And he wanted to share his story with her. Only her. She could listen to his story and learn. 'There was a house fire. I escaped relatively unscathed, considering. Imagine this happening all over your body.' He remembered the sight so vividly it was an open wound that never healed. 'Imagine your body so charred no one can recognise you, not even your own son.

'Or imagine you suffer forty per cent burns, like my sister did, and you live. Permanently disabled, with pain a daily struggle. If only I could have got her out sooner. Now do you understand why I reacted the way I did?'

She reached out, her eyes moist, touching his scars. Touching his soul. 'Your mother? I'm so very sorry. How old were you?'

'Eighteen.'

'And you saved your sister's life,' she murmured in wonder.

'I'm no hero. Can we get back on track here?' He pulled her close, felt her naked flesh against his for the first time warm and close and soothing against his. He kissed her long and deep. He was alive.

Then he let her go and walked to the room's CD player, facing away from her. 'When I turn around I want all that stuff gone. Finished. Because I want to be inside you but I don't want to be inside you with my past coming between us.'

He remained that way a moment to settle them both, then switched the player on. Mellow sax floated out.

When he turned back she'd lowered herself to the carpet. She nodded. 'We're good.' Using her hands behind her head as a pillow, she spread herself out like a banquet of sugar and spicy delights and stared up at him, a smile on her lips. 'Come on down.'

His fingers were shaking as he shoved his jeans off and joined her on the floor, banging his knee on the leg of an armchair on the way. Swearing, he rolled onto his back. 'You got an aversion to beds?'

'No, they're great for sleeping.' His minor mishap had broken the tension and she laughed. From her supine position, she raised herself onto her elbows. 'Ouch. Want me to kiss that better for you?'

His pulse beat fast and harsh in his ears. 'Yeah, but it's not my knee that's hurting.'

'I know,' she said and shuffled up beside him, tapped his nose with a fingertip. 'Close your eyes.'

'I—'

'Remember that conversation? The one where I own the dance floor? And I'm not going to lie back and let you do all the work, so man up, Leo, and let me be me for you.'

'I never said…you assumed…' He trailed off, his whole body tightening as her intention became clear, and closed his eyes as requested.

He heard the soft *shoosh* of the room's air conditioning, a busker playing the bagpipes down at Salamanca, Brie's not-quite-steady breathing near his ear. He drew in the scent of her bare skin and struggled with the primitive urge to tumble her onto her back and finish it, but he'd given his word and he owed her.

Then warm lips were dropping a path of petal-soft kisses as she slithered over him, silky skin abrading his. Smooth hands, capable fingers, tracing his collarbones, circling his nipples. A harsh groan tore from his throat but she didn't stop.

Lower.

Lightly touching his scarred torso, running her fingers over his hip's damaged and knotted skin. His eyes snapped open. Just simple acceptance in hers. She smiled as she lowered her lips there, to kiss the puckered surface. 'It's your story here and it's a magnificent one,' she said. 'One of courage and sacrifice.'

Leo thought he nodded but his eyes blurred and he closed them again so she wouldn't see a man reduced to the humiliation of something close to tears by a woman's tender words and understanding touch.

Lower.

Mindless mayhem, drugging delights. 'Breanna,' he gritted through his teeth, filling his greedy, restless hands with her hair, twisting and bunching the silky strands in his fists. Taking him far away from the ugliness.

And as she shot him skyward with her mouth and tongue, teeth and hands, every dark fantasy he'd had about her faded in the brilliance of the real thing.

Then just when he thought he couldn't last another second, she rose up, straddled herself over him and sank slowly down his length. Tight, hot, wet. He opened his eyes to watch. Her heavy breasts hung free, hair in disarray around her shoulders, the black ends caressing her olive skin and wine-dark nipples.

Their gazes tangled, reflected, entwined. Neither spoke in that breathless hiatus. Neither moved.

The earth stopped turning. Or maybe it spun out of its orbit—he didn't know—but he *did* know in that skipped heartbeat his world changed forever.

Brie saw the instant his eyes changed. Darkened, deepened. She told herself it was a shifting of the light, a cloud drifting over the sun, that she was imagining it. But she couldn't seem to get her breath; her heart felt swollen, too big for her chest.

Simple seduction was no longer the only thing happening in this convenient hotel room. Not after he'd shared his story. They were bonded in some inexplicable way. She knew there were other forces fuelling their passion as she began to move. Slowly. Over him, with him, for him, their movements in perfect sync, as if he'd been made for her at some exclusive Tiffany's in the sky.

Their fast demands and desperation yielded to something that flowed slower, richer, stronger. Something that came with consequences because the parameters of their relationship had shifted forever.

She knew she couldn't allow it, that she'd have to end it and move on, but right now she'd never felt more free, more alive. *Live in the moment,* she reminded herself as they crested the wave, tumbled over the other side and slid into a lazy fulfilment.

Moments later, side by side, they lay staring at the foam-speckled soundproofing on the ceiling. What had happened wasn't supposed to have happened. Not the sex—the other thing. But she couldn't walk away from this amazing connection yet. Not yet.

She exhaled slowly, her body still throbbing, her mind reeling. It took a monumental effort to keep it casual, the way she wanted it. The way she knew he wanted it. 'I know I said I wanted post-coital conversation, but I think we just said it all with that performance.'

'What did we say?' He spoke with care, as if worried what she meant.

'You're good. We're good. Shall we get going?'

'What's the rush?' He traced a tempting finger over her breasts and she very nearly changed her mind.

'You're not a woman, you wouldn't understand.' She rose, grabbing items of clothing and dragging them on, needing to be gone *now.* Before she had time to *think.*

'I need to find my passport at some stage...' She trailed off as his hand wrapped around her ankle then shook her head and moved away with a mountain of regret to tug on her boots. 'You've seen the state of my house. Some stuff's

there, some's at Jett's place.' She gave a half-laugh. 'Lo-
cating it could take a while.'

'You want me to check West Wind?'

She felt a little shiver at the thought of him checking
out her underwear drawer. Some things were simply too
private. 'If you could just look in the living room and
kitchen? And my home office is next to the bedroom, the
key's in the top drawer of the kitchen dresser. I'll search
the rest if you don't find it.'

'You locked me out?'

Reassured at his almost wounded expression, she
smiled. He'd never tried to gain entry to the rooms she'd
told him were private. Kudos to him. It meant a lot that she
could trust him. 'That was before. I know you better now.'

In the early hours of Thursday morning, Leo was still
awake. In Breanna's bed in West Wind trying not to notice
her lingering perfume, which he couldn't seem to eradi-
cate from his nostrils.

Breanna. He'd tried consistently but he didn't think he'd
ever get used to calling her Brie. Yet the casual name suited
her personality so well. When he was intimate with her,
or thinking intimate thoughts, which was ninety-nine per
cent of the time, she was Brie. Perhaps that was why he
preferred to use Breanna when interacting with her at other
times? It was more formal, one step removed. Maintaining an emotional distance.

You sure about that distance, Leonardo?

His mind spun back to the hotel. In that life-changing
moment when his emotions had been all over the shop.
She was different from anyone he'd ever met and he didn't
seem to know how to be himself around her. She wasn't
like other women he knew who gushed over receiving
flowers. Now he knew why. And who else would argue
over the free installation of a fire alarm?

He wasn't used to independent, confident women. He didn't understand them. The kind of women he'd dated had never done a striptease in front of a wall of windows in the glare of full sunlight. They'd never tried to seduce him in a lift.

Most hadn't acknowledged his scars, preferring to ignore them altogether than ask the awkward questions. He'd seen distaste in the eyes of some who had. Not Breanna. She'd embraced them as a part of who he was, and wasn't that refreshing?

None of those women knew his story. None had ever tugged on his heartstrings. Shoving back the quilt, he stalked to the window and stared at East Wind, silhouetted against the night sky. *Heartstrings?* That was new.

But then he'd never been with a woman like Breanna Black.

Brie.

The instant he'd caught sight of her last Saturday after just a few days of not seeing her, he'd realised how much he'd missed her sassiness, her directness. You knew where you stood with her. If she didn't like something, you knew about it. For a mad moment, he'd had this crazy notion that he could get used to seeing her every day.

Was it so crazy?

On an oath he swung away, headed downstairs for a glass of water. Time to think seriously about what she meant to him. How she might fit into his life.

Brie.

Busy, energetic and professional. She put others' needs before her own. But the tornado-swept room she called her home office, her living spaces, which should be havens of relaxation: all total chaos. Anathema to him. Gulping water, he started upstairs once more. He sincerely hoped she found her passport.

Brie.

Hopelessly disorganised.

He'd searched where she'd asked, without success. In the meantime, he'd reorganised her garden shed and purchased a palm for the front veranda and a few exotic herbs missing from her collection. The least he could do to repay her for the convenience of allowing him to stay here. He'd made a start on sorting her library but decided to postpone. He could be overstepping the mark.

All of which had left him seriously behind schedule.

On Thursday afternoon, Leo was at Breanna's dining-room table still finishing the project report he needed to take with him before they left the country tomorrow afternoon. He'd never been so disorganised before an important business meeting.

After last night's soul-searching he'd spent the morning relocating his gear to East Wind. The renovations had been finished for a few days but he'd dragged his feet moving back, telling himself he had too much work to catch up on. Plus he'd been to Freycinet then on to Launceston to meet with clients.

Now, he knew, it was time; too much had changed between them. With Sunny's furniture not here yet, he'd sleep on the floor when they returned from Singapore. Preferable to lying awake in Breanna's bed with nothing to do but think.

His heart skipped a beat when her personalised chime sounded on his mobile. 'Breanna. How's—?'

'I can't find my passport.'

'Are you serious?'

'I've been to West Wind while you were away like I told you—just very quickly, to search my room. I didn't snoop through your stuff, bu—'

'I know you didn't snoop, Breanna.' He drummed his fingers on the dining table. 'You've left it till twenty-four hours before we leave to inform me you still haven't found your passport?'

'You said you'd be busy. I didn't want to bother you with my little problem. And I was packing,' she said, defensive. 'I have to dress to impress. What if one of your important colleagues sees me? I think I'll get a new bikini…'

'*Little* problem?' He rubbed a hand over gritty eyes. To erase the swimsuit image or was it frustration with her skewed priorities? 'You don't need to wear anything but skin to impress me and you won't be meeting my colleagues, so stop with the packing and start with the hunting. Have you any idea where you saw it last?'

'So you hide your dates from your colleagues?'

'We were talking about your passport?'

'I haven't used it since I went to Bali three years ago.'

'Breanna.' He rolled his gaze to the ceiling. How could he have even contemplated being involved with such a disorganised person? 'Do you want me to look anywhere else?'

'Would you? I'm pretty sure now that it's in the kitchen. I had this flash—'

He hit Save and pushed back his chair. 'I scoured the kitchen.'

'Have you checked the biscuit barrel with the fifties girl picture on the front? The brunette in the spotty dress? Top shelf right up high next to the fridge.'

He snapped his fingers. 'Now why didn't I think of that?'

CHAPTER ELEVEN

BRIE DANGLED HER legs over the edge of the opulent Marina Bay Sands Hotel's infinity pool and watched the early morning sun paint Singapore's unique skyscrapers pink and gold.

She wriggled her toes in the water while she admired her tropical-print bikini, newly purchased from the Skypark shop. Leo had left for his meeting thirty minutes ago. The poor guy had looked whacked this morning. She grinned to herself—probably because they'd not reached their room till just before one a.m. after the long flight. It was now seven-thirty and they'd put those few hours to good use. Not a lot of sleeping had been involved.

She'd zoned out for most of the journey in her spacious business-class seat whereas Leo had been working like a fever on his laptop. So she was super refreshed and ready to hit The Shoppes at the bottom of the spectacular structure as soon as she'd eaten what promised to be a delicious breakfast in one of the restaurants conveniently close to the pool.

The morning passed too quickly: a frivolous shopping spree, a thirty-minute massage, morning tea in a speciality chocolate café.

At two p.m. Leo met her in the lobby and they were chauffeured by limo to the famous Raffles Hotel with its attractive British architecture. They enjoyed the Tiffin

Room's curry buffet sitting at one of the black lacquered bamboo tables and swapping stories about their respective mornings.

After lunch Leo enjoyed showing Breanna the stunning Gardens by the Bay. They wandered through the two conservatories—climate-controlled biomes aptly named the Flower Dome and the Cloud Forest.

He explained to his rapt audience of one that a sustainable feature was the horticultural waste generated within the Flower Dome, which in turn generated electricity to maintain its cool, temperate mini-climate.

Then they took an open-air vehicle to the solar-powered Supertrees nearby. He'd visited the vertical gardens half a dozen times and their other-worldly beauty still captured his enthusiasm and imagination. Today was a bonus; he was sharing it with a first-time visitor who obviously enjoyed it as much as he.

'Amazing, aren't they?' She turned a circle gazing up at the impressive steel structures covered in ferns and tropical blooms. 'They remind me of that movie, Avatar.'

'Yes, they are a bit Pandora-like.' He took her hand. 'There's a spectacular view from the skywalk.'

'So what's your professional interest in them?' she asked as they viewed the Bay Gardens from the sky bridge connecting some of the fifty-metre-high structures.

He explained how they mimicked real trees by harnessing solar energy, which was used for their attractive lighting, and how rainwater was collected for irrigation and water displays. 'My business colleagues and I are working on a plan for something similar in Australia. Probably somewhere along Sydney Harbour or nearby.'

He filled her in on his meeting with his Singaporean counterparts. Their combined plan to create similar structures in Australia within the next five years. His particular expertise in this innovative and specialised field was somewhat unique—he'd put forward a bold initiative for the Aussie Outback, which had been received with cautious optimism.

They stopped to buy ice creams. When had he talked about his business life with anyone beyond the occasional colleague? He'd discussed aspects with Sunny, but only when she'd asked, which wasn't often since she said getting info from him was as painful as chopping off her violinist's fingers one by one with a rusty blade.

He worked alone and liked it that way. But he found sharing his work with Breanna, seeing the genuine interest in her lively eyes, and answering her intelligent questions, a rewarding and energising experience. Almost as good as sex. He remembered last night's marathon—the way she'd unravelled beneath him—and smiled to himself. Almost as good but not quite.

'What's going on in there?' She tapped his temple, a sultry look in her midnight eyes. 'It's obviously wicked and debauched.'

'Wildly.' He pressed his lips to her forehead, tasted her skin's salty glow. 'Far too wicked to tell you in public.'

'So let's go back to our room and we can have Show and Tell.' She shifted against him in the growing dimness. 'I can't wait.'

'Soon.' He took her hand, tugged her close so that her hard little nipples grazed his shirt, an appetiser before the main course later. 'I want you to see the light and sound show first.'

'We'll make our own,' she murmured against his ear.

Sensitive body parts constricted at the husky promise. 'I'm counting on it.'

As dusk came, the trees' solar lights began to glimmer like colourful glow-worms, then the featured show lit up the sky. The audience oohed and aahed. Leo preferred to watch the rainbow reflections playing over Breanna's animated face.

Afterwards, he wined and dined her at Boat Quay, a vibrant open-air restaurant strip along the Singapore River that reminded him of Sydney's bustling Darling Harbour.

When they at last stepped into their suite, Brie entered first and left the lights off. She set her handbag down on her way to admire the night view, her eyes drifting inevitably to the king-sized bed as she passed.

It seemed an age since she'd left those rumpled sheets that smelled of sweet sin this morning. In other ways, it seemed like a minute, and the minutes were ticking away. This was their last night here. *Better make the most of it.* The bed was now as smooth as a lake, the edge of the crisp white sheet folded down in invitation, butter-coloured Singapore orchids on the pillow.

In the dimness, she stripped off her clothes where she stood. She walked to the full-length sliding doors that led to their balcony, which was bedecked with a profusion of purple bougainvillaea. Singapore's cityscape of lights dazzled.

'Brie.' Leo's voice was close but not intimately so, even though he was using her shortened name—which seemed to stick in his throat. She could see his reflection over her shoulder.

'Don't turn around,' he said, so quickly that she barely picked up on the thread of tension tightening his vocal chords.

'This trip's been amazing,' he said. 'You've been amazing. You *are* amazing.'

She watched in astonishment as he slid something heavy around her neck. A necklace. And not just any necklace. Tiny rainbows twinkled on her décolletage. She'd have sworn he'd stolen it from some royal collection except that this wasn't ornate and overdone. It was a modern asymmetrical design in gold with a row of diamonds along one edge. Simple yet striking. Astonishment swiftly turned to panic.

Oh. No. 'What have you done?' Shaking her head, she turned to him, flung her hands in the air. 'What does this mean?'

'That I... That I'd like to keep seeing you when we get back.'

'What do you mean? I don't understand what you mean by that.' Her voice rose a couple of notches as she fought the conflicting emotions twisting like razor ribbons inside her. 'Or this.' She lifted the heavy gold away from her skin, felt the runaway pulse at her neck as she did so.

'It means I'd like us to be more. It means I want to explore us further and see where it leads.'

Her heart turned over, her blood ran hot then cold. She couldn't look at him and turned away. 'I thought we wanted the same thing. A no-strings kind of thing. A fun kind of thing. We agreed that day in my office, remember? You looked horrified with the notion that it should be anything other than just sex.'

'Who says we can't change our minds?' he said behind her.

'You've changed your mind?' She stared at his reflection behind her. He'd changed his mind. 'Oh my *God*...' She shoved at the balcony door so she wouldn't see his reflection and it slid open silently. She barely noticed the clammy evening air on her naked skin. All she could feel was the necklace's heavy weight. *The String.* 'I thought you understood already—I'm not like other women. I don't *want* gifts.'

'What *do* you want, Breanna?'

It hurt, irrationally so, that he'd reverted to the safety of his formality. Cool, *displeased* formality. 'I want us to continue the way we have been.'

'And we can,' he assured her. 'I'm not talking marriage

and everlasting, I'm simply suggesting a more stable ongoing arrangement. A more exclusive arrangement.'

His last words chilled her. Just like the boys back in her teens who assumed... She spun to face him. 'I *don't* sleep around. I already told you: if I'm sleeping with a guy, he's the only guy I'm sleeping with. And I expect the same from that guy.'

'I crossed that possibility off the list a long time ago, baby doll.'

'There you go again—*baby doll*? For heaven's sakes, I'm hardly petite.' To divert the topic of old prejudices, she reached deep down inside for aggravation.

'What I meant was I want *you* to feel you can trust *me* to be exclusive. Don't take it off,' he said, when she reached behind for the necklace's clasp.

'It was a no-strings deal.' She lifted the gold away from her skin. 'You do realise this is a *string* in our no-strings agreement, don't you?'

His brows lifted in genuine surprise. 'It's no such thing. Calm down. We can keep it as simple as you want.'

She did as he requested and left The String alone because she didn't want to spoil this night and, judging by his response, maybe she *was* overreacting. He'd just promised to keep it as simple as she wanted. 'I don't need a pet name. Unless it's Brie.'

'You're still a shorty to me. *Brie*. And we'll do this however you want, so don't stress.'

Her smile came slowly at the reassurance in his voice and the laughter lines crinkling around his eyes; she was relieved they seemed to be on track once more. 'There'll be no stressing tonight,' she promised him. 'And maybe I am petite after all coz you're the tallest man I've ever been with.'

'And you're the tallest woman I've been with. But you're

still a shorty.' He patted her head. 'With me you'll always be a shorty.'

With me. Always. The words rolled off his tongue as if he meant forever and was totally comfortable with it. As if he'd made up his mind and expected her to fall in with his decisions.

She didn't want forever. She wanted freedom. She wanted to leave her options open in case... In case. *No heart, no hurt.*

But forever was no closer, no more substantial than hopes and wishes. *Now* was in her grasp. She could feel it. *Now* surrounded her, the way Leo surrounded her. His scent, his touch, the sound of his quickened breathing near her ear.

And for now, for once, she'd forget he'd tried to change the rules they'd agreed to play by. She lifted her arms around his neck and clung tight. 'For tonight, can we just be lovers?'

Leo thought he heard an edge of desperation to her plea. In answer, he hauled her naked body flush against him. He filled his hands with her breasts while he nuzzled behind her ear and murmured, 'Where do you want me to start?'

'Right there's just fine,' she breathed. 'And make it slow, make it last, you're so good at that.'

He smiled into her hair. Damned if he understood this perplexing woman, but at least he knew what she wanted in the bedroom. She smelled of sweet tropical blooms and midnight and he set about filling her request to the best of his ability.

They landed in Sydney at seven-thirty on Monday morning. Once through Customs, Brie was continuing to Hobart without Leo. Seemed he had a connecting flight to Melbourne that he'd neglected to tell her about.

'So when will you be back in Hobart?' she asked as they manoeuvred their luggage towards the taxi stand.

'A couple of days. I need to help Sunny pack and since I've not heard back from her…' mini hesitation—unusual for a man who was always in charge of everything and everyone '…I want to check everything's on schedule.' Swinging his cabin bag over his shoulder, he opened a taxi door for her. 'Any plans for this week?'

'Apart from working my butt off to make up for lost time?'

His smile was fleeting. 'I meant evenings.'

She knew that. It was time to pull back; she needed breathing space. Just space. 'A charity event and three parties.' She didn't know who was socialising yet but she'd find them. She always did. 'I'll need tonight off to find Party Babe Brie—she's been MIA lately. Oh…' She pulled out The String tucked inside its velvet box, held it out. 'I don't need gifts to remember what a wonderful time I had, but I do appreciate the sentiment behind it.'

His whole body tightened, stiffened.

Brutally offended.

'Do what you want with it. Sell it. Or auction it for your charity.'

She didn't need to see his eyes behind his sunglasses to read his emotions in his body language and tone of voice and she wanted to weep and rage with frustration. She knew no sane woman would have refused such a gift. He still didn't get it—still didn't understand that she wasn't like other women. And right now, a little *in*sane.

Did he still not realise he'd broken the rules of their agreement? 'Leo…' she ventured, then paused, lost for words.

'You getting in, buddy?' she heard the cabbie ask.

Leo shook his head once. 'Domestic terminal for the lady, please,' he said. And pushed the door shut.

* * *

Leo opened the front door of his Melbourne home an hour later to discover the entire hallway lined with packing boxes, sealed and ready for transportation.

He dumped his cabin bag at his feet and bellowed, 'Sunny!' And instantly regretted his lapse. Given their shared pasts any show of temper towards his sister was an unforgivable sin. He'd seen what damage runaway emotions could do by watching his father.

But today something tore free and wouldn't be leashed. 'What's going on?'

'Leo. Hi.' She came out of the lounge. 'I was—'

He swept a hand over her belongings. 'I told you to wait.'

'Didn't need to.' Her awkward gait was more pronounced today as she moved towards him on her crutch.

He wanted to hit something but curled his fists instead. 'Overdoing it as usual, Miss Independent?'

She blinked, but to her credit she didn't react to his outburst. 'Not at all,' she said. 'I'm fine. I'm not sure about you though.'

'You didn't return my call.' Dammit, he *wanted* an argument from her.

'A friend helped me. I knew you were busy and I wanted to get it done.' She looked up at him, concern in her blue eyes. 'Weekend didn't go well?'

He waved it off. He didn't want to talk about the weekend. He'd told her he was going to Singapore for business and might have mentioned he might take a friend along. A mistake to tell her. Bigger mistake to have tried to combine business with pleasure. He focused on the more immediate concern. 'It appears you're ready to leave.'

'The moving van should be here any minute.'

'You were going to leave without telling me.' Something twisted inside him. She really was branching out into the

world on her own. He wanted to put his arms around her
and protect her as he'd always done but she didn't need him
any more—hadn't for some time. He'd chosen not to notice
but now the reality was staring him in the face, literally.

'No, Leo. Of course not,' she soothed. 'The stuff's going
but I'm catching tomorrow afternoon's flight. I couldn't
leave without sharing a last supper with my favourite
brother. You will be here tonight, won't you? Mrs J's making our favourite dumpling stew.'

He breathed out slowly. 'I'll be here. Tell me your flight
details, I've got a meeting in the city tomorrow afternoon
but I'll change it and come back when I've got you settled in.'

'Leo. I'm flying down with a friend from the new orchestra,' she said gently. 'I'm staying with him until my
stuff arrives. At least a week or two.'

Leo felt as if he'd turned to stone. *'He.'* He watched her
wait for some sign of support from him, but he knew it
wouldn't make a difference. She didn't need his permission or his approval. 'Gregor Goldsworthy.'

'He'll take good care of me.'

Suck it up, big brother, and say nothing *to dim that smile
on her face.* 'Make sure he does or he'll answer to me.'

Her smile widened, reaching her sparkling blue eyes.
'It's a good feeling knowing I have my brother at my back
if I need him.'

If she needed him. Something brighter burned in her
eyes, he noticed now, and it tore at something deep. Big
changes were coming. He felt as if everything was slipping
away from him. 'Why the sudden decision to leave now?'

'You said the renovation was finished. I decided to move
straight away so you'll have this place to yourself.' She
smiled. 'That way you won't have to sneak around any
more when you want to bring someone home with you.'

The only person he wanted to bring home was Brie.

'I've had to put my stuff in East Wind for a bit, so it could be a case of reversed situations. I've taken a spare room and in the meantime I promise to stay out of your way.'

'What happened to the arrangement with…Breanna, isn't it?'

'Wasn't working out.'

'Aah.' A woman's knowing eyes focused on him, which was odd, since they were his little sister's eyes. 'So Breanna's the mystery girl who's had you tied up in knots.' Her smile sobered; her blue eyes sympathised. 'What happened?'

He shrugged, his shoulders tense. 'No mystery. I took her out a couple of times. So what?'

'So Singapore's no ordinary date, that's what.'

'I didn't…' He leaned a tight shoulder against the wall. He'd never slide this one past Sunny. Defeat—it felt a lot like defeat, and it was an unfamiliar sensation. But she was the only person he'd ever confided in. 'If someone gave you a diamond necklace,' he said slowly, 'what would you do?'

'Diamonds.' She tapped her chin, her eyes searching his. 'That's serious bling.'

'No.' He waved a dismissive hand. 'It was just a souvenir. Token. Something simple. How would you receive it? And don't overanalyse.'

'It would depend on who he was and how we defined our relationship.'

There she went, all deep and meaningful again. He shook his head. 'Forget it, it's not important.'

'Are you talking about the relationship or the diamonds?'

'Neither. Both.' Hell. 'A simple answer without the psychobabble would have sufficed.'

He turned on his heel but she reached out with her crutch, tapped his arm, forcing him to turn back. 'You didn't let me finish. If I wasn't sure where I stood with the guy concerned, or where the relationship was headed, or even if I thought we might want different things from such a relationship, I might be wary of accepting such a gift.'

Considering, he scratched his bristled jaw. Had he got too intense too soon? Was Brie simply being cautious? Or was she guarded and hiding how she really felt behind that nonchalant attitude she was so good at because she was afraid?

For a guy who dated often, he was clueless about this particular woman who was the polar opposite of the sort he was accustomed to. 'Thanks.' He lifted a finger. 'If this *friend* of yours—the one whose home you're going to be staying in—if he gave you a…token of his…' He lifted a hand, dropped it.

'I'd say thank you and wear it with love.'

'Love?'

She nodded and something burned in her eyes.

He turned, muttered, 'Let me get used to it,' and headed back the way he'd come.

'It's okay to show you care, Leo,' Sunny said behind him. 'Whether it works out the way you want it to or not, expressing your feelings—however you do that—is not a weakness. When are you going to get that through that stubborn head of yours?'

CHAPTER TWELVE

BRIE WAS EXTREMELY busy the first couple of days after their return. She was grateful for it. But the evenings were a different story. Solo and filled with the fast clack of her knitting needles rather than party sounds. Chamomile tea instead of red wine.

She hadn't even wanted Sam's company. Or maybe she didn't want to foist her poor humour onto her friend.

She'd returned to West Wind as soon as she'd read Leo's brief text explaining he'd moved out. No matter how spacious and elegant and modern the retreat was, West Wind was home and she'd missed it. Its solitude and class. The smell of fresh pine cones in the fireplace. The wind song through the row of pencil pines that divided the two homes. There was something so comforting about the familiar.

She couldn't believe what he'd done with her garden shed. Everything tidy and sorted and shelved from empty pots to fertiliser to tools. Plastic labels on those shelves. A pretty sign on the inside of the door: *A place for everything and everything in its place.* Was he *serious*?

Why would he go to those lengths for her?

The more she thought about it, the faster her needles clacked. It was another kind of String. She'd be indebted to him for taking time out of his busy schedule and away from all those other people depending on his vast experience. She'd be obliged to thank him in some way for his kindness and generosity—which wasn't the problem—except that she hadn't asked for his help.

She was independent by choice. Free. Unencumbered. Uncommitted. And she loved it that way. She *did*.

Tossing her knitting down, she stood, flexing cramped fingers. Without words, Leo was saying she didn't know what she was doing in any aspect of her life and needed him to help her out of her mess. That he was just the man for the job.

Leo was trying to change her into someone she wasn't. Someone she didn't want to be. He'd stripped her naked in more ways than one and exposed her shortcomings and insecurities.

She swiped up the radio's remote, aimed and pressed, but she found the music's happy beat irritating and switched it off. Where was Party Babe Brie when she needed her distraction? No one distracted Brie better than her party persona and yet she seemed to have disappeared.

He'd made her lie.

The truth? Leo Hamilton was a good man. A dependable, responsible, kind, caring, generous, witty, sexy, clever, creative and amazing man.

He was just bad for her.

Leo had an appointment in country Victoria on Tuesday, and back-to-back meetings in Melbourne's CBD, on Wednesday, so he didn't make it back to Hobart until late Wednesday evening.

He lay on his inflatable mattress in the dark. He could've stayed in a hotel for the night but he'd wanted to check on East Wind. And he'd wanted to be close to West Wind.

His usual evening leisure activities hadn't worked for him in Melbourne; they weren't working here. Since returning from Singapore, no amount of reading or killer

Sudokus—not even Sunny's enchanting violin CD—could prevent his thoughts from wandering to Brie.

Because things had been up in the air and awkward when they'd said goodbye at Sydney airport, he'd sent her a text message to say he'd moved out of her place and into East Wind and left her a note advising her of same on her kitchen table. He still had her spare set of house keys.

He'd had a brief text reply thanking him for letting her know and for an 'amazing weekend'. Not another word about what was happening between them or any suggestion they get together soon. Nothing.

At least she'd replied. He told himself she was busy with rescheduled clients and her hectic social life.

Right.

Staring at the ceiling, he wondered, was she doing her party thing with another guy tonight?

If I'm sleeping with a guy, he's the only guy I'm sleeping with.

If there was one thing Leo knew about this woman it was that Brie did not lie.

Tonight the hushed still of the night and his solitude were all he had. He'd always been content with that. Until he'd met Brie and she'd worked her way under his skin like a prickle, then an itch.

Then all the way right into his heart.

He rubbed a fist over the place where on cue it throbbed and burned and ached.

Flinging back his quilt, he pushed up and stalked to the window and stared at West Wind's darkened windows. He shook his head, refusing to acknowledge the only possible reason why his entire chest felt as if it were caught in a vice. It couldn't be.

She wasn't his type. She wasn't anyone's type—she was unique. She was Brie.

Strong and smart and sexy. Messy. Honest and open

with a wicked sense of humour. A woman whose company inspired and entertained him. A whirlwind and a challenge. A woman he never tired of gazing at or sparring with or making love to.

Because love was exactly what he felt when they were together. When he buried himself inside her and held her close, looked into her bottomless black eyes. And denied it every time.

Not any more.

He tried on the word for size. 'Love…' The murmur felt foreign on his tongue but it fitted. With Brie, it fitted.

It was as if Sunny's words had unlocked something inside him. Freed him to examine his thoughts and emotions in a different way. And it didn't make him feel weak—he felt strong, invincible. A Superman.

Pulling on a T-shirt and jeans, he let himself out into the chilly air and headed to West Wind to wait for Brie. Whatever time she came home, he intended to be there. To tell her how he felt.

As he walked up the path to the front door, a slant of light coming from the room she liked to call The Parlour on the far side of the house caught his attention.

He walked along the path in that direction to check if her car was in the garage or if she'd been picked up, glancing in the window to check if everything was in order in the room on his way past.

Through the gauzy curtain, he saw Brie sitting on the overstuffed couch, hunched over as if in pain, the heels of her hands pressed to her brow.

Was she ill? Not wanting to give her a heart attack by knocking on the pane, he jogged to the front door, let himself in with his keys, calling her name as he headed down the passage.

'Brie…' He stopped in the doorway. The scene was

not the scene he'd viewed through the window less than thirty seconds ago.

Surrounded by a sea of natural yarn, she looked up at him, all casual composure. So, the outward calm she presented wasn't always the way she felt inside.

She picked up a ball of driftwood-coloured wool and said, 'I thought you'd moved out?'

'I thought you were ill.'

'I'm perfectly well, as you can see.'

As he came further into the room, he could see her eyes were red and swollen. 'Not from where I'm standing.'

She didn't answer him, knotting the end of the wool in her hand to the charcoal yarn and picking up a pair of lethal-looking knitting needles he'd not noticed earlier.

'That's going to be some scarf when it's done.' He moved closer, willing her to look at him, but she lowered her head to her work. 'You made it abundantly clear your social calendar was chock-a-block this week,' he said. 'You've accused me of making assumptions, so I'm going to ask you to tell me if I've got it wrong in assuming you told me that to avoid seeing me.'

Her head bent further, her hands faltered and she nodded.

She might as well have plunged her knitting needles into his chest because they wouldn't have hurt as much as the pain that arced through his heart. 'Why?'

Setting her knitting aside, she shook her head. 'This. Us.' She made a to-and-fro movement between them with her hands. 'It's better to end it now.'

'Why?' He heard the curt demand in his voice, reined himself in, tried again, calmer this time though his insides were cramping and everything was unravelling like her wool. 'Can I ask why?'

'You rearranged my garden shed.'

What? 'Yes. But—'

'You don't get it, do you?' She lifted devastated eyes to his. 'When someone just comes in and takes it on himself to change everything. When someone tries to reorder my life?'

'Your *garden shed*,' he corrected. 'Or are you talking about something else?'

She shook her head. 'I *like* messy. I'm comfortable with messy—it's who I am.' She rose, pinned him with an accusing look. 'I bet you arrange your DVDs in alphabetical order and woe betide anyone who forgets to put them back in their correct niches.'

'Chronological, actually.' He tried a smile but his lips wouldn't cooperate. 'What else? Surely one mistake on my part can't have changed your mind.'

'Your grand gestures.' She ground a fist into her open palm against her chest. 'Flowers, diamonds. I don't need them. Don't want them.'

'Is it a crime to want to show a person I appreciate her?'

'So it makes *you* feel good?'

'Wrong.' But he thought of other times with other women when it had been exactly that. It was different with Brie. 'You want me to go away—is that what you're trying to tell me?'

'I don't need a regular man in my life. I'm happy the way I am. Freedom's what I want.'

To his surprise—and hers, apparently—her eyes filled with tears.

'So why are you crying?'

'I'm not crying.' She swiped at her cheeks, swore under her breath. 'Okay, I'm crying.'

'You lied to me about your activities this week. The one person I trusted not to lie.'

'That's why you're bad for me.'

'I don't understand.'

'You took it upon yourself and changed the terms of our

relationship without giving me a say. You always have to be the boss; you can't let others make their own choices.'

'That's who I am.'

'A control freak's who you are.'

The truth of her words, unfair, struck at his core and anger simmered just below the surface. 'Let me tell you about control. My entire life was dictated by my father's actions. He'd turn up on Mum's pay day and take our rent money then disappear for weeks till the cash ran out. When I was old enough I took an after-school job to help.

'I was eighteen when I came home after work one night to find the bastard laying into her. When I intervened, he goaded me into swinging a punch and I just lost it. For the first time in my life I let the man get the better of me. I think I broke his nose. And it felt so friggin' good. So well deserved.'

Brie's swollen eyes filled with moisture. 'Leo…it's—'

'I'm not done.' Leo slashed the space between them with his hand. 'He left off Mum and staggered out like the coward he was. Great—I was prepared to do it again. Whatever it took to get him away from us.'

'That w—'

'I was wrong. He came back later that night when we were asleep and set fire to the place. *Because I lost control.*'

'*No.*'

She rose from the couch, reached a hand towards him but he held up a hand. 'Not now.'

Her arm fell to her side. 'You were protecting the ones you love.' Her voice was barely audible. 'Where is he now?'

'Dead. Killed by the fire he started.'

'I'm sorry,' she whispered. 'I shouldn't h—'

'I've cared for Sunny ever since. After surgery and physio and counsellors, she needed someone there for her, someone to make the decisions. In the absence of any other family, that person was me and I won't apologise for that.'

'I'm not asking for apologies.'

'So what are you asking for?' He narrowed his eyes, searching for some clue. 'Or are you too afraid to risk asking the question?'

What little colour she had drained from her face, leaving her chalk-white. Hugging defensive arms to her chest, she turned away from him, paced to the end of the sofa. 'It's better if you leave.'

'Better for who, Brie? You're not the woman you show to the world.' He waved a hand at her craftwork. 'Hiding away here after you made sure I thought you were out socialising this week.'

'I—'

'You're not only lying to me, you're lying to yourself. And that's the real tragedy.' He moved closer—one small step for a man. He saw fear in her eyes, and pain as she backed away further. 'You don't have to be afraid, Brie. Trust m—'

'Please. Just go. Go now.'

The finality in her plea hit him full force and he turned to do just that. But he stopped at the doorway. He wasn't leaving without saying what he'd come here to say. 'So you want to toss what we have away before we find out where it goes?'

'You're a very special man, Leo Hamilton, and it's been an amazing ride. But I like my freedom more.'

Freedom. A bitter laugh rose up his throat at the irony. How many times had he told himself he wanted the same? 'I came here tonight to wait for you to come home, no matter how long it took. To tell you I'm in love with you, and want you in my life permanently. I want it all. With you. The real kicker is that Sunny told me to lay my feelings for you on the line and just go for it.'

She stared at him, aghast, as if he had some contagious fatal disease. 'You can't be in love with me.'

'Why the hell not? I'll be the judge of who I'm in love with.'

'No.' The word fell from parched lips. 'Even if that were true, sooner or later you'll fall out of love and leave—emotionally if not physically. And that's the very worst kind of absence. The kind that drains your essence, drop by drop until there's nothing left but a shell.'

'Is that what Elliot did? Your parents?' The agony he saw in her eyes slayed him but she was measuring him against others. 'I'm not like that. What's more you *know* I'm not like that. One attribute I do have is stickability— ask Sunny. You're not being fair to me. To us.'

She wasn't listening to him, her gaze focused inwards. 'It's emotional abandonment,' she said, her voice trembling. 'And I won't let it happen to me. Not again.' She buried her face in her hands.

'You mean you're not prepared to take a risk even after I've bared my heart and soul to you.'

'Can't,' she whispered. 'Won't.'

'Life's a risk. Stepping out the front door in the morning's a risk. Coming here tonight was a risk.' He tossed her set of house keys on the nearest chair. 'When you're ready to take that risk, let me know. But don't take too long about it. Life's not only a risk, it's also short.'

As soon as Brie heard the front door close, her legs gave way and she sank to the floor, curled up into a ball and rocked. The world had officially gone crazy.

She'd just listened to the saddest story she'd ever heard. How much more pain had he endured than her? She'd wanted to reach out to him in that moment but he'd pushed her away, mentally shut her out. Ten seconds later he'd done an about-turn and said he was in love with her. He wanted her in his life forever.

The man who only a few days ago had assured her they could keep things as simple as she wanted—which just went to show men didn't know what they wanted and were incapable of keeping their word.

Simple as falling in love? She coughed out a bitter laugh. She'd been falling down that slippery slope since that fateful evening at East Wind when she'd introduced herself to Mr Perfect. Falling, sliding, scrambling—to keep her feet on the ground, her head in control of her stupid heart that wanted what it couldn't have.

And ultimately failing.

Where Leo was concerned, *no heart, no hurt* wouldn't work. She'd known that from the start. But Brie the Great Pretender had gone ahead and played her game of *let's stick to casual fun because I'm too afraid to trust anything deeper* anyway. And now she was going to pay the price for the rest of her life.

Because that was how long it would take to get over him.

A few weeks later, Brie glared at the catastrophe she called her salon's tiny office and flipped through another pile of miscellaneous papers strewn across her desk. A new client had made an appointment with Jodie only an hour ago and was due in ten minutes and Brie couldn't find the product order she'd printed out yesterday for the delivery guy who was turning up any minute now.

She could really do with Leo's organisational skills here.

The thought of Leo sent shards of pain shooting through her body for the fiftieth time this morning. He hadn't contacted her since that last horrible night. She could admit, now that it was too late to tell him, that she loved what he'd done with her garden shed. One day when things between them weren't so damaged—in a million years—

she'd let him know how much she appreciated his efforts. She pounced on the wayward paper beneath an empty takeaway coffee cup and headed to the shared reception area with it.

A young blonde woman with clear blue eyes stood at the desk. She leaned on an elbow crutch and smiled as Brie approached. There was something about that smile that reminded her of someone.

'Good morning.' Brie checked her new client's name on the information sheet Jodie handed her. 'Sky? Welcome. I'm Brie.' As she ushered Sky into her treatment room Brie noted beneath her black trousers one leg was deformed in some way. 'Have a seat and we'll have a quick chat.' She lit her Balinese Temple aromatherapy candles and switched on her calming CD. 'I see here you've chosen to try the chamomile and fruit facial and a hand massage?'

'Yes.' Sky set her crutch on the floor beside her.

Brie skimmed the form. 'You're from Primrose Bay.' A forty-minute drive away.

'I'm staying with a friend temporarily.'

Brie looked up. 'Not that I'm complaining, but why come all this way?'

'I looked up Eve's Naturally online. I like your use of natural products. Oh, and I admire what you're doing with Pink Snowflake, which you mentioned there too.' She smiled.

Brie smiled back. 'Let's get started, then.'

Brie always left it to her client to choose whether she wanted to talk or close her eyes and relax during treatments.

Sky was a talker. Brie asked the usual questions and answered Sky's responses on autopilot. But as usual, she couldn't seem to concentrate because she was thinking of Leo. How he was, what he was doing now, whether he'd found somewhere to live because she hadn't seen him near East Wind.

'Do you have a regular guy in your life?'

Brie heard the end of Sky's question and pulled herself back to the present. 'No.' She squirted lotion onto Sky's palm and worked it in with her thumb. 'You?'

'I do. We've been seeing each other for four months now. He's an amazing and gifted person.'

So is Leo. 'That's great.' Working her way up each of Sky's fingers in turn, Brie reminded herself she'd glimpsed what gave Sky that inner radiance and slammed the door on the possibility for herself.

Then Sky grimaced. 'I just wish my overprotective, control-freak brother thought so.'

'Some guys can be like that,' Brie said, thinking of one guy in particular. 'I'm sure your brother doesn't mean to be controlling.'

Sky coughed out a laugh. 'You reckon?'

'And dictatorial and overbearing too?' Brie suggested.

'Yeah.' Sky's smile turned wistful. 'But he's the best brother in the world and I wouldn't swap him for anything. Sometimes I forget to tell him.'

'I'm sure he knows. Maybe he's so focused on doing what he considers is in your best interests, he simply doesn't understand how he comes across.' Brie blinked at her own perceptiveness. 'Sorry,' she murmured. 'Enough of the psych talk.'

'Not at all. It's good to meet someone who understands. He's still getting used to the fact that I'm an adult now and want to do my own thing,' Sky went on. 'I think he just needs to be needed.' She cocked her head, bright eyes filled with interest. 'You've never had a guy in your life that you thought could be someone special?'

Brie's chest cramped while she squeezed and kneaded

Sky's hand, pressed deep into the palm. 'Yes. But I didn't want commitment. I wanted my freedom.'

'So is freedom still what you want or are you afraid of making the wrong decision?'

'I'm still thinking about that.' And why were Sky's questions so similar to those Leo had asked her? Those same questions she'd asked herself over and over since he'd walked out of her life.

'Men aren't good at expressing emotion,' Sky said. 'They don't want to talk about their feelings; they don't want to know about yours; it freaks them out and makes them feel like they've lost face somehow.'

'If they were more like women…'

'I'd say it would be kind of boring, wouldn't you? Does he love you, do you think?'

'Yes. I think he does. *Did.*'

'Did he tell you?'

'Yes.'

Sky's eyebrows shot skyward. 'Wow, I'm impressed,' she murmured thoughtfully. 'It takes guts for a guy to confess his love, you know? So if he told you that, I reckon he won't have changed his mind in the space of a few weeks.'

Brie prided herself on understanding men but she'd never looked further than skin-deep. Except with Leo. Every time she'd started looking beyond their initial attraction, she'd pushed such thoughts away.

She'd not thanked him as he deserved to be thanked for the fire alarms she'd given him such grief about. His efforts at organising her garden shed—who'd go to all that trouble for someone else unless they were really special to them? And she'd repaid him with the kind of appalling social skills she'd accused him of having. She'd refused to view it in the way she should have.

Because she was a coward.

She wiped the lotion off of Sky's fingers with a damp

towel. Maybe, as Sky said, Leo just needed to be needed—
Hang on a bit. Brie frowned. 'How did you know it was
only a few weeks ago?'

Sky regarded her a moment, then said, 'Because Leo
Hamilton's my brother and I can't stand seeing him so
unhappy.'

Stunned into silence, Brie stared at Sky while confused
thoughts raced through her head. Finally, she managed,
'But his sister's name's—'

'Yeah. Sunny-Sky. Hyphenated.' She shrugged, gave
a small smile. 'Mum thought it was cute. And Camp-
bell's her maiden name. I apologise for the deception but
I wanted to meet this special woman Leo's so hung up on.
He doesn't know I'm here, by the way, so if we can keep
this between—'

'Leo's unhappy?' Why did that make Brie feel so much
better?

'I haven't seen much of him lately. He's given himself a
massive workload this past week, but we had lunch yesterday and his mood wasn't pretty. Still, he talked, and for a
guy like Leo that's a way big deal. And this control thing
he's got going on? Pretty irritating, believe me, I know.
But it stems from our childhood. Why don't you call him?'

'I don't think he'll—'

'Yes—he will. Trust me. Better yet, trust him.'

CHAPTER THIRTEEN

AFTER FALLING INTO bed at midnight, Brie woke again at just after one in the morning. Sleep was impossible with so much stuff spinning around inside her head. She went downstairs, made a mug of warm milk and honey, her favourite comfort food, then carried it to the living room. Snuggling into a comfy armchair, she switched on the wall furnace and warmed her bare toes while she sipped.

Sunny-Sky's surprise visit had knocked Brie sideways and she was still reeling. Brie had to admire her for having the guts to pull off such a stunt. The simple pretext had been for a noble reason and Brie knew she'd always intended coming clean before leaving. It showed Brie just how much love existed between the siblings and had given Brie a new insight into the man who'd stolen her heart.

And unexpectedly enough, into herself.

Sunny, as she preferred to be called, had held a mirror up to Brie's doubts and questions and fears and insecurities. She'd forced Brie to look deeply and honestly at herself—and she acknowledged it was way past time.

She didn't like what she saw.

Because her father's decisions and choices had had such a negative impact on her life, her motives and the way she'd conducted herself where Leo was concerned were a coward's way. Time to change that.

To trust him.

ANNE OLIVER 173

Sunny's powerful words swept away some of Brie's insecurities. Leo was nothing like her father. But her insides were churning as she pulled a note pad off the coffee table. She wanted to show him once and for all that she was ready to take that risk he'd told her to think about. The one she'd been too afraid to take a few weeks ago. If only she wasn't too late...

The following morning, Brie waited until she had a break between clients to ring Leo. Heart pounding into her throat, she waited for him to answer. What if she'd taken too long to get back to him? What if he saw her name and ignored her call? No, that was Brie's MO.

'Breanna, good morning. This is a surprise—and a coincidence.'

Oh? At the familiar sound of his deep voice, she gripped the phone tighter. 'Good morning, Leo.' How formal. How stilted. How wrong given what they'd been to one another. 'A coincidence?'

'I was going to call you today with an idea. But firstly, how have you been?'

'Fine.' She hesitated then told the truth. 'Not fine.'

'Sorry to hear that.'

He didn't sound sorry. He sounded pleased. She squeezed her eyes shut and said, 'What were you going to call me about?'

'We'll start with why you called me.'

'I have a favour to ask—it's not urgent.' His reason might affect her plans. 'You?'

'It's essentially a business call.'

She ignored the stab of disappointment and said, 'How can I help?'

'I've been giving the Pink Snowflake Foundation a lot of thought. I have a proposal you might be interested in.'

Not that kind of proposal, Brie. 'I'm always interested in anything that supports Pink Snowflake.'

'I'd like to discuss it with you, hear your opinion. We'll keep it business.'

'Definitely. Business.'

'Would tomorrow suit? Five o'clock, at your salon?'

It couldn't have worked out better if she'd organised his meeting herself. 'I have a late client so I'd prefer six. But I've got something happening after.' She hoped.

'Okay.' His tone was brisk. 'Six o'clock. I'll see you then.'

Brie was ready and waiting when Leo tapped on her open office door at precisely six the following evening. Without thought, she lifted her hand to check the formal knot of hair on the top of her head. 'Good evening, Leo. Come in.'

'Evening, Brie.'

She wasn't quite ready for her heart-racing response to his use of her informal name. Nor was she prepared for the sight of his masculine allure in his charcoal suit and snowy shirt and neat-as-a-pin maroon tie. 'Dressed to impress,' she said. 'And I am. Impressed, that is.' And rushed on with, 'This must be an important proposal. *Business* proposal.'

'It is,' he said, voice as crisp as a dress shirt.

Brie bit her lip. Leo had always had that destabilising effect on her. Beneath her black buttoned-up jacket she was anything but the cool, calm, in-control woman she wanted to be with him tonight.

Then it hit her and she wanted to die of humiliation and embarrassment. He hadn't suited up for her. He was dressed for some social function or other—which more than likely included female company—and was simply calling past here on the way. *Great going, Brie.* He wasn't the only one who jumped to the wrong conclusions.

He stepped into the tiny room, which wasn't much bigger than a closet. He cocked his head as if to ask if she usually wore a business jacket in her line of work, then his gaze drifted lower to the short hemline of her shiny new party dress and he said nothing. Just lifted his eyes back to her face. For an instant, she saw his eyes darken with emotions she couldn't guess at, yet he'd laid it all out for her not so long ago. For a few brief shiny moments she'd seen the real Leo Hamilton.

She missed that man.

Her glimmering red dress and the sophisticated hair was all part of the plan to win that man back. She sat on her stool, indicated an office chair she'd brought from the shared lunch room, and invited him to have a seat.

He did, while looking at the mess sprawled over most of her desk which was pushed up against one wall.

'I know.' She looked him straight in those enigmatic silver eyes. 'I didn't thank you for tidying up my garden. And my books. And the kitchen. I was rude and I apologise.'

'You're welcome. Sometimes I came on too strong.'

She smiled. 'I'm getting used to the way it works with you. With us. Maybe I can start again, put the messy bits behind me...'

He didn't react the way she'd hoped and barbed wire tightened around her heart. She realised, now, that she wanted that life he'd offered her, and she was willing to risk everything for it. She wanted to tell him she loved him back. If he hadn't changed his mind. Even if he had.

He got straight down to business. 'The reason I'm here is to suggest a fundraiser for Pink Snowflake. I'm asking Hope Strings to do a charity performance and they're more than happy to donate their time for a worthy cause. I thought an evening with fine music, dining and dancing. So I've booked the classiest venue in Hobart—it's Sunrise-Sunset on the fourteenth of June.'

She blinked while she caught up. 'You've gone ahead and booked Sunrise-Sunset. Without asking me?'

'The thing is,' he said slowly, resolutely, 'I admire Pink Snowflake's vision and I intend to proceed with my fundraising idea with or without you. Having said that, I'd love to have you work alongside me on this.'

He was pledging himself to the cause dearest to her heart and was willing to go ahead with his plans alone if necessary. 'Of course I want to be involved. Tell me more.'

He smiled. 'Thought you'd say that. Eight weeks should be enough time to get organised. I'm thinking a glittering event with a couple of big-name Aussie celebrities I can call on at short notice.'

'I'm in. Glittering events are my forte.' She clapped her hands together, brought them to her lips to keep her smile from flying away. She still had a chance. 'One thing, though. Hope Strings is classical. What about those of us who like to shake their booty on a dance floor?'

'Don't worry, Hope Strings is nothing if not versatile. There'll be plenty of time for dirty dancing.'

She did a little finger clap in front of her lips. 'Excellent.'

He glanced at the clock on her wall, shifted on his chair as if in a hurry to leave. 'There was a favour you wanted to ask me?'

'It can wait.' Actually, no. It couldn't. She had to tell him now, before he walked out of here in his special suit and tie for his maybe special date. Sunny had told her Leo was a man who needed to be needed. 'I need someone who lives and breathes organisation. You know someone like that?'

He nodded once. 'I'm your man.'

'The office needs some structure before I relocate it to the McPherson retreat.' She waved an encompassing hand. 'If you could, maybe, help me create some order out of the chaos some time soon, I'd be very grateful.'

'How grateful?'

'Very.' He watched her for a moment without answering, his expression giving nothing away.

She wished she knew what he'd meant by that question. She wished she knew what he thought *she* meant. Because honestly? She didn't mean it in a sexual way. She'd be grateful for any contact, no matter how fleeting.

'I'll do it,' he said at last. 'As a special favour to you.' He spoke casually, his long-fingered hands on his knees. 'You want to work with me on it?'

'Not necessary.' She breathed a sigh of relief and optimism. 'I trust you to do an amazing job. You can even organise your own filing system, so long as you teach me how to use it.' It was her turn to glance at her diamond watch. Her plan was still on schedule. 'I'll put the date for the fundraiser in my diary and we'll make another time to go over the details, but right now I've got something more important happening.'

She rose, watching his eyes darken as she unbuttoned her jacket and took it off. She tossed it onto her desk, slid open her top desk drawer and pulled out a glitzy evening purse.

Leo's eyes didn't know where to look first. At the silky fabric clinging to her womanly curves, or the long legs encased in shimmery stockings or the spiked heels on her feet.

Her strapless fire-engine-red dress enhanced her toned shoulders and prominent collarbones; the upswept hair revealed her slender neck to perfection.

'I'm not the only one dressed to impress,' he murmured, lifting his hungry eyes to her jewelled midnight ones, struggling hard not to let possessiveness get the upper hand.

He wanted to beat his chest and roar to the world that she was his, and only his. He wanted to reach out, loosen her hair and let the silken strands tumble into his hands. He wanted to yank her to him and hold her prisoner until she yielded to him and admitted what he already knew in his heart and wanted to hear aloud—that she loved him.

Or had he got it spectacularly wrong?

'Looks like it's some party you've got lined up.'

'It is.' She opened her purse and drew out the necklace he'd given her in Singapore, held it out. 'I was having trouble with the clasp. Will you do this up for me?' She turned.

'So you've decided to keep it.'

'Yes.'

Clenching his jaw, he performed the task even though the tiny rational part that was left of his brain told him to get the hell out before he made an idiot of himself. Again. Why was he letting her play him for a fool?

Never more a fool than a man in crazy, impossible love.

She turned back, the diamonds glittering at her throat, her eyes focused on his. She pressed the intercom. 'Jodie, thanks. That'll be all. I'll see you tomorrow.'

His cue to leave too? 'I'll get going, then.'

'There's something else I need you to do,' she said softly. 'Do you trust me? I trust you. *I trust you, Leo Hamilton.*'

He stared into her fathomless eyes and saw hope. He nodded, because frankly he wasn't sure he could get his voice to work.

He followed her out of her office to her treatment room, hardly daring to look at the stunning vision in front of him. She stopped at the closed door, pressed her lips together and turned to look at him. For the first time, her heart was in her eyes. Unguarded, open, still so achingly vulnerable.

'If you had plans for tonight, I don't care how important they were, cancel them.'

He'd made none but said, 'Consider them cancelled.'

She nodded, then murmured, 'One party coming up,' and pushed the door open. Dozens of tea-lights flickered on all available surfaces, giving the room an intimate golden glow. A bottle of bubbly chilled on a pedestal in the corner. And all he could think to say was, 'You left these candles burning unattended?'

Her laugh was a full-throated sound of genuine amusement. And no candle could shine brighter than Brie's smile, which lit up her face like he'd never seen.

'Would I do that? No, Jodie kept an eye out till I was ready, so zip that totally kissable mouth of yours and let me do the talking. I remembered you liked parties for two, so here we are. There's a rule though: there'll be no sex here.'

His brows rose. 'No sex?' He saw the sunshine in her eyes—and the clouds of uncertainty beneath. He tsk-tsked. 'That's a bad rule, Brie.'

She tapped his lips. 'And no interruptions till I say so.'

He set his lips against the intercepting fingers and nodded.

She paced away a little then turned to him. 'You were right when you accused me of hiding the real Brie from the world. I've spent my life perfecting the art and it's a form of lying—you were right about that too. I've been lying to myself. I've been playing in a world I thought I wanted, free to please myself but ending my relationships before they got serious. And I really thought I was happy.'

She shook her head. 'Not any more. I've realised that true freedom comes not from a long list of casual, meaningless acquaintances but with an honest, open commitment to one. So I want to thank you. Very much. I'm free because of you. I understand myself—even if no one else does.

'I'm not bound by fear of "what-if", because I've learned to trust. To trust *you*. That night when you came to me with your story and your heart and soul in your words, you showed me it's safe to fall in love.'

'Brie—'

'Please, don't interrupt.' She held up a hand. 'I need to get it out. My parents were totally focused on their own misery. They threw gifts and money at me and hoped I'd go away and leave them alone. I felt abandoned and invisible. So I partied, rebelled and garnered often inappropriate attention but at least it was attention—just for all the wrong reasons. And I've already told you about Elliot.

'Which is why I viewed your flowers as an easy apology for standing me up, and I apologise because no one should come before your sister. The diamonds…' she touched the sparkling jewels at her neck '…brought back the bad old days.'

'Enough.' Two steps and he was in front of her, brushing loose hair from her brow, kissing away her hurts, soothing away her fears. 'Enough. Relax, breathe. You're shivering.' He rubbed her upper arms.

'I'm not cold, just emotional. It's okay.' Brie could barely see through the veil of tears. She'd never felt so treasured, so safe as she did in that moment. And her entire body was indeed shivering.

With sheer paralysing fear of what he'd say next.

'I love you too,' she said, determined to finish what she'd started. 'And I want to spend the rest of my life with you. If it's not too late. So I have a proposal of my own.' She reached into her purse and pulled out a black velvet box, pushed it into his hand. 'I'm asking you to marry me.'

His eyebrows rose. 'You're proposing marriage to me?'

'Isn't that what people want to do when they love each other? Show their commitment? Announce to the whole world that they're officially off the market?' Her breath rushed out and embarrassing despair rushed in to fill its place. Her cheeks burned. 'Oh, *no*. Stupid, stupid me. You don't want to get married. I am *such* an idiot. Of course you don't. Why would you?'

She tried to snatch her box back but his fist tightened

around it. 'No. You don't give someone a gift then take it back. Didn't anyone tell you it's bad manners?'

'I never gave a man a gift before. Except Jett, and that first time didn't go so well. And this…this isn't…' She trailed off beneath his gaze.

His eyes looked deep into hers, so deep, she felt the love from them touch her soul. Then he said, 'Let's open it, shall we?'

'I…' She pressed her lips together as he flipped the lid open.

His mouth kicked up at one corner. 'Well, now.' With great care and a million stuttering heartbeats later, he lifted the ring out of its box. The cluster of rubies and diamonds winked in the candlelight. He slid it onto the tip of his pinkie and shook his head. 'It doesn't fit me. You'll have to wear it.'

He lifted his eyes to hers and smiled. 'What do you say?'

Thank you? No. She batted his chest. 'You're confusing me; it's what do *you* say.'

'I say I love you right back and let's get married.' He slid the ring onto her left finger. 'It suits your bright and shiny personality. And it's stunning, just like you. But I'll pay for it.'

'No, no, no.'

'I insist. No pay, no marriage contract.'

'You can buy an eternity ring for our first wedding anniversary.'

'I'll buy that too.'

She settled against his chest. 'Since you insist, I'll let you win. This time.'

'Deal.' Leo sealed it with a kiss, then swept her off her feet and up, before blowing out candles.

'What are you doing?'

'I want to make love to you and you've said this place

is off-limits so I'm taking you home.' He swung past the ice bucket. 'Grab that bottle of bubbly.'

'Home?'

He kissed her as he carried her to the door. 'To West Wind.'

Hours later, Leo awoke. They lay together, their limbs entwined in the dimness. Brie had agreed to share his Melbourne house on occasional weekends, and he'd be there when he worked in Victoria, but they were making their home West Wind. She'd even agreed to let Mrs J come over and keep house for them. With her heavy workload and commitments to Pink Snowflake, he knew Brie needed someone to help, and Mrs J was more than keen.

He turned his head on the pillow and watched her sleeping. Her breasts were warm and soft against his chest, and his erection was nudging her hip. He rolled over, pinning her beneath him and stroking her hair from her face. 'Wake up, baby doll.'

Sleepy eyes opened, her full inviting lips curved. 'I wasn't asleep. I was thinking.'

He cupped a breast, rolled the nipple between thumb and forefinger. 'About this?'

Her smile widened against his roaming lips. 'About your constant need to be on top of things.'

'I let you be on top last time.'

'You did,' she agreed. 'But it's not sex I'm talking about right now, Mr Must-stay-in-control-at-all-times Hamilton.' Wriggling out from beneath him and rolling onto her side, she propped her head on her elbow and studied him in the semi-darkness. 'Did you thank Sunny, or give her a lecture about interfering in your love life?'

'Sunny? What do you mean?'

'She didn't tell you?'

Brie looked so horrified, he bit back a smile. 'Tell me what?'

'That she came to see me at the salon.'

'When was this?'

'Oh.' She rolled onto her back. 'I think I just messed up a beautiful sibling relationship.'

'You mean when Sunny-Sky went to extraordinary lengths to beg you to give me a chance?' His hand found and stroked her belly button.

'Yes.' She visibly relaxed. 'Sunny-Sky. You weren't mad?'

'Why would I be? She convinced you I was the one, didn't she?' He touched her little piercing. 'Why a strawberry?'

'My sixteen-year-old self's little rebellion. My parents hated body decoration. And I love strawberries. They're pretty and dainty and they taste sweet.'

'Since you possess all three attributes, it suits you perfectly.'

She snorted. 'I thought we were going to be honest with each other?'

'Okay, maybe dainty's—'

'Fine, if you think it suits me, I'm happy.'

'So am I.' He spread his hand over her flat belly. Would they ever have their own children? He hoped so. 'You know something? Mum would have loved you. Almost as much as I do.'

Her smile was brilliant against the dimness. 'See? Easy. I don't need flowers and fancy gifts, just the words. Just the love. And I adore you right back.'

EPILOGUE

THE SUNRISE-SUNSET ballroom was a glittering collision of sensory delights. Rainbows bounced off glassware and jewels sparkled beneath chandeliers dripping crystals. Hope Strings entertained with a selection of Vivaldi and Purcell while the guests, who'd paid big bucks to attend, enjoyed canapés including such delicacies as chicken and coriander dumplings, lemon-myrtle-dusted fish goujons with tartare sauce and lobster onion pâté with lavoche, to be followed throughout the evening by three more courses of equally sumptuous fare.

Brie saw her brother—a head taller than everyone else bar the man at her side—near the window overlooking the harbour and glimpsed Olivia's flaming red hair alongside. 'They're here,' she told Leo and, grabbing his hand, she tugged him through the crowd.

The four of them had caught up a month ago when Jett and Olivia had returned from their honeymoon, and the newlyweds were almost as excited as Brie and Leo about the upcoming wedding.

Jett's face lit when he turned and saw her heading towards him. 'Hey, Brie.'

Brie would never get sick of her big brother's smile. 'Hey, there, yourself.' She hugged Jett first, then turned to Olivia. 'How are you feeling today, honey?'

'Not bad *now*. Pretty awful for the rest of the day.'

Livvy looked amazing, as usual, but there were smudges beneath her eyes. There was a reason for that and it made Brie smile. 'How's my little niece or nephew coming along in there?' Brie patted the small mound covered in sky-blue silk.

'It's a he,' Olivia muttered. 'A female would never give me such a hard time. Don't let me put you off having babies though.'

Brie smiled up at Leo. 'As if.' She hugged his arm. 'Just not yet though.'

Olivia grimaced. 'That's what I said and look at me.' She glared at her husband, who just shrugged as if he'd had nothing to do with it.

Brie slung an arm around Jett. 'Go on, you were both thrilled. Did you purchase that little cradle you were looking at?'

'Yes.' Livvy's expression brightened. 'And while we were there we saw some adorable wallpaper with teddies.'

Leo exchanged a look with Jett and raised his glass. 'Anyone for a refill?'

Talk of cradles and babies obviously made Brie's future husband uneasy and she smiled to herself.

Jett jerked a thumb. 'There's a guy over there who wants to talk to you about his environmental concerns on the north-west coast, if you've got a minute.'

Brie caught Jett's glint of humour directed her way then watched the two most important guys in her life merge into the crowd. She smiled and turned to Olivia. 'How's Jett with all this baby talk?'

'He's as thrilled as me, he just doesn't want to show it in public. So Eve's Naturally is doing okay?'

Brie's business had moved to the McPherson retreat last month. 'We're almost on track after Leo's hard work with the filing system.' Brie groaned. 'I swear I didn't inherit the organisational gene.'

'You don't need to—you have a slave at your beck and call now.'

Brie laughed. 'Don't let him hear you say that.'

Hours later, the Blue Menagerie jazz band provided an easy syncopated beat and Leo got Brie onto the dance floor, more as an excuse to have her up close than to dance. Sunny and Gregor were taking a well-deserved break near the orchestra and waved as Leo guided Brie past.

He loved whatever she wore but tonight she looked extra special. She was wearing the dress she'd proposed to him in. A grin twitched at the corner of his mouth. And it wasn't even a leap year...

'See? I *am* capable of allowing a man to lead on the dance floor,' she told him, batting her lashes coquettishly.

'And I'm thinking of lying back in bed and letting you do all the work tonight,' he replied.

She looked at her watch in mock surprise. 'Goodness, it's getting late. We should go. Now.'

'Not so fast.' He tugged her closer, ran his hands over her bare shoulder blades. 'It's nice, holding you like this.' They moved slowly to the music, wrapped in each other's arms and lost in the moment. 'Don't ever change, baby doll. You're perfect just as you are.'

'That goes for you too.' She smoothed his lapel and stared up at him. 'We'll have that for our wedding waltz.'

'Have what?'

'Billy Joel's "Just the Way You Are".'

'We'll make a list and vote on them.'

'Okay. So long as we both vote for Billy.'

'One thing's for sure, we're going to take forever to get bored.'

She pressed her lips to his chin. 'Sounds perfect to me.'

* * * * *

THE FLAT IN NOTTING HILL

Love and lust in the city that never sleeps!

Izzy, Tori and Poppy are living the London dream—
sharing a big flat in Notting Hill, they have good
jobs, wild nights out…and each other.

They couldn't be more different, but one thing is for
sure: when they start falling in love they're going to
be very glad they've got such good friends around to
help them survive the rollercoaster…!

THE MORNING AFTER THE NIGHT BEFORE
by Nikki Logan

SLEEPING WITH THE SOLDIER
by Charlotte Phillips

YOUR BED OR MINE?
by Joss Wood

ENEMIES WITH BENEFITS
by Louisa George

Don't miss this fabulous new continuity from
Modern Tempted™!

Dear Reader

Well, here we are again—but this time I'm part of a team! This is the first book I've ever written in collaboration with other authors, and I hope you have as much fun reading it as I did planning and writing it.

Writing is usually very solitary—just me and my laptop—but with this book I've had three other fab authors to brainstorm and chat with. We shared photos and decor plans for the flat in Notting Hill, and bounced around ideas for the café where all the flatmates meet up.

The best bit has been seeing glimpses of Lara and Alex in the other books in *The Flat in Notting Hill* series. For once the road to happy-ever-after for my couple isn't the limit of their story, and I can see a bigger picture of their friendships and their lives together. Add to that the wonderful vibrancy of the Notting Hill setting and this story really leapt off the page for me. I hope it does for you too!

Love

Charlotte x

SLEEPING WITH
THE SOLDIER

BY
CHARLOTTE PHILLIPS

Published in Great Britain 2014
by Mills & Boon, an imprint of Harlequin (UK) Limited,
Eton House, 18-24 Paradise Road, Richmond, Surrey, TW9 1SR

© 2014 Harlequin Books S.A.

Special thanks and acknowledgement are given to Charlotte Phillips
for her contribution to *The Flat in Notting Hill* series.

ISBN: 978-0-263-25023-7

Charlotte Phillips has been reading romantic fiction since her teens, and she adores upbeat stories with happy endings. Writing them for Mills & Boon® is her dream job. She combines writing with looking after her fabulous husband, two teenagers, a four-year-old and a dachshund. When something has to give, it's usually housework. She lives in Wiltshire.

Other Modern Tempted™ titles by Charlotte Phillips:

THE PLUS-ONE AGREEMENT

**This and other books by Charlotte Phillips
are available in eBook format
from www.millsandboon.co.uk**

DEDICATION

For Sam, who keeps me smiling
when I think I'm rubbish. I am so proud of you.

CHAPTER ONE

LARA CONNOR WAS aiming to corner the rich Notting Hill market in boutique lingerie and she wasn't about to achieve that heady dream with French knickers that looked as if a club-fingered chimp had sewn them together.

She stared in disbelief at the mass of pale pink silk and delicate lace now rucked up in a tangle of mad stitches beneath the foot of her sewing machine and gritted her teeth hard enough to make her jaw ache. Above her head the banging started again with a new urgency that really brought out the hostility in her.

She liked to think she was a glass-half-full kind of person, laid-back, live and let live, default mood: happy. But the noise pollution emanating from the flat above all night, every night, had meant her sleep had been broken for weeks now. Tiredness had pushed her normally sunny attitude to the brink of her patience and, frankly, if it didn't stop now, murder might be on the cards.

She lifted the foot of the machine, disentangled the ball of expensive fabric from the needle and examined it. Beyond saving. She lobbed it across the room into the 'remnants' bin. The knickers weren't even salvageable enough to go into the 'seconds' bin. And having sunk every penny into this venture, she couldn't afford to keep slipping up like this. The 'remnants' bin was looking far too full for her liking, and it was all the fault of the Lothario upstairs, who apparently couldn't let a day pass by without getting laid.

The clanking and banging in the pipes had begun a few weeks ago, not long after Lara had moved in. The sudden increase in noise coincided with the return of the soldier brother of Poppy, who owned the flat upstairs. Lara had got to know Poppy quite well over the last four or five weeks, and her flatmate, Izzy. A brief hello on the stairs had quickly progressed to coffee and chat in the downstairs café. Both girls were excited to hear about Lara's lingerie designs. Izzy had even bought a couple of samples. On her own in a new place, Lara was especially pleased to have made friends. If only Poppy's brother could have a *smidge* of her consideration.

Sitting in Ignite, the ground-floor café, while Lara updated her blog courtesy of the free Wi-Fi, she'd picked up plenty of gossip from the other old-fire-station residents about Alex. He was rumoured to be some military hero, honourably discharged from the army after frontline action abroad. The building was also awash with gossip about his endless stream of women; the word was that he bedded a different one every night! And two or three times she'd actually seen said women, sporting that giveaway combination of evening clothes, bed hair and smug smile, making the walk of shame when she'd nipped down to the café for a takeaway coffee first thing in the morning. Lara had watched pityingly; she couldn't think of anything more pointless. With all this evidence taken as a whole, there was no real question as to the source of the noise pollution that was tiring her out, disrupting her work and thus costing her money, of which she had absolutely no more.

The first couple of times it might even have been funny. His bed must be shoved right up against the radiator, because the water pipes for the top flat were clearly shared by her own little studio flat below. At first she'd rolled her eyes in exasperation and—possibly—a hint of wistful envy. Not that it had anything to do with the military hero himself, of course; in her opinion he sounded far too attractive for his own good. But still, it had been a long time since she'd last seen any action in that department. That was what big aspirations did to your life. There had to be sacrifices; something had to give. Lara Connor had plans and ambitions, and she intended to keep her eye on the prize.

The next step on that journey to success was the small shop she'd managed to secure in Notting Hill for the next two months. Her own pop-up shop to showcase her own line of vintage-inspired lingerie. The rent on this little flat was extortionate and had eaten away at her savings, but it was worth it so she could live near the premises and she'd been working all the hours she could muster. Sewing was only a part of it—there was marketing to think of, the shop to fit and decorate. Night and day her mind was filled with nothing else. She was already exhausted, just with the workload she had to shoulder, but she cared about none of it because this was the next step in her game plan, from which she would not be distracted.

Certainly not by some inconsiderate love god living upstairs. The endless noise was beginning to jeopardise her carefully laid plans, and she quite simply was not going to stand for it any longer. Especially since it now seemed that all night was no longer adequate for his needs. This morning she'd heard the familiar slam of the door as his most recent conquest left the building. But this time it hadn't been followed by the welcome peace that she needed to produce the intricate lingerie she designed herself to the exacting standards she demanded. She worked with delicate, fine fabrics. Silks, lace, ribbons, velvet. The kind of garments she made took skill and close attention to detail. Absolute concentration was required.

Instead, what she'd had was half an hour of mad hammering. For the first few minutes she'd tried to ignore it, waiting to see if one of the other residents would intervene. Surely she couldn't be the only one driven mad by this? But as the minutes ticked by and the noise didn't abate she came to realise that clearly no one else *was* around to intervene. They'd all gone out to work, of course, while work for Lara took place right here. She needed to concentrate on her sewing. Everything was riding on this stock being perfect. Seconds were not an option.

As she pushed her chair back grimly and grabbed her door key from the table the bashing overhead began again in earnest, bringing a fresh wave of anger to bubble up inside her.

All night, every night was one thing. Was she now expected to put up with this racket all day too?

Enough was enough.

Shoulders squared, teeth gritted, she took the stairs up to the top floor grimly, ready to give Poppy's inconsiderate brother a piece of her sleep-deprived mind, and the planned outburst screeched to a halt on the tip of her tongue as she rounded the corner at the top of the stairs. The hinge on her jaw seemed to be suddenly loose.

Poppy's inconsiderate brother?

Correction: Poppy's all but naked, roped with muscle, fit and breathtakingly gorgeous soldier hero brother. His modesty was saved only by a very small white towel, which was held up on his muscular hips by a single fold. Hard muscle twined the tanned biceps and broad shoulders. His stomach was drum-tight and his short dark hair was damply tousled. Smoothly tanned skin gave away the fact he'd spent months abroad in action before coming here. By sheer will she fixed her eyes above his neck when all they wanted to do was dip lower and check out those perfect abs.

And OK, for a moment she *might* have been stunned into silence by the revelation that, actually, the rumours were true, Poppy's brother really *was* drop-dead gorgeous, and by the fact that his modesty was hidden by the tiniest of white towels, but then he'd gone on to ruin the effect by raising his clenched fist and hammering on the closed door of the flat, reproducing the sound that had driven her to the edge of her sanity for the past half an hour. Up close it was monstrously loud and her already aching head throbbed in protest.

'I think,' she snapped, in the coldest voice she could muster, 'we can safely assume that everyone who lives on the other side of that door is either out or deaf.'

Alex Spencer stopped, knuckles poised mid-hammer, and turned sideways to look at her. Her thick blond hair was piled up messily on her head with a pencil stuck through the middle of it, she had a full rosebud mouth, and wide china-blue eyes that would have been captivating if they hadn't got an expression in them that implied she'd quite like to see him decomposing in a ditch. She wore a pale pink cardigan with the top two buttons undone, revealing a silky smooth expanse of flawless porcelain décolletage, cropped jeans and bare feet. And even though he was so tired he could hardly see straight, and not only because he'd just spent a very active night in bed that involved anything but sleep, his pulse managed a jolt of interest.

'And you are…?' he said, raising sarcastic eyebrows as if she were the one who looked out of place and it were perfectly normal to be walking the corridors wearing a bath towel.

'The poor sap who lives downstairs,' she snapped. '*Directly* downstairs, to be specific. Right below *you*.'

He stared at her, his tired brain struggling to process what she was saying. It felt as if he were thinking through a very large wad of cotton wool. Technically, thanks to the way his sickening insomnia had progressed, night time for him had pretty much now turned into day and vice versa. Thus it was currently an hour or so past his bedtime and his patience was balanced on a knife edge.

'What are you talking about?'

The question opened the floodgates and he took a defensive step backwards.

'Your night-time action is ruining my *life*,' she wailed. 'All night, every night, crashing and clanking pipes while you get your rocks off with whatever girl you happen to have brought back. Your bed must be right up against the radiator or something. The noise travels down the pipes and echoes round my bedroom as if I'm in the bloody room with you. It's utter selfishness! I can hear *every move you make* and I can't take it anymore!' She raised her hands up and pressed them to the sides of her head as if she thought it might explode. 'I can't *have* this kind of distraction. I've only got a week or so left before the shop launches and I'm going to go crazy if I don't get some uninterrupted *sleep*.'

The blue eyes took on a hint of madness, and an unexpected twinge of sympathy twisted his stomach because restful sleep was currently an elusive thing for him too. It had been since he'd returned from his recent overseas tour via the hospital. He'd worked his way through convalescence at breakneck speed after the chest injuries he'd sustained in a roadside bomb, only to learn that he wouldn't be going back. Physical injury was one thing, an early end to his career was quite another. Discharge from the army had not been what he wanted, no matter that it was honourable. He had a lot on his mind, he kept telling himself—it was no wonder that he didn't sleep like a baby at night.

'The shop?' he said.

'I'm in the middle of launching a pop-up shop in Portobello Road. It's my first try at moving into proper retail instead of market stalls. I need it to be a success and *nothing's* going to stop me, including your libido!'

Her angry explanation of her business commitments brought a lurching reminder that currently his own life was cruising along rudderless. It wasn't as if he had a direction right now, or plans to consider. Lack of sleep had no consequence in *his* life, aside from the fact that his routine was getting a bit out of kilter, and who really cared about that? Since his social circle currently consisted of a group of girly flatmates, an old friend who was hardly ever there, and his kid sister, concern about his sleep pattern wasn't exactly a buzzing topic of conversation. And since his sleep problems were rooted in an unrelenting spate of cold-sweat nightmares that made staying awake through the dark hours extremely attractive, he'd quite like to keep it that way.

After operations to remove shrapnel and four months of medical care, his physical recovery was as complete as it was going to get. He'd worked hard to regain his fitness, thinking that would be an end to it, believing he'd got off lightly. He hadn't counted on the nightmares continuing. He hadn't told anyone about them, not even Poppy, vaguely thinking that verbalising their existence might somehow give them even more of a grip on him. Easier to just evade sleep and hope they would subside. To help things along, he filled his waking hours with distracting activity, taking full advantage of the sudden lack of discipline and routine in his life after years of moulding to the requirements first of boarding school and then the armed forces.

The sense of purpose and the camaraderie that he'd come to take for granted in the army left a gaping hole in his life now it was unexpectedly gone. Hence the appeal of filling his time with far less challenging distractions. For the first time in his life he'd thrown himself into having fun, losing all sense of his current pointless existence by bedding as many women as possible. It wasn't difficult. Women seemed to fall at his feet with minimal effort on his part, just the way they always had done.

Except, possibly, for this one.

'If this carries on I'll report you to the local council for noise pollution,' she was snarling. 'Can't you phone Poppy?'

He cast exasperated hands down at himself in the small towel.

'With what, exactly? Do I look like I've got a phone

stashed on my person? If my sister would just haul her-self out of her pit and *answer the bloody door*, I wouldn't *need* to be making any noise,' he yelled at the closed door, pressing his point by adding in another quick bash on it, which made the crazy neighbour from downstairs stiffen like a meerkat.

'Will you *stop* with the knocking?' she hollered. 'Is Poppy deaf?'

'Not as far as I'm aware.'

'Then she's not bloody *in there*, is she? You've been hammering on that door for half an hour and it's loud enough to wake the dead.' She threw her hands up in a gesture of exasperation. 'For Pete's sake, she must be at *work*. I saw her the other day and she mentioned she was on call this week.'

The implications of that information burst through his mind in a flurry of exasperation. Poppy could be gone for hours and he couldn't bring himself to interrupt her work as a medic for something as ludicrously embarrassing as locking himself out. Her flatmate, Izzy, had just moved out and the only other person with a key was his friend Isaac, who was supposedly crashing in the extra room but who actually spent more time away than he did at home. He was currently globetrotting between swanky new po-tential continental venues for his chain of cocktail bars.

He had to face facts. He could hang out in the hall-way in a towel for a chunk of the day until Poppy got back. Or he could sweet-talk the interfering neighbour, who looked as if she'd be glad to see his head on a spike.

He stepped away from the door, anticipating that an apol-ogy might not have quite the clout it needed if he was still within hammering distance of it.

He spread his hands.

'Look, I'm sorry. What's your name?'

She narrowed suspicious eyes at his newly amenable tone.

'Lara Connor.'

'Lara. I'm Alex.'

She nodded at him, not a hint of a smile, so he tried a bit harder, attempting to mould his face into an apologetic expression.

'I'm sorry for the noise. The *disruption*. I had no idea I was bothering anyone. It's not as if anyone else has complained.'

Quite the opposite. The biggest problem he had was wriggling out of any follow-up dates. He had absolutely no desire to ruin what was a very nice distraction plan by bringing anything so emotionally demanding as a proper *relationship* into the situation.

As apologies went it was all a bit pants in Lara's opinion.

'Why *would* anyone else complain? No one else has a bed directly below yours,' she said. 'And I don't need an apology or a load of rubbish excuses. What I really want is some kind of assurance that you'll make an effort and stop the racket.'

'I'll move my bed away from the wall,' he conceded. His voice was clipped and very British. She noticed he didn't offer to interrupt the endless flow of women through his bedroom.

'Right,' she said. 'And what about now? You can't keep hammering on that door—my sanity is hanging by a thread. What are you going to do until Poppy gets back?'

She folded her arms and frowned at him.

He shrugged resignedly.

'I'll just have to wait it out. Unless you'd like to take pity on me.'

'I don't think so,' she said, smoothing her hair back from her face.

'It could be hours.' His expression took on a pitiful look. 'I don't even have a jacket.'

'Tough,' she said. 'It'll do you good to put up with a bit of discomfort for a change.' She made a move towards the stairs, wondering how far he might go with the grovelling, enjoying the upper hand. She'd let him suffer a bit longer and then offer to let him wait in her flat.

His grovelling had apparently reached its limit. Silence as she descended the top step and then a sudden flurry of bangs on the door started up again. She turned back to him incredulously.

He shrugged, his upraised knuckles poised at chest level.

'You know, I'm really not *convinced* Poppy isn't in there,' he said. 'Maybe if I knock long enough, she might show.'

He put enormous emphasis on the words 'long enough', making it crystal clear he was prepared to knock all day if necessary.

Anger bubbled hotly through her as she stared at him, seeing the challenge in his eyes and knowing that if she wanted to get any work done today at all she would have to give on this. It was all she could do to force herself to act rationally, when what she wanted to do was snarl at him like a fishwife. She would give on this because it was in her best interest, thereby retaining the upper hand rather than dragging herself down to his level, but he needn't think this was over. Not for *one moment*.

'Come on, then,' she said, turning back towards the wrought-iron staircase.

She glanced around to see him looking after her. The few paces extra distance would have given her an eye-wateringly fantastic full body view of him if she hadn't bitten her lip in her determination to keep her eyes fixed from the neck up.

'What?'

'I give in. You win. I've got more important things to do than stand here arguing with you. You can use my phone if you want to try and get hold of Poppy.' The words stuck in her craw because she really didn't *need* a half-naked ex-soldier blagging his way into her flat when she had a mountain of silk knickers with velvet ribbons and frills to sew on the back. 'I haven't got her work number, but you must know it, right? Or I think I've got Izzy's number somewhere. Maybe we can get her to drop by if she still has a key. You can wait in my flat if you like,' she added grudgingly.

She led the way down the wrought-iron stairs before he could say anything triumphant. If he did that she might be tempted to call the police.

CHAPTER TWO

ALEX FOLLOWED HER down the narrow stairwell and into her flat, and, if he'd thought a few bras hanging over the bathtub in Poppy's flat was a girly step too far, this was a whole new ballgame.

There was an enormous clothes rail directly opposite, stuffed to breaking point with clothes. And not just any clothes. Everything seemed to be made of silk, satin, lace and velvet. Subtle pinks and creams hung alongside vampy deep reds, peacock blues and purples. There were spools of silk and velvet ribbon in every colour imaginable. In one corner of the room was a headless manne-quin wearing a black silky bra with tassels along the cups and matching knickers. He stared at it for an incredulous moment. Rolls of fabric were stacked against the wall and hung over the back of the sofa in the corner and the room was dominated by an enormous trestle table with two different kinds of sewing machine on it.

'Is it just you living here?' he asked as she crossed the cramped room to the kitchen area at the other end. He was used to Poppy's roomy flat. This was a shoebox in comparison.

She nodded.

'It's a one-bed studio. There isn't much space but it's

in such a perfect location for my shop. The time I'm saving by living so close kind of makes the lack of space worth it.' She nodded towards the sofa. 'Have a seat. I'll make some tea.'

'And what exactly is it that you do?' he said, picking his way through the clutter to the overstuffed sofa. It was covered in a brightly coloured patchwork throw and he had to move a huge pile of silk and lace remnants before there was room to sit down.

She was clattering about in the tiny kitchen area in the corner. There was a doorway at the side of the room with a length of some filmy cream fabric hanging across it as a curtain. He narrowed his eyes, trying to get his bearings. Her bedroom must be down there on the right if it really was situated underneath his, as she claimed. He shook his head lightly because he had absolutely zero interest in how she spent her nights.

This was a means to an end, nothing more, a marginal step up from waiting it out in the hallway upstairs. He had no desire whatsoever to find out more about the infuriating woman from downstairs. He sank onto the sofa, shifted to one side uncomfortably and tugged out a pale pink feather boa from underneath him. For Pete's sake.

'I design and make my own line of boutique lingerie,' she said.

It was impossible to miss the faint trace of pride in her voice.

'Knickers, camisoles, nightgowns, slips, bustiers, basques. You name it.' She counted them off on her fingers. 'Vintage inspired, Hollywood glamour, that kind of thing. I like to make the most of the female figure.'

His mind reeled a little. She might as well have been speaking in some foreign language and he'd felt enough of a fish out of water already in the past couple of weeks, thank you very much. After living at close quarters with soldiers for the best part of the last few years, much of that time in the roughest of conditions, moving in with a group of girls was like living with a gaggle of aliens. Everything was scented. *Everything.* There was girly underwear hanging over the radiators. The fridge was full of hummus, low-fat yogurt and other hideous foodstuffs that filled him with distaste, the topics of conversation mystified him and the bathroom was full of perfumed toiletries. He'd grabbed the opportunity when Poppy's friend Izzy had moved rooms a few weeks ago to draft in male back-up in the form of his old schoolfriend Isaac, but in reality it had made little difference because Isaac was hardly ever there. Alex was out of his depth as it was, and now he was catapulted into a room full of lingerie.

'I've been selling from market stalls for ages now, building up a customer base,' Lara was saying. 'And I have a blog—*"Boudoir Fashionista".*' She made a frame in the air with her hands as if imagining the title on a shop sign.

'A blog?' he repeated. The conversation was becoming more surreal by the minute. He leaned his head back against the sofa. His headache seemed to be intensifying.

'Mmm…' She continued to clatter about in the kitchen, not turning round. 'I showcase my lingerie, blog about fashion and beauty. I've been wanting to expand the business for a while, try my hand at retail, but it's such a gamble in terms of cost, you have no idea. And then I started looking into pop-up shops.'

He didn't answer. Her voice was sweet, melodic even, pleasant to listen to. He closed his heavy eyes to ease the thumping headache, a side effect of his crazy off-kilter sleep pattern that seemed to be becoming a regular thing.

'It's just a short-term thing, so less risk. There are places that advertise opportunities. You take on empty premises, sometimes even just for a day. I couldn't believe it when I found the place on Portobello Road—it was like a dream. I've got it for the next couple of months. Perfect timing for me to take advantage of the run up to Christmas and long enough to see if I can make it work.'

Lara gave the tea a final stir. Busying herself in the kitchen was an autopilot way of taking her mind off how much tinier the already minuscule flat suddenly felt with him in it. Small it might be but it had still been at the absolute limit of what she could afford. Desperate to give everything to the pop-up shop opportunity, she'd quickly realised that living nearby would be a huge advantage. Failure was absolutely *not* an option.

She'd give him the tea and then try to track down Izzy. The thought of having him here under her feet all day made her stomach feel squiggly. She had *tons* of work to do and she'd lost nearly an hour this morning already to first his noise and now the follow-up chaos. She didn't have *time* to step in as rescue party for neighbours. She turned back to cross the room to him. Three paces in and she came to a stop, smile fading from her face, mug of tea in each hand.

He was fast asleep.

He looked completely out of place among the frills, ribbons and lace that festooned the sofa. He had the most tightly honed muscular physique she'd ever seen outside a glossy fashion magazine, his shoulders were huge, his abs perfectly defined. One huge hand rested against his chiselled jaw as if he'd been propping his chin up when he nodded off.

She watched him for a moment. In sleep the defensive expression on his face when he'd given her his half-arsed apology for the noise was nowhere to be seen. The dark hair was dry now, the short cut totally in keeping with his military background; she could easily imagine him in uniform. The face below was classically handsome. His cheekbones were sharply defined, followed up with a firm jawline and strong mouth. Her eyes roamed lower and she caught her breath in surprise.

The upstairs landing was pretty shadowy and he'd been turned away from her for much of the time. Add in the fact that she'd been making a heroic effort to keep her eyes from wandering below his neckline and as a result she only now got a proper view of his body. A twist of sympathy surged through her.

The left-hand side of the tautly muscled chest was heavily puckered and ruched with a web of scar tissue. She pressed her lips together hard. Of course she'd heard from Poppy that Alex had been injured in action but, having heard and seen the evidence of his sexual prowess, she'd assumed whatever had happened to him must have been pretty minor.

Whatever had happened to cause that scarring could most certainly *not* be pretty minor.

She put the two mugs down on the edge of the sewing table and moved closer to him, hand outstretched towards his shoulder to shake him gently awake, and then her eyes stuttered over the shadows beneath the dark eyelashes. He looked exhausted, and no wonder. From what she knew of him, he barely ever slept. His breathing now was rested and even. She withdrew her hand.

Why not let him sleep? Yes, she could try and contact Izzy or Poppy, but really she'd wasted enough time today already on this situation.

She tugged the multi-coloured patchwork throw from the side of the sofa. Her foster mother had made it for her and it was deliciously huge and comforting to snuggle into. She tucked it gently over him. He didn't even stir.

Five minutes later and she had her own mug of tea at her elbow as she got back to her sewing. She had the finishing touches to do on fifty-odd pairs of silk knickers. And that was just for starters.

It felt as if hours had passed when a moan of distress made her foot slip from the pedal of the sewing machine. She'd been so engrossed in her work that she'd almost forgotten she had a house guest. The room had grown dark now in the late afternoon; the small light from the sewing machine and the angled lamp above her workspace were the only sources of light. She stood up and looked curiously at Poppy's brother, sprawled in the shadows on the sofa. Deciding she must have imagined it, she moved to sit back down.

He twisted in his sleep.

She frowned. Abandoning her chair, she took a step towards him. His hands were twisting in the throw she'd draped over him and he let out another cry. Almost a shout this time, enough to make her jump. She watched his face as it contorted. Sympathy twisted in her stomach as she caught sight again of his scarred chest in the dim light. Where was he right now in his mind? In the middle of some hideous battle?

His body twisted sharply again and she couldn't stand

it any longer. She reached out to shake him awake, to take him away from whatever horror he was reliving.

First there was the vague impression of something stroking his upper arm. Tentative, not rough. And then there was the scent, something clean and flowery, like roses. It reminded Alex vaguely of his mother's dressing room back at their country home, with its antique dressing table and ornate perfume bottles and he flinched at the thought. It had been years since he'd visited the family home and he had absolutely no plans to do so in the foreseeable future. Why would he? For a place filled on and off with so many people, so many offshoots of the family, it had been bloody lonely for a kid.

He opened his eyes, disorientation making his mind reel.

He struggled to place himself in a panic. Not his army quarters. And not his room in his sister's flat, with its calming military organisation. Instead he was in a room that could only really be described as a *boudoir*. And it was getting dark.

He struggled to his feet, his mind whirling. Of course, he'd been locked out of Poppy's flat and the downstairs neighbour had offered to make him tea. That was the last thing he remembered. He looked down at himself as the quilt covering him fell away and saw that the towel around his hips was hanging askew. He snatched it closed again. Horrified, he realised he'd been sleeping here in a stranger's flat with his scars on show for her to view at her leisure.

The blonde neighbour was standing a few feet away, an expression of concern on her pretty face. The sewing machine was lit up on the desk by a bright angled lamp. A neatly folded pile of pink silk lay further down the table. A tentative smile touched the corners of her rosebud mouth.

'Are you OK?' she asked. 'You were…' a light frown touched her eyebrows '…calling out in your sleep.'

The heat of humiliation began at his neck and climbed burningly upwards as he regained a grip on reality. He'd had a nightmare. In full view of her. Had he shouted? What had he said? How could he have been so stupid as to let himself fall asleep here?

'What time is it?' he managed, rubbing a hand through his hair as if it might somehow help to clear his foggy head.

'Nearly six,' she said. 'I was just about to wake you. Poppy's home, I think—I heard her go up the stairs to the flat. So you should be able to get back in now.'

Six?

He'd slept the entire day. He avoided her eyes. What must she *think* of him, just falling asleep like that? And then having a bad dream, like some kid. He couldn't quite believe that he could relax enough to fall asleep in a strange place with a strange person. His tiredness must be a lot more ingrained than he'd thought it was.

'I can't believe I fell asleep,' he blustered. 'You should have woken me.'

'I couldn't really believe it either,' she said. 'Of course *I* think my business plan is the most interesting topic of discussion on the planet.' She smiled. 'But it made you nod off in the space of about ten minutes.'

He shook his head. What the hell must she be thinking?

'I'm sorry.'

'It's a *joke*,' she said, making a where's-your-sense-of-humour? face. 'I'm joking?'

'Right,' he said. Awkwardness filled the room, making it feel heavy and tense. He had to get out of here.

'I *was* going to wake you,' she said, 'but I didn't have the heart.'

'Oh, really?' He zeroed in on that comment. Was this some kind of sympathy vote because she'd seen his awful scars? Or worse, because he'd cried out in his sleep? He didn't do sympathy. And he didn't do bursts of emotion either. Nearly thirty years in the stiff-upper-lip environment of his military-obsessed family did that for a person. Stoicism was essential. His father had made that pretty damn clear when Alex was just a kid, an attitude later reinforced at boarding school and then in the army. Emotion was something you stamped on, definitely not something to be expressed among strangers.

'You looked so peaceful,' she went on. 'And you've clearly been getting hardly any sleep if your noise pollution is anything to go by.'

There was an edge to her voice that told him she was still narked about that. He didn't let it penetrate, there was no need to, since he had absolutely no intention of running into her again after today.

'Cup of tea?' she asked him. 'Your last one got cold. Are you sure you're OK?'

He shook his head, automatically folding the enormous throw and placing it neatly at the side of the sofa. He had no idea how she could live in such a cluttered room without going mad. It jarred his military sense of order.

'I am perfectly fine,' he snapped. 'And I've taken up

enough of your time. Now I know Poppy's back I'll get out of your way.'

He headed for the door as she watched him, a bemused expression on the pretty face.

'Bye, then,' he heard her call after him as he pulled the door shut.

A thank-you might have been nice.

Then again, she didn't have time for niceties. Neither did she give a stuff as long as Alex curbed the disruptive noise from upstairs.

Forty-eight hours had now passed with a definite reduction in noise levels although she'd seen no corresponding drop in the stream of disposable girls visiting. That was the thing about working from home for all waking hours—the comings and goings of other residents in the building amounted to distractions, and she couldn't fail to notice them. He must have moved his bed away from the radiator because the endless clanking had ceased. Not, of course, that she was dwelling on Alex Spencer's bedroom activities.

What mattered was that normal sleep quality had been resumed and thank goodness, because the launch of the shop was only a week away now. Just time to fit in a quick shower this morning and then she would head over there to add a few more finishing touches to the décor before she began to move stock in. She'd managed to track down a beautiful French-style dressing screen, the kind you might find in a lady's bedroom, gorgeously romantic. No run-of-the-mill changing cubicles for her little shop. Still, she wanted to try it out in different positions until she found the perfect location for it.

She rubbed shampoo into her hair, closing her eyes

against the soap bubbles and running through a mental list of the hundred-plus things she needed to get done today. A full-length gilt-framed mirror had been delivered the previous day; it would provide the perfect vintage centrepiece for the small shop floor, and she needed to decide where best to put that too. Then there were garlands of silk flowers to hang and some tiny white pin lights to add to the girly atmosphere she wanted to achieve.

The torrent of water rinsing through her hair seemed to be losing its force. She opened one eye and squinted through the bubbles up at the shower head. Yep. The usual nice flow was definitely diminishing. And without the sound of the running water she was suddenly able to hear a monstrous clanking noise coming from behind the wall and above her head.

'What the hell…?' she said aloud as the water reduced to little more than a trickle. The clanking built to a crescendo.

Oh, just bloody *perfect*. Naked, covered in bubbles and with her hair a bird's nest of shampoo, she climbed out of the shower unit and wrapped a towel around her. A quick twist of the sink tap gave a loud clanking spurt of water followed by nothing. She grabbed her kimono from the hook on the back of the bathroom door and shrugged it on as she took the few paces to the kitchen to check the water pressure there.

She didn't make it as far as the sink. Horrified shock stopped her in her tracks as she took in the torrent of water pouring down the wall of the living room, pooling into a flood and soaking merrily into a pile of silk camisoles she'd left in a stack on the floor.

'No-o-o!' she squawked, dashing across the floor,

picking up armfuls of her lovingly made garments and moving them to safety on the other side of the room. She kicked the metal clothes rail out of the way as she passed it, the few garments hanging at one end already splashed by the ensuing torrent of water.

She rushed to the cabinet under the sink, found the stopcock and turned off the water supply as she tried madly to rationalise what could have happened, then she stood, hand plastered to her forehead as her mind worked through the implications of all this. Some of her garments had been soaked through—there went hours of work down the drain. The water continued to spread across the floor in a slow-moving pool. She knew instinctively from the clanking in the pipes that this wasn't going to be some five-minute do-it-yourself quick-fix job. The building was ancient. Behind the glossy makeover of the flat conversion was interlinked original pipework. That much was obvious from the racket they made when the love god upstairs was entertaining.

She had absolutely no money to spare for a plumber. She wondered if any of the rest of the building was affected. Surely it wasn't just her? In a panic she opened the flat door with the intention of knocking on the door opposite and instead ran smack into Poppy, who was on her way up to her own flat with a chocolate croissant in one hand and a takeaway coffee in the other. Poppy's mouth fell open at her insane appearance.

'What the hell happened to you?'

'My flat's flooded,' Lara gabbled. 'It's like the deck of the sodding *Titanic* in there. I've got a shedload of stock in the room, my shop launches next week and I've got no hot water.'

Poppy didn't so much as flinch. She exuded utter calm.

Maybe it was a side-effect of medical training that you simply became good in any crisis. Lara shifted from one foot to the other while she leaned around her to see into the living room.

'Have you turned off the water?'

Lara nodded.

'It seems to have stopped it getting any worse. But just look at the mess.'

Poppy walked into the room and put her coffee down on the trestle table.

'I see what you mean,' she said, peering at the enormous spreading puddle on the floor and the piles of silk and velvet clothing now strewn haphazardly on the other side of the room.

'I need this room to work in and now I'll be behind with my stock levels,' Lara wailed.

The full implications of the situation began to sink in. She'd been running at her absolute limit to get the pop-up shop off the ground in so many ways, working all hours, hocked to the eyeballs financially, using her living accommodation as workspace. She had absolutely no back-up plan. Despair made her stomach churn sickly and she clutched at her hair in frustration. It felt matted and sticky from the puddle of shampoo she'd been unable to rinse out.

'Not to mention the lack of running water,' she added. 'I'll have to stick my head under the tap in the café toilets downstairs.'

'You rent, don't you?' Poppy said, unruffled, crossing the room to look at the huge dark patch on the wallpaper. 'Have you called the landlord?'

Lara sat down on the sofa and put her head in her

hands. She'd been far too busy having a meltdown of major proportions to do anything as practical as that.

'Not yet.'

'It will be down to the landlord to get it sorted, not you. You don't need to stress about cost.'

That was lucky, because *cost* was one thing she really couldn't do any more of right now.

'It isn't just that,' Lara said, pressing a hand to her forehead and trying to think rationally. Already there was a musty smell drifting from the soaked wood floor and bubbling wallpaper. 'It stinks in here—it'll permeate my stock. I'm hardly going to dominate the market with seductive lingerie that smells like a damp garden shed, am I? Not exactly alluring and sensuous, is it? And even if I could leave it here, there'll be workmen traipsing through. I can't risk any further damage. My back's against the wall with the shop opening next week. And I can't stay here anyway if there's no running water.'

She could hear the upset nasal tone in her own voice and bit down hard on her lip to suppress it. She didn't do emotional outbursts. That kind of thing elicited sympathy and she was far too self-reliant to want or need any of that. But she'd given her everything to this shop project and now it felt as if all her hard work had hit standstill in the space of ten minutes.

Poppy, who clearly didn't know or care about the not-liking-sympathy thing, joined her on the sofa, put an arm around her shoulders and gave her an encouraging smile and a squeeze.

'Come and stay with us for a few days, then, until it's sorted out,' she said. 'The boxroom's free—you'd be welcome to it. It's pretty titchy, but at least it's dry. And even better...' she waited until Lara looked at her and threw her hands up triumphantly '…I have running water! Cheer up, it'll all seem better when your hair doesn't look like a ferret's nest.'

Lara felt her lip twitch.

Poppy's grin was warm and friendly. But still the shake of the head came automatically to her, like a tic or an ingrained stock reaction. Lara Connor didn't take help or charity. She'd got where she was relying only on herself.

'I couldn't possibly impose on you like that,' she said. 'I'll be perfectly fine. I'll figure something out myself.'

Figuring something out herself had featured in a big way on her path in life. Taking offers of help didn't come easily to Lara. Relying on other people was a sure-fire route to finding yourself let down.

'You've got a headful of shampoo and no running water,' Poppy pointed out.

Lara touched her hair lightly with one hand. It was beginning to itch now, and seemed to be drying to a hideous crispy cotton-wool kind of texture. She hesitated. Her back really was against the wall over the shop. She groped for some kind of alternative solution that she could handle on her own but none presented itself. Even if she had enough room at the pop-up shop to store all her extra stock, she couldn't exactly move in and live there, could she? There was one tiny back room with a toilet, no furniture, no space, no chance.

'Stop being ridiculous,' Poppy said in a case-closed tone of voice. 'It really is *not* such a big deal. It makes perfect sense. I've got a spare room and you're stuck for a day or two. Where's the problem?'

'I don't like to impose,' Lara evaded.

Poppy made a dismissive chuffing noise.

'If you were imposing, I wouldn't ask you,' she said. 'Come on, it'll be a laugh. Things have been a bit quiet since Izzy moved in with Harry—it'll be nice to have someone else around for a bit.' She stood up. 'You can get straight in the shower and rinse that shampoo out, and then you can ring your landlord and sort out a plumber.' She made for the door as if the subject was closed.

Poppy made it all sound so straightforward. But then of course she had a proper family background, supportive childhood and, let's not forget, her big brother on the premises. She had no need to let coping with a crisis be complicated by things like pride and self-reliance and managing by yourself.

'Just a couple of days, though,' Lara qualified, finally giving in and following her. 'Just until the water's sorted out, and I'll pay rent, of course.'

With what exactly, she wasn't sure. But she would find a way. She always did. Being indebted to someone really wasn't her.

'It's only small, I know...' Poppy said apologetically.

'It's absolutely perfect,' Lara said, wondering vaguely how she could possibly fit all her stock in here. The room was tiny, the only furnishings a small dresser and lamp and the narrowest single bed Lara had ever seen. But in terms of living space, it was a gift. She supposed it might seem small to Poppy and her friends. Lara had heard them talk about boarding school and their families; spacious living was clearly the norm. Lara had had many bedrooms over the years. The dispensable bedroom was part of the package when you were working your way through the care system. She'd lived with a succession of foster families over the years and a room of your own still felt like something to be prized. And after the flood debacle, it really was. 'I can't thank you enough,' she said. 'All I need to do now is source some storage for the rest of my stock. Until the shop gets going I've got a bit of a stockpile. I'll have a look and see if there's somewhere locally that I can keep it cheaply.'

Poppy flapped a hand at her.

'There's no need for that. You don't want to be putting those gorgeous clothes in some hideous manky lockup. You can keep them in Alex's room—there's tons of space in there.' She led the way along the hall and opened the door on what was possibly the neatest room Lara had ever seen. The bed was made with symmetrical coin-bouncing perfection, the top sheet neatly folded back in a perfect white stripe across the top of the quilt. She narrowed her eyes as she took in the radiator, the ends of which were visible either side of the headboard. Goodness knew what acrobatics he'd been performing in this room to make the hideous racket she'd had to put up with.

After the cosy bohemian colour of the rest of the flat, the room was practically austere. Poppy moved to one side so Lara could see properly. Open shelving ran the length of the opposite wall, filled with perfectly folded rectangles of knitwear and T-shirts. Gleamingly polished shoes were lined up neatly in pairs along the lowest shelf. A shelf was devoted to books, their spines lined up in order of height. Not an item was out of place, not a speck of dust marred the clear floor space. A dark oak wardrobe stood at the side of the window. Lara imagined his shirts and jackets would be hung in colour co-ordinated perfection if she were to look inside.

'Wow,' she breathed.

'I know,' Poppy said, completely unfazed. 'He's a million times more tidy and organised than I am. That's what comes of being packed off to boarding school at the age of five and then later going into the military. He's the most organised, methodical person I know.'

A pang of sympathy twisted in Lara's chest at the thought of Alex as a five-year-old fending for himself when he had a family of his own back at home. She'd been forced into that situation by necessity; there simply hadn't been an alternative for her mother. She couldn't comprehend why anyone would want to send their child away when they didn't have to, and they probably paid a fortune for the privilege too.

'He does all his own washing and ironing,' Poppy was saying. 'He just needs a bit of, well, female influence in his life.'

Lara looked at her with raised eyebrows. Female influence? Poppy grinned at her.

'Maybe not *that* kind of female influence. I'm not sure he's short of that.'

He certainly wasn't, judging by the frequency of his overnight guests.

'He needs someone a bit more long-term in my opinion. He's spent far too long with only blokes for company. Who knows? Perhaps a roomful of lingerie might put him in touch with his feminine side a bit more.'

'Are you sure he won't mind having the clothes rails in here?' Lara said doubtfully. 'I mean, it's so *tidy*. I've got quite a lot of loose stuff too.'

Poppy shrugged.

'I'm doing him a favour here, letting him stay. It's my flat, after all.' She tossed her hair back. 'Do you want a hand moving in?'

CHAPTER THREE

HEADING TOWARDS MIDNIGHT, and the landing and stairs were customarily dark as Alex propelled his latest evening companion towards the top flat—Name: Susie; Age: Twenty-six; Occupation: Medical Secretary; Favourite Drink: Strawberry Daiquiri…whatever the hell that was. He'd need to ask Isaac—although he'd bought a few this evening.

He opened the front door and ushered Susie down the dimly lit hallway to his bedroom. The rest of the flat was quiet. Poppy could sleep for England and Isaac was still out of the country. This last week after his encounter with the quiet freak downstairs, Alex had found himself grudgingly attempting to keep the noise down and so he skipped his usual stop-off in the kitchen for a nightcap. Not that it had anything to do with any personal regard for Lara Connor, of course, although he had to admit to a nod of admiration for her business drive. It was more a desire to keep her off his back and live an easy life. And after the embarrassment of sleeping the day away in her flat, he'd done his best to avoid bumping into her again. To that end, he'd also shifted his bed away from the wall a little. Apparently it had worked, since he hadn't heard a word from her since.

As he opened his bedroom door it was the scent that hit him first. It assaulted him even before he flipped the light switch and it put him immediately on edge. Sweet floral notes that took him right back to the rose garden at his family home in the country. The memory wasn't a particularly welcome one. Then again there were precious few childhood memories that were. Susie hung on to his arm and stifled a tipsy giggle, which trailed away as light flooded the room.

'*This* is your room?' Her voice registered shocked disgust, and the fun tone was completely gone, as if he'd lobbed a jug of cold water over her for perfect instant sobriety. She let go of his arm. 'Oh, my God, you *live with someone*,' she wailed. 'I knew it was too good to be true. Where is she—out somewhere? Working?'

The perfect order by which he'd lived his life since he was just a small kid at boarding school, reinforced first by the cadets and then by the army, had been completely in evidence when he'd left the flat some six hours ago for his usual Friday night out. A place for everything and everything squarely in its place. In his absence the room had been inexplicably turned into what looked like a bordello. Clothes racks full of silk and satin nightwear stood alongside the wall; the floor space to one side of the room was stacked with baskets of frilly knickers and lacy bras; there was an overflowing box full of bars of ladies' French soap from which the cloying girly smell was emanating and, most unbelievably, there was a padded clothes hanger over the door of his wardrobe on which hung a long and flowing peacock-blue silk dressing-gown thing trimmed with matching marabou feathers. He felt as if he'd stumbled into some insane dream world.

He suddenly remembered Susie standing next to him and shook his head lightly as if to clear it.

'I'm not with anyone,' he said. 'I'm single.'

Her tone now shifted to sickened.

'You mean this stuff is *yours*? I should have listened to my friends, all those warnings about one-night stands and weirdos. Where's my phone?' She opened her handbag and began to paw through it. 'What are you, some kind of cross-dresser?'

'Of course not,' he said, exasperated. 'For Pete's sake, do I *look* like I might enjoy wearing women's clothing?'

'They never do,' she said, pulling out her phone and scrolling through it. 'I've watched enough reality TV to know that the ones to watch out for are the masculine types. And they never choose the kind of clothes that blend in either, oh, no. It's always a bloody prom dress.' She pointed an emphatic finger at him. 'Or a silk negligee.'

The situation was careering way out of control. He held up placating hands.

'There's obviously been some kind of a mix-up,' he said.

'Too right there has.' She turned away from him. 'Taxi, please,' she snapped into the phone. 'I'll be waiting outside Ignite, Lancaster Road, Notting Hill.'

'It's probably something to do with my sister,' he called after her as she marched back down the hallway to the front door.

'Yeah, yeah. I bet that's what they all say!' she yelled back over her shoulder.

He heard her high-heeled shoes clattering down the stairs as she made a swift exit. He turned back to his room, took in the clutter of girly clothing and breathed in the head-reeling scent of roses.

He'd had enough trouble sleeping when the room was the epitome of calm and orderliness. How the hell was he meant to manage now?

Lara woke to the muffled banging of knuckles on a door and floundered for a moment to get her bearings in the dark. She felt vaguely closed in.

It came slowly back to her overtired brain.

Flooded studio. Damaged stock. Poppy's boxroom.

The knocking continued and she wondered vaguely if it was the front door. Sex-god Alex must have locked himself out again. There was a hint of self-righteous satisfaction in that thought, especially after what she'd learned this afternoon from the emergency plumber who'd investigated the root cause of her flooded flat. A ten-minute conversation had made it clear the flood problem went a lot deeper than a need for a new washer. The old fire station might have had a modern makeover when it was converted to flats but it turned out the glossy living space papered over some serious cracks in the original pipe network. It all made perfect sense now. The pipes servicing her flat were clearly linked to those above and below, hence the insane racket from Alex's bedroom activities travelling down so effectively to her bedroom underneath.

In fact, according to the plumber, the pipework showed signs of recent stress—clearly this was what had caused the plumbing to give up the ghost. So not only was her lack of sleep down to Poppy's sex-crazed brother, but now the flooding of her flat could be attributed to him too. He was fast becoming her least favourite person and therefore any initial guilt she might have felt about imposing on him by using his bedroom to store her stuff had been very easily suppressed.

The brief temptation to just let him knock all night was trumped by the desire to tell him exactly what she thought of his nocturnal activities, the damage of which had now surpassed simple noise pollution. She threw the covers back and grabbed her robe from the back of the door.

Turned out the knocking was coming from inside the flat. She'd been right about one thing though: it was Alex again.

'Is no disruption too inconsiderate for you?' she snapped. He jumped and turned to look at her. She had a mad sense of déjà vu at the sight of him with upraised knuckles hammering on Poppy's bedroom door. Except that this time he was fully dressed. The dark blue shirt made his eyes look almost slate in the dim hallway light and her stomach gave an unexpected flip.

The ability to speak momentarily disappeared because it felt as if his tongue was stuck to the roof of his mouth. Lara's soft blond hair lay in messy bed-head waves over her shoulders. She wore a pink silk dressing gown, with wide sleeves, that ended a good couple of inches above her knees. His eyes dipped to her legs before he could stop them. The slight sheen of the silk against her skin seemed to give it a porcelain quality and the pink colour of the gown picked out the soft fullness of her mouth. He floundered for speech as the unexplained transformation of his bedroom made sudden sense. Was she somehow *staying* here? Why the hell would she be doing that when she had her own perfectly good bedroom down one flight of stairs?

The door clicked open behind him and Poppy finally staggered out, yawning and squinting at the light.

'What the hell's all the noise about? I'm on duty in a few hours.'

He took his eyes off Lara, not without some difficulty, and rounded on his sister. She looked at him with one half-lidded eye.

'My bedroom looks like a tart's boudoir,' he snapped. 'What the hell is going on?'

'For Pete's sake, it's just a few pairs of knickers,' she protested, an incredulous tone to her voice as if his room didn't look like some vintage cathouse. 'There's been a flood in Lara's flat so I've invited her to stay in the boxroom. She needed to store some of her stock for a bit and since there's *masses* of spare space in your bedroom, I couldn't see the problem. Can't this wait until the morning?'

'No, it can't,' he snapped back. 'Have you seen it in there? You didn't even ask me. It's an invasion of my privacy and I'm not going to stand for it.'

He'd always known Poppy's patience was not at its best when she was tired and he braced himself for a sibling argument of monumental proportions.

She drew herself up to her full height.

'Don't, then. Find yourself another flat if you don't like it. Or you could go back home.'

A low blow, and he could tell by the way she shifted her eyes away from him that she knew it. The subject of their inheritance from their grandparents hung between them as strongly as if it had been a visible sack of cash in the corner of the hallway. After getting access to it at the age of twenty-one, Poppy had put hers away, stashed it sensibly for the future, and now she had this flat to show for it. Living for the moment, he'd frittered his away on swanky nights out with Isaac while at university and later while on leave from the army. Expensive holidays were the order of the day. When he had time to himself, he made that time count. One particular ill-judged week in Las Vegas with the lads had reduced the pot considerably. He hadn't given it a thought at the time, hadn't needed to, because he'd had a *career*. Now that career was cut short he found he didn't have the funds any longer for a house deposit, and he needed what was left to start over. Without Poppy's offer of a place to stay he really would be reduced to returning to the family home and the thought filled him with distaste. If it was a choice between that and living in a room full of knickers, he'd just have to put up.

Poppy cast exasperated hands up at the ceiling when he didn't respond.

'I can't *do* this. I am *not* discussing your sleeping arrangements at one in the morning when I've got to be at work in a few hours. The underwear stays. You either put up with it or you move out.' She turned away and stopped any further argument by shutting her bedroom door on him. He stared at the panelled wood, feeling Lara's eyes on his back.

'She loves me really,' he said.

'I'll be out of your hair as soon as the plumbing's fixed in my flat,' Lara said, and instead of what should surely be an apologetic tone he picked up an undeniable pointed edge to her voice.

'Plumbing?'

She leaned against the hallway wall and crossed her arms. His mind insisted on noticing how the silk of the gown lovingly clung to her perfect curves. By act of sheer will, he kept his eyes on her face.

'Yes, plumbing,' she said. 'Turns out your energetic nocturnal activities have put the pipe network under too much strain.'

He stared at her.

'What the hell are you talking about?'

'Half the plumbing in this place is years old—it dates back way before the flat conversion. They might have built things to last back then, but no one reckoned on your bed being shoved up against it. The pipe running down from your bedroom radiator finally gave up the ghost today. It dislodged and because my flat's directly below it caused a flood. I've got no running water down there and damaged stock, and if it wasn't for Poppy I haven't a clue what I'd do.'

'I moved the bed away from the radiator,' he protested.

'Too little too late,' she said, and as she spoke he noticed the dark smudges beneath the indignant eyes. A twist of guilt spiked in his stomach because he'd seen how completely immersed she was in her damned pop-up-shop project. In terms of actually living a productive life right now, he'd just slipped into negative territory. Living a quiet life and not hacking anyone off surely wasn't meant to be this hard. The feeling of uselessness and lack of direction that he'd been shoving away pretty much since he'd returned to London made a sudden gut-churning comeback.

She looked on as he passed a hand tiredly over his forehead. She could feel the climb down as he spread his hands.

'Look, I'm sorry about the flood. You're sure it was down to me?'

An apology? And a marginally more genuine one this time since he really didn't have anything to gain from it. He wasn't shut out on the landing half naked now, was he? In acknowledgement she curbed her angry tone a little.

'According to the emergency plumber, the problem originated in the area of pipework attached to your radiator, so that would be a yes.'

He made a move towards the kitchen and she followed him and watched from the doorway as he filled the kettle.

'Hot drink?' he said, eyebrows raised.

She shook her head and he took a single mug from the drainer.

'Any idea on timescale?' he said. 'How long do I have to live in a *frou-frou* bordello?'

'Do you mind? My stuff is classy, not tarty,' she snapped.

He sighed. 'Of course it is.'

'The plumber did that thing where they suck in their breath and shake their head pityingly,' she said. 'I'm guessing at least a few days. Plus you have to factor in the weekend. He's made it safe but he's not going to actually *do* much else until Monday.'

He thrust an enormous heaped spoonful of instant coffee into the mug and topped it up with hot water.

'You're really going to drink that now?' she said, eyeing it. 'You'll be buzzing.'

He glanced at her. She could see the dark circles beneath his eyes even from here. Why would anyone who looked that tired want a caffeine boost?

'Yup.'

He turned around to face her, leaning back against the worktop. Her heart rate upped its pace a notch at the intense look in the grey eyes. The last time she'd been this close to him he'd been asleep, his face relaxed. Now he looked drawn and tense. He looked as if he needed a good night's sleep.

'You mentioned some stock was damaged,' he said.

She nodded and sighed.

'Some camisoles,' she said and, seeing his questioning frown, added, 'like vest tops, you know, with the string-type shoulder straps. Also some silk knickers.'

There was no denying it had been a setback. The water marks had ruined them.

He shifted awkwardly on his feet, clearly not massively comfortable with discussing women's underwear in the early hours of the morning.

'Look, I know I can't make up for the time you've lost but at least let me pay for the damage,' he said, his hand sliding around to the back pocket of his jeans. He produced a wallet and opened it.

She looked at him, surprised. An apology *and* an offer to make amends.

'It's fine,' she said, shaking her head. 'It's enough that Poppy's letting me stay here. That's a massive help. I hadn't a clue what I was going to do.'

'That doesn't help with your stock damage, though, does it?' Completely ignoring her, he pulled a wad of notes free. She stared at them, a hundred different things running through her mind that she could do if she had an extra cash injection. She rejected them all.

How easy it must be to just have access to that kind of money whenever you needed it, just paying off your problems when they arose. He probably had a massive trust fund at his disposal. She might have her back against the wall and no ready cash but what she had to show for it had never been handed to her on a plate. Everything she had was the result of hard graft. That was the way she wanted it. She didn't want to feel beholden to anyone else, that way she knew any success was hers alone and couldn't be snatched away. Yes, the pipes breaking might have been down to Alex but the whole pipe system was shot to hell as it was and there was no way she would be accepting his money. She would never have taken up Poppy's offer if she hadn't been desperate.

'I don't want your money,' she said, holding a hand up to stop his outstretched handful of notes.

He hesitated a moment, watching her face intently, and then put the money away.

'OK, then.' He took a sip of the coffee that was so black it looked like engine oil. 'But if there's anything I can do to help, let me know.'

Throwaway comment or genuine offer, she didn't know. At least he'd accepted responsibility. Her opinion of him stepped up the tiniest notch.

'I will,' she said, knowing she wouldn't. She turned for the door and headed back to bed, leaving him to sip his horrible drink and wondering what the hell problem he had with normal sleep patterns.

Sleeping in the daytime had a major drawback, Alex now found. Pitch darkness was almost impossible to achieve, background noise kept rousing him, and every time he came awake he was faced with the hideous violation of his ordered personal space. Staring at the four walls of his room in Poppy's flat was a great deal less palatable and restful now that they were festooned with women's underwear.

He eventually gave up at around three in the afternoon, showered, dressed and headed out for a head-clearing walk. The October Saturday afternoon was crisp and sunny as he turned onto Portobello Road with its buzz of shoppers. The colour and pace was rousing. He was almost past the shop before he realised it was Lara's, his overtired brain only processing the eye-catching pink and black sign when he'd taken half a dozen paces onwards.

He stopped in his tracks and backed up, looking up above the gleaming glass window, to where 'Boudoir Fashionista' was painted in a curly black handwritten font on a pink background. Another sign hung on the closed door. 'Opening Soon', it said.

Not that he hadn't had his absolute *fill* of frilly underwear back in his own home, but curiosity nonetheless meant he couldn't stop himself from just having a quick look to see what her big dream of a pop-up shop looked like inside. He moved to the glass and framed his hands around his eyes to see in.

Inside, with just a couple of overhead lights on, he could make out a counter at the back of the small shop floor, open shelving that was currently empty, some stacks of boxes, and, in the middle of it all, Lara, apparently trying to heft a package that was at least twice as big as she was across the floor. It teetered on one corner and looked momentarily as if it might topple through the plate-glass window taking her with it. What the hell was she thinking?

Before he knew what he was doing he was trying the door, and when it didn't open he knocked on it, hard. He watched as she heaved the package to lean against the wall and then practically saw her eyes roll as she clocked him watching her. She crossed to the door, undid a few bolts and opened it.

'What are you doing here?' she said. She certainly didn't sound pleased to see him.

'One wrong move and you'll be pinned under that thing for a week,' he said 'What the hell are you doing humping furniture like that around on your own?'

She glanced across at the six-foot-high package of tape and bubble wrap.

'It's a full-length mirror. I'm trying to decide where I want it.' She tilted her chin up indignantly. 'And I'm not an invalid. I'm perfectly capable of moving a few sticks of furniture around.'

Sticks of furniture? The mirror was enormous, a good couple of feet taller than she was and generously wide.

'Don't be ridiculous, you'll end up in traction. And then where will your damn pop-up shop be?' He walked straight past her into the shop and crossed to the packaged mirror. 'Where do you want it?'

For the umpteenth time he rested the mirror against the wall of the shop and watched as Lara leaned back and surveyed the floor as a whole. The shop door was closed again, but through the plate-glass window he could see shoppers rubbernecking in interest at them. She'd painted the walls the palest of rose pink. The floor was polished wood and there was an original fireplace to one side. Lara had made the most of the feature, stringing it with pale pink silk flowers and white pin lights. In the centre of the small floor space there was now a low oval French-style table painted cream. The small counter at the back of the shop had a tongue-and-groove effect in cream-painted wood and there was a painted wooden dressing screen with scrolled edging that Lara kept moving around because she couldn't decide where she wanted the changing-room area to be. The whole effect was girly enough to have him feeling completely out of his comfort zone.

'What about there?' he asked, without much hope. She'd had him move the damn thing all over the place, trying out all four walls and every corner.

She shook her head, one finger tapping at the side of her chin.

'No, I think I liked it best the way we had it first.'

He squashed his exasperation, not without some difficulty. He could appreciate perfectionism as much as the next military man but this...

He caught her looking at him, an apologetic smile playing at the corner of the lush mouth.

'I'm sorry. I'm a nightmare, I know. I just want so much for it to be perfect.'

'No problem.'

He moved the mirror back to where it had started nearly an hour ago. In the interim she'd got on with decorating the shop around him, stopping every now and then to order him about. There was a part of him that couldn't fail to be impressed by her drive and determination. Not to mention the fact that her dreams were mapped out. She had a game plan that she was clearly taking in stages. And no wonder he was intrigued by that in light of the fact that his life was currently cruising along with absolutely zero direction.

'So what's the big deal about refusing help?' he said, glancing at her as she watched him heft the mirror around. 'I mean, I did *offer* the other night. You could have just spoken up then that you needed some fittings moving around.'

'I didn't want to impose. I'm doing enough of that just by staying at the flat.'

He shrugged.

'It's no big deal. Poppy wouldn't have offered if it was. She'd do the same for any of her friends.'

His blasé tone made it clear he thought she was making a mountain out of nothing. Of course he would think that. The rich were surrounded by freeloaders, weren't they? Hangers-on probably came with the territory, and she couldn't bear the thought of being seen like that.

'I guess I'm just used to doing things by myself, that's all,' she said. 'Problems come up, I find my own way round them. I don't like to take anything or anyone for granted, so I get things done myself.'

She'd made that mistake far too often when she was a kid to make it again now.

'Even if it means getting trapped under something heavy?' he said. 'You can't shift furniture like this about yourself,' he added, his tone appalled. 'You really will injure yourself.'

'Of course I can,' she said indignantly. 'I put up the shelves myself. I painted the walls myself. I can hump and bump a bit of furniture around.'

Not that it hadn't been too heavy for her. He was right about that: it had been a struggle. Whereas he could clearly shift furniture around all day without breaking a sweat.

'Yeah, well,' he said gruffly. 'Any more of that needs doing and I want you to ask me.'

She opened her mouth to politely decline the offer and he held up a hand to stop her.

'As a favour,' he said. 'For Pete's sake, accept some help. I'm not asking you to sign your name in blood.'

His tone was final, subject closed and she found herself inclining her head in acknowledgement, not that she

would stick at it if the situation arose. She couldn't deny
it was nice to have the fittings finished in here and it
would have taken her twice as long on her own, but she
certainly didn't intend to make a habit of leaning on anyone else. Especially him.

'You're very driven,' he said, changing the subject.

She crossed to the wooden counter and pulled herself
up so she was sitting on it.

'Yeah, well, it's been a dream for a long time. Finally
trialling a shop is a really big deal for me. There's a lot
riding on it.'

Her entire savings just for starters.

'How did you get into it?' he said. 'I mean, isn't it a
pretty niche market, underwear?'

His tone was vaguely awkward and a smile rose on her
lips at his obvious fish-out-of-waterness when it came
to discussing lingerie. She imagined he would be the
type of man she sometimes encountered on her market
stall, obviously out of their depth as they chose underwear for a wife or girlfriend with no clue about bra size
or colour choice.

'I've always been into sewing,' she said. 'It's grown
from that really. Specialising in lingerie came later when
I went to college. I'm inspired by vintage fashion, that
Hollywood era where women were glossy, curvy, glamorous. When I designed my first collection I based my
ideas on that.'

She watched him positioning the mirror, not looking
at her, and her mind drifted back down the years. She
hadn't been into much of anything really as a child, apart
from keeping her head down. Until she'd been fostered by
Bridget, that was. The last in a long line of foster homes

where Lara had apparently not been a good fit. Being a *good fit* was a hideously elusive thing. She'd tried everything over the years to be that. Living with Bridget was the one and only time she'd come even close. She'd ended up staying there until she was old enough to go to college. Bridget had been a seamstress and had taught Lara everything she knew. And finding something she was not only good at but was also passionate about had been the biggest turning point in her life.

She'd realised while at college that she was talented at dressmaking. On the heels of that came the realisation that she could make a living at this if she wanted to. She could make her own stability, her own home life, without having to rely on anyone else. If she worked hard enough she'd never need to worry about being a good fit ever again. She'd have a life of her own.

'You decided against working for anyone else?' he said.

She shrugged.

'I started out that way, did some time for a high-street fashion line. But I'm a bit of a control freak. I like doing things my way. I like the idea of making my own success. I know I can rely on myself, you see. I won't be letting myself down.'

'And you learned to sew before college?'

The mirror was in place. He took a step back.

'That's perfect,' she said, jumping down from the counter. She crossed the shop to join him and began tugging the polystyrene corners and protective film off the mirror, revealing a gilt scrolled frame and flawless glass. He moved in to help her. 'I learned to sew when I was about fourteen.'

'Your mum taught you?'

She looked at him for a moment. He'd shifted a bit of furniture around. Was she really going to kid herself that he wanted to hear her life story? He was probably just being polite, filling the silences.

'Something like that,' she said.

She bundled the packaging up into a ball and shoved it into the corner next to a couple of bin bags, then turned back to survey her shop floor. It was exactly as she wanted it and excitement sparkled through her at how the project was coming together. Before she could stop herself she'd reached out to touch his arm. He looked down at her hand in surprise.

'Thanks for helping out,' she said. 'I owe you a favour.'

For the first time since she'd met him, she got a smile that didn't have an undertone of exasperation about it. It creased his grey eyes at the corner and lifted the strong mouth. He really was gorgeous and her stomach gave an unexpected flutter.

'I'll think of something,' he said.

CHAPTER FOUR

ALEX THREW HIMSELF bolt upright, panic racing through his veins, certain he'd just shouted out loud.

It had been the same as always. The windows bursting into cracks, held in place by their film covering. The feeling and sound of massive pressure beneath the vehicle as the explosion ripped through it. Smoke and dust filling the space around him, the air thick with it. He could taste the explosives in his mouth. Then the aftermath, the melting hot asphalt on the road beneath him and the disorientation as he staggered through smoke and wreckage to look for Sam and for the driver of the vehicle. Private Sam Walker had been accompanying him. One of his unit, one of his own.

He stared around him in panic, a twist of sheet clutched in one fist and the pillows damp against his back.

There was a book open to one side of the bed where he'd been trying to stave off sleep by reading. Late autumn's golden sunlight slanted through the gap in the curtains. And the bedroom was full of ladies' underwear.

His pulse slowly began to climb down towards normal, his breathing began to level. Somehow the festooning of his room with lingerie and nightwear put such a mad skew on his surroundings that it calmed him in a way

his usual military-ordered bedroom didn't. This was reality. There was no way of confusing this room with his
army existence. He was home. He was no longer part of
the army. His responsibility was discharged.

He checked his watch. Late morning. He must have finally dropped off to sleep around five. It could be worse.
Six hours' uninterrupted sleep wasn't a bad count by
recent standards. And he couldn't have shouted aloud.
Poppy and Lara were probably hanging around the flat;
they would have heard, Poppy would have burst in here
without a moment's thought. He swung his feet off the
bed and headed for the shower, stood under the torrent of
hot water. Maybe this was what counted for an improvement; maybe he would be able to get longer and longer
stretches of sleep until he could find some level of normality. He would not succumb to these nightmares. He
would get through this.

Strong coffee. That was what he needed now to get rid
of the last grasping tendrils of the dream. Five minutes
later and he was heading downstairs to the ground-floor
café and its industrial-strength espresso.

Ignite channelled quirky but cosy with a nod to the history of the building from the original fireman's pole still
in the middle of the shop. Framed black and white wall
prints hung on the exposed brickwork of the walls, showing the building when it was a fire station instead of a
block of flats. It ran a steady trade in Sunday brunch, the
air was filled with the delicious smell of frying bacon and
hot coffee and Lara was sitting at the corner table with a
pot of tea, a laptop and an untouched blueberry muffin.

She didn't even glance up as he walked in, and he
watched her at his leisure as he waited to pay for his

coffee. Her blond hair was piled up on her head today, a pink fabric flower pinned at one side, and she was wearing a fitted floral blouse that showed off her curves to perfection. In terms of distraction she easily beat Marco, who stood behind the counter, and a surge of heated interest spiked through him—interest that hadn't really come to the fore when he'd had her pegged as annoying neighbour. There was no need to fudge the fact he was looking at her because her entire attention was focused on the open laptop screen. Did she never do downtime?

'It's Sunday,' he said, coming to a standstill, coffee in hand, next to her table.

She looked up at him, china-blue eyes wide.

'And your point?'

'You're working,' he said. 'Again. Do you never take a break?'

'I *am* taking a break,' she protested. 'I'm updating my blog and I'm checking over my launch fliers and thinking about where I can hand them out.' She pushed the opposite chair out with one of her ballet flats. 'Sit down—you can tell me what you think.'

'Not sure I like what it says about me, that you think my opinion on women's lingerie might have value,' he said. Then the immediate need for coffee won over and he sat down and took the pale pink piece of stiff card she held out.

'You'd be surprised how many of my customers are men,' she said. 'Hanging round the market stall looking awkward, usually on a quest for something red with peepholes. I soon put them straight. Women like classy and glamorous, not tarty.' She pointed at him with her pen. 'So, actually, I'd be interested in your feedback.'

He looked over the invitation with its loopy black handwriting and silhouette image of a curvy female form.

'You're having a launch party on Thursday night?' he said.

She nodded.

'I'm opening from six until eight. Late-night shopping with pink champagne and nibbles, that kind of thing. You'll come, won't you?' She swept on breezily before he could get in an immediate thanks-but-no-thanks. 'I've invited half the building to drop by. Poppy's coming, and Izzy and Tori. I just need to drum up as much interest as I can, need to think about where I can hand these out. Marco says I can put a stack of them on the counter in here.' She pressed a hand to her forehead. 'And I'm doing a big post about it on my blog, and then I need to keep building up the anticipation on the Facebook page. Not to mention tweeting about it…'

He held up a hand to stop the stream-of-consciousness torrent.

'You'll drive yourself into an early grave. When did you last take a break?'

She waved a hand at the untouched blueberry muffin and half-full teacup and raised her eyebrows.

'This is *not* a break,' he said, exasperated. 'You're putting yourself under far too much pressure. What you need is fresh air and exercise.' The words were out of his mouth before he registered what he was doing. 'Come for a run with me this afternoon.'

She stared at him as if he'd just suggested she jog naked down Portobello Road.

'Are you insane? I don't do running.'

'I know,' he said. 'I can tell by the way you're so manic. Physical fitness feeds the mind. You'll be able to work twice as efficiently afterwards.' He nodded at her muffin. 'Much better than the sugar rush you'll get from eating that stodge.'

She narrowed her eyes at him, as if trying to decide whether he was joking.

'Really?'

He nodded, taking a huge swig of his coffee.

'One hour. You can spare one hour. And you do owe me a favour. I'm fed up with running on my own.'

It was becoming clear that being alone with his thoughts might not be the best therapy for dwelling on the past. And testing though it might have been heaving furniture around her shop the previous day, it had also been the first hour in a while that he'd been engaged enough by something that the past hadn't encroached on his thoughts. The rest of the day yawned emptily ahead of him without his current distraction of choice—female company. And it occurred to him as she leaned forward to speak to him, giving him a fabulous view of her perfect creamy cleavage, that he was a fool. There was no sense in trawling bars and clubs on Sunday daytime when he had a perfectly good contender right here.

'I meant cooking you lunch or buying you a coffee,' she said. 'Not letting you distract me from my work to run round Notting Hill like a headless chicken.'

'My runs are structured, not some random dash,' he countered. 'You're so manic that you'll probably find it calming to do something physical for a change.'

She paused.

'And we can distribute some leaflets while we're out,' he said.

She tilted her chin upwards in a way that told him *that* was the real pull for her in this scenario. Everything she did seemed to be about furthering her damn business plan.

'Done,' she said. 'And I am *not* bloody manic.'

She slammed the downstairs door of the flats behind her and saw that he was already there. Ready and waiting for her in running gear that was worn in enough to show he took his fitness extremely seriously. She glanced longingly through the window of Ignite, where she could be sitting right now with her laptop and a doughnut. She forced a smile, turned to face him and clocked his bemused expression.

'What?' she said as he looked her up and down. 'I'm not some gym bunny, you know, with all the kit. I did the best I could in the time.' She looked down at herself. 'I borrowed the running shoes and shorts from Poppy. The T-shirt's my own. I embellished it myself.'

'You don't say,' Alex said, staring at the loose cotton T-shirt, the front of which was smothered in a sprinkling of pink sequins. Her hair was caught up in a ponytail and tied with a pink scarf and she was wearing pink lipstick. He wondered for a moment why the hell he had thought this would be a good idea.

She moved behind him and unzipped his backpack.

'What the hell are you doing now?'

A wave of her floral perfume as she leaned in close to him knocked his senses off-kilter. He craned around to see her stuff a wad of her pink leaflets into the bag.

'This is meant to be for an energy drink, or an iPod, or a mobile phone, not masses of stuff,' he grumbled.

'It's just a few leaflets,' she said, totally ignoring him and zipping it back up. 'No need to roll your eyes—you must be used to lugging ten-stone backpacks across deserts for days at a time. A few slips of paper are hardly going to weigh you down.'

He nodded down the street.

'Holland Park's in that direction. Brisk walk first,' he said as she began limbering up and jogging from foot to foot. 'You need to warm up properly, don't want to pull any muscles.'

She kept pace with him as he started down the road, and five minutes later they turned into the park. Holland Park was quiet and peaceful with lots of open green space, but also nature trails and walkways and a stunning Japanese garden. The ground was covered in temptingly kickable autumn leaves in red and gold and the air was crisp and clear. Trees filtered golden sunshine. The appeal of running, which had so far eluded her, kicked in. This place was a real haven from the buzz of the city.

There was something about his hugely muscled frame in its well-worn sportswear that made walking fast look cool as opposed to looking as if he were late for a bus or rushing for a toilet. She really wasn't sure she could pull cool off in Poppy's shorts, which were really on the small side for her curvy hips but gaped massively at her waist. She retied the drawstring grimly and tugged her T-shirt down as far as she could.

She must have been mad to agree to this. She could have been spending this time drafting the next couple of days' worth of Facebook posts, uploading the photos she'd taken of some of the new raspberry silk knickers she'd designed with the frills on the butt.

Alex made a valiant effort not to let his eyes slide continually down to her bare legs. This close it was impossible not to notice the smooth cream of her thighs, and there was a fragility to the porcelain skin and blond hair, blue eyes colouring that belied how strong-willed and driven she really was.

'Have you done any running before?' he asked.

She shrugged.

'I've been able to do it since I was a toddler.' She sighed as he pulled an unimpressed face. 'No, I haven't. Not proper running. Not since I was at school. I'm not some madly fit exercise freak—it has to fit around everything else in my life.'

'Any exercise at all?'

'I like swimming,' she said unexpectedly. 'I used to go a lot. No time for it since I came here though. I let everything slide really that isn't related to the business. It's only a couple of months. I wanted to throw everything I've got into it.'

A spike of envy at her sense of purpose jabbed him behind the ribs. He couldn't help admiring her focus and determination, that refusal to let anything divert her from her goal.

'We'll take it steady, then,' he said. 'One minute gentle jogging, then one minute walking. Ready?'

He broke into a slow jog and she followed suit next to him.

'What about relationships?' he said after a moment.

Just because he'd never seen her with a man, didn't mean there wasn't one.

She let out an amused noise alongside her speedy breathing.

'Some of us just don't have time for that stuff,' she panted.

He couldn't fail to miss the barb in that comment.

'Meaning that I do—right?' he said.

He glanced at his watch and slowed down into a walking session, keeping it brisk to maintain the heart rate. She kept pace next to him, clearly not as unfit as she'd made herself sound. Then again, he couldn't remember the last time he'd met anyone with so much energy. She was constantly on the go.

She took the bottle of water he passed to her and took a sip. He was aware of her watching him over the bottle.

'I suppose everyone's entitled to *some* time out,' she conceded. 'How long will you be staying with Poppy? She said something about an honourable discharge. Is that permanent? No going back to the army?' She handed the bottle back.

He gritted his teeth.

'I won't be going back. The discharge is an end to it. That chapter of my life is well and truly over.'

Saying it out loud made it no more palatable. It still felt vaguely unreal, even months later, with everything tied up.

'You don't sound so pleased about that.'

He shrugged.

'I'm not. I didn't want to be discharged—the army was my life.'

She didn't comment for a minute or two, but he could feel her eyes on him.

'I saw your scars,' she said at last. 'When you fell asleep in my flat.' Her voice was full of sympathy. 'I'm really sorry.'

He carried on walking in silence for a moment, noticing she didn't push for any more details. The gap sat there in the conversation, and she was leaving it to him to elaborate.

'There was an incident,' he said eventually. That word seemed so inadequate as a description. The relentless guilt churned sickly in his stomach as he recalled it. Guilt that he was walking through this glorious park while Sam, who he'd promised to look out for, had been gone in an instant on Alex's watch.

'A roadside bomb,' he clarified.

He indicated the left side of his chest lightly. 'This was down to shrapnel—it sliced below my shoulder blade and then settled in my chest muscle. The medics removed it but there wasn't much they could do about the scarring.'

The physical side of the injuries he could talk about. She certainly wasn't the first woman to ask about them. Coping with them and recovering at breakneck speed had been his way of proving his strength, to himself as much as anyone. He clenched his fists lightly. If only putting the experience out of his mind could be as straightforward. Nagging doubt about his mental strength continued to plague him. The sickening guilt that he'd failed Sam was never far away, seething beneath the surface of his mind. He had offered encouragement to that young soldier when he'd struggled at first with his posting. He had helped him get a handle on his fears. He had assured Sam he would look out for him and he'd let him down on an epic scale.

The frustration that he couldn't seem to just fast-track the recovery of his mind in the same way as his body was relentless, and worse was what that said about his strength or weakness as a soldier.

'You're lucky to have your family to support you through something like that,' she said.

The ludicrousness of that comment brought a laugh that he failed to suppress.

'Did I say something funny?'

He glanced sideways at her, saw her puzzled frown and shook his head.

'I'm not laughing at you. My family aren't really like that, except for Poppy. We're not close. Stiff upper lip and all that.'

He kept walking, wondering if she'd let the subject drop now.

'What are your plans now, then?' she said. 'If the army's out of the question.'

Apparently not. He shook his head.

'I haven't got a clue. I've known exactly how my life would play out since I was knee high. There was a long line of military family members to live up to when I was growing up, never any question that was the route I'd take. Tons of army anecdotes bandied around at family gatherings. I enrolled at Sandhurst when I finished university and then pushed myself up the ranks. My future was mapped out. To suddenly not have one is a bit of a curved ball, to be honest.'

Understatement of the year.

'OK, then, well, what was your Plan B? You have to have a back-up plan. Like me, for example, if this pop-up shop doesn't work out then I'll probably look into building up an online presence more, try pushing the internet shopping angle. You must have at least an idea of the direction you want to take, even if you haven't pinned it down to a specific career path.'

'I've never needed a Plan B. What would be the point? My Plan A spanned pretty much the whole of my life. I thought if I took a bit of time out and stayed with Poppy I could work out my next move.' He thought for a moment. 'It would have to be something active, I think. I'm not sure I'm suited to sitting behind a desk.'

She didn't answer and he checked his watch.

'Time's up, let's pick up the pace again,' he said.

Twenty minutes of alternating jogging and brisk walking and he had to admit she wasn't the ditsy glamour girl
she seemed. Not entirely anyway. Although he could see
from the flush high up on her cheekbones and the damp
tendrils of blond hair escaping her ponytail that she'd
pushed herself, she'd nonetheless kept pace with him for
the full distance.

'You've done well,' he said. 'You sound like you have zero
time for exercise but you must be doing something right.'

She shrugged and smiled, pushed a damp lock of hair
out of her eyes.

'I'm always on the go. The business keeps me really
busy, especially at the moment. I've thrown everything
I've got at this pop-up shop. All my spare money's tied
up in it. I've got no choice but to make it work.'

'Doesn't that worry you, having so much invested in
it?'

She smiled.

'If I stopped to worry about everything that could go
wrong, I'd never get anywhere. You can't get rid of any
risk completely. I mean, I'd planned this move into retail within an inch of its life but I hadn't factored in the
problem with the plumbing in my flat. If it hadn't been
for Poppy offering me the boxroom I would have been
in serious trouble there.' She shrugged. 'But you have
to accept some risk if you're going to move forward.
Sometimes you just have to put yourself out there to
reach your goal.'

It was hard not to get swept along by her drive. That
dogged refusal to contemplate failure. She made any-

thing seem possible. Spending time with her was like having an injection of optimism and, goodness knew, he had been in dire need of some of that these past months.

He slowed to a standstill as they approached a fenced-off playground area and nodded at a park bench.

'Need to cool down now,' he said. 'Stretches. Last thing you need is to pull a muscle.'

She followed him reluctantly to the bench and gripped the back of it in the same way he was, self-consciousness kicking back in. A stone's throw away the sandy-floored playground was jam-packed with small children clambering over wooden equipment and rubbernecking Notting Hill mums. Alex Spencer, ex-army, with his honed body hot and sweaty in muscle-hugging sportswear, was clearly a big distraction to the female species at large.

'Now stand on one leg and hold the other leg behind you, hold your foot above the ankle,' he instructed, oblivious to the fluster he was causing in the playground.

Clearly her attempt at the exercise was inadequate because he was suddenly in her personal space, one hand pressed softly at her lower back, holding her steady and the other covering her hand as she gripped her own ankle, holding her foot high behind her. She felt envious eyes boring into her back from the direction of the playground.

'Feel that stretch?' he said.

Maybe she would do, if she weren't too busy feeling unexpectedly *melty* at the closeness of his muscular body and his huge hands on her. There really was no denying how breathtakingly gorgeous he was. There was also no way she was going to have a swooning moment over him. She had far too much on her plate to let *that* kind of distraction slip past her guard.

'Absolutely,' she said loudly.

* * *

Another half-dozen or so stretches out of the way and it occurred to Lara that she was missing a trick right there with Alex's captive audience. Unzipping his small rucksack, she removed a wad of leaflets and crossed to the playground while he leaned against the back of the bench and swigged from a bottle of water.

She walked into the playground and handed a leaflet to anyone who made eye contact.

'Lingerie?' A dark-haired woman with a designer pushchair took a leaflet and read it with interest.

'It's a pop-up shop,' Lara said, full of pride. 'In Portobello Road. Boutique lingerie and nightwear. Vintage inspired. I'm having a launch party on Thursday and I'll be there for the next couple of months. I'd love it if you'd drop in. And tell your friends.'

'Maybe that's the secret, then. I need to get me some boutique lingerie.'

She nodded in Alex's direction with a knowing wink.

Lara laughed out loud, glossing over a deep-down glimmer of pride that it clearly wasn't *that* outrageous a suggestion that she could be the other half of someone who looked like an Adonis.

'We're not together! He's just my...' she searched for the right description '...*running partner*.' As if she had time for daily jogs around parks and sets of stretches. 'Military-style personal training,' she added, purely off the top of her head.

She followed the gaze of the yummy-mummy contingent as Alex, seemingly oblivious to the attention, poured a few lugs of the water over his head and tousled it through his short hair.

The dark-haired woman leaned in towards her.

'Bloody hell, having him as a personal trainer would be way more motivating than the gym.'

'There you go, doesn't your head feel clearer for that?' he said as they headed back to the flat.

Well, she hadn't thought about the shop for half an hour or so, if that was what he meant. Not that it had anything to do with exercise, more about being fascinated by the reality of what she'd simply assumed was a privileged and fabulous upbringing. Plus there was the physical diversion provided simply by looking at him. Of course, she hadn't been the only one seduced by that—he'd had half the playground drooling over him.

'That could be your Plan B, right there,' Lara said, nodding back towards the park as they walked away.

Alex looked sideways at her.

'What do you mean?'

'Personal training,' she said. 'You wouldn't be short of clients. I mean, just look at you. You're a bored lady-who-lunches' dream. You could be the new Zumba.'

'I'm not sure if that's a compliment or an insult,' he said. 'On the whole I'm leaning towards insult.'

'Who cares which it is if you can make money out of it?' she said, her eyes shining. He could almost see her mind ticking over as she thought through whatever insane idea it was she was trying to pitch. 'You could make a killing. Once I'd told them you were just taking me for a run and they got past the fact that we weren't an item I nearly got trampled in the rush. You did *say* you didn't fancy some desk job. You're bored with exercising on your own instead of bawling out squaddies on route marches or whatever, so take on a couple of clients and earn some cash while you're at it. At the very least it could be a stopgap until you decide what you really want to do.'

'I'm not sure,' he said doubtfully, struggling to keep up with the torrential pace of her mind. She totally ignored him.

'OK, then, maybe not *exactly* that, but what I'm saying is you need to put yourself out there, try out some ideas, maybe think outside the box and make your own opportunity. The perfect job isn't just going to materialise like magic and drop in your lap while you hibernate in your sister's flat and pop out every now and then to pull women. What about a fitness boot camp for kids? You've got that military presence thing going on—no one would dare backchat you. The country's full of overweight teenagers sitting playing Call of Duty or chatting on Facebook. You could be a one-man combat for the obesity crisis. I can see it now—*Rid Notting Hill of Couch Potatoes.*' She held her hands up as if imagining the slogan as a headline.

The first spark of positivity he'd had in weeks unexpectedly lifted his spirits. Insane though some of her stream-of-consciousness ideas were, it was hard not to get swept along by her enthusiasm. She made anything seem possible and she was becoming more distracting by the second.

'Oh, and you have to come to the launch now,' she said airily. 'A few of them asked for business cards and, of course, you don't have any, so I handed out my leaflets instead. You could literally *see* their ears prick up when I mentioned you'd be there.'

Oh, just bloody *great*.

As he followed her up the stairs to the flat the rest of the afternoon now seemed to lie empty ahead of him, especially as he was actually feeling positive for a change. Optimistic, even. A half-hour chat with Lara and her energy and enthusiasm was infectious. Already his mind was running with the idea of some kind of business centred around fitness; it could fit his skills set on so many levels.

He didn't want their encounter to be over. It wasn't just that she was so distracting, it was how cute she looked with her blond hair dishevelled for once instead of polished, the flush of her cheeks from the exercise, the smooth shapely legs in the shorts. It was how she made anything seem possible. He liked her. On every level. And since his own fitness level was way above a thirty-minute jog-walk session, he was now a mass of pent-up mental and physical energy. He was at a loose end until the end of the day. Taking all of this into account, the perfect afternoon scenario was obvious.

Prolonging the afternoon with her in his bed would be the perfect solution.

'Would you like to get a drink?' he said, thinking ahead. Drink, chat in the sitting room, ending up in his bedroom.

'Ooh, yes, that would be perfect,' she said. 'Could you make me a pint of lemon squash while I have a quick shower?'

Not exactly what he had in mind. He followed her past the kitchen and she turned back to him at the door of the boxroom, tugging the band out of her hair and ruffling it. Anticipatory sparks were simmering hotly in his stomach at the thought of where this could lead.

'Thanks for the run,' she said. 'I'm expecting my productivity to at least double this afternoon now, otherwise I'll be lodging an official complaint.' She was looking up at him, smile on her face, her eyes shining and cheeks pink from the fresh air and exercise. The relaxed look was such a contrast to her usual polished style and it suited her. She looked absolutely adorable and he reached a hand out to tuck a stray lock of hair behind her ear.

Her initial reaction was shocked surprise at the unexpected touch, and as a result sensibility took a few moments to kick in. A few moments in which he cradled the nape of her neck in one of his huge hands and executed the most deliciously bone-melting kiss she'd ever had. Her body clearly couldn't give a toss about sensibility and kicked straight in with a hike in her heart rate and a mass of hot fluttering in her stomach.

Her mind had been set so resolutely in work mode these last weeks that all thoughts of her personal life had been swept under the carpet. It simply hadn't entered her radar that there could be any more to this than…well, than a *run*. Also, he looked like a sportswear model and she was currently hot, sweaty and wearing a hideous ill-fitting shorts and T-shirt combo. All of which might not have mattered one bit if the fact that he usually picked his women up for one night only hadn't popped into her mind. That last thought brought common sense whizzing back and she disentangled herself from him just as he was sliding his free hand around her waist.

He was clearly at a loose end for the rest of the day and couldn't see the point in going out on the pull when he now had someone living in. Whereas she had three days and counting before the shop launch and a million and one things to do in that short space of time.

She'd had enough disposable people dip in and out of her life to add another one. Relationships in her opinion should be about stability, not about shallow motives, not something that could be picked up and put down on a whim. Not that she hadn't partaken in an occasional flurry of dating, always when she was between projects or had a bit of extra time on her hands, but so far none of those flurries had translated into anything that could survive being shoved aside by what was *really* important in her life: her work ambitions. That held true more than ever right now because things were at such a pivotal point. More than anything she needed to keep focus, keep her wits about her. No being distracted from her goals because she'd been propositioned by the fittest guy she'd come across in years.

She locked her knees before they could slide out from under her.

There was no denying her attraction to him. He could see it in the speed of her breathing and the hard peaks of her nipples through the thin sequinned T-shirt. Nonetheless, deny it she did.

'I'm sorry, Alex.' Just the way she said his name upped the heat in his stomach a notch. 'I've got too much to do to while away an afternoon in bed with you.'

'I wasn't thinking about being idle.'

He saw the blush that comment invoked and liked it.

'And attractive though a hot fling might be to some people, I'm not that kind of girl. And even if I was, I'm juggling enough things as it is right now. I daren't add sex to the mix or the whole lot could go tits up.'

He shrugged.

'There's no need for it to be complicated,' he said. The worst thing he could have said, apparently, because she took an extra pace back and gave him a my-mind-is-made-up smile.

'Why does that not surprise me?' she said. 'I know your routine better than you do. I've lived downstairs from it for weeks. I'm not interested in being one of your disposable pickups, making the walk of shame the morning after. I'm better than that. I don't do one-night stands or shallow flings. If and when I meet someone I intend it to have some meaning a bit deeper than a quick tumble in your bed.' She shrugged. 'Plus I'd like to be able to live in the same flat as you without things getting awkward. I'd like to have coffee with you or go running with you without any tension. I don't need any hassle in my life.'

Hassle? He stared after her as she headed for the bathroom.

'Where does that leave us, then?' he called, just before she shut the door on him.

'Exactly where it did before,' she called back. '*Flatmates*, Alex. I'm going to take a shower and get back to work.'

He hadn't expected a knockback. Mainly because they never happened.

From his room he could hear the shower running, his mind insisting on imagining her naked curves wet and covered in soap bubbles, and then various doors opening and closing as she returned to the boxroom, changed clothes and left the flat, presumably on her way to the shop. He lay on his bed with his hands clenched, his entire body a coiled spring of latent sexual tension. He could still feel the full softness of her top lip between his own, could imagine the creamy silk of her bare thighs beneath his hands. And kicking around the empty flat was making him feel worse by the second.

He left his room for the bathroom, showered, dressed and headed for the front door. What the hell? There were plenty of other single women out there who weren't work-aholics.

CHAPTER FIVE

So much for fresh air and exercise aiding productivity. Lara had spent the past few hours shoving Alex Spencer and his delicious kiss firmly out of her mind only to find him right back there again five minutes later. Which only made her even more furious with herself when she eventually returned to the flat to discover the woody scent of his aftershave still lingering in the bathroom and no sign of him in the place. Based on what she knew of him, there was only one explanation: Her knockback a few hours earlier hadn't fazed him one tiny bit. He'd simply refocused his efforts in the usual direction. He'd clearly gone out on the pull.

Why did it bother her so much?

The churning deep in her stomach felt an awful lot like disappointment. Had she really been hoping that the interest he'd shown in her—moving fittings around for her in the shop, cajoling her into taking time out—might stem from genuine liking and concern? It was plain as day that what he really was hoping to gain from it was an easy lay. She should never have expected anything else and she didn't have time to spare to be sucked into this stupid debate with herself.

Poppy was making toast in the kitchen.

'No Alex?' she said, smiling as Lara walked in. 'You two seemed to be getting on like a house on fire.'

Lara shook her head and uttered a light laugh.

'No, he's just been giving me a hand shifting stock, that's all. I don't think he wants to get to know me beyond flatmate levels. Plus he seems to have a crazy social life and I'm up to my eyeballs in work.'

She could hear herself gabbling, protesting too much, and forced herself to stop before Poppy picked up on it. She had absolutely zero interest in how Alex Spencer was spending his evening. She crossed to the counter and concentrated on putting the kettle on.

Poppy sat down at the table.

'I'm not sure his social life is all it seems, to be honest,' she said, nodding her head as Lara held up a mug with a questioning expression. 'He's been through a lot these last few months.'

Lara busied herself, getting together instant coffee and milk from the fridge.

'You mean his injuries? He hasn't really mentioned them.'

Poppy shook her head.

'He wouldn't. He wouldn't let anyone fuss over him, even when he was in the hospital. He doesn't want sympathy, thinks that should all be directed at the soldier who lost his life. The lad was younger than Alex, such a waste.' She looked up at Lara. 'You have to understand his army mates were like family to him. I think that made it a lot harder. He feels responsible.'

Lara's mind reeled with the information. What exactly had Alex been through?

'It's not just the physical injuries. To him they're part of the job. He accepted that risk when he signed up. If

anything, leaving the army seems to have been more of
a wrench.'

Lara nodded.

'He did mention he was looking for a new direction.
I tried to brainstorm a few work suggestions for him.'

Poppy stared at her in surprise.

'Did you? It's more than he's let any of us do.'

And what exactly did *that* mean? That he was interested in what she had to say? Her heart gave a tiny and
poorly judged skip because it was a far more likely scenario that Lara was too pushy and hadn't let him get a
word in.

'Just because we come from a big family doesn't necessarily mean there's a big support network going on
there,' Poppy went on. 'And it's especially difficult for
Alex when it comes to army stuff. My father's had an in-
credibly successful army career, really full-on stuff. He
works for the United Nations as a military advisor and
that's meant a lot of travel over the years, for him and for
my mother. Alex and I had a nanny when we were very
young, then boarding school when we were old enough.
Alex went from school to university to Sandhurst then
straight into the army. He had his whole life mapped
out—right from the get-go he knew where he was heading and he seemed happy with that. He threw himself into
army life, climbed the ranks at breakneck speed. It was
like he was born to do it.' She gave Lara a rueful smile.
'In a way I suppose he was.'

Lara looked down at her coffee mug.

'He can be a bit gruff sometimes but don't be too hard
on him. His whole life has changed, his whole future,
and not through his choice. I'm not sure he's having an
easy time coming to terms with that—that's partly why

I offered him the room here. The last thing he needs is
my father harping on about military careers when Alex
has had to give his up.'

Fresh air and exercise had also failed epically at living
up to the promised restful sleep. One ear cocked for the
expected arrival of Alex with unnamed conquest, furious with herself for actually being *interested*, Lara finally
dropped off somewhere in the small hours. And now her
alarm was going off, it was still dark and it occurred to
her as she stared one-eyed at her own haggard reflection in the bathroom mirror while she brushed her teeth
that she'd been so preoccupied with Alex's behaviour the
previous day that she'd forgotten today's plans involved
moving her stock from the flat to the shop.

Stock that was currently being stored in his bedroom.
Where he was, presumably, holed up with whatever conquest he'd managed to pull the previous night. She might
not have heard him make it home but that didn't make
her any less certain he was in there. And since he had
the most erratic sleep routine of anyone she'd ever met,
he could sleep in for *hours* yet.

She didn't have hours. Time was, as usual, of the essence. She couldn't just tiptoe around him; she had work
commitments. That the thought of seeing him in bed with
another woman made her feel icky had absolutely no
place in the debate, and she crushed the unhappy churn
in her stomach as she walked down the darkened hallway.

She paused outside his bedroom door. Should she
knock? On one hand it would be the polite thing to do,
but then again it was only just coming up to six o' clock
in the morning. October mornings included pretty full-
on darkness at this time. Surely it would be far easier

and much quicker to just tiptoe into the room and start by taking the stock nearest the door, mainly stuff that was boxed. She could leave the big clothing rails and the boxes near the window until later, when hopefully he would be up and his bedroom companion had been dispatched.

She held her breath and pressed the door handle down, eased the door open a crack and crept into the room.

As sleepless nights went, it made a change to be kept awake by something other than nightmares or sex.

Alex had undertaken his usual strategy the evening before, and he'd had no trouble finding company in the bar he went to. He never did. Unfortunately the rest of the evening hadn't panned out in the usual way. Engaging in conversation was even more wearing than usual and, worse, he seemed to have no real interest in where the evening was heading. He felt antsier than ever and the company just wasn't cutting it. At a little past midnight he'd made his excuses and returned to the flat. Alone. And sleep had eluded him ever since.

That Lara had knocked him back needled at his pride, yes, but it wasn't just about the snub. Nor was it the physical pull of her. She was very pretty, of course, and the girly, glamorous clothes she chose with her curvy figure and creamy skin really did it for him. It was both those things but more than that too. He *liked* her. More than he was used to liking someone. She had a zest for life that was intoxicating to him in this limbo state he felt so trapped in. She had her own goals, her own standards, without reference to anyone else's. And she made him feel as if he could have that too.

Somewhere before dawn, as he was finally drifting

towards dropping off through sheer exhaustion, he heard the bedroom door snick open.

The dim light from the hallway lit her up in silhouette and her light perfume drifted across the room, putting his senses right back on standby.

Lara was creeping into his room under cover of darkness and surely there could be only one explanation why she might do that. Perfectly understandably, she'd spent the rest of yesterday having second thoughts about knocking him back, probably followed by a sleepless night, and now she'd decided to take matters into her own hands.

He watched, his eyes completely accustomed to the darkness, since he'd been lying in it for the past five hours. She tiptoed to the side of the bed, and, really, was that her best attempt at stealth?

There was a clatter as she caught her foot on one of the wretched metal clothes rails and then a moment later a muffled yelp as she fell over a box. And then she picked herself up and paused, obviously gauging whether she'd woken him or not. He saw her head on one side in the semi darkness, as if she was listening closely.

In one swift movement, he leaned up from the bed, caught her around the waist and pulled her into his lap. Waited for her to melt into his arms as he groped for her mouth with his, his whole body firing up with hot anticipation.

Instead of the anticipated breathy sigh she let out an anguished squawk that wouldn't have gone amiss on a throttled parrot and karate-chopped him in the neck.

Thirty seconds later and Lara had disengaged herself from him, scrambled across to the light switch and snapped it on, all the while hideous thoughts tumbling through her mind of threesomes and goodness knew what else. She stared across the room at him as he blinked in the bright light, sheets pooled around his waist, super-toned naked torso, short hair lightly dishevelled. And she couldn't stop herself exclaiming in surprise.

'You're on your own!' she said.

Alex, sitting at the scrubbed kitchen table in a T-shirt and shorts, held up two fingers as she spooned instant coffee into a mug for each of them and she rolled her eyes as she added a second spoonful for him.

'No wonder you're perpetually awake,' she remarked.

'Yeah, well.' He looked at her over the rim of his coffee mug as she handed it to him. 'My sleep pattern may have become a bit...' he paused '...off balance since I got back. And don't change the subject. What the hell were you doing sneaking around my bedroom in the small hours if you weren't planning on jumping my bones?'

Was there no end to his arrogance when it came to women?

'I can't believe you'd just assume that,' she said.

He continued to look at her, eyebrows raised, and she took a big sip of her coffee.

'I was coming in to get my stock,' she said. 'I want to start taking it over to the shop today. There's still so much to do to get the shop ready before Thursday and I've still got to organise food for the launch evening to hand round with the pink champagne but I haven't even looked at it yet.' She sighed. 'I'm sorry I woke you. I was trying to be as quiet as I could.'

A herd of elephants might have a better line in stealth than she did, in his opinion.

'You didn't wake me,' he said shortly. 'I couldn't sleep.'

'Even without a…' she paused to pull a disapproving face '…*companion*, you're still awake half the night? Don't you *ever* sleep?'

He had absolutely no desire to discuss his sleep patterns with her or anyone else.

'And there was no need to sound so damn shocked,' he carried on, ignoring the question. 'I don't bring women back every night.'

She was watching him steadily, eyes narrowed.

'And even if I did, I don't see that there's anything wrong with that. We're all consenting adults.'

She shrugged, not meeting his eyes, but her body language screamed disapproval.

'Whatever floats your boat, I suppose.'

'What's that supposed to mean?'

She tipped the rest of her coffee down the sink and put the mug in the dishwasher. He could literally see her disengaging from the conversation.

'Nothing. Just that having disposable people in my life isn't really my bag. To me it just seems like a horrendous waste of time. Time I haven't got to spare.'

'That's because you obviously haven't had a *disposable person* in your life who's any good,' he countered, holding her gaze until he saw the blush climb up her cheekbones. Nothing was easy with her. He couldn't remember coming across someone who felt so damned challenging and it was clear that talking the talk wasn't going to cut any ice when it came to impressing her. He'd have to try a more practical approach.

He stood up and walked round the table towards her and rinsed his mug out at the sink. The heady floral scent of her French perfume made his senses reel.

'Come on, then,' he said, leading the way back to his room. 'If you need to get your damn stock.'

'Back to bed, is it, now?' she called after him.

'Well, I'm hardly going to get any sleep now with you clattering in and out, am I? Tell me what needs shifting and I'll give you a hand.'

His third navigation of the narrow stairwell and of all the bloody people to bump into when he was loaded down with boxes of knickers.

Isaac slung his duffel bag over his other shoulder and stared.

'You're back, then,' Alex said, stating the obvious.

'What the hell are those? And that?'

He pointed out the clear polythene clothes cover hanging over Alex's arm, through which peacock-blue satin and feathers were visible.

'It's a negligee,' Alex said. Since he'd moved in with a gang of women it felt as if a whole new world of vocabulary had opened up. 'And these are ladies' knickers.'

'Seriously?' Isaac pulled a shocked face. 'I leave the country for a couple of weeks and suddenly you're the authority on women's underwear. Is there something you're not telling me?'

For Pete's sake.

'I'm moving some stock for the girl who lives downstairs. *Lived* downstairs,' he corrected. 'She's taken Poppy's boxroom. Long story. She runs an underwear shop.'

Lara chose that moment to back out of the flat door behind him with an armful of lacy bras.

'Lara, this is Isaac.'

She nodded at him, squeezed past them on a cloud

of delicious perfume and disappeared down the stairs. Isaac watched her go.

'I take it all back,' he said, clapping Alex on the shoulder. 'Nice work.'

'It's not like that,' he said. He was beginning to wonder what the hell it *was* like.

CHAPTER SIX

LARA HAD DECIDED on a pale pink fitted dress that she'd designed herself, hoping it would hit the right note of old-school Hollywood glamour, and teamed it with heels that would kill her feet after a couple of hours but which gave the perfect impression. Drinks and nibbles were laid out on a temporary table in the middle of the shop, fairy lights were in place and switched on, lending a soft girly note to the shop floor. Every item of stock was lovingly hung or folded in exactly the right place. Fliers had been distributed everywhere she could think of. All that was left to do now was wait, and hope she would be buried in the rush of customers.

Her stomach was a knot of tension as she unlocked the shop door and positioned the stand-up sign on the pavement outside. The pink and black helium balloons fastened to it bobbed in the evening breeze.

She leaned back against the counter. Nothing yet. Worry began to gnaw at her insides that this had all been a crazy idea, that she'd sunk her entire savings into a venture that would never get off the ground, no matter how hard she worked. She struggled to crush it back down as she stared at her perfect but deserted shop floor and then Poppy and Alex were sweeping into the shop,

followed by a couple of other fire-station residents. Two
minutes later and a group of women dressed for the office crowded in, clearly on their way home from work.
She noticed Alex pouring champagne into glasses and
managed a smile at last. Worry was gone, the shop was
buzzing and she was on her way.

Poppy, standing in the middle of the shop, leaned around
Alex and pinched a breadstick, dunked it in one of the
bowls of dip and ate it. Next thing he knew she was standing still and staring at the table, which was covered in
bite-size nibbles.

'You helped Lara with the food?'

She stared at him with an incredulous expression and
he ran a defensive hand through his hair. Somewhere
along the line, helping Lara shift a few boxes of stock
had graduated today into collecting a case of sale or return champagne and helping her organise the food. After
all, what else did he have to be doing? Lying in bed staring at four walls? Walking or running aimlessly around
Notting Hill?

'No, not really,' he evaded.

'Don't deny it! That's your signature dip. The one with
the secret recipe that you always said you'd take to the
grave.' As if to confirm it to herself she fumbled another
breadstick from the pot and used it to lever an enormous
scoop of dip into her mouth.

He shrugged and grabbed a cheese tartlet so he
wouldn't have to look at her knowing grin.

'What's the big deal?'

'No big deal. Just that the last time I clocked your
views on Lara's lingerie business you weren't quite so en-

thusiastic.' She took a sip of her pink champagne. *'Tart's boudoir*, wasn't it?' she said.

He looked at her in exasperation and saw the smile on her face, knew she was teasing. She touched his arm and leaned in.

'She's lovely, Alex. Makes a nice change.'

'Yeah, well, it would do. Except it's not like that. We're friends.'

She waved across the shop floor at Izzy, who'd just arrived.

'God knows what you've been doing traipsing round half the bars in Notting Hill as if your life depended on it,' she said with ill-hidden disapproval, putting her empty glass down. 'Friends is a bloody good start.'

Question was, would friends be enough?

He had to hand it to Lara: she was good at what she did.

He'd watched her for the last half hour, moving effortlessly from customer to customer, greeting people with a smile as they entered the softly lit shop from the cold darkness of the street outside. Nothing was too much trouble. Determination to make the venture a success was obvious in her every move.

'So you can offer tailored running classes?' the darkhaired woman at his elbow said. 'Would that be as part of a group or is it on a one-to-one basis?'

He tore his eyes away from Lara, who was holding up a raspberry lace vest and smiling on the other side of the shop.

'Either,' he said distractedly.

Whatever Lara had said at the playground, she'd obviously given him a great sales pitch. He'd been inundated with thirty-something women asking him about personal training, certainly enough inquiries to demonstrate that he could have a viable business here, if he chose to pursue it.

It felt vaguely against the natural order of things to be handing out his phone number to women when he had no intention of going to bed with them. Exhausted with their questions, he glanced around for an escape route and realised Tori had entered the shop while he was pre-occupied. Just what he needed. She couldn't have timed it better if she'd tried. He immediately excused himself from the crowd of women, and headed straight over to her via the counter, where he took a couple of fresh glasses of pink champagne.

She looked up at him as she flipped randomly through the clothes rail near the door.

'You look tired,' he said, handing her one of the glasses.

Truth be told he was quite taken aback by the change in her demeanour since he'd last seen her at Izzy's house party. That had been over a month ago now and she'd been full of enthusiasm about her fabulous new boyfriend.

'Just for future reference,' she said, taking an enormous slug of champagne, 'when you say "you look tired" to a woman, what she actually hears is "you look like crap".'

He laughed.

'You don't look like crap. You never have.'

She raised her glass in acknowledgement. She was the life and soul of every party she ever went to and yet here she was looking through the rails by herself in the corner. Even the stripes in her hair seemed less vibrant than usual. He'd known her long enough to pick up immediately that something wasn't right. Maybe there was trouble in paradise.

'You've got it bad,' Tori commented.

He stood back a little.

'Got what bad?'

She gave him an exasperated look.

'Lara,' she said, making his stomach do a crazy back-flip. 'I've been watching you for the last five minutes. For Pete's sake, Alex, we've known each other since we were kids. I've got eyes. I can tell.'

'How can you tell?'

'You mean besides the fact you're actually *attending* a party in a ladies' knicker shop? Let me think…' She tapped one finger against her jaw in an exaggerated gesture of consideration. 'You can't take your eyes off her. And last time we met you tried to resurrect our friends-with-benefits agreement but you haven't so much as given me a second glance so far tonight. Don't suppose you want to revisit that conversation now?'

He had absolutely no inclination whatsoever to do that. And having it pointed out to him brought any delusions about how much he liked Lara crashing down around his ears. He had zero interest in pursuing Tori, or anyone else for that matter. Tori was waiting for an answer, an expectant look on her face. *Awkward.* He spread his hands apologetically.

'Tori, I'd love to but—'

She punched the air in a gesture of triumph.

'There you go. I rest my case.'

For all the jokey posturing he still thought for a moment that there was a hint of disappointment in her smile, but of course he had to be mistaken. She'd made herself quite clear at Izzy's party. Mark was, for her, the real deal. The *benefits* part of their friendship was, for her, well and truly over with.

'It's not like that,' he protested. 'She thinks I'm only after one thing and, to be perfectly honest, I'm not sure I'm up to offering more than that right now.'

He could see from Tori's smile that he wasn't fooling either of them. They'd always had an easy confidence like this; he knew he could trust her.

'I'm damaged goods, Tori,' he said at last. 'I don't want to put that on her.'

He watched over Tori's shoulder as Lara crossed the shop towards them, smiling and chatting to customers, working the room like an expert. Tori moved a pace sideways to block his view and grab his full attention.

'That's such crap, Alex,' she said. 'Damaged goods? For Pete's sake, everyone has a past. We've all got baggage, and you've decided that she'd make a judgement call about yours without even *asking* her opinion. That's really not fair, is it?' She turned away from him and began flipping through a rail of pastel silk dressing gowns. He watched as she rejected each one. 'Take your time, get to know her properly and show her there can be more between the two of you than just sex,' she said. 'You're here, aren't you? Offering support, helping her out. I'd say that's a step in the right direction.'

Lara finally reached them and Tori dropped her voice quickly and held up a short pink silk nightie.

'Have you got anything…*edgier*?' Tori asked her.

After a while smiling made your cheeks ache, and it really should come a lot more naturally based on the fact the launch was turning out to be a fantastic success. The turnout was brilliant, the buzz around her stock delighted her, and she'd already made lots of sales.

Lara caught herself looking over at Alex yet again and dragged her eyes back to the counter, forced herself to focus on processing the sale and talking to the customer. He'd made a real effort on her behalf this last couple of days, while taking great care to keep things on a friendly level between them. No more flirting or invading her personal space. She'd begun to wonder if he was trying to impress her, somehow show that she meant more to him than his usual conquests, maybe even prove that his interest in her went beyond disposable fling. Helping her shift her stock, for example, even pitching in with the catering. She hadn't expected that, hadn't expected him to *cook*, for Pete's sake!

Now it seemed that all he'd been doing was passing the time because, let's face it, he had nothing better to do.

He'd spent the early part of the evening surrounded by prospective fitness clients; she'd picked up snippets of the conversation herself every time she walked past him and she was secretly delighted at his new positivity. He'd also turned out to be a brilliant side attraction to her designs. Note to self: keep a hot guy on the shop floor at all times to maximise female footfall. And then somewhere in the last twenty minutes or so, Tori had arrived, and suddenly networking for a prospective fitness business seemed to have gone out of the window. She could see them in her peripheral vision, talking quietly, in each other's personal space. They obviously knew each other *extremely* well.

And that was when the unhappy churning in Lara's stomach had kicked off.

Now Tori stood at the counter paying for a beautiful

but undeniably racy basque and French knickers set in black silk, decorated with intricate lace and feathers, and some lace-topped silk stockings.

Poppy, looking on, sighed wistfully as Lara wrapped the delicate garments in pink tissue paper.

'It must be lovely to have someone in mind when you buy this kind of thing,' she said. 'They are *so* beautiful. Not that I need anything like that.' She nodded towards the nightwear rail on the other side of the shop. 'I'm going to buy a pair of those silk pyjamas.'

'They're so gorgeous, aren't they?' Tori said. 'Not that there's any point in me looking at them. Silk pyjamas would be a bit run of the mill for Mark's taste, no matter how lovely.' There was a resigned edge to her tone. 'In Mark's opinion, the saucier, the better.'

'All of this is for Mark's benefit, then?' Alex said, joining them.

Lara's stomach gave another twist at his obvious interest in Tori's relationship. First he'd spent ages talking quietly to her in the corner and now this. Try as she might to deny it, maybe dismiss it as first-night nerves, deep down she knew perfectly well what it was and she might as well face facts.

She was jealous.

'How are things with Mark?' Concern showed on Poppy's face. 'It feels like we've hardly seen you recently. Is everything OK?'

'Of course!'

Tori's smile was a little too broad, her tone a little too light-hearted to really sound genuine. Poppy was waiting for her to elaborate, as she always did. Instead she simply handed over her credit card to Lara. For the first time in history, it seemed, Tori was reluctant to talk about herself.

* * *

Lara's feet ached inside the skyscraper heels but she couldn't have cared less. Poppy had left a while ago with Izzy, each of them carrying a pink and black ribbon-tied carrier bag. Tori had disappeared back home to Mark. But even after all the potential fitness clients had gone, Alex had stayed. From beginning to end he'd been there for her shop launch, not giving it a miss or dropping in for a grudging half hour or so because she'd cajoled him into it. His support had gone above and beyond a favour. With the shop launch occupying every spare space in her mind, she hadn't allowed herself to consider what, if anything, *that* might mean. Maybe he was just being polite. Maybe he had nothing better to do.

It was full dark now outside and cold, a little past nine. She supposed he would go straight on to the pub now. Or the bar. Or wherever it was he disappeared to during his evenings out. The thought brought a twist of disappointment, which had no place amid her euphoria at the way the evening had gone.

She focused her mind on her work. All that was left to do now was tidy the shop and cash up. Alex carried the pavement sign in from the darkness of the street.

'Thanks for all your help today,' she said, crossing to the counter breezily to avoid looking at him. 'It's been a fantastic success. You can get off now. I'll just cash up and tidy round a bit.'

The shop floor seemed suddenly still and quiet after the buzz of the evening. His voice came from behind her.

'I'll stay while you lock up and then I'll walk you back.'

So she'd been wrong about him finishing the evening with his usual routine. Her stomach gave a slow and deliberate flip at that throwaway comment and what it might mean if she let it.

'There's no need.'

She heard his exasperated intake of breath.

'It's pitch dark out there and I assume you'll be carrying your takings? Don't argue.'

She moved around the shop, tidying up. Just turning the sign on the door around to read 'Closed' gave her a spark of happiness. This was *her* business, *her* shop. She'd worked so hard for this evening and it had gone well. She was acutely aware of him beside her as she cashed up and put the takings in her bag. He made her feel protected, cared about, and that touched her on a level she rarely allowed anyone to reach. She'd allowed that to happen, of course, accepting his help when she took help from no one. There was danger inherent in that, but she'd believed herself immune to it because she wasn't interested in the quick shallow flings he favoured. Now he'd moved the goalposts, his usual routine and line-up of conquests interrupted, and as a result her opinion of him was no longer such a great defence. Watching him with Tori had shown her she liked him a lot more than she admitted, to him and to herself.

Now that some of the stress of the project had been alleviated her consciousness of him seemed to have increased a hundredfold.

'It's been a huge success,' Lara said. Her eyes sparkled and she looked absolutely radiant in the soft pink lighting of the shop. Alex's heart turned over softly. He waited while she flicked the shop lights off and locked up and then she was next to him, walking the icy pavement in the clear night air.

'You seem to get on well with Tori,' she said after a moment.

His interest sharpened instantly that she'd even noticed.

'I've known her a long time,' he said. 'She used to come and stay with us in the school holidays when Poppy and I were kids.' He paused. 'We've dated on and off over the years. Actually, not even dated really, more ended up together when both of us happened to be free. Nothing heavy.'

She uttered a little laugh.

'Nothing ever *is* heavy with you, is it?'

He considered that for a moment, dug his hands deep in his pockets as they walked.

'You have to understand what my life was like, in the army. I was away so much, and I put so much of myself into it that there wasn't much left for anything or anyone else. And it's a very regimented way of living. For as long as I can remember I've had someone else to answer to—be it a housemaster at school or a senior officer. Suddenly having all this freedom was weird. I could do whatever I wanted, whenever I wanted. I'd had years of heavy. I decided to make up for lost time.'

Silence for a moment.

'So is that what you were doing? Tonight with Tori. Making up for lost time?'

His heart was picking up the pace tentatively.

'No, we were just catching up. That side of things was never such a big deal and it's in the past now. We're friends, nothing more.'

'Because she's with Mark?'

'Not just that, no. What's with all the questions?' He

threw caution aside with a throwaway comment that he could pass off as a joke if he needed to. 'Jealous?'

'No!'

Her immediate sharp denial told him all he needed to know and tendrils of hope began to climb through him.

A pause.

'Just interested,' she qualified.

'It might have escaped your notice but I haven't been out with anyone recently, Tori included. It's kind of lost its charm.'

'Why's that?'

'Isn't it obvious?' he said, exasperated at last by the interrogation. 'Do you think I make a habit of hanging around ladies' clothes shops? Don't you think I'd rather be out at the pub right now, keeping it simple? I've spent my whole life answering to other people, living by the rules, and these last few weeks have been the first time in my life I've been free to live it up without regard for anyone else. And now I find I don't bloody *want* to. I'd rather be chatting to a gang of women and drinking pink champagne if it means being with you.' He stared up at the sky. 'What have you done to me?'

For a moment there was silence and he chanced a glance sideways. She wasn't looking troubled or as if she was gearing up to give another rendition of her rejection speech. She was smiling up at him and that was all the encouragement he needed. He stopped walking, tugged her into his arms and kissed her.

His room back at the flat was channelling its usual sparse military as Alex crossed the room to close the curtains. The soft glow from the bedside light highlighted the ordered shelves and perfectly made bed.

'This room is in dire need of soft furnishings...' Lara began as he moved back towards her, and then he stopped her mouth with a kiss and all thoughts of décor disappeared from her mind like smoke. He cradled her face in both hands, his thumbs stroking her jaw softly as he caught the curve of her lips in his, easing them apart and caressing her with his tongue. Sparks of heat spread slowly through her body to melt in her stomach and tingle between her legs. His shoulders were huge and broad, tightly muscled. She let her hands slide up his chest and around his neck, let her fingertips slip through his hair as he curled huge arms around her. Reservations about disposable relationships melted from her consciousness; they required presence of mind, and the all-encompassing force of her physical response to him had swept that away. Her past relationships had never stifled her ability to keep her head, not like this. What was it about him that made her rational mind switch off?

Her perfume filled his senses.

It was like unwrapping the most decadent of luxury gifts. Layer by gorgeous layer, velvet, lace, silk, crystals. He found the zip at the nape of her neck and slid it smoothly down to the base of her spine. The silk dress slipped easily from her shoulders and fell into a soft gleaming pool at her feet. Beneath it he found a slip so thin it was almost translucent. The soft glow of the lamp on his bedside table gave her skin a creamy sheen against its peach silk and he caught his breath. He was used to living in the roughest of conditions and everything about her exuded luxury, the decadent scent of her skin, the soft slinky fabrics unfamiliar beneath his fingers. There was a femininity about her that was so intoxicating it made his senses reel.

He slipped the thin straps of her slip off her shoulders, and followed his progress with soft kisses, tracing her collarbone, moving lower. Her skin was as smooth and flawless as the silk clothes she wore. Beneath the slip there was a delicate lace bra, and he moved his lips across its roughness to suck her nipples gently through the gossamer-thin fabric. She moaned softly and arched her back, and desire surged through his body at her reaction. He slipped the straps of her bra off her shoulders as her fingertips found the buttons of his shirt and pushed it from his shoulders, then she slid her hands lower to tug the button of his jeans, remove them and free his erection. Her fingertips played lightly over his length, making nerves flutter softly in his groin, and he caught her hand before he could lose control. Curling an arm around her waist, he lowered her to the bed, and there she lay before him in the soft lamplight, the beautifully cut bra and knickers highlighting her curves perfectly. Her underwear was made to be seen, and he found her self-confidence in her body intoxicating.

He let his hands play over her body, exploring, revelling in the hitch of her breath as his fingertips found the silky skin of her inner thighs, in the tensing of her body as he teased his fingers beneath the soft lace of her panties, stroking her apart and then sliding two fingers inside her. She gasped against his neck as he found the sensitive nub at the very core of her and circled it lightly with his thumb as his fingers picked up a deliberately slow rhythm. With his free hand he cupped her breast, pinching the hard point of a nipple lightly between his fingers, pushing her slowly higher until she tensed against him as she found her climax.

A moment passed as she lay curled against him, and

then she tipped her head back and found his mouth with hers, her tongue slipping softly against his, firing him up even further. Then she leaned upwards, moving above him, her blonde hair silky against his cheek as her lips moved to his neck. Then lower still. He failed to stop himself tensing as her kisses strayed towards the ruined skin on the left-hand side of his chest, his fists clenching tightly at his sides. He hadn't given it a thought before, hadn't cared what any of his partners since the accident might think about him.

She mattered.

She was so beautiful, so perfect, and the thought that she might find him repellent filled him with sudden dread.

Her progress didn't falter. The line of kisses continued softly over his chest as if the twisted and puckered skin weren't even there. Relief washed over him, and with it desire for her that swept away all restraint. In one swift movement he turned her gently on her back, then leaned away briefly to find a condom in the drawer to one side of the bed.

Lara's heart thundered so fast and hard that she fancied he might hear it. As he slowly circled her slick entrance with his rigid erection she wanted him so much that she raised her hips from the bed, trying to take control and push him forward, yet he made her wait, teasing her until she thought she might cry out before he finally thrust forward, taking her in one deep fluid movement. His hands found hers on either side of her head, twining her fingers in his own as he found his rhythm, thrusting forward smoothly again and again, all the while holding her gaze with his own until she could hold back no longer and she cried her pleasure against his neck as he took her over that delicious edge. A moment later and his body tensed against her own as he followed her.

As her breathing evened she curled her body against him, tugging the blanket free of its perfect hospital corners and snuggling into him deliciously, already her thoughts breaking up into sleep.

Faint notes of her perfume still clung to her hair and Alex closed his eyes and breathed them in. Her fingers entwined in his, and he felt a sense of peace that had eluded him since he'd arrived home.

For the first time in weeks he didn't fight sleep when it came.

Big mistake.

CHAPTER SEVEN

IT STARTED WITH a couple of shivers as he lay next to her. Not enough to drag her fully back to consciousness from the delicious deep, sated sleep, but just enough for awareness of his presence to seep in, for the deliciousness of the previous evening to surface in her mind and make her stomach flutter before she sank back down into slumber.

And then there it was again. Soft muttering. This time she opened her eyes and frowned in the dim light of the very early morning. She was curled snugly against Alex, his arm curled protectively around her, her head nestled comfortably in the hollow beneath his jaw. She inhaled the warm, musky scent of his body. The feeling of warmth and safety warmed her to her toes.

She moved up onto one elbow and screwed her eyes up, looking down at his face in the semi-darkness with its strong bone structure. No longer pinned down by her, he suddenly flailed his arms and shouted aloud, making her jump, and she scrambled into a sitting position. Her mind backtracked madly to the day they met—had it really only been a week or so ago? He'd fallen asleep in her flat while she worked. His sleep had been disturbed then too.

She leaned across and clicked on the lamp on the bed-

side table. Deep in sleep, he didn't wake. And little wonder—he was clearly so sleep-deprived that once sleep had
him in its grasp it wouldn't let go easily. Worry twisted
in her chest as she watched a frown cross his face. Beads
of perspiration shone on his brow. Muttering kicked back
in, louder this time. Vague, garbled words, none of it in-
telligible.

Unable to bear the anguished twisting of his body
a moment longer, she reached a hand out to shake his
shoulder, and when that didn't work she began patting
his cheek lightly.

'Alex?' she ventured.

His arms flew back against the headboard and a strangled shout that was leaning towards a scream left his lips.
In a panic, Lara did the only thing she could think of.

The dream had Alex right in its dark grasp, fear and despair pelting through his veins as he staggered through
the smoke, tasting its acrid bite at the back of his throat
as he tried to call out for Sam, desperately searching for
him and for their driver.

And then a sudden flood of icy coldness dashed full-
force into his face and he was scrambling to sit up, dis-
orientated, water dripping from his face onto the sheets.
He screwed his eyes up and tried to focus in the unexpected bright light.

'What the hell...?' he spluttered. The fragments of the
dream were still whirling in his mind, his heart pounding thickly in his chest.

His eyes slowly began to adjust. Poppy's flat. His bedroom. Present day. Lara was sitting a few feet away from
him on the bed, the sheet clutched against her chest, the
empty glass from his bedside table in her hand and an

apologetic look on her face that did nothing to mask the underlying fright.

'I tried shaking you,' she said apologetically. 'You were muttering in your sleep and thrashing about. Nothing worked. And then you really shouted and I kind of acted on reflex.'

Her voice trailed away. Her hair lay in loose waves over her bare shoulders and her china-blue eyes were wide with worry. She looked utterly beautiful and hideous shame boiled through his veins as he comprehended what had happened. Making love to her had lulled him into such a state of euphoric hope that he'd stupidly thought he might have beaten off some demons. What a fool he was for thinking he might have turned a corner with his nightmares just because Lara was in his bed. What the hell must she think of him, crying out in his sleep like a baby?

His flailing mind chose that moment to treat him to a hideous memory of his father, one of thousands of similar memories, berating him as a seven-year-old for crying as he was decamped back to school yet again. His face burned in spite of the cold water that still clung to his cheeks. Emotional displays were shameful, something to be avoided at all costs, and avoiding them had become second nature. When he was awake. Apparently his unconscious self still needed a few lessons in self-control.

He attempted to joke his way out of it.

'Your reflex reaction is a bit sledgehammer-to-crack-a-nut, isn't it? Remind me not to get on the wrong side of you.' His hair was damply sweaty as he ran a hand through it.

She didn't smile. Her pretty face was full of sympathy,

fuelling the humiliation all the more. He couldn't bear to have her pity him.

'What's going on with you, Alex? Is this to do with your injuries? The roadside bomb? Poppy mentioned how difficult it's been.' She put her hand on his arm gently. 'You can talk to me, you know.'

'You've been discussing me with Poppy on the quiet?' Mortification kicked up another notch.

'Not in a negative way,' she said. 'She was concerned about you, that's all. She could see we were becoming friends.'

'It's nothing to do with Poppy or anyone else,' he snapped. 'There's nothing to talk about.' It came out more strongly than he'd meant it and he caught the tiny recoil on her face. She took her hand away and cut her eyes away from his. He forced his voice into a light tone. 'So I had a bit of a disturbed night—I probably drank too much at the launch. No big deal.'

He avoided her eyes, instead swinging his legs off the bed and putting on shorts. The silence in the room was heavy with tension. He needed to get out of here for a few minutes, calm down. Then when he came back the moment would be over with.

'I'll be right back,' he mumbled, heading out to the bathroom.

Lara watched the door close behind him and gritted her teeth against the wave of miserable disappointment churning in her stomach. Two words: *Unrealistic expectations*. Had she really thought that after his romantic declaration of feelings for her, followed by the most unbelievable stomach-melting night, things might actually be rainbows and butterflies from now on?

No. But it might have been nice if they could get past the morning after before her hopes were dashed. She of all people should know better than to expect more. This was *her* life after all. Rainbows and butterflies had never featured before—why the hell should they be putting in an appearance now?

Her mind was working overtime. There was more to this than a one-off or a glass too many of pink champagne. From what she'd seen and heard of him last night he certainly hadn't drunk that much. Her thoughts kept going back to the unsettled sleep he'd had back on the sofa in her flat. And now something else clicked into place in her mind. His major overuse of caffeine. The odd hours he kept—sleeping in the daytime, up and about half the night. Try to palm this off as a one-off or a phase, he might, but she knew better.

Whatever this was, he apparently didn't have enough regard for her to be straight with her about it. And really—was that such a big ask? She pushed her fingers back into her hair, trying to think clearly. The way he'd helped her with the launch, their growing friendship, the way he'd been with her last night. Had all that just been a stepping stone to bed after all? Had he just upped the ante after she'd knocked him back after their run, playing the game, pretending he wanted to get to know her until he got what he wanted? Anything deeper than that was apparently not on the agenda.

Self-preservation kicked sharply in and she threw the covers back from the bed. She padded quietly around the room, picking up her clothes, finding her shoes, all the while squashing the feeling of hurt stupidity for thinking there might be more to this than just sex.

* * *

In the bathroom Alex filled his palms with cold water and held them against his face, wondering how the hell to play this now. He could kick himself for falling asleep. So wrapped up in the deliciousness of having Lara cuddled up to him, he'd relaxed for once, not even sparing a thought for his nightmares. He was filled with hot shame at what he might have done or said in his sleep; it had certainly disturbed her enough that she'd lobbed water over him. In any other situation it might have been funny.

His immediate reaction was to back off. At speed. He'd intended to have fun for a while, not to get in so deep with a girl that he actually cared what they thought of him. In getting to know Lara he'd somehow lost sight of that objective. The sensible thing now would be to draw a line under the whole thing. Go back to being nothing more than neighbours who made small talk. Yet the thought of not seeing her again except in passing, of just being acquaintances, made his stomach lurch with disappointment.

He gripped the edges of the sink and looked down at his hands. He would have to find another way to deal with this instead of ending it. He just needed to put in a bit of distance. His best option was surely to fob her off, dismiss the nightmare as one of those things, and then find a way to make sure it didn't happen again.

He took a deep breath as he walked back down the hall and pushed open the bedroom door.

She was dressed. Or at least dressed enough to indicate the night was well and truly over. She wore her pink frock from the launch party and the beautiful undergarments hung over one arm. Her shoes were in her other hand. Worse, her face was full of disappointment. Clearly in him. And who could blame her? Had he really assumed she would still be interested in him after this? Naturally being woken up to his girly screaming had put her off.

'You're leaving,' he said, stating the obvious. His stomach churned with despair at the realisation that he'd blown this.

'I should never have stayed,' she said. 'Last night was a mistake.'

'There's no need for you to go,' he said quickly. 'I'm sorry if I overreacted or scared you. It was just a dream, just one of those things. This doesn't normally happen.' OK, so that was stretching the truth more than a little but he'd worry about that later; if he had to stay awake twenty-four-seven from now on to hide his weakness from her then he would manage it somehow. He held a hand out to her. 'Come back to bed.'

She rolled her eyes at the ceiling.

'So you want to dumb down this whole thing between us until all it's about is sex,' she said. 'I don't know why I'm even *surprised*.' She took a step nearer the door, then turned back and flung a hand up in a gesture of exasperation. 'It's not the bloody *dream* that's the problem. It's your reaction. It's the way you've just fobbed me off and then suggested bed as if sex might just divert me from getting to know you on any deeper level than that. *A bit of a disturbed night?* It was way more than that. And you can try and pass it off as a blip or a one-off if you want, but I'm not an idiot. This isn't the first time it's happened, is it? What about when you fell asleep back in my flat—you had a nightmare then too, didn't you? And that's why you're always trying to stay awake. Why didn't you just say you're having trouble sleeping? Don't you think I *care* about that?'

He groped for an answer that wouldn't make him look a total arse. He'd thought he'd got away with the sleep disturbance in the flat that day. She'd never mentioned it since. It felt suddenly as if he were under the spotlight and defensiveness kicked in.

'What is this—twenty questions?'

Disappointment filled the blue eyes at his curt tone.

'No, this is me wondering why you're not being straight with me and realising I already know the answer. You said it yourself the other day. You've never been with a disposable person who's any good. That's how you see yourself, how you see this, isn't it? A quick fling. OK, you might have had to jump through a few extra hoops this time to get your way, but you got there in the end, didn't you? Like an idiot I thought there might be more to us than that.'

She headed for the door while he stared after her in horror, seeing how the conclusion she'd reached must look so obvious to her in the light of his previous behaviour, his string of one-night-only girlfriends.

'There *is* more to us than that,' he called after her.

She paused. Turned to look back at him from the open doorway.

'OK, then, prove it,' she said. 'Sit down with me now and be straight with me about what just happened.'

He stared at her, groping for something to say that would turn the situation around and failing. Because he knew exactly what she'd think of him if he sat down opposite her and told her all about his night terrors. About the bomb blast and his broken promise to look out for a nervous soldier who looked up to him. About his failure to be of any use whatsoever to those whose safety was ultimately his responsibility. The silence yawned between them until she shook her head.

'I've got work to do,' she snapped.

The door clicked shut behind her.

It didn't have the best flouncing-out value when you were only going feet away down the hall but she'd given it her all anyway, cutting her eyes sharply away from him and slamming the door behind her. At least the walk of shame was only a few paces. Bloody Alex. She should be euphoric after yesterday's success but instead she was filled with stomach-wrenching disappointment.

Back in the boxroom she sank onto the narrow bed and rubbed her scratchy eyes with her fingers. The clock on the dresser told her it was a little before six. Five minutes later and she was heading into the shower, mind forcibly refocused back where it should have been all along. Her work.

Coffee in Ignite accompanied by an enormous *pain au chocolat* that would undoubtedly go straight to her hips, then she would head in to open the shop. She ate it anyway, because the size of her hips was irrelevant now that she wasn't intending to get naked with a man again any time soon. Had to go and sleep with him, didn't she? She should have known better. She stared at her laptop screen and focused hard on updating her blog with photos from the launch. Anything to crush the feeling of stupidity, and the underlying prickle of concern for him that he really didn't deserve, because however hard he might try to brush it off those nightmares were no picnic.

Somehow the concern was worst of all because it told her she actually *cared* about him.

Try as she might to concentrate on writing a blog post, her eyes kept wandering to the door. Which of course was insane because he hadn't exactly beaten the box-room door down upstairs to try and talk to her. She'd heard nothing from him from the moment she slammed his bedroom door. And why would she? It all fitted. He'd got what he wanted—why would he want anything more to do with her? The only difference between her and all his other walk-of-shame girls was that she'd slammed the door on the way out instead of kissing him goodbye.

As she polished off the last of the pastry, not really wanting it but grimly eating it out of principle, the door of the café opened and her stomach gave a disorienting flip. She bit her lip hard enough to hurt because her eyes might have been glued to the door but she hadn't for one moment thought he actually might walk through it. He crossed the room towards her via the counter, where she heard him put in his usual order of coffee strong enough to strip wallpaper. And then he came to a standstill next to her table, by which time her heart was thundering so loudly in her ears that it was a wonder she could hear him when he spoke.

'I'm sorry,' Alex said.

Her hair was loosely tied at one side, curling over her shoulder, and the porcelain cheekbones were without their usual touch of colour. She looked tired and frag-ile. *His fault.* A prickle of guilt spiked inside him and he wondered briefly if it would be better to just leave her be instead of subjecting her to his attempts to move on with his life. Then Tori's words from the previous evening flit-ted through his head. *We've all got baggage, and you've decided that she'd make a judgement call about yours without even* asking *her opinion. That's really not fair...*

Lara looked up at him, pen clenched in one hand, face carefully neutral. Her posture was stiff and guarded, giving nothing away.

'For what?'

'For everything. Can I sit down?'

A pause. And then she nodded at the opposite chair. He pulled it out and sat opposite her, looked down at the table for a moment, gathering his thoughts, then looked up and into her cautious blue gaze.

'I know how it looks, but you're wrong,' he said. 'This is not just about a one-night stand or a quick fling for me. I told you that last night and I meant it.'

She held his gaze levelly, giving nothing away.

'But that didn't make it any easier for me to tell you about my nightmares. What the hell would you have thought if I'd dropped in a quick warning before we went to sleep? If I'd told you that I might freak out somewhere in the small hours? You'd think I was a complete nutter.'

He looked back down at the table.

'Truth is, I'd had such a great time last night that for once I didn't stress about going to sleep. I didn't think I could have a nightmare when I was feeling so…well, so relaxed.'

He glanced up to see her expression soften a little. He tried hard not to see it as a sympathy look. If he did that, he might not be able to continue.

'I haven't told anyone about the dreams. Not even Poppy. I didn't want to worry her. It's my problem, no one else's and I'm dealing with it in my own way,' he said.

The counter girl chose that moment to walk past and place a supersized mug of black coffee in front of him. He nodded his thanks as he took a huge slug of it, relishing its strong bitter taste and waiting for the buzz to kick in and sharpen his senses.

She nodded at the mug, a cynical expression on her face.

'That's you dealing with it your own way, is it? Over-dosing on caffeine and avoiding sleep.'

'Short-term management,' he said. 'In actual fact things have improved. Already the dreams are getting less frequent, I just need to give it more time.'

Not strictly true. They were less frequent because he *slept* less frequently. But he had no wish to undermine the improvement by analysing it too deeply. He was convinced he just needed to give it time. Surely the longer he spent out of the army, the less he would dwell on it, right?

'What are they like? The dreams?' she ventured. Her voice was tentative, as if she was worried he might snap at her.

His stomach churned a little at the question. Verbalising what happened hadn't really been on his agenda when he'd come to find her; he'd simply hoped to apologise and talk her round. But here it was, his chance to prove he was totally on top of this. Totally in control. He gripped the mug of coffee hard in one hand and curled the other into a fist, forced what he hoped was an I'm-in-total-control-of-this neutral expression onto his face.

'They're always the same,' he began, keeping it short. Keeping it *vague*. That was best. 'The explosion, the heat and the smoke. And then this awful sense of disorientation.' He dug his fingernails into his palm and glanced around the café. Chatting customers, background music, *reality*. 'And then I wake up.' He forced a grin. 'Or in this instance, I *get* woken up by being dunked in cold water.'

She smiled back, but the smile was a size too small.

'You scared me half to death,' she said.

'I'm sorry.'

She shook her head slowly.

'It must have been an awful time for you. I can't possibly imagine what it must be like to have that in your head. Have you had any counselling? Don't they offer that kind of thing?'

'I'm not some basket case,' he said defensively.

She rolled her eyes.

'I'm not suggesting you are. I want to help, that's all. I want to understand. I'm not passing judgement.'

He wasn't about to confide in her beyond the most basic level. Better by far to keep things simple between them, to keep it fun. For neither of them to get too attached. Wasn't her independence part of what was so attractive about her? She had her own life, her own agenda that had absolutely nothing to do with him. She was far too preoccupied with her own goals to really *need* him and he found that so appealing about her, that she demanded sole responsibility for her own life.

'I thought you of all people would understand that this is something I want to handle myself,' he said.

An indignant frown touched her eyebrows.

'What's that supposed to mean?'

'Miss I'll Shift My Own Furniture,' he said. 'Didn't you tell me you hated relying on anyone else's help?'

A grin twitched at the corner of her mouth and his spirits lifted. He pressed on.

'Is it so wrong to try and get through it myself first before I drag anyone else into it? It wasn't a personal judgement about you—I haven't told *anyone*.'

'No, it's not so wrong.'

He covered her hand with his, noticing she didn't pull her fingers away.

'Does that mean I'm forgiven?' he said.

She looked up at him through narrowed eyes.

'Depends.'

'On what?'

'That you don't try and hide it from me. Or anything else, for that matter. I need you to be straight with me. And you stop trying to stay awake twenty-four-seven.'

'Anything else?'

'You buy me another pastry.'

'Done.'

CHAPTER EIGHT

NORMAL COUPLE. HE COULD do that. In those early days when he'd left the army, keeping it casual had been the automatic choice. Freedom to go where he chose, when he chose, with whomever he chose had held a novelty value that was intoxicating after the years of rigid structure in his life. Yet throughout that time of shallow one-night stands and partying, he'd found no real sense of satisfaction. There had still been that uncomfortable sensation of being rootless, of having no direction.

Now he understood why. When it came down to it, he had missed it. The sense of *belonging* that school and the army had provided. He only truly realised that now he was beginning to regain it. He revelled in the sense of direction that the new business gave him, in the steadiness that living with Poppy offered, and now in the happiness that being with Lara brought. Casual really wasn't him. He had a sense of moving forward now instead of living a disposable, inconsequential, limbo life, and he wanted that feeling to stay. Letting his relationship with Lara become steadier was the inevitable next step.

Now that things were sorted between the two of them he felt more certain of that than ever, confident that he'd taken another step towards building a normal life outside the regimens of the army, putting the past further behind him. He'd been frank with Lara, right? Just a couple of nightmares and he was handling them himself, no biggie. Surely it was only a matter of time now before they disappeared completely.

Girlfriend—*check*. New and promising fitness business—*check*. Place to live that had no bearing on his past—*check*.

A group of people were just drifting into Ignite for wine and tapas as Alex passed them and climbed the stairs to the flat. He'd just finished his very first personal training session—up until now it had all been about assessing fitness levels and planning exercise schedules and diets. Now he'd actually embarked on proper fitness sessions with a couple of clients. Things were moving forward. With every step he insisted to himself that life was back on the right track.

The laughter and chat could be heard as soon as he walked through the door and he followed it to the kitchen. Isaac was sitting at the table, leaning back in his chair with a grin on his face, Poppy was busy at the stove, whirling a huge wok around, and Lara was at the counter opening a bottle of wine.

'You're back again, then, mate,' he said to Isaac, crossing the kitchen and sweeping Lara's blond hair to one side so he could kiss her cheek.

Poppy made retching sounds from the other side of the kitchen.

'What are you, twelve?' he asked her. 'Just because you're perpetually single.'

She shot him a look and turned back to the stove. Lara held up a wine glass and raised her eyebrows but he shook his head and crossed to the fridge instead for an energy drink. Wine was not a good option if you wanted to disprove all suspicion of sleep deprivation. He'd end up falling asleep at the kitchen table.

'How did it go, then?' Lara said. 'Your first full-on personal training session.'

In his experience commanding soldiers was infinitely easier. For a start they didn't question his authority or answer back. Or stop to reapply lipstick. Yet at the same time he couldn't deny it was nice to actually have a sense of worth and purpose again. OK, so it might only be short term, he hadn't absolutely decided where he might go with it yet, but at least he was earning now. At least he could feel he was moving forward. And the more he thought about it, the idea of running some kind of boot-camp-style class was really appealing, dealing with groups of people at a time. Maybe he could try it out on adults first and if that worked think about pitching the idea to schools.

'Challenging,' he said. 'Having my orders questioned at every turn is a new and interesting experience, but yeah.' He shrugged. 'On the whole it went well.'

'I thought I'd cook,' Poppy said. 'Since you've got your first session to celebrate. And Isaac's back, of course,' she added as an afterthought, glancing at him. 'We haven't had a group meal since Izzy left. I'm doing Thai green curry, fragrant rice and a slaw. Lara's bought cakes from the café and Isaac…'

'I've got the drink angle covered,' Isaac said easily. 'Pull up a chair.'

Poppy dished the curry up into huge bowls and joined them around the table.

'How long you staying this time?' Alex asked Isaac, forking up some rice.

Lara noticed Poppy glance up sharply at him from her

plate. She could see how it might be annoying that Isaac
essentially treated Poppy's flat like a hotel. Things had
changed quite a bit now from when Lara had first moved
into her studio flat downstairs. Izzy had still been living with Poppy; Tori had been forever dropping in; there
were constant parties and girly chats.

Isaac shrugged.

'Couple of days. Depends what comes up.' He winked
at Lara. 'No two days are ever the same. I'm heading to
Blue later. You should all come along.'

'Blue?' Lara said. What the hell was that?

'Isaac's bars have a colour theme,' Poppy supplied.
'Blue is in Islington.'

'How long have you all known each other?' Lara said.
Isaac only seemed to stay over the odd night, despite
the fact he was obviously stumping up for the rent. How
lovely it must be not to have to think where every penny
was coming from. It was clear he and Alex got on like a
house on fire. Although, glancing at her, she didn't think
Poppy looked quite as comfortable.

Isaac leaned back in his chair, swirling white wine
around his glass.

'I've known Alex and Poppy for years,' he said. 'Alex
and I were at school together. I used to crash at their place
every school holidays. You've no idea the dirt I could dish
on the pair of them.'

Out of the corner of her eye, she saw Poppy visibly
tense at that comment. Next thing she was on her feet,
heading to the fridge with her back to them. She returned
to the table with a bottle of water.

'Dirt?' Lara said.

Isaac shrugged easily.

'Nights out, holidays, that kind of thing. Trip of a life-time to Las Vegas.'

'Hah, you're so funny,' Alex said with tones of deepest sarcasm. She threw him a questioning look and he flung up a hand. 'I blew half my inheritance on an ill-judged week away with him and the guys. Let's just say Lady Luck wasn't in my corner in the casinos.' His tone was throwaway.

He might as well be speaking in some kind of foreign language. Lara had zero comprehension of a world where there was such a thing as an inheritance, let alone a swanky holiday to blow it on.

Isaac topped up their drinks, hovering the neck of the wine bottle briefly over Poppy's glass as she put her hand over it. The camaraderie between him and Alex meant the kitchen was full of laughter as they reminisced. By the time the meal was finished Lara had built up a picture in her mind of a rich childhood and adolescence, of an enormous country pile in the Cotswolds, of posh holidays and a friendship group, all of whom were too cool for school. With every anecdote she felt more and more like a fish out of water. At last Poppy stood up and began clearing plates from the table.

'Want some help?' Isaac offered.

'That's OK, I've got it,' Lara said quickly, getting up. Relief surged through her that the meal was over, closely followed by irritation at herself for being so bothered. This wasn't school. She wasn't the perpetual new girl anymore. Why should she even care whether she fitted in here or not? Living in Notting Hill was a strategic career move, not a popularity test. She opened the dishwasher and started stacking crockery.

'In that case—' Isaac looked at his watch '—I'm heading into the city. The night is young and all that. Anyone want to come along?'

Poppy shook her head immediately.

'I'm on duty in an hour,' she said. 'Night shift. I need to get moving.'

'You go,' Lara said. 'I'll finish clearing up.'

'Laters, then,' Isaac said, holding a hand up and heading out of the door. Moments later the front door of the flat slammed behind him. Poppy headed to her room to get ready to leave for work.

Alex cleared the glasses from the table as Lara wiped the surfaces.

'You were quiet,' he said.

'Was I?' She kept her back to him as she stood at the counter. Her life was a whole different ballgame from his. Apart from the fact they happened to have ended up in the same flat, they had absolutely nothing in common. Their lives were literally miles apart. How could she possibly expect to fit into his world once the first flush of novelty wore off? An unhappy prickle of doubt climbed her spine. How long could a relationship survive before those kinds of fundamental differences started to cause cracks?

'Yes, you were.' He moved across to her at the counter, and tugged her by the hand to sit down next to him. She could see the concerned expression on his face. 'What's up?'

She pitched her tone of voice at light, hoping to make it look as if it really weren't such a big deal. *That's it, Lara. Shrug it off.*

'Your upbringing was just so different from mine,' she said simply. 'Yours and Poppy's. Big family, loads of relatives, friends down for the holidays.' She paused. 'It was just interesting, listening to you all talking about it, reminiscing. I couldn't really relate to any of it.'

He shrugged.

'Yeah, well. It had its downside too,' he said shortly. 'What about you, then? You haven't told me much about your background. Except that your mother taught you how to sew, didn't she?'

'Not my mum. Not exactly,' she said.

She smiled cautiously back at him and took a sip of her wine.

'Foster mum,' she corrected.

'You were fostered?'

He sat up straight; she'd spiked his interest now. Her background had had the ability to do that when she was a kid too. In many a school playground she'd been a new and interesting life form. New starts were hard.

'My mum was very young when she had me.' She watched for his reaction. 'She was only fifteen, just a kid.'

To his credit he didn't flinch, so she carried on.

'She tried her best but she just couldn't look after me properly. It wasn't that she didn't want to, she just didn't have any support. Her own parents weren't much help.' She shrugged. 'Long story short, I ended up being taken into care.'

His face was full of concern and her stomach lurched a little despairingly. So far he'd only seen strong Lara, independent, driven Lara who made things happen for herself. She didn't want to be seen as weak or in need of sympathy.

'And then you were fostered?'

'I was.'

'What about your father?'

She shook her head. *Who?*

'I never knew him. I'm still in touch with my mother, we see each other now and then, but we're not close. We never really had a chance to be. I don't blame her. She had everything working against her and she wasn't much more than a child herself. I didn't have any brothers or sisters, like you have Poppy. It's always been just me.'

'What was your foster mother like?'

Which one? For Lara, there had only been one who mattered. The others didn't deserve a mention; they barely even registered for a thought.

When she thought of that time, the time when she'd at last felt settled, the smile came more easily. 'Her name is Bridget. I went to live with her and her husband and they were lovely. Warm and friendly. Bridget was the one who taught me how to sew—she'd worked for years as a seamstress and she was brilliant at it. She made all her own clothes, toys, soft furnishings, you name it. Up until then I'd drifted through life with no real direction and then suddenly I found something I was good at and someone who was actually interested in me.'

She thought back to the hours she'd spent learning how to shape seams, put in darts, sew button holes. Bridget's endless patience with her stream of questions. The enthusiasm for her new skill that almost bordered on greed in her eagerness to learn more, practise more. 'My whole business has stemmed from there. I did a costume design course at college, got some work experience, then started making my own stuff.'

'Are you still in touch? She must be really proud of you.'

She nodded.

'I see them when I can. Talk on the phone, and visit,

that kind of thing. When I hit sixteen and went to college I moved out of their house and found a room to rent. I started building up my own life, looking out for myself, and I've been doing that ever since.'

Alex watched her as she swirled the wine slowly around her glass. Had he ever come across someone so independent, so determinedly self-reliant? It gave a very attractive sense of security to what was happening between them—he was comfortable in the knowledge there was no way her happiness and well-being could ever be totally dependent on *him*. No need for him to worry about things stepping up a notch between them because he knew she could manage perfectly well—and perfectly happily—without him.

'So you can see it was a bit like an alien world to me, listening to you and Poppy and Isaac chat through your childhood,' she said. 'I didn't really know how to engage with that. We're really very different, you and me.'

He could tell by the tone of her voice that she didn't consider that to be a good thing.

'Your childhood sounds idyllic,' she carried on. 'You were so lucky growing up, having this massive family, financial security, a big country home.'

He couldn't hold back a cynical laugh.

'Yeah, well, it might look Pollyanna from the outside, but it's really not.' He lobbed aside his reservations about alcohol and sleep and poured a splash of wine into an empty glass for himself. 'I don't think security and happiness is about having blood relations, not really. Poppy and I are up to our ears in relatives but scraping the bottom of the barrel when it comes to support and family love.' He smiled at her frown. 'Money helps, of course, but up until now I've never been brilliant with that. I got my inheritance at the same time as Poppy but it's mostly gone now. She was the sensible one, investing it in bricks and mortar. I never really thought ahead that far—my whole life revolved around the army. I never thought for a second I might need the money for a back-up plan. Instead I frittered it away on holidays with the lads, lost a whole load of it back there in Las Vegas—Isaac wasn't joking about that. All in the name of fun.'

He looked at her small, indignant face. She'd been up against so much as a kid and she'd triumphed in the face of it. He couldn't help but be impressed by that kind of tenacity. He'd had all the financial trappings and foot-in-the-door family reputation that anyone could want to get him ahead in life. Just look how far she'd got without any of that.

He reached out across the table top and took her hand in his.

'You've pushed yourself to get where you are and that's something to be proud of—you didn't get there on the strength of your family name or your father's reputation. When you look at your business and your shop, at everything you've achieved, you know that you've done all of that on your own. The credit's yours.' He paused. 'I wish I could say that.'

'You can. You were a captain in the army. They don't just hand things like that out on a plate.'

He shrugged cynically.

'I come from an old military family—we go way back. My father has contacts at the highest level. I'd be a fool to think my family's reputation hadn't helped me get where I am.' He paused and swallowed. 'Where I *was*. Unfortunately it doesn't count for much anymore. And since I left the army any interest I did have from my family has melted away. Do you know that since I left hospital my parents haven't visited even once?'

Was it worse, Lara wondered, having all that prospective love and support just sitting there but having it withheld? How was that better than not having it at all? At least she knew where she stood. There was no disappointment because she had no one to be disappointed *in*.

'I guess what I'm saying is that you and I are not so different,' he said. 'It might seem like that on the surface. I've got relatives coming out of my ears and you've got none to speak of, but mine are completely useless. They have nothing to do with my life, no interest in me. We might come at it from different directions, but basically both of us are on our own.'

He downed the glass of wine in one and stood up from the table, his face set. Saying it out loud dragged it out from the recesses of his mind and the familiar taste of bitter disappointment rose in his mouth. For the longest time he'd had institutions in his life to replace what his family lacked. First school, then university, then the army. A circle of long-term friends to give that feeling of belonging. The floundering feeling he'd experienced in those first weeks after discharge from the army, the rootless feeling that he was going it alone, made an unwanted comeback. He'd made inroads since then, settling into Notting Hill with Poppy, finding Lara, finding a new direction in his business plans. The last thing he needed was to revisit that pointlessness.

She looked up at him with a questioning expression and he leaned over to smooth her hair back from her forehead and kiss the creamy softness of her brow.

'I'm going to take a shower,' he said.

Lara's rose-tinted view of his perfect upper-class

childhood felt suddenly skewed and her heart twisted a little for him as he left the room. She could tell he was unsettled. All those people in his life to support and love him were really people to live up to or to disappoint. She felt a new and unexpected affinity with Alex, a closeness that she hadn't realised was there. Maybe they weren't so far removed from each other after all. The thought of that brought a surge of heated desire for him deep inside her at a level beyond that provoked by his gorgeous face and his muscular body.

Without thinking what she was doing, she put the dish cloth down on the counter and left the kitchen to walk slowly down the hallway towards the bathroom. The strength of her need for him somehow transcended her usual presence of mind, breaking down her self-control. When had she ever let her guard down like this with a man, revelled in the physical deliciousness of being with someone unfettered by the endless thoughts of self-preservation by which she lived her life?

The thundering sound of water from the shower was audible from outside the door. She tried the door before knocking and it opened smoothly. With Isaac gone and Poppy at work until the morning, he clearly wasn't bothered about privacy. She was. The last thing she wanted was Isaac dropping back and bursting in unexpectedly. She closed the door behind her and twisted the spring lock.

The room was warm and the air heavy and damp with scented steam from the shower. It smelled fresh and spicy and made her heart skip into double time. The undeniably male shower gel, which he used as an antidote, he said, to all the pink and pretty girly toiletries that cluttered every surface in here.

Behind the steamed glass of the shower cubicle she could see the shadow of his huge shoulders tapering down to the tightly muscled torso. Heat began to course through her and pooled tinglingly between her legs. Slowly she stepped out of her clothes and padded barefoot across the cold tile of the floor to slide open the glass door.

She stepped into the shower unit beside Alex as if it were the most natural thing in the world and his initial surprise was quickly followed by a surge of arousal at her smooth nakedness. As the shower spray soaked her blond hair, darkening it, he slid his hands across her wet skin, circling her waist and pulling her tightly against him. He groped for her mouth with his, found it and crushed his lips against hers, hot need for her crashing through him. She knew exactly what she wanted from the moment and she took it on her terms. He found that completely mesmerising about her.

The masculine scent of his shower gel hung on the steamy air, citrus and bergamot filling her senses as she slid her hands over his soapy skin, feeling the rock-hard muscle beneath. He pushed her gently back against the wall, the smooth stone tile pressing cold against her shoulders and butt. His hands were everywhere now, exploring her, moving to cup her breasts, to hold them close together while he gently sucked their hard tips, sending dizzying sparks right through her to burn hotly between her legs.

Warm water sluiced over them as he moved slowly lower, taking his time, trailing a line of kisses softly down the hollow between her breasts, over her flat stomach and lower still. Kneeling before her now in the shower stall, he ran his hand down the length of her legs, and lifted one of her heels until her knee lay supported over his shoulder. Her legs were held firmly apart now, the better to expose her fully to his attention.

Lara leaned her head against the hard tile of the wall, the shower spray missing her face now, instead sluicing in a torrent down her body and over his. Nerve endings jumped and sparked between her legs as he kissed his way up her inner thighs, taking his time, making her wait. Then with one delicate stroke of his tongue he parted her swollen core and she heard her own sharp intake of breath as her head rolled deliciously back and her eyes fluttered shut. He found the sensitive nub and began to circle it softly with his tongue, one hand holding her against his mouth, the other first teasing lower and then sliding two fingers deep inside her in one smooth movement. He seemed attuned to her every response, moving his fingers in a slow and delicious rhythm, caressing her with his tongue until she felt herself climb towards that elusive height of sensation. Losing control, she curled her fingers into his dripping-wet hair and in response he increased his smooth pace until she cried her pleasure at the ceiling.

Before she could fold on her jellified knees into the bottom of the shower stall, waves of deliciousness still coursing through her, he'd slid the glass door of the stall open and grabbed a condom from the cupboard beside the sink. As the water thundered on in the empty stall behind them, he lifted her gently from the shower. Water splashed and pooled across the bathroom floor as he turned her to face the bathroom wall, clasping a firm hand around her waist, the other at her inner thigh. She felt the press of his rigid erection against her slick core and then he was inside her, filling her completely, taking her in long, slow strokes, his muscular torso firm against her back as he swept her wet hair aside and kissed the nape of her neck. The cold, smooth tile of the wall pressed against her hard nipples, her fingers traced marks in the condensation on either side of her face as she began to climb again. With him this time, feeling his breath quicken with every stroke he took. And as he finally tipped her back over that dizzying height of pleasure she felt him cry out his own ecstasy against her bare shoulder.

CHAPTER NINE

SHE LAY CURLED now into the crook of Alex's arm, in the soft pool of light from his beside lamp. His fingers entwined in hers, deliciously warm, sated and comfortable. Her things were starting to trickle into his room. Not much yet, just her robe and a few items of clothing. Funny how it felt like no big deal. Sleeping with Alex every night was spared full-on scary seriousness because she had her own room just down the hall and a separate shelf in the fridge. Not to mention a flat just downstairs that should be ready to move back into in a day or two. Outside the door the flat was quiet; there was no sign of Isaac returning. Then again, by the sound of it, when Isaac partied he didn't do it in small measures.

She frowned a little as she thought of Isaac, recalling Poppy's behaviour at dinner.

'Poppy seems a bit tense around Isaac,' she commented. 'Is there something going on between them?'

She felt him shake his head.

'She seemed OK to me,' he said. 'Fab scoff, as per. She's always been a great cook.'

'Typical brother, you are,' she said, exasperated. 'Completely oblivious. You could have put the atmosphere in that kitchen through a mincer. And Poppy couldn't get out of there fast enough. Honestly, men are so insensitive sometimes.'

He laughed softly into her hair.

'I can be sensitive when I want to be,' he said. She looked up into his grey eyes as he shifted in the bed, turning her gently and leaning up on one elbow to place an arm either side of her head. He tangled his fingers in her hair and kissed her so tenderly she thought her stomach might melt. She wrapped her limbs around his body, loving the fact that he was so tall and broad-shouldered, so heavily roped with muscle. She felt protected. Warm and safe. It wasn't just in the way he was with her in bed, it was in the little things he did, in not allowing her to walk a couple of streets home in the dark, in stepping in to move furniture around for her.

It was a sensation she wasn't used to experiencing, had in fact *avoided* feeling, instead substituting the need for it with her own drive and ambition. Letting herself relax into feeling safe had been something she'd learned to avoid growing up because it usually preceded the figurative rug being jerked out from underneath her. The feeling of contentment, of trusting someone else with her feelings, was something she'd learned to be wary of. She was older now, though, and wiser. She had her own life well and truly under control, providing for herself without the need for anyone else. She told herself this thing with Alex, whatever it was, didn't need to have any detrimental effect on that.

As sleep began to break her thoughts up she cuddled into him and let her guard slip a little. She could afford it.

Alex lay against her, breathing in the sweet scent of her hair in the darkness as she nestled her head beneath his chin, and stared at the ceiling. Through sheer will he held his eyes open, grimly refusing to let the comfort and warmth of his bed, of Lara curled against him, drag him into sleep. He wouldn't be making that mistake again. He listened as her breathing evened and gradually let the stroke of his fingers against the silky skin of her bare shoulder slow until it stilled. She didn't flinch. The room was silent.

Then he added on another twenty minutes just to be sure.

When he was certain she was fully asleep he shifted her gently from his chest and waited quietly while she snuggled into the pillows, then he moved across to the edge of the bed. Smooth, slow movements so as not to disturb her. There was no tripping over random items on the floor or bumping into furniture. When it came to moving in the darkness with stealth, Lara could learn a thing or two from him. He closed the bedroom door quietly behind him and headed to the kitchen, his laptop and a large mug of strong black coffee.

There was a surprising amount of admin and red tape associated with starting up a small business, even a fledgling one like his. At first the personal training thing really hadn't been much more than a way of buying some time, perhaps earning a bit of money while he decided on a proper new direction. Not to mention a way of keeping Lara and Poppy off his back with their seemingly endless career advice and suggestions of how he should be spending his time. Yet this last week, having taken his first couple of one-to-one clients out, talking through their hopes for weight loss and improved fitness and formulating a tailored fitness plan for each of them, he'd been surprised at how enthusiastic he was about the whole

venture. Already he was planning to trial group running classes, and after that possibly week-long intensive
boot-camp-style courses. The possibilities were endless.

Unfortunately there was more to it than spending all
his time outdoors handling the practical one-to-one fitness stuff. There was advertising to think of, public li-
ability insurance to consider; he needed to record his
income and expenses. The list went on and on, and Lara
had been impressed at his organisational skills, not knowing of course that he'd had hours to spare for designing a
website, setting up accounting software, scouting around
online for the best insurance deals.

When you slept less than four out of every twenty-
four hours it was amazing how much you could get done.

Lara was so tired from her in-your-face working day
that once asleep there was no waking her until her alarm
went off at some godforsaken dark hour of the morning, and at which point she would leap out of bed and
the whole damn work routine would start all over again.
The last few nights he'd been able to slip back into bed
shortly before her alarm, simply getting back up again for
an early run as soon as she was up and about. He scheduled his fitness clients in the morning, usually after nine
when the school run was out of the way, and before lunch.
Then he would grab a few hours' sleep in the afternoon
while Lara was occupied at the lingerie shop. By the time
she was finished he was up and about and she was none
the wiser. And that way, he could limit any sleep disturbance to when she wasn't there.

Lara would be able to move back into her own flat in
days, now that the plumbing was fixed and the replas-
tering of the water-damaged wall was under way. That
would take the pressure off even further. After over a

week of sharing each other's living space, that would be a step back. Staying together all night every night would likely become less of an automatic choice. Just a few more days of managing his routine and it would be easier.

In the meantime this was turning out to be the perfect solution to his nightmares. Squeeze them out. If he gave them as little opportunity as possible it stood to reason that they would happen less, that they would relinquish their grip on him. There had been no sleep disturbance at all for the last two days. And so the strategy, complicated though it was, appeared to be working. Until he could be sure he was rid of the nightmares, he intended to rigidly control his sleep pattern. Whatever it took to achieve surface normality, he was prepared to do it. Hope began to grow at last in his heart that the whole hellish experience might finally be behind him.

Isaac expertly popped the cork from the bottle of Perrier-Jouet to the background sound of cheers and claps filling the sitting room. Lara had never met anyone before so adept at producing like magic the perfect bottle to suit any occasion. She wondered if he kept a stack of bottles hidden away in his room, ready to whip out with a flourish when required. Relaxed shared flatmates' dinner? Chilled bottle of Pinot Grigio. Announcement of former flatmate's whirlwind engagement? Top-notch champagne, nothing but the best would do.

He filled flutes one by one as Poppy held them out to him.

'I bloody well told you so!' Poppy said triumphantly, passing a flute first to Alex, then to Lara. 'Didn't I say that ring on Izzy's right hand was fooling nobody? Finally she puts me out of my misery and moves it to the correct finger.'

Lara could see excitement on Poppy's face mingling with a measure of relief that things had obviously worked out so wonderfully for Izzy. She looked blissfully happy with Harry's hand resting around her waist. Lara offered her own congratulations as she examined the swirl of silver on Izzy's left hand.

'It's beautiful, Izzy,' she said. 'Just so elegant.'

A pang of unexpected wistfulness surged through her stomach as she examined the ring, silver with a couple of diamonds, gorgeous in its simplicity. Not wistfulness for the ring, gorgeous though it was, but for how lovely it must be to have someone make that commitment to you, to be able to look forward to a shared future instead of a solitary one.

'Izzy and Harry,' Isaac said, raising his glass. They all followed suit.

'How's your father doing, Harry?' Alex asked.

Harry smile tightened almost imperceptibly.

'On the mend, thanks,' he said. 'Touch and go for a while back there but he's over the worst now. I guess we'll see when we go back in a few weeks for the wedding.'

There was an immediate shocked gasp from Poppy.

'*For the wedding?* You mean you're getting hitched in Australia, not here? You can't!'

'We're doing both,' Izzy said, smiling.

'Both? How's that going to work?'

'We're getting married in London first,' Harry said. 'Something more intimate, so Izzy can have all her friends and family there, and then we'll decamp to Australia afterwards for the full-on "official" take on it.'

'So chill out,' Izzy said, 'no one's going to miss out,

you'll all be there. And actually, Lara, can I have a quick word?'

Izzy drew Lara quietly to one side as Isaac refilled glasses.

'I was wondering if you'd consider making my wedding dress?' she ventured.

A flush of genuine pleasure warmed Lara's cheeks. She was thrilled to be asked, to be trusted with such an important part of their day.

'Seriously?'

'Absolutely. Your lingerie is just gorgeous. And you do other clothes too, right, not just underwear? I'm right, aren't I? That dress you wore at the shop launch?'

Lara nodded.

'I make some of my own clothes, yes.' She clasped her hands together to contain her excitement. 'I'd *love* to do your wedding dress. It would be an absolute dream. What kind of thing did you have in mind?'

Lara sat down on the sofa and Izzy perched next to her, opening her tote bag and spreading a pile of wedding magazines out in front of her. As Izzy flipped through some cuttings Lara grabbed a pen and notepad and made notes furiously.

'I was hoping we could come up with a design that could double up for both weddings,' Izzy said. 'Nothing fussy, just simple lines.' She pointed to a magazine clipping of a full-length, elegant sheath dress, stunning in its simplicity. 'Kind of like this, but maybe with more of a drapey neckline.'

'Like this?' In a few strokes Lara sketched a draping column of a dress with a cowl neckline.

'Yes, exactly like that.' She clapped her hands together excitedly. 'I'm going to have an angora sweater for the service here—it'll be a very fine knit that I can wear over my dress. Hand-made. I've outsourced it to my mother!'

Lara smiled.

'And then the second wedding in Australia is going to be hot so I can just wear the dress without the sweater.'

'I'll put together some proper drawings for you and then we can fine-tune the design from there,' Lara said. 'I'll need to take full measurements from you. I'll need to know what shoes you're wearing, work out what lingerie will be best, that kind of thing. And we'll do fittings as we go along so we can make sure it's exactly what you want.'

'Perfect!'

Izzy's enthusiasm and excitement filled the room and another stab of envy poked Lara sharply behind the ribs. Izzy and Harry had been together for, what—a couple of months? And yet they were so utterly sure of each other that they were storming forward with wedding plans.

'It must be lovely to be so certain of something,' she said, before she could stop herself. 'Of *someone*.'

Izzy glanced up from the sketches and smiled.

'You're loved-up with Alex, aren't you?' she said.

'Of course.' Lara shrugged. 'But I haven't a clue really where we're headed. I've got so much on at the moment and the business always comes first. I don't have time to think about the future of any relationship. Not right now.'

Saying it out loud felt vaguely reassuring. There was a niggling sense of unease at her current situation that she'd tried hard to ignore. She hadn't counted on how happy it would make her feel, how secure, being with Alex. She looked across the sitting room to where he was joking around with Isaac, and her feelings for him bowled her over with their strong, confident depth. For the first time since her childhood she let her dogged tunnel vision slip and allowed herself to wonder if a solitary future really *was* the only option for her. There was no harm in dreaming, right? Maybe even in playing out the dream a little—why rule anything out? Surely Lara, with every aspect of her life under full control, could be open to seeing where this thing with Alex led without committing herself fully? In fact it would be odd if hopes and dreams *didn't* enter her mind right now—they were exactly what weddings were all about after all.

Mutual support. There was something deliciously couple-ish about it. Something that made Lara feel warm and happy deep inside, the unfamiliar sensation of being part of a team. Alex had been there for her at the shop launch, and now it was her turn to step up to the plate and return the favour.

Shame really that, in her case, mutual support had to include gruelling exercise. How much more palatable it would be if, for example, Alex ran a wine bar, like Isaac. She could quite happily envisage herself socialising, dressed in something sophisticated with a cocktail in her hand. She would be perfect for the role. Instead, here she was again, dressed in her mishmash of borrowed sportswear and bringing up the rear of a group of eight thirty-something women, all of whom looked a billion times more attractive than she did. Honestly, wasn't the whole *point* of needing to go to boot camp that you *didn't* already look your best?

This was Alex's attempt to diversify his test market from one-to-one personal training into fitness classes, leading a sample group of women on a cross-country run through the woodland of Holland Park. It had undoubtedly been preceded by one of his customary sessions of gruelling warm-up exercises and, possibly, instructions on how to keep up without turning into a sweating mess. Unfortunately she'd missed all that so she'd just have to wing it. She'd lost track of the time, sorting out loose ends at the shop instead of rushing here straight after closing. Alex had timed the half-hour run carefully to make the most of the last hour or so of daylight.

The woman directly in front of her had chestnut-brown hair caught up in a perfect high ponytail and co-ordinating pink and black designer sportswear. As Alex led them uphill Lara was treated to an unwelcome view of her perfect pert bottom emphasised by skintight leggings. Insecurity stabbed her sharply in the stomach and she grimly did her best to ignore it and plod on through the mud and leaves. Since the night of the launch, nearly a week ago now, Alex had been there for her on every level. He'd given her no reason to think he'd be interested in anyone else, no matter how good they might look in Lycra.

She made a special effort to pull her posture together, hold her head high and present a bouncy jogging motion instead of her body's default attitude of staggering along. Unfortunately holding her head high meant she didn't spot a sudden hollow in the squelchy ground preceded by a protruding tree root. Didn't spot it, that was, until her foot had caught in it and she'd performed a dying-swan sort of movement that ended in a muddy splat as she fell flat on her face. Mercifully, being at the back of the group meant no one realised she was floundering on the ground behind them.

The running group jogged on ahead of her in perfect unison, manoeuvring through the trees with Alex's voice counting out the pace in loud shouts from the front. Lara

scrambled back to her feet as quickly as she could, only
to fold immediately back onto her knees the moment she
attempted to put weight on her left ankle. The pain was
horrible, making her head spin and sending stars across
her field of vision. She watched the group putting more
and more distance between them.

The main path was only a few hundred metres away,
the end of the run a short distance along it. The choice
was perfectly simple. Either she could draw attention to
herself as the weakest link in the team, distract Alex from
his very first test class, which up until now had clearly
gone perfectly to plan, or she could do her best to limp
to the end of the course.

No contest.

In her mind there wasn't even a decision to be made.
She attempted gingerly to test her foot again and bit her
lip. Painful, but manageable as long as she didn't keep
her weight on it for too long. She pulled herself grimly
into what could only be described as a limping jog, con-
centrating hard on not falling too far behind the group,
and forced herself over the final leg of the run. By the
time Alex brought the group to a standstill at the finishing point, she was reduced to lurching along like a total
moron. Fortunately he was so engrossed in leading the
cool-down exercises that he didn't notice her limping appearance at the back.

She leaned against a tree a short distance away and
closed her eyes briefly. The cool-down exercises could
go to hell. With no weight on it her ankle didn't feel
too bad. Perhaps she just needed to give it a minute or
two to recover. She waved at him from the sidelines as
he caught her eye, and watched him talk to his adoring
class. She could hear him bandying motivational phrases

around. And then as the class finally dispersed he made his way over to her, an exhilarated grin lighting up his handsome face.

'You made it,' he said. 'I thought you'd got held up at the shop.' Then, eyes narrowing, 'Just how late were you? Did you do the warm up?'

'Just about caught it,' she lied, taking the bottle of water he offered and sipping it gratefully. 'I thought the class went brilliantly, didn't you? Just wait until the word gets around at the school gates—you'll be inundated.' She pasted on a beaming smile.

He turned back towards the path, zipping up his hoodie, ready to get back to the flat. Dusk was beginning to fall now and the street lamps were kicking in. Lara tried her weight on her ankle carefully and pressed her lips together. The pain was monstrous. She gritted her teeth and limped along anyway a foot or so behind him, which was fine for a few seconds until he turned back and put an arm around her shoulders. Oh, the bliss of having something to lean on. She shoved her arm around his waist and used him as a crutch. And just a couple of paces was enough.

'What the bloody hell is going on with your foot?' he said, stopping immediately. She could hear exasperation fighting with concern in his tone of voice.

She drew herself up to her full height. Not easy when only one of your ankles could bear your weight. She pasted a breezy smile on her face.

'I slipped a bit on the way round. It's nothing.'

Totally ignoring her, he was already on his knees in the mud, loosening the laces of her trainer. She couldn't stop a yelp as he eased it off.

'Lara, it's swollen. When did you fall?'

'Near the end,' she said. 'Just when we turned back onto the main path.'

'That was way back,' he said. 'Why the hell did you keep going? Why didn't you stop the class?'

And make a total fool of herself in front of Notting Hill's yummy-mummy set? Did he know *nothing* at all about female pride?

'There was no need,' she said. 'I wasn't about to make a fuss and put a stop to the class, not when it was going so well.'

He slid an arm gently around her waist and took her other arm over his shoulder.

'Let's get back to the flat. With any luck Poppy will be there and we can get her to look at it.'

'I don't need Poppy to look at it, I'm perfectly all right. Don't fuss.'

He stopped then and looked her in the eye. She saw with some surprise that he was fighting to control his temper. Just what the hell was the big deal?

'*Don't fuss?*' he snapped. 'You were part of my class and that makes you *my* responsibility.'

'And how exactly are *you* meant to be responsible when I didn't tell you what I'd done?' she said. 'Nothing would have made me pipe up in front of that gang of middle-class mums in their DKNY sportswear that I'd just slipped in the mud in my too big cast-off trainers. I'm over eighteen, Alex, I'm not made of *glass*, and I don't need Poppy looking at my foot.'

'However you try and dress it up, I'm accountable for this,' he said, as if he hadn't heard a word. 'For you *and* your foot. So for once in your damned independent life, accept some help. This isn't a laughing matter. If I'm going to be running these classes professionally then health and safety has to be paramount.' He shook his head and frowned. 'Maybe I should have done another risk assessment.'

Oh, for Pete's sake.

'Can you just stop with the health and safety?' she said, holding up a hand. 'A thank-you might have been nice instead of a dressing down. Perhaps you'd like me to get down in the mud and give you fifty press-ups? Do you really think I *wanted* to turn out in the freezing cold and schlep round Holland Park? I came because I wanted to give you some moral support.'

He stared at her.

'I appreciate that, but I can't have *my* responsibility compromised because *your* mind isn't on the class,' he said. 'If you've just come along for a jolly and you're not going to take it seriously then it's probably best you don't come at all.'

A *jolly*?

Despite the rapidly cooling air, a rush of boiling heat suffused her from the neck up.

She disentangled herself from his arm, elbowed him aside and limped ahead at speed. The pain in her foot was awful but the way she felt right now she'd rather walk fifty miles on it than spend one more minute leaning on him.

'Lara, stop,' he said, jogging alongside to keep up with her. 'Let me help you.'

She stopped next to him.

'There was nothing *jolly* about hauling myself around Holland Park in the freezing cold,' she said through gritted teeth. She shook him off as he tried to take her arm. 'I wanted to be there for you, the same way you were there for me when I was biting my nails to the quick over my shop launch. But now I know you don't want me to bother unless I've got some kind of *fitness* objective, I'll stay out of the way in future. Risk assess *that*!'

She stormed off again and this time he didn't follow her.

CHAPTER TEN

ALEX LET HIMSELF into the flat and found Lara in the kitchen with her foot up on one of the chairs and Poppy strapping the ankle up with elasticated bandage. Lara's arms were folded and she had a mulish expression on her face.

'What happened to not needing Poppy to look at it?' he said, exasperated. 'You were having none of it back at the park.'

'Oh, she tried her best to limp past me,' Poppy said, glancing up. 'Lucky for you it isn't broken,' she told Lara. 'Just a strain. Take it easy for a day or two and it will be fine.'

He knew just by the expression on Lara's face that hell would be freezing over before she took it easy. Poppy covered the whole thing with a tube bandage and stood up to pack away her first-aid kit.

He could feel the indignant vibes radiating from Lara. The instant Poppy left the room she put her foot on the floor.

Alex had begun the solo walk back to the fire station fired up with exasperation at Lara for not taking better care of herself and, worse, with fury at himself for not being in better control of the class. How the hell had he not noticed whether she was at the warm up or not? Irritation gave way to thinking through the situation. This had been a test class after all, a chance for him to fine-tune the running of things. Maybe Lara had done him a favour. Better that he picked up on any loopholes like this now, before a paying client had some kind of accident on his watch. He resolved to tighten up his protocol before going any further with the boot-camp model. But then calm thought returned, and with it came a stab of guilt at the way he'd gone off at her. Lara Connor with her single-minded attitude, determined to run her life on her own without letting anyone in, had turned out to support him in his new business venture, a business venture that by the way she'd been instrumental in setting up. When did Lara ever make time for anything except her own business plans? Yet she'd made time to come and support him.

'How is it?' he asked.

'It's perfectly fine,' she said in tones of pure frost.

He pulled out the chair opposite and sat down.

'I'm sorry,' he said. 'I didn't mean it to sound like I'm ungrateful for your support—'

'But you'd just rather take the *personal* out of personal training,' she cut in. She held her hands up. 'It's fine. I'm *more* than happy not to come to any more of your classes.'

'It wasn't about not wanting you at the class.'

She simply stared at him with a sceptical expression on her face. *Yeah, right,* it said. He ran a hand uncomfortably through his hair.

'It wasn't actually about *you* at all,' he said. 'It's about accountability. You have to understand I've spent years taking decisions that affect other people. The army was all about that for me—having people rely on me, following my orders without question or thought for the consequences. It was all about not letting people down, because when you stuff up with that kind of thing in an army situation people get hurt.'

He knew that better than anyone. His mind sideslipped madly back to that final tour before he could stop it. Private Sam Walker looking at him with that half grin on his face. *'I know you've got my back, sir. And I've got yours.'* He blinked hard and forced himself to refocus on the present, on Lara. Her expression softened a little, the cynical slant melting away.

'You're not in the forces anymore, Alex,' she said patiently. 'Lives aren't at stake. You don't have control of what other people do or say. You can do all you can to make sure things are safe, and you're doing that. You've covered the insurance angle, you're up together on warm-up exercises and risk assessments. But you can't control the fact that I turned up late and bent the rules, or that my heart wasn't in the run. You can't take the blame because I screwed up. You're not responsible for the rest of the world.'

'You're more than just the rest of the world,' he said. 'I care what happens to you.'

A warm and fuzzy stomach flip kicked right in and Lara pressed her hands over her tummy hard. He *cared*. She was used to taking care of herself on every level, taking responsibility for every aspect of her life herself; his downright refusal to let her go her own way without voicing his concern was completely new to her. The sensation of being looked after, of being *cared about*, was one that she'd denied herself for so long that she'd forgotten just how lovely it was.

Or how dangerous.

What exactly was she doing here, letting herself get so close to someone that being *cared about* came into the equation? It was the living-in thing, of course. That was why it had slipped past her guard. Circumstance and not conscious choice had meant they'd ended up sharing a flat. And maybe it was the Izzy-and-Harry thing a bit too. Being part of the whirlwind excitement of their fairy-tale happiness made anything seem possible. The warm and happy feeling was intoxicating. Would it really be so dangerous to just run with this and see where it led?

When he reached across the table and covered her hand with his, she didn't take it away.

Two hours later and if she had to put up with one more minute of sitting still in the flat with a constantly re-filled cup of tea and a magazine, Lara thought she might scream. Not that she'd had any big plans for this evening except possibly to sort through some stock and then cook a meal, but now she was unable to do either of those things she felt hemmed in.

Still, when he appeared in the sitting room showered and changed she smiled at him through gritted, *bored* teeth because, actually, his concern was something she was liking very much. If only he could exhibit it in an-other way than ensuring her bladder stayed above the pint level with his endless cups of tea.

He smiled back, crossed the room towards her, and before she could make any comment he leaned down and picked her up from the sofa as if she weighed abso-lutely nothing. She was treated to a delicious wave of his aftershave, something woody and fresh, and she curled her arms around his neck immediately, her stomach beginning to fill with heat. Now *this* beat reading women's magazines.

'Where are you taking me?' she said in surprise as he failed to take the expected route to his bedroom. He kicked open the door of the flat and proceeded to carry her down the stairs.

'Ignite,' he said. 'I could see you were climbing the walls in there.'

'Could you?' she said, interested that he could be that perceptive.

'Yep. It was that tight voice you used when you thanked me for the tea.'

'I'm sorry,' she said, feeling guilty. 'It *was* the fourth cup in the space of an hour. I am grateful, really I am. I just don't *do* bed rest. It just isn't me.'

'You don't say,' he said, pausing in the stairwell to smile into her face. She smiled back and he planted a soft kiss at the corner of her mouth.

'I did think about Isaac's bar followed by dancing but I thought that might finish you off,' he said, taking the stairs again. At the bottom he pushed open the door of Ignite with one foot and carried her across the restaurant to a corner table while the staff and customers looked at them with interest. He set her down gently.

'I can actually get around by limping, you know,' she protested. He raised sarcastic eyebrows at her and she backed down with a grin. 'But Ignite is perfect.' Just knowing her well enough to see that she'd been going stir crazy was enough to melt her heart. Dinner out was an unexpected bonus.

Ignite did a great line in wine and tapas when it wasn't being a coffee lounge and, tucking into a shared platter over glasses of chilled white wine, it was easy to let herself relax in Alex's company. She let her guard take the evening off, knowing normal self-reliance would be back in charge the moment she could put her weight back on her ankle. She didn't argue at his insistence throughout the evening that she keep her foot up on the opposite chair, or at his refusal to let her walk back up the stairs to the flat when the evening was over. Yes, there was a growing closeness between them, but she was fully conscious of it, that was the most important thing here. And she should be able to move back into her own flat at the end of this week. That would put a bit of distance right back into the situation. And so surely there was absolutely no harm in feeling a little bit cared about until then.

When sleep arrived later that evening, it was in his arms.

Lara stretched deliciously, blinked her eyes open, and tried to pull her scrambled sleep-fuzzy brain together. She felt well rested for once. None of the usual hankering from her body for more sleep, which she always steadfastly ignored. No disorientation about where she was—it seemed after years of sleeping, of doing everything alone, all it took was a few nights to get used to sharing her bed with someone else. *His* bed, if she wanted to split hairs. The golden autumn sunshine slanted through the curtains and into the military order, which was only tempered a tiny bit by the items of her own clothing slung randomly over the back of a chair. She turned her head to the left then and realised Alex wasn't there. His side of the bed had the covers thrown back.

Frowning, she leaned up on one elbow. The flat was quiet. None of the clattering from the kitchen that signified Alex making one of his endless cups of coffee. And it occurred to her that the room was unusually bright. She was used to scrambling around in the semi-darkness when she got up in the mornings. And then, as her mind began to focus properly, her stomach kicked in with a hideous lurching sensation. The kind of lurch that came when you overslept on the morning of an exam or missed a really important meeting. The kind of lurch that she never experienced because Lara Connor did not *do* lateness or poor organisational skills. Ever.

She was across the bed in one swift scrambling movement, grabbing at Alex's alarm clock with a flash of horror. Two facts careered madly through her brain: it was five minutes shy of ten o'clock and someone had switched the alarm off. Right about now she should be standing, perfectly groomed, behind the counter of her shop greeting the morning customers with a smile. Instead her hair was in its first-thing fright-wig mode, there was sleep in the corners of her eyes and her hard-won clientele would be greeted by a locked door and a 'Closed' sign.

She'd thrown herself out of the bed, plonked both feet to the floor and stood up before she remembered the previous day's injury. She yelped in pain and hopped back onto the bed, one hand clamped to her throbbing ankle, the other scraping through her hair as she put two and two together.

Alex had obviously, without so much as a whisper in her direction, taken a unilateral decision to let her have a lie-in, probably because of some personal-trainer opinion about resting injured limbs for *days*. Clearly it would be perfectly fine for him with the balance of his trust fund as a cushion to take a morning off work whenever he felt like it. She, on the other hand, had no back-up plan worth beans. Did he not understand she had a *business* to run?

Limping out to the kitchen, she found no trace of either him or Poppy, although his enormous coffee mug was upended in the sink.

She also found no trace of the keys to the shop despite turning the kitchen counter upside down. Her frantic call to his mobile phone went straight to voice mail and the only explanation was so unthinkable that she came to a shocked standstill in the middle of the room.

Alex wouldn't have opened the shop, would he?

The sign on the door read 'Open' and she could see through the glass door that Alex was standing behind the counter at the back of the shop.

'What the hell is going on?' She stormed through the door on the wave of anger and frustration that had built to a crest during the taxi ride. 'Who the hell do you think you are, opening my shop without even asking me? Taking my keys? Letting me oversleep?'

His welcoming smile disappeared like smoke.

'Thank you, Alex, for looking after the shop for me while I took a much-needed rest,' he said loudly. 'You twisted your ankle yesterday. That kind of injury needs to be rested, not squashed into a four-inch heel.'

He glanced downward at that moment to see she was wearing a pair of soft leather ballet flats and made a backtracking chuffing sound through his nose. 'Well, I see you've at least decided to be sensible about footwear,' he conceded.

She didn't bother to enlighten him that she'd tried half a dozen heeled pairs before admitting to herself that limping was a whole lot easier and less attention-grabbing in flat shoes. No way was she just passing across the upper hand. He was the one in the wrong here.

'But you should still be resting up,' he carried on. 'You never take a break. You're always on the go. And since I don't have any training sessions today, I thought I'd help you out. I've sold half a dozen pairs of those knickers that look like shorts and one of those sets of pyjamas.' He spoke with the triumphant air of someone who'd just discovered a natural flair for sales that would floor Alan Sugar.

'Without even *asking* me?' she snapped incredulously. 'Would it have *killed* you to ask me my opinion before you took over my business? You didn't even leave a note, for Pete's sake.'

'I was trying to do you a favour,' he said. He waved a hand around at the shop floor. 'The place didn't spontaneously combust just because you weren't at the helm for *one bloody hour*. I am not a total imbecile.'

His voice had suddenly taken on an icy cold and even more clipped tone than usual. She realised with a jolt of surprise how angry he actually was. It filtered through to her one-track work-obsessed mind that she might be overreacting here the teeniest bit, and she made a too-late effort to curb her tongue.

'It's my business, Alex,' she said, attempting to explain. 'It's all I've got.'

'So it's fine for me to take you out to dinner and pamper you a bit but when it comes to trusting me with something that actually *matters* to you, you revert to control freak,' he snapped, walking out from behind the counter and storming past her towards the door. 'Since this place is the only thing that's remotely important to you, I'll leave you to get the hell on with it.'

He was out of the shop before she had time to say

anything else and slammed the door behind him so hard she was surprised the plate-glass window didn't shatter.

It took ten minutes to reorganise the counter back to her own liking instead of in his right-angles–lined-up obsessive military neatness. Ten minutes during which seething and self-righteousness gradually gave way to niggling doubt about who was in the wrong here and who exactly had overstepped the mark in terms of reasonable behaviour.

She couldn't fail to see that he'd made a careful list of the items he'd sold, and when she did a quick check of the till it balanced perfectly. He'd managed without a hitch. When you got right down to it, he was trying to do something nice for her, looking out for her. And of course he was confused as hell because last night she'd allowed that without complaint. But then it hadn't been about her beloved lingerie business, had it? Big difference between letting him spoil her with a meal and letting him take the reins of the most important thing in her life. The alarm bells that had started ringing yesterday when he'd helped her home after she'd twisted her ankle had gone into overdrive and she'd acted without thinking, concerned only with looking after the safe and secure little world she'd built for herself, believing that only *she* was capable of doing that.

She'd overreacted. He'd been spot on when he'd called her a control freak. And now she had to find a way of climbing down.

She managed until lunchtime. Her interim attempts to get hold of Alex went straight to voice mail and even a short rush of late-morning customers failed to stop the unhappy churning in her stomach. Her mind constantly picked at the situation, at her own behaviour. A bolt of ivory silk had been delivered for Izzy's wedding dress and she found herself staring at it miserably. Had she actually been daydreaming about having a future like that herself? Only now did she see how far beyond her that was, how unsuited she was with her present attitude to being part of a proper couple. If she couldn't relinquish control and put her trust in someone else, how could she ever hope to share her life with someone?

She ran her shop, her life, her world in her own way. The problem was, she wasn't really sure that was what she wanted, not anymore.

The first step towards change would be to apologise, of course. If he would listen after the spoilt-brat way she'd behaved towards him. And unfortunately, it became slowly clear to her that the only way to climb down and convince him she wasn't just talking the talk but was actually serious would be to put her money where her mouth was. Or, more accurately, her shop.

If anything proved to her that she was in too deep here it was this one tiny action of turning the sign on the glass door of the shop to read 'Closed' when it was currently two o'clock in the afternoon. Three hours' business time left and she was sacrificing a chunk of it to sort out her personal life. She who didn't even *have* a personal life, let alone one whose importance interfered with shop opening hours. She did it anyway.

There was a moment where she faltered as she walked past the door of her own studio flat on the fire station stairs, a floor below Poppy's flat. A couple of weeks ago and everything had been so straightforward. The pop-up shop had consumed her every waking thought; she'd been utterly focused. She couldn't have imagined anything distracting her from that. And now look at her, back here when she could be working, because when it came right down to it she just couldn't let the situation lie.

Alex was in the kitchen at the flat, the open laptop on the table displaying some kind of fitness website. He glanced up at her in amazement.

'What are you doing back here?'

'We need to talk,' she said, putting her keys and bag down on the table and sitting down. His face was completely inscrutable, which didn't help at all. She had no clue if she was in with a chance of turning the situation around.

'You've shut the shop? In the middle of the day? Bloody hell, call CNN,' he said. She let that slide. She deserved it.

She looked down at her fingers.

'I may have overreacted,' she began. 'A little.'

His face didn't change in the slightest.

'What the hell happened to you that you can't even let someone lend you a hand for a morning?' he said. 'I've never known such a control freak.'

'It's not about being a control freak,' she protested. 'It's about being professional.'

'It's about having a chip on your shoulder about accepting help.'

She bit back the indignant denials that rose to her lips. She could deny it all she wanted but her behaviour today had spoken volumes. To herself as well as to him.

'I'm just not used to delegating and the shock of waking up and finding that you'd gone ahead and opened up without even asking what I thought—'

'What exactly are you trying to say?' he snapped, making it perfectly clear that edging around an apology simply wasn't going to cut the mustard.

'I'm trying to say I'm sorry,' she blurted out. 'I know you were trying to help. I'm just not used to people doing that.' She paused, and then corrected, 'I'm not used to *letting* people do that.'

'You don't say.'

She put her elbows on the table and pushed her hands into her hair, looking down at the scrubbed wood table top.

'Accepting help from people, handing over responsibility for things, that isn't something I do lightly,' she said. 'I promised myself a long time ago that I'd make my own success in life, that I'd get where I wanted to be on my own, without having to rely on anyone else's input.' She shrugged. 'I may have become a bit rabid about that.'

A smile twitched at the corner of his lips and her heart turned softly over.

'You think?'

She smiled back.

'I made the mistake too many times when I was growing up. Of trusting people, thinking I knew where I was and then having everything change again.'

'You mean your mother?' His gaze sharpened and he reached out and shut the lid of the laptop. 'I do get that, Lara. It must have been tough when you were small, but when you talked about it I kind of got the impression that things were much more settled after you were fostered.'

Of course he had. It was exactly the impression she'd intended to give. If only it had been that simple. Straight into care, touch base and straight out again to the perfect foster family. Accepted and loved. Integrated easily at school. Grew up well-adjusted with lasting supportive family ties. This was the real world though, and she'd quickly seen that life just wasn't that warm and fuzzy. Verbalising the reality didn't come easily but she forced herself.

'I gave you the airbrushed version,' she said. 'The bits I think are worth remembering.' She held a hand up in response to his questioning expression. 'You're not the only one with baggage, Alex. We've all got it. We all have to find our own way to deal with it. For me, it's about being in control, about making my own decisions and building a secure life. And for a long time that's been something that I've done on my own. I'm way past believing that anyone else is going to do it for me.'

She took a deep breath.

'I told you my mother couldn't look after me,' she said. 'I spent some time in a children's home and then I was fostered.' She paused. 'And then when that didn't work it was back into the care system until I was fostered again.' She managed a strangled laugh. 'And again. Unfortunately there must have been something about me that meant I didn't fit in. It takes time to settle in with new people and I'd just about start to get a handle on it, then it wouldn't work out and back I'd go. It was so unsettling. I was constantly changing schools, as fast as I made any friends it felt like I moved on again. Eventually I gave up trying.'

A surge of sympathy tugged at Alex's chest as he imagined her as a little kid being shifted from one household to the next. And something else, the oddest thing: the sensation of things falling into place, of *understanding*. Because once he'd been a kid of five arriving at boarding school loaded down with a trunk and a tuck box and rejection. That sense of not being wanted hollowed you out deep inside. He'd been able to fill the gap before long, with friends, with the teachers and pastoral assistants at school. Then later with his comrades in the army. He'd been lucky in that at least there had been continuity for him: he'd stayed at the same school throughout his childhood, had made lifelong enduring friends. Isaac was a case in point. For Alex, it had become his home and family. Lara hadn't even had that. Little wonder that she was so determined now to go it alone.

'It carried on until I hit my teens, backwards and forwards to this placement or that, and then one day I ended up with Bridget and her husband,' Lara said. He could hear the affection for these people in her voice. 'I stayed with them right up until I started college. That was the only place that lasted.' She gave him a rueful smile. 'By then I think the damage was done though. And there's still this niggling doubt that maybe I moved out before they could get fed up with me, and *that's* the real reason it worked with them and not the others.'

'Do you really believe that?'

She thought of Bridget's kindness, the time and effort she'd given to helping Lara settle in, and finding something she could focus on. She shook her head.

'No, I don't really believe that. It's just that for some reason the times I was sent back resonate more with me than the one time I got to stay. Like any criticism, I suppose. You always take more notice of the bad stuff—did you ever notice that?'

He stretched across the table and took her hand in his.

'By the time I went to live with Bridget I was only a couple of years away from college age. And when I found I had a flair for sewing and I could actually *make money* at it, well, that was like finding the perfect answer. If I took charge of my own life and made my own security, I'd never have to leave it. My mistake was looking for someone else to make that life for me. Thinking that I could somehow slot into someone else's perfect family. I decided I'd make my own future that no one could take away from me. There would be no more lurking fear that just as I got close to people I'd be moving on.'

'That's why you're so work-obsessed,' he said. It made perfect sense now.

'I don't see it as *obsessed*,' she said. 'I know I'm driven but it's not about making millions—it's just about making enough for me to put down some roots, so I can have some security.' She lifted her chin a little and gave him a look of triumph. 'Maybe buy a place and get settled. And it will be all the sweeter because I got there myself.'

'I get where you're coming from now,' he said. 'Your determination to do every minute little thing on your own, no matter what the cost. I can understand that. But you don't need to go it alone. Not anymore.'

She looked up at him and the expression on her face made his heart turn softly over.

'I'm sorry,' she said. 'I'm just not used to people being there for me.'

He stood up and rounded the table, pulled her to her feet and tugged her against him. She tucked her head beneath his chin as he wrapped his arms around her.

'Then get used to it,' he said.

CHAPTER ELEVEN

EVENINGS OUT ON the town were a thing of the past. His growing business brought with it a new routine. Clients in the morning and boot-camp groups a couple of afternoons a week. Lara had got the go-ahead to move back into the studio flat and now they split their time between his place and hers. Normal couple. Normal *life*. October was almost at an end now, soon winter would be kicking in, but Poppy had told him she was happy for him to stay put in the flat as long as he wanted. The sense of belonging somewhere again, of having a purpose, felt like finding his way home after being cast adrift and floundering for months.

And tonight, Lara was home first. He'd had a late training session and so she'd decided to treat him to a home-cooked dinner in his own flat. He was greeted by the delicious aroma of salmon with ginger, lime and coriander. There was a green salad and chilled white wine.

'The personal training sessions are really taking off,' he said as she sat down opposite him. He poured them each a glass of wine. 'Offering a taster session for free is really working out well. I picked up another new client today, word of mouth.'

'That's great,' she said.

There was a troubled undertone to her voice that belied the breezy smile. In fact now he came to think about it, she'd been a bit detached and quiet this last couple of days. He'd assumed it was just that she was tired.

'What's up?' he said. 'Everything all right at the shop?'

Asking him about future plans made a cold little pebble of dread land in Lara's chest and she forced herself to carry on regardless. These last few weeks had been so great, for the first time in years she'd actually begun to let someone else's presence slip into her life. The temptation to just let it carry on, not questioning what it was or where it might lead, was overwhelming. Because that way she wouldn't have to run the risk of an answer she didn't want to hear.

Unfortunately the situation wouldn't allow for them to just drift along much further with no direction. The lease would be up before she knew it on the pop-up shop. Already she was halfway through. She needed to consider what her next steps should be with the business. And it wasn't just that—there was the flat to consider. She'd only intended on renting it for the duration of the shop lease and that had been done on the strength of her savings. There was no way she could afford to keep renting in Notting Hill in the long term.

'I've been thinking about the future,' she said, not looking at him. 'The pop-up shop is a really short-term lease, remember. Just until the end of November and then I'll have to ship out. Someone else will move into the premises, probably some Christmas shop or other.'

He frowned a little as he forked up some of his fish.

'OK, so what are you thinking of doing after that? Knowing you, you've probably got the next ten years mapped out.'

She took a deep breath and kept a neutral expression on her face.

OK, so he hadn't immediately leapt in with an enthusiastic torrent of suggestions of how they might proceed from here—*together*. She bit the inside of her cheek to distract herself from the surge of disappointment that brought. Just because she was making a conscious effort to take a step back from control freak didn't mean she had to flip to the other end of the scale and start working needy. He probably wasn't thinking beyond the next week or so, but his lack of future plans didn't necessarily have to have anything to do with his regard for her, right?

'That's the thing,' she said. 'I need to start thinking about where I'm going with it next.'

He tucked into the salad.

'The shop's doing well, isn't it?'

She nodded and took a sip of her wine.

'It's done really well, but it was only ever really an experiment. I need to start planning where I'm going with it next, whether I run with the retail thing and look for another shop or maybe trial internet sales on a wider scale.'

'Why not put some figures together for the different options and then we can talk it through?' he said. 'Weigh up the pros and cons.'

The long-ingrained urge to politely decline any offer of help rose to her lips just as it always did. This time she swallowed it. He was in her corner. In time sharing things with him would surely become less conscious and more natural.

'Great,' she said. And it was great. She felt more settled than she had in years, secure and happy.

As they finished the meal she stood up to make coffee and he joined her, curling his arms around her waist, kiss-

ing her neck from behind, making her so deliciously hot.
She turned in his arms and he tilted her face up gently to
meet his. Not fast or furious this time, no rushing. His
mouth found hers and she melted against him. He picked
her up and carried her down the hall to his room as if she
weighed nothing at all.

Undressing her was an indulgent pleasure and Alex
lingered over it, revelled in it, kissing her skin inch by
silken inch until she was squirming with desire. Then he
lay above her, feeling the soft curl of her arms and legs
around him, binding him to her. Her soft cry of pleasure
at his first thrust deep inside her thrilled him on a vis-
ceral level that drove his own arousal to an ever higher
level. He plunged both hands into her hair and cradled
her face as he took her, in long, slow, delicious strokes.
Her china-blue eyes were wide as he looked down at
her, holding his own gaze steadily, sharing every sensation with him. Feeling her writhe in ecstasy beneath
him sent him careering beside her towards that shared
height of pleasure.

Crazy, hot, short-term sex, this wasn't. This sex had
strings. This was making love, savouring every touch,
every inch of her skin. Wanting to please her more than
himself. This was what it was like to let someone in.

The joy in that sensation was tinged with a gnawing
edge of danger that he tried hard to ignore. Afterwards
they lay sated in each other's arms and he felt her urgent
grip on his shoulders slowly relax.

'I think I could get used to this,' she whispered against
his hair as his breathing began to level. He could feel her
own breath warm against his skin.

She settled lower, curling up into the crook of his arm,

and he felt her smile against his shoulder as she twined his fingers into her own.

'These past few weeks have been great,' she said. 'I've been on my own for so long that I'd got used to managing everything. I actually thought I liked living that way. I used to tell myself that was the best way to be—no one to answer to but myself, no one to let me down. I never thought I could have this sense of belonging—I thought it was beyond me. It's so lovely, feeling protected and looked after by you, knowing it's not just me against the world for a change.'

She leaned up on one elbow and smiled into his eyes.

'I love knowing you've got my back,' she said. 'And you know I've got yours.'

She pulled away a little so she could find his mouth and kiss him. As the words registered in his mind a hideous black sense of déjà vu stormed through his veins like ice water, picking up speed as it reached his heart.

What the hell had he been thinking?

You've got my back...and I've got yours.

The words filled him with fear as he recalled the last time he'd heard them. Private Sam Walker, now deceased. He'd been unable to save him, unable even to *find* him in the aftermath of the bomb. He'd failed to look out for him after all.

She'd come to rely on him.

Lara Connor, who relied on no one, who did everything for herself, who decided what she wanted from life and found a way to take it without enlisting anyone else's help. And in a flash of unsettling clarity it came to him. That was what he'd found most alluring about her all along. Lara was someone who could manage perfectly well without him. She didn't need him to protect her or look out for her. He had to force her to accept help, such was her level of perfect control freak. As such, the prospect of letting her down or failing her hadn't come into play. And in encouraging her to change, in pushing her to lean on him and let him look out for her, he'd ruled himself completely out of the game.

He lay rigid in the bed next to her long after she'd fallen asleep, curled up in a warm ball against his chest, wanting the façade he'd created. Desperately wanting to be that man with that perfect life—beautiful girlfriend, fledgling new business, new life all mapped out just there for the taking. Knowing he couldn't be, knowing it was all for show and that underneath the exterior he'd created so carefully that he'd actually begun to believe in it himself, he wasn't that man at all.

The revelation that now she *needed* him, that she felt protected, that she was revelling in having someone looking out for her for once, that she saw a future with him, made tendrils of cold dread begin to curl through him. He wasn't up to that challenge. The last person he'd encouraged to depend on him had died on his watch. Just what the hell had he been thinking?

There was no struggle to stay awake tonight while he waited for her to fall asleep. He lay next to her in the bed, tense with shock at his own arrogant stupidity. So determined to channel normality that he'd actually begun to *believe* in his own fiction.

Her talk this evening over dinner about the next move for her business came back to him. Her lease would be up in a matter of weeks. Was that why he'd let this get so far when he really should have known better? Because, subconsciously, he'd always seen an end point in sight to this? He'd known from their first meeting that she was here for a couple of months, no more. She'd told him, that day he'd fallen asleep in her flat, that she'd sunk her savings into this couple of months. *Couple of months.* Deep down had he believed this to be temporary? Just another longer version of his flings, commitment free? And therefore safe.

As her breathing evened, he eased his way out of the bed and moved to the kitchen, the same way he had for the past few nights.

The old single bed in Poppy's boxroom was so narrow that Lara hadn't been able to turn over without bashing herself on the wall of the boxroom. Sharing Alex's big double bed after that was pure luxury and as she surfaced from sleep somewhere in the small hours she stretched deliciously to her toes before turning over to snuggle back up to him.

His side of the bed was empty.

For a disoriented moment she wondered if she'd over-slept again and he'd got up to open the shop without ask-ing her, like some crazy Groundhog Day rerun of the other morning. But no, the other morning the room had been light with sunshine, not pitch dark as it was now. She came awake more fully and pulled herself up onto her elbow, screwing her eyes up to read the digital clock on Alex's bedside table. A little past three in the morn-ing. She lay for a few minutes, assuming he must be in the bathroom, or maybe getting a drink from the kitchen, but nothing. The minutes stretched ahead and she was wide awake now. Maybe he was ill.

That thought galvanised her into action and she threw the covers back and grabbed her robe from where it lay over a chair. The hallway was as dark as the bedroom. Poppy's bedroom door was closed and the bathroom was empty and silent. She padded down to the kitchen and immediately saw the slice of light cutting out beneath the closed door. She opened it and went into the room.

Alex visibly jumped as she came in. He was sitting at the table behind his laptop, a mug of coffee the size of a small bucket next to his hand, and a look on his face of pure guilt. *I'm caught,* it said. The guilt thing was so obvious that it shut out all other details as her mind searched madly for a simple explanation. What reason could a man have for sitting at his laptop in the middle of the night, sporting a guilty expression, except possibly for porn?

The instant that thought hit her brain, she marched across the room and took in his laptop screen. Not porn but the website for his new business. There was a notepad next to his hand and he was clearly working. Maybe he just couldn't sleep.

That thought in itself tripped some kind of alarm in her mind.

'What are you doing up?' she asked. 'I was worried. I thought you might be ill.'

He smiled at her.

'I just couldn't sleep. Thought I might as well get up and do something else.'

He pushed up from the table and attempted to sweep her into a hug. She batted his hands aside. Her mind was working overtime now.

She noticed with new clarity the dark shadows under his eyes as he failed to meet her gaze, shadows she'd noticed back in her flat when they first met, and like a bucket of cold water being sloshed over her she realised that those dark shadows had never really gone away. Her mind picked up other telltale details. The enormous coffee mug by his hand. The documents that strewed the table. His amazing ability to start up a business and cope with all the associated admin when she'd always felt as if she never had enough hours in the day.

'I couldn't sleep either,' she said. 'But I do what most normal people who can't sleep do at three in the morning. Warm milk and counting sheep. Whereas you've launched yourself into the working day.'

She waved a hand at the table, covered in papers, lists of figures, business card and poster samples. Her sleep-addled brain continued to make connections.

'I woke up three nights ago and you weren't there,' she said. 'It was some godforsaken small hour of the morning. I assumed you'd gone to the bathroom so I just turned over but you weren't there, were you? You were in here. Working. And your coffee addiction. On the whole, it's worse. I've never known anyone guzzle so much caffeine.'

She paused.

'This is about your nightmares, isn't it?' she said simply.

The words made Alex's stomach begin to churn.

'I'm dealing with it,' he said, clenching his hands.

'You told me you were dealing with it weeks ago,' she said. 'But staying awake isn't the answer. You're burying your head in the sand. That is *not* dealing with it.'

He sat down at the table and she tugged her silk dressing gown tighter around her and sank into the chair next to him, reached out to touch his wrist. He stared down at her hand, intended to comfort him, and shame began to climb burningly upward from his neck.

'You can't keep denying you have a problem,' she said

firmly. 'I let you fob me off last time because I thought things were getting better but by the look of it they're worse than ever.' Her smile was supportive. 'You don't need to worry,' she said. 'I'm here for you. We'll get you all the help you need.'

On the back of his fears about being able to take care of her now came this. He was a total basket case. He needed *help*. In her offer to get him support, she'd just inadvertently confirmed his failure. He was a failure as a soldier, as a comrade and friend. And if he stayed in her life, he would fail her too. She deserved better than that after the constant let-downs she'd already endured throughout her childhood. He gritted his teeth hard and forged ahead with his only option.

'This isn't going to work between us,' he said.

She was close enough for him to hear her catch her breath.

'What?' she whispered.

He pulled his arm away from her hand, stood up and backed away to lean against the kitchen counter, wanting to put distance between them now, steeling himself to go through with this, knowing it was for the best.

'I've been pretending that it could. Playing at normality,' he said. 'Kidding myself that I could work a normal relationship. Dating, supporting each other, sitting round the table eating dinner while we talk about our day. Sleeping together. All those things that *normal* people do. But all the time I've just been using it to hide reality.'

'From me?'

He shook his head and ran a hand briefly through his hair.

'Worse than that. From *me*. I've been kidding myself that I can be the man you deserve, that I can look after you in the way you need. I'm not up to that, Lara. I'll let you down—it's inevitable. Just a matter of time.'

'You're *dumping* me?' she said, her tone incredulous.

'A clean break is best,' he said. 'I'm not good for you, Lara. I'm not what you need.'

She held up a hand at that and he saw anger rush to her face.

'Don't you dare!' she snapped. 'Don't you *dare* spin me that it's-not-you-it's-me line. I should have listened to my instincts when I twisted my ankle. You let me think I could *count* on you. Have you any idea how hard it was for me to accept that? And now you're just saying you didn't mean it after all? I should never have let this get off the ground. I mean, have I not learned *anything*?' She tipped her head back and laughed sarcastically at the ceiling.

'It's not a line.'

'How can this *possibly* be about you?' she asked him then. She waved a hand at him. 'I mean, look at you— you've got half of Notting Hill's women salivating after you. You're smart, brave, funny, gorgeous.'

He was shaking his head.

'It *is* about me. I can't be the person you need me to be.' He lifted his hands in an all-encompassing gesture. 'None of this is real,' he said. 'This thing we have. Relationship. Whatever you want to call it. I thought I was doing such a great job. I thought that by going through the motions I could actually *be* normal, but it doesn't work. It's all a façade. I'm not the person you think I am and I'm not right for you.'

The words fell on Lara like stones. In other words, she didn't fit with him. And as a knock-on effect, she supposed, with his sister or his friends. And he clearly thought he could spare her a rundown of her personal failings to live up by blaming himself.

She bit the inside of her cheek to stop the burning sensation at the back of her throat from turning into anything more obvious. Funny how the age-old survival techniques kicked right back in. It felt as if she were twelve again, another foster home not working out, holding her head up high as she packed her things up, all ready to move on and insisting to herself that she didn't care; *she didn't care*. It wasn't about *her,* oh, no, it was about finding the right situation, the right family setting for her needs, the right *fit*.

When it came right down to it, none of his excuses really mattered. At best, even if she accepted what he was saying, it meant he'd never been straight with her. If manufacturing some ludicrous normality and hiding his sleep loss was preferable to just being honest with her, then he had a very different view of how important this relationship was. Whatever the reasons were, she wasn't right for him. She didn't want or need to hear any more excuses, in the same way as she hadn't wanted or needed to hear the explanations throughout her childhood. She wasn't a good fit, either now or back then, and she never should have kidded herself that she could be.

She stood up from the table and pushed the chair carefully back into place.

'I'm not bothered, Alex,' she said. She didn't raise her voice. She dug deep for all the dignity she could muster. 'I don't *need* to talk about this. I don't need any of your excuses. It was good while it lasted but my work has always come first. No big deal.'

She backed away from the table and out of the door and then she heard her practically sprint downstairs to her own flat. He was on his feet before he'd given it a moment's thought, ready to run after her. He hadn't reckoned on this. Hadn't thought for a second she would make it about *her*. This was *his* screw-up. How could she possibly believe this could be due to some failing of hers?

Then instinct was pushed away by reason. This was for the best; he was letting her off the hook, doing her a favour. Clean break, as he'd said to her. He could go down that hallway, bang on her door and talk with her all night, but the conclusion would be the same. This couldn't continue. He'd been a fool to let it go on as long as it had. He simply couldn't have people relying on him and she really was better off without him. The only way forward now was on his own. He really should have known that from the start.

CHAPTER TWELVE

'How are you holding up?'

Lara could feel Izzy's eyes looking down on her from where she stood on one of the old second-hand dining chairs in the middle of her studio flat. Putting her heart and soul into making a wedding dress, the epitome of a happy-ever-after, wasn't the automatic choice of therapy for a broken heart, but she was fine. She could do this. She was a *professional*. Faking a breezy 'I'm over him' wasn't that much of a challenge, she found. But then again she was a past master of toughing things out with a brave face.

'I'm absolutely fine,' she said, around a mouthful of pins. 'It's for the best. I'm not cut out to be one of a couple. I never have been.'

Perhaps if she said that often enough to herself and everyone else, it might actually start to make her feel better. Some time this century might be nice.

Wedding-dress fittings from now would take place in her own little flat, a venue change from that first talk she'd had with Izzy about dress styles, up in Poppy's living room, champagne in hand, surrounded by her new friends. Lara hadn't set foot in the flat upstairs since things had ended with Alex. No matter that he was away somewhere right now, accompanying Isaac at the last minute on one of his endless bar scouting trips, running away from his problems. Apparently a flight of stairs wasn't enough distance for him; he'd decided to leave the country rather than run the gauntlet of bumping into her in the hallway. Her stomach gave its now familiar miserable churn as she failed yet again to squash him from her mind. Somehow that was the worst part of all, the lingering concern for him, reminding her just how far she'd fallen for him, just how much she cared.

Poppy's flat and the friends who shared it were as much a part of what was lost to her as he was. Her stupidity in thinking that misfit Lara Connor could fit in here, in rich Notting Hill, now amazed her. She should have known better. All that was left now was to see out the lease on the pop-up shop and this flat, and to finish Izzy's dress, of course.

She'd had to bring the big guns back into play. The old tactics she'd learned as a kid, shunted back and forth, never feeling settled or wanted. Withdrawal into her own company and refocusing on the one thing that had brought her answers: work. She'd committed to making Izzy's dress, and although she longed to run for the hills she was also a professional who took pride in her work. She wouldn't let Izzy down. Shame she wouldn't see the wedding itself though; she'd be long gone by then.

She took a step back, hands on hips, and surveyed the gown, currently pinned and tacked together so that she could easily adjust seams. Even half finished, it looked great.

'Oh, Iz.' Poppy sighed from the sofa. 'It's just gorgeous.'

Glamour. Excitement. Freedom. Full-on whirlwind distraction from the real world. When you got down to it, that was what Isaac's chain of bars was all about, providing his clientele with the ultimate distraction through sophisticated entertainment and leisure. *That* was what Alex needed. That was what he should have been aiming for all along. No ties. No responsibilities. For the first few days away, living it up in Isaac's world, the relief at relinquishing accountability for anyone else was overwhelming. No need to worry about letting Lara down, or anyone else for that matter.

She was better off without him.

For the first few days, he'd been convinced that he'd done the right thing by walking away. He'd thrown himself with abandon into a few all-nighters at the clubs, surrounded by pretty girls. Had told himself that he was having a *great time*.

Unfortunately there was only one direction to go when you were at the pinnacle of *great time*.

Without his carefully honed sleep pattern, the nightmares began to creep back in. Last night had been the most gut-wrenching, hideous one yet, leaving him cold and shaking in his hotel room. It seemed there was no end to it, no way of putting the past behind him.

Lara had made him feel as if he could conquer anything.

He kept coming across that thought unexpectedly, popping up from nowhere, despite his efforts to keep her out of his mind. The thought of her made his stomach clench with misery. Before he'd met her he'd been stuck in limbo, no clue how to move forward, his mind constantly occupied by his past. Her reassurance and help had got his business off the ground, had given his life some focus again. His nightmares might still have plagued him, but they'd felt somehow more manageable because he'd had a new life to anchor himself to.

Lara had had confidence in him when he'd had none left in himself, and without her encouragement, her endless optimism, he was utterly lost. He'd tagged along on this trip with Isaac at the last minute, anything to get away and maybe get some perspective. He'd called his fitness clients and told them he'd be gone for a few weeks. Yet living it up and playing the field wasn't the answer and he had absolutely no idea what was. And finally black despair surged through him as he fumbled his wallet from his pocket.

He sat on the edge of his bed in the nondescript hotel room and flipped through until he found the card. Just to look at it, not necessarily to *call* the number on it. A military charity, offering help for soldiers under stress. He'd taken the number out of politeness when he'd left hospital months ago, brushing off the slightest mention of PTSD, never intending to call it, never believing he would need to. To call that number would be to admit defeat, to acknowledge that he couldn't do this on his own.

He picked up his phone.

He'd flown back to London alone, declining Isaac's offer to accompany him on the second leg of the trip. The flat was exactly as he'd left it, his room tidy to military standards of precision. The comfort that had once given him seemed to have diminished a little now. Lara had come with endless *stuff* that began to seep into his room. Clothes left hanging over chairs, cosmetics on the dresser. He'd had to fight the urge to tidy up after her, but now he kind of missed the mess.

He dumped his bag and headed straight to Portobello

Road, determined to give this his best shot. He knew now that honesty was the only path open to him. By the time he'd finished she might be congratulating herself on her lucky escape. He came to a standstill outside the little shop with the pink and black sign, composing himself. Well, here went everything. Hadn't that been one of the most attractive things about Lara? That her reactions were never predictable? And she was used to being on her own, that much he knew. None of it gave him much confidence in the outcome. But damn it, he had to *try*.

He pushed open the door of the shop and went in. The usual floral scent of the French soaps and perfumes she stocked smacked him immediately between the eyes, the way it always did. Lara was at the back of the shop behind the little counter, gift-wrapping something pink and silky for a middle-aged woman, who glanced his way with interest. He saw Lara stiffen almost imperceptibly as she saw him, her blue eyes widening, and then her inscrutable expression locked into place. Not a single clue as to what his reception might be. As he approached she handed over one of her signature pink and black bags with the black silk ribbon handles to her customer and turned to him.

'Yes, sir?' She gave him a breezy smile. 'How can I help you? Looking for something for a girlfriend? You look like the quick throwaway-fling type. Let me guess— something red with peepholes.' Her just-served customer was looking on with interest and Lara swept past Alex to the front of the shop to hold the door open for her. 'I'm sorry but I don't think I'll be able to help,' she called back to him over her shoulder. 'I'm not sure what you were expecting but that kind of thing *really isn't me*.'

The emphasis on those last few words made it crystal

clear that if he'd thought talking her round was going to be a piece of cake, he was sadly mistaken. She closed the door behind her customer, turned the sign around to read 'Closed', and turned back to him.

'Make it quick,' she said. 'Say what you've got to say. Time is money. Every minute I close the shop I'm losing sales.'

'I came to say I'm sorry,' he said.

He saw her press her lips together.

'For what?' she said. 'For letting me think we actually had some kind of relationship there, letting me buy into all of that, when it was all for show?'

He closed his eyes briefly.

'It wasn't all for show. The way I feel about you was and is not just for show. I'm sorry for hiding my problems from you but I truly thought I could deal with them on my own. And you have to understand that, in my family, throughout my life, that's the way it's been done. As far back as I can remember, emotional outbursts have been a sign of weakness. By the time I was seven years old I'd worked out that crying only made my father angry—it certainly didn't elicit any sympathy or affection. Soldiers don't cry. They don't show emotion.'

She was watching him steadily. He had no idea if any of this was counting for anything at all with her. He crossed the shop towards the counter, took a breath and turned back to her. She was watching him steadily.

'I thought I could put the past behind me and have this fantastic life with you,' he said. '*That* was the problem. I was kidding myself that I could actually do that. On my own, without help from anyone else. I thought if I lived a normal life with you, starting a new business, moving on, pretty soon it would become exactly that.'

'Pretending things are normal won't make them normal,' she said, her voice carefully neutral. She walked slowly across the shop towards him, her arms folded defensively across her body. 'You can't just gloss over the bad stuff and expect it to go away.'

'I know that now,' he said. 'It was partly my pride. I just couldn't bear your suggestion that I get help. You have to understand that was the last thing I wanted to hear. I'd spent so long denying I had a problem that agreeing to get help was unthinkable. I thought I'd rather manage on my own than admit that. I decided to throw myself into partying with Isaac and I lasted less than a week. I don't want that life. But if I'm ever going to have more than that I have to face up to my past. I realise that now.'

He held her gaze carefully and a tug of sympathy pulled at Lara's heart. Yet still she steeled herself.

'Have you any idea what a big deal it was to let you into my life?' she asked him quietly. 'How much that cost me? I've never been able to take my eye off the ball and relax with someone, not since I was a kid. I'd had too many times, you see, where I'd done that, where I'd put my trust in someone, when I thought I could put down roots and be part of a family. And then the whole thing would come tumbling down around me.

'That's why I don't like to rely on other people. I've never *had* anyone to rely on. Whenever I thought I was settling in somewhere, or I got used to a new school or made a friend, before I knew it I'd be swept back into care and the whole damn thing would start all over again with another family. I just…wasn't a good fit.' She held her head high and carried on boldly, 'I made up my mind a long time ago that I'd make my own life, that I'd work hard and get my own security without having to look to anyone else's help to get me there. I knew I wouldn't let myself down. And then you came along and made me rethink all of that. And for you to just walk away from it as if it meant nothing...' she caught her breath '...that was the worst thing that could happen to me.'

She sank into the chair next to the dressing screen. Just what did he expect from her? How could he expect her to give this another try when he'd messed with her trust, that thing that was so difficult for her to give?

'There were three of us in the vehicle,' he said then, and her fingers clenched on the arms of the chair. She turned slowly to look up at him in stunned surprise, understanding what he was about to tell her.

She could pick up the tiniest falter in his clipped deep voice and her heart turned over in spite of the way she was trying to steel it against him.

'Alex, you don't need to put yourself through this,' she said. 'I don't need to hear this stuff. It's not relevant anymore.'

'I want you to understand,' he said, his expression steady. 'I don't want any more secrets. There were three of us. Driver, another soldier, and me. Same kind of journey taken countless times, no big difference about that day, nothing that made it stand out.' He shrugged. 'My memories of the bomb are sketchy. I remember a sense of building pressure, as if I could feel the explosion coming from beneath us before it really hit. I remember the smoke, the smell of explosives burning at the back of my throat. My eyes stung. And the disorientation, that was the most hideous part. I couldn't find the others. I couldn't see. I was staggering around. It was chaos.'

'It must have been terrifying.'

'It was. But at the same time it was no more than I'd

signed up for. I knew the risks. We all did. I went into it with my eyes open. And I wasn't about to have some kind of meltdown after the event. Not when I still had *my* life, that would have been a mockery of the soldier who lost his.'

He looked down at the floor.

'Private Sam Walker, his name was. The soldier who was killed.'

There was a long pause before he said any more and when he did she could hear the strain in his voice.

'It was his first tour and sometimes it takes time to adjust. Suddenly it isn't a training exercise anymore, it's the real thing and people…well, some people struggle, that's all. If I became aware of that I always tried to step in where I could, give some kind of encouragement. He'd…well, he'd had some problems and I told him I'd look out for him. That I had his back.'

He drew in a rasping breath and at last he looked up at her. His grey eyes held a tortured expression that made her heart ache for him.

'When you said that to me the other night, about having my back, it brought it all rushing back. I panicked. That's why I backed away so quickly, why I wouldn't discuss it with you or listen to reason. That's what I meant when I said it was about me not being what you need. I was determined to get well in record time after the bomb. I pushed myself like crazy in rehab. I told you I was handling it myself, that I had it under control, that it was improving, and I meant all of those things when I said them.' He shrugged. 'I think maybe I was trying to convince myself as much as you. And I know I should have got some help but I was ashamed.'

She shook her head, but he talked over her, as though if he stopped talking now he might never revisit this.

'I felt so *weak*,' he groaned, his head tilting up at the ceiling as he ran a shaky hand through his hair. 'I was an exemplary soldier, Lara. I was determined to better my father and I'd pushed myself up the ranks with sheer hard graft, I wanted to prove that I wasn't just there because of the family name. Without all of that I had no idea who the hell I was anymore, and I certainly didn't feel like I was good enough for someone as lovely as you. I got off lightly, Lara. The driver suffered terrible injuries and Sam was killed. I was the most senior person in that vehicle and there was nothing I could do for either of them.'

He was shaking all over now, both his hands clutched at the sides of his head. She was up from the chair before she knew what she was doing, pulling him tightly against her. She felt him grip her tightly, his breath heaving.

'How could I possibly trust myself to look after you when I'd failed so hideously?' His broken whisper was hot against her neck.

'You didn't fail,' she said, holding him tight. 'You didn't plant that bomb. None of what happened was your fault.'

She continued to hold him, feeling the tension in his shoulders slowly relax.

'I can't sort this out on my own,' he said after a minute, his voice muffled. 'And I know I threw your offer of support back in your face but I'm asking you to reconsider.'

She disengaged herself from his embrace and took a careful step back.

'What's changed?' she said. She searched his face. 'Why should I believe this isn't just you talking the talk and then necking off to swig espresso and pop caffeine pills?'

'Because I've got help this time,' he said. He looked away from her while he tugged a wad of paperwork from the pocket of his jacket and handed it to her. She took it and scanned it.

'A military charity?' she said.

'They run a helpline. Support for ex-servicemen who are suffering from stress. The dreams, the anxiety, they're common PTSD symptoms. I'm going to take counselling, whatever they can offer me to deal with it. No more pretending I'm improving by avoiding sleep. I know it's not going to be easy, and I'm not asking you to give me an answer right away. I just couldn't bear to have you thinking this was somehow down to some shortfall of *yours*. I'm the one with the problem here, not you.' He reached across and took her hand in his. 'I want to be with you. But I still don't feel like I'm good enough for that.'

Accepting you had a problem, wasn't that the first step to recovery?

She looked at him.

'I don't need rescuing, or looking after, Alex, so you can quit thinking I have any need for you to do that. I've done perfectly well by myself all this time. If we're going to be together then what I want is to be part of a team for once. To not be on my own. But that means we give it our best shot, the bad stuff and the good stuff included, not some stupid idea of what you think it should be like where I'm wrapped in cotton wool and you hide anything from me that you think I won't like.'

'Is that a yes?'

A tentative grin touched his lips.

'It's not as simple as that.' She'd had a good dose of

reality these last few days since he'd gone. It had made her refocus on her business plans and ambitions. 'Even if it was a yes, I'll be moving out in a few weeks. I've no idea what my plans are next. I need to give that some serious thought.'

'Move in with me at the flat,' he said immediately, grabbing both her hands in his. 'At least for now. Poppy won't mind—I know she won't. She's loved having you around. I know it all sounds like our plans are short term but that's just logistics. I'm in this for the long haul if you are. If you can give me a second chance. No secrets.'

That he'd been open with her about his past touched her deeply. That couldn't have been easy after denying it so vehemently to everyone including himself. And it still wasn't going to be rainbows and butterflies, at least for the time being. But, hell, when had her life ever been that?

She squeezed his hands. Maybe in each other they could finally find the security they both needed.

'OK,' she said at last, and then she was pulled into his arms. Her stomach melted as he kissed and kissed her.

'With one condition,' she said, coming up for air. 'No boot camp for me. Ever.'

He smiled down at her.

'Done.'

* * * * *

*If you loved this book,
make sure you catch the rest of the incredible
THE FLAT IN NOTTING HILL miniseries!*

*THE MORNING AFTER THE NIGHT BEFORE
by Nikki Logan, available August 2014*

*SLEEPING WITH THE SOLDIER
by Charlotte Phillips, available September 2014*

*YOUR BED OR MINE?
by Joss Wood, available October 2014*

*ENEMIES WITH BENEFITS
by Louisa George, available November 2014*

MILLS & BOON®

Maybe This Christmas

Author of *Sleigh Bells in the Snow*

Sarah Morgan

Maybe this Christmas

COMING SOON
OCTOBER 2014

* cover in development

Let Sarah Morgan sweep you away to a perfect winter wonderland with this wonderful Christmas tale filled with unforgettable characters, wit, charm and heart-melting romance!
Pick up your copy today!

www.millsandboon.co.uk/xmas

MILLS & BOON®

Why shop at millsandboon.co.uk?

Each year, thousands of romance readers find their perfect read at millsandboon.co.uk. That's because we're passionate about bringing you the very best romantic fiction. Here are some of the advantages of shopping at www.millsandboon.co.uk:

* **Get new books first**—you'll be able to buy your favourite books one month before they hit the shops

* **Get exclusive discounts**—you'll also be able to buy our specially created monthly collections, with up to 50% off the RRP

* **Find your favourite authors**—latest news, interviews and new releases for all your favourite authors and series on our website, plus ideas for what to try next

* **Join in**—once you've bought your favourite books, don't forget to register with us to rate, review and join in the discussions

Visit **www.millsandboon.co.uk**
for all this and more today!